Rachael Stewart adores conjuring up stories, from heartwarmingly romantic to wildly erotic. She's been writing since she could put pen to paper—as the stacks of scrawled-on pages in her loft will attest to. A Welsh lass at heart, she now lives in Yorkshire, with her very own hero and three awesome kids—and if she's not tapping out a story she's wrapped up in one or enjoying the great outdoors. Reach her on Facebook, Twitter @rach_b52, or at rachaelstewartauthor.com.

Nina Milne has always dreamed of writing for Mills & Boon—ever since she played libraries with her mother's stacks of Mills & Boon romances as a child. On her way to this dream Nina acquired an English degree, a hero of her own, three gorgeous children and—somehow!—an accountancy qualification. She lives in Brighton and has filled her house with stacks of books—her very own *real* library.

MY YEAR WITH THE BILLIONAIRE

RACHAEL STEWART

FALLING FOR HIS STAND-IN FIANCÉE

NINA MILNE

MILLS & BOON

First published in Great Britain 2022
by Mills & Boon, an imprint of HarperCollins*Publishers* Ltd,
1 London Bridge Street, London, SE1 9GF

www.harpercollins.co.uk

HarperCollins*Publishers*
1st Floor, Watermarque Building,
Ringsend Road, Dublin 4, Ireland

My Year with the Billionaire © 2022 Rachael Stewart

Falling for His Stand-In Fiancée © 2022 Nina Milne

ISBN: 978-0-263-30226-4

This t   r

For

Print

MY YEAR WITH THE BILLIONAIRE

RACHAEL STEWART

MILLS & BOON

For Pippa, my sanity. xxx

PROLOGUE

Edward

I KNOW I SHOULDN'T STARE. That I should keep on walking and pretend I haven't seen. But I can't tear my eyes away.

I also can't believe what I'm seeing.

Summer Evans, my gran's new foster child, is taking a *swim*. I get that it's hot, the summer heatwave unusually oppressive, but a swim…in the *loch*? I've been visiting the castle every year of my life—twenty years and counting—and not once have I considered dipping my toes, let alone diving in headfirst.

I shouldn't be surprised. I've met enough of Gran's foster children to expect the unexpected. But this…

She can't be that much younger than me, yet her actions set her a world apart and I'm entranced. My fear that I might have to dive in and rescue her abating as she gracefully cuts through the water, her easy stroke belying the weight of her clothing. Not that there's much of that either. Just a simple white T-shirt and denim shorts, her trainers abandoned at the end of the rickety wooden dock.

I head to the water's edge, watch the sun play over the ripples she creates and have the wildest urge to join her.

But wildness isn't in me…

And then she turns and bright blue eyes collide with

mine, their flecks of gold glinting up at me as they widen, her gasp drowned out by the water splashing around her.

Now she might need rescuing...

My heart jerks in my chest, failing to settle as her expression lifts, her movements calm and she cracks the widest of grins.

'You must be Edward?'

Her voice rings out across the loch, her accent hard to identify. It's not quite Scottish, not quite English. A mashing together of sorts.

'That's me.' I clear my throat, which feels strangely tight. 'Gran sent me to tell you dinner will be ready in half an hour.'

She cocks her head to the side as she treads water. 'Half an hour. Got it.'

I shift from one foot to the other, feel the weight of her stare, and can't seem to find the inclination to leave. I've done my duty—now I should go. Instead, I find myself asking. 'Do you have a towel I can fetch...?' Because she can't seriously mean to walk back into the house, clothes all wet. 'Or fresh clothes?'

She laughs. 'Does it look like I came prepared?'

She's got you there...

'Not particularly.' Her spontaneity is as enthralling as it is alien to me. 'But I'm not sure you want to be traipsing back through the castle leaving puddles in your wake.'

She closes the distance between us and I take a step back.

'Don't worry...the sun will dry me off soon enough.'

She reaches for the rungs of the makeshift ladder at the dock's edge and I realise she's about to get out...with her top so see-through she might as well be naked.

I spin on my heel, tug my sweater from around my shoulders, eager to give her something, anything, to stop me seeing more than I should. 'You're welcome to use this.'

I offer it up without turning, my brain working overtime as it persists in painting a picture I don't want to see—of her clothes clinging to her every curve, her smile bright, her eyes full of spark...

I blame my intense reaction on my life of late. All work and no play...it's a saying for a reason. I've had my head down for so long I've forgotten that life exists outside of my university dorm. Coming here is meant to be a break from it all, a chance to let off steam—something this Summer looks to be quite proficient at.

I'm accosted by a fierce pang of envy, cut short by her sudden laughter that urges me to turn—though I won't, not until she's covered up.

'You're quite the gentleman.' The jumper slips from my hand into hers.

'I try.' I swallow, my ears attuned to the water dripping over the wooden boards, and I imagine her shaking out her short blonde hair, wringing out her sodden shirt. The slightest droplet catches on my arm and goosebumps prickle beneath the path it takes down my arm.

'You going to stand there for ever?'

'Huh?' Now I turn and look and... What the...? I give a disbelieving cough. 'I didn't mean for you to sit on it.'

'Oh...' She looks down at where my sweater is stretched out beneath her, her palms pressed into the delicate cashmere, her wet denim-clad behind too. 'Sorry.' She winces up at me. 'Would you like it back?'

'Would I...?' I'm unable to finish. My head is shaking as my lips twist up into a smile—the first genuine smile I've felt in ages. 'No. No, I don't want it back.'

'Good.' She grins once more, her eyes going back to the view. The sun lights her up from top to toe, beads of water leaving glistening trails over her bare skin that my eyes are keen to follow. My throat tightens further, my chest too. Is she doing it on purpose?

I tug my gaze back to her face, to where her lashes create dark crescents over her high cheekbones, and she breathes in deep. She acts like she hasn't a care in the world, but that can't be true. As my mother always says, Gran's foster children come with enough baggage to sink a ship. You steer clear—*well* clear.

'Want to join me?'

She doesn't open her eyes as she says it and I look away, to the far less provocative horizon, and tell myself to walk away, to reset the unfamiliar buzz she's sparked in my veins.

But I don't want to. There's an ease about her, an ease that's also wild and unfettered, and I want to stay in its orbit just a little longer.

I contemplate going back inside, being robbed of her presence, which is as warm as the sun itself, and my blood runs cold. She's Summer through and through, and I lower myself to the dock before my common sense dictates otherwise.

'Was it so hard to decide?' she murmurs, ripe with teasing.

Teasing that has the smile returning to my lips as I rack my floundering brain for a slick retort. I'm not usually this inept with the opposite sex, but then… I've never met a girl quite like her.

She turns away to rummage inside her shoe, draws out a cigarette. 'Want one?'

I screw my face up, the magic somewhat dampened. 'No. Thank you.'

'It's only been in my trainer for a minute or two.'

'It's not the trainer I object to.'

'Ah…' She cocks a brow. 'So it's the smoking. Not the done thing in your hoity-toity circles, hey?'

I know she's mocking me; I can see it in her eyes as she catches the cigarette between her teeth and pulls out a lighter. 'Suit yourself.'

She sparks it up as I watch on—fascinated, disgusted, amazed…

'You know Gran doesn't approve, right?'

Is that really my voice? So gravel-like and hoarse? And why can't I tear my eyes from her lips? The plump bed on which the cigarette rests and the perfect cupid's bow above…all luscious and pink.

She takes a slow puff, wets her lips to torment me further. 'Not my problem.'

A defiant fire comes alive behind her eyes, warring with her relaxed ease and I frown, uncaring that I can see the black outline of her bra through the clinging white T-shirt—who wears black under white anyway?

Someone who doesn't like to conform…a rebel… And heaven knows Gran has seen her fair share of them over the years. Seems Summer is no exception.

'You're living under her care, under her roof, don't you think that makes it your problem?'

She meets my gaze, all steel and ice, and then her eyes trail over me as though she's seeing me properly for the first time and her lips quirk, her eyes warm. 'Are you going to discipline me?'

I bite back a curse, smother the excited kick to my gut—*Definitely* a rebel and *definitely* trouble with a capital T.

Is she toying with me? Mocking me some more? The public schoolboy, born and bred. Not a hair out of place, my chinos and pale blue polo shirt perfectly pressed… Or is she genuinely flirting, liking what she sees?

Whatever the case, there's no answer I can give. None that feels safe and correct. And I'm all about that.

My silence has her laughing softly, releasing me from her provocative stare as she looks to the water and flicks it with her toes. 'How long are you stopping for?'

It takes me a second to trust my voice, another to form a response. 'Didn't Gran say?'

'Nope.'

She settles back on her elbows, stretching her body out languorously, and I'm caught up in her, my brain and voice silenced by the heat that rushes into my veins. I forget myself, forget what we're talking about, and too late, she's caught me looking where I shouldn't. Heat streaks my cheeks, my pulse pounds…

Not that she cares. She's revelling in it. Her breathless chuckle is all flirtatious, the nip she gives the corner of her mouth even more so.

Speak, you fool, before she labels you as one.

'September. I'm staying until September. When term starts up again.'

'Edinburgh Uni, right?'

I nod and she gives a low whistle, her gaze raking back over me. Her own pulse flickers in her throat as her eyes darken. I know that look. I know it and I want to act on it. The urge burns through me even as I acknowledge that it's a line I should not cross…even if it's a line she has probably crossed herself many times over.

'So…' she breaks the heated silence, rakes her teeth over her lower lip '…we have the entire summer together. How fun.'

Swallow. Speak. 'You think so?'

'Don't you?'

Her eyes collide with mine and images dance through my mind. Wrong. Tempting. Crazy. It's like she's projecting her idea of fun at me—but her kind of fun and my kind of fun are not one and the same.

Maybe they should be, the devil on my shoulder argues.

She gives a soft *hmm*. 'You know, my stay here just got a whole lot better.'

I focus on her words and not the heat she's stirring up. 'You sound like it's just a fleeting visit for you?'

She shrugs, but there's an edge to it, an awkwardness that doesn't fit with her confidence. 'It always is.'

I don't contradict her. I don't tell her that Gran's track record of long-term fostering says otherwise. I'll let her believe what she wants to believe until life proves otherwise.

She turns to me then, a curious look in her eye. I wait for her to say something, but nothing comes. Instead her blue eyes draw me in, deeper and deeper still, until I can't quite catch my breath and I'm forced to break her spell.

'What?'

She smiles, her eyes alight with it. 'We really are chalk and cheese, you and I.'

I give a tight laugh. 'That's one way to put it.'

'You say that like it's a bad thing.'

'No, not bad…'

Risky. Because she intrigues me, fascinates me. To the point that my body is overriding my good sense and all the warning signs telling me to keep her at a safe distance.

'What, then?'

I smile as I find my voice, my mind made up. 'Well, to use your phrase, it either makes me as dry as chalk or as pungent as cheese, and personally I don't fancy being classified as either.'

Her laugh is as brilliant as the sun and my body thrives on it.

'Oh, Edward, we're going to get along famously.'

'You think?'

She gives me a playful wink, leans in close, her voice a husky whisper. 'Oh, I know.'

She pinches her lip in her teeth, her eyes fall to my mouth, and I swear I could kiss her...

I want to—my entire body thrums with the energy to do just that—but I don't.

I want something more.

I want to get to know her.

I want to dig beneath the confident rebel front with its hairline fractures and get to the girl beneath.

And now I have the entire summer to do so...

CHAPTER ONE

Summer

'COME ON, come on, come on…'

I drum my fingers against my knee, my eyes hooked on the blazing green digits that make up the minicab's dash-board clock. I'm going to be late—so late. The traffic's bumper to bumper and we're going nowhere.

Is it always like this? It's been years since I've visited Edinburgh—years since I've been in the UK, even. Everything is just so frantic.

I'm used to open spaces—mountains, beaches, bars—and to people who act like they have all the time in the world and the freedom to enjoy it.

Not here, though. Through the drizzle, people are dashing from one building to the next. Suited and booted. Grey and grouchy.

My eyes drift back to the ticking clock and I chew my lip.

I never should've helped the woman with the missing luggage, or the child with the vending machine that wouldn't play ball, or paused to donate some loose change to the busker singing his heart out in the rain before airport security took him down.

But I did…and there's no going back to rewrite history.

I sigh. It feels like the story of my life—only this time it pains me more than usual.

I should have been here a month ago. Not now, and at the request of a man I don't know, on behalf of the only woman I have ever loved. My foster mother. Katherine.

Not that she loved *me*. Not enough to give me the chance to say goodbye.

My nails bite into my palms, their sting worse for the burn behind my eyes.

No, that's not fair.

I know why she didn't tell me.

But it doesn't make it hurt any less.

Katherine was the closest thing to family I have ever known and now she's gone.

It's back to me...*just me*.

I shrug it off. I don't do sad. It's such a waste of life. We only get one, and we have to live it to the full, right? Cram in as much as possible, see the world, no time to pause...

At least that's the way I see it...even if it's making me late right now.

I lean forward and meet the cabby's eye in the rear-view mirror.

'How much longer?'

He gives a shrug. 'Ten minutes. Twenty. They're tearing up roads all over the city—it's carnage.'

I thrust back into my seat, my knees bobbing. A horn sounds, another chimes in, and I can't take it any more. Even with my luggage I can walk it faster than this. I look at the satnav, see where I need to be.

Rummaging through my satchel for my purse, I pull out some notes and shove them at him. 'It's enough, right?' I gesture to the meter and he nods, twisting in his seat to eye my luggage sceptically.

'But...'

'It's fine. I've got it.'

I shimmy along the seat and shove open the door. It's a relief just to be out in the fresh air again, and for one brief second I raise my face to the rain and breathe in deep, give the hint of a smile as I feel free again. I've spent too long cooped up on planes and public transport, with the journey from Kuala Lumpur seeming to take for ever when it was twenty-four hours tops.

The desire to check in to a hotel and hit a shower is almost enough to see me doing just that. All it would take was a simple call to Mr McAllister to request that the meeting be put off until tomorrow…

Ah, avoidance, thy name is Summer!

I ignore the inner gibe and slam the door closed as the car behind my taxi gives an impatient honk.

'Yeah, yeah…okay.' What is it with this place?

I wave at them and sling my bag onto my back, strike off in the direction of the solicitor's office. One upside to being heavily laden is that people—those who are looking up from their various devices, at least—clear a path for you. Definitely the right decision to get out of the cab. Even if the weather and the exertion will see me turning up looking less than best.

Less than best… I laugh. As if I even *have* a best.

Maybe I should have made more of an effort.

Maybe I should have flown in a day earlier, prepared more—physically and mentally.

But then, I've never been one for putting on a show, and Katherine respected me for that. Why change now?

And what if he's there?

I falter on the pavement, catch my shoulder on a streetlamp and wince.

'There's no reason he should be there,' I grumble under my breath, then right my backpack and my stride.

Whatever it is Mr McAllister wants to pass on, it doesn't necessary follow that Edward will be in attendance too. And if he is going to be present, wouldn't it have been polite for Katherine's solicitor to mention it in his email?

Polite, yes. Necessary, no.

My pulse skips a beat and I grit my teeth. I've been going round in circles with this ever since I received the email and I'm sick of it. If he's there, he's there. I'll simply have to deal with it. I'm a thirty-eight-year-old woman who knows her own mind and her own worth. I'm not an insecure eighteen-year-old running scared. And I'm more than capable of standing my ground and having a civilised conversation, in Edward's presence or not.

You weren't the one who was wronged, though...

I grimace, and the man walking towards me takes a wide berth. Not that I can blame him. I must look half crazed. But debating the past— especially *that* part—always sends me a little loopy. My mind races ahead, wondering if he's married now. A father. Happy. Settled.

I feel the answer in my gut. He has to be. A man like him—kind, wealthy, sexy—is an absolute catch. And if he's happy and settled, maybe he'll be grateful that I left the way I did.

Yup, you keep telling yourself that, sugar!

I up my pace and ignore the pressing feeling in my chest that the past is finally catching up with me...

Edward

Charles clears his throat for the umpteenth time and my eyes narrow on the beads of sweat breaking out over his brow. He hurries to dab it dry with his monogrammed handkerchief, but I've seen enough and it's teasing out an uneasy sweat of my own.

Charles is the epitome of cool—level-headed, dependable, pragmatic. It's why my grandmother chose him to manage the legal affairs of her estate. He wasn't just her lawyer, he was her closest friend too, which makes his discomfort now all the more concerning.

He tries to smile at me, the wrinkles around his grey eyes deepening behind his wire-framed spectacles. He looks like he's stepped out of the nineteen-thirties, his office too, but I'm not here to appraise his dress or choice of décor. I'm here for the reading of my grandmother's will. If only he'd get on with it…

I understand that it's hard for him. Hell, it's hard for us both. But the quicker we get this done with, the better.

It's bad enough that my parents didn't deem the reading important enough to cut their travels short. Enough that for all my grandmother loved and cared for others it's just me sat here now. Me and whoever it is Charles has insisted we wait for. Not that he will tell me. I've asked. He's denied.

Curiouser and curiouser, as my *Alice-in-Wonderland*-loving grandmother would have said.

I don't return his edgy smile. I adjust my tie and glance at the old grandfather clock that has been a feature of this room for as long as I have known him.

Twenty minutes late. Just how long does he want to wait? I have places to be, people to see, distractions to pursue…

'We're both busy, Charles.'

I drag my gaze back to his, ignore the weight of the lie. Because the truth is I'm not busy enough. It's been a month since Gran died—a month. And nothing can fill the void she's left behind. And I've tried. I've tried everything.

Though none of my grief slips into my voice. It never pays to appear weak. My mother taught me that and life reinforced it. 'I don't see why we can't get this over and done with now.'

He chokes on thin air and wets his lips—the gesture tests my patience and my nerves further.

'I'm sure they will be here very soon. They promised they would be. And I promised your grandmother I would abide by their wishes.'

'If I'm to be made to wait for this person, surely I deserve a name?'

My ears are primed for their identity…yet, nothing. What's he so afraid of?

'Come now, Charles. I must know them. Unless you've managed to dig up some distant relative that no one has ever heard of and declare Katherine's entire—'

'I'm so sorry I'm late!'

The breathless voice permeates the heavy oak door to Charles's office and the man himself shoots up out of his seat, wiping his palms down his trousers as the door opens on his secretary.

'Miss Evans has arrived, Mr McAllister.'

'Thank you, Tracy.'

He's already striding forward, his smile warm as he looks past Tracy to the woman I've heard but haven't yet set eyes on.

Miss Evans?

Who on earth is…?

The faintest of bells ring in the deepest, darkest recesses of my mind… The slight rasp to that feminine tone…the unidentifiable accent…

I rise and turn, good manners overriding my mental flurry as I seek to greet our new arrival, but the ground shifts beneath my feet, my vision narrowing until all I see is her.

Summer.

It's not… It can't be…

I force my body to straighten, smooth out my tie on impulse as my head refuses to believe what my eyes are seeing. At first all I register is an abundance of blonde hair and bronze skin—far too much skin for autumn in Scotland—and clothing that seems so mismatched it's like she's walked into a charity shop and paid no heed to size nor colour. Her walking boots are as worn as her backpack, which is almost as big as her and likely weighs much more.

Where the hell does she think she is? Her whole get-up is better suited to a trek across the sunny beaches of Bali than the streets of Edinburgh in the damp and dreary depths of autumn.

Does she not realise what season we're in? Does she not care that she looks so out of place?

Did she ever?

My head taunts me, reminds me, teases me.

This is Summer, who never cared for anyone's opinion but her own.

And that's when I meet her gaze and it truly hits home. Summer. Summer Evans. She's the person we've been waiting for. She's the person Gran insisted be here for this.

A thousand memories surge forth as my heart stutters in my chest.

The grin she gives me is accentuated by lines that suggest she smiles often. The nose that has seen a bump or two lifts marginally and her eyes…her eyes transport me back twenty years, to those same bright blue eyes, the same rebellious grin…

I snap my gaze away.

'What the hell is she doing here?' I fire at Charles, and his sweat makes a prompt return, his smile falters.

'Well, if you'll both sit down,' he blusters, 'I can explain just that.'

'It's a pleasure to see you too,' she directs at me, and

although her voice is strong, her eyes show a hint of what I'd like to think is remorse.

Though she hasn't got the heart for remorse.

I'm the one choking on thin air now, and she has the decency to look away, to hesitate. She combs unsteady fingers through her hair, sweeps the rain-dampened strands off her flushed cheeks and she secures it back with some brightly coloured cloth.

Where on earth has she come from? Where has she been all this time? And, more importantly, why is she here?

She grips her backpack tightly now, her knuckles flashing white, and I realise the room has fallen silent and all eyes are on me. Waiting on me.

Her throat bobs, her lashes flutter. 'Well, shall we sit?'

Sit? With *her*? To hear my grandmother's will? This has to be a joke. Some weird, twisted joke.

'Yes, let's sit.'

Charles is all over the idea, ushering her to a seat, helping her deposit her bag on the floor, and I'm… I'm stood there like some bloody lemon. My eyes tracking her, devouring her. Does the woman not own a coat? It's raining cats and dogs out there and her bare arms shine with it, her clothes cling to her skin…

And just like that I'm back at the loch over two decades ago, and the fire is as immediate as it is unwelcome.

'Can I get you a drink, Miss Evans?'

Charles persists in trying to make her welcome…trying to make up for my obvious hostility, I'm sure.

'A coffee? Tea? Water…?'

I can almost sense Gran looking down on me in disapproval, her *tut-tut-tut* echoing through my soul.

If Gran wants her here, my mind tries to reason, *you need to play nice.*

'Water would be lovely,' she murmurs softly, and I want

to shut myself off from the way her voice sings through my blood. 'Thank you.'

'Sparkling? Still?'

'Either's fine,' she says, her eyes returning to me, hesitant, wary…

She's completely out of her depth.

It should make me feel better.

It doesn't.

It does make me move, though.

Dragging a hand over my face, I return to my seat and force normal service to resume—the projection of an outward calm strong enough to mask the inner storm.

Oh, Gran, what have you done?

CHAPTER TWO

Summer

'GRAN'S DONE *WHAT*?'

I leap a little in my seat at Edward's outburst. I'm not sure what's worse: his initial greeting or his response to the will.

Not that I can blame him for either.

And I'm just as stunned. Speechless, in fact. Not a trait I'm experienced in, let alone know how to handle. But I'm still struggling to believe we're in the same room together…never mind the unbelievable news Mr McAllister has just delivered.

'Would y-you like me to re-read it from the beginning?'

McAllister dabs at his forehead, his wrinkles deepening. Poor man. Edward is fierce. Like, seriously fierce. The sharp cut of his deep blue suit adds to his severity, and his carefully groomed brown hair is unmoving in its swept-back style, the hard angle to his designer stubble precise and accentuating his prominent cheekbones and strong jaw.

Gone is the twenty-year-old I met all those years ago. The clean-shaven, ex-public schoolboy with his foppish hair, quiet, reserved smiles and sweet nature.

This is a man with the full weight of his years, wealth

and success behind him. Not to mention his obvious dislike of me…

'No. No, I don't need you to read it from the beginning, Charles. I understood. I just—'

His chocolate-brown eyes flit to me, razor-sharp, and my heart gives an involuntary flip. I don't even have time to recover before he's looking back at McAllister, accusation flaring in his depths.

'She can't have been thinking straight. You were supposed to…' he waves a hand at the man '…make sure she was in her right mind when she made such decisions.'

'Edward!' I erupt, driven by my innate need to defend her. 'Don't you dare question Katherine's mind; she was perfectly sane.'

'Really?'

His eyes return to me and I can't breathe for the emotion I see there. Anger. Hatred. Pain…

He clenches the end of the armrest closest to me, the veins in his hand popping, his entire body emanating a physical strength he didn't possess before.

'And what would you know of her mind when you haven't seen her in twenty years?'

Bullseye—he might as well have thrown a dart straight through my grieving heart.

'I've always been around,' I say quietly, my cheeks burning with the direct hit.

'Around?' His mouth lifts into a chilling one-sided smile. 'Is that what you call it?'

'Now, now…'

McAllister comes to my rescue. I half expect him to add *children* to the end and inwardly cringe. I don't need him to fight my battles. Especially in front of Edward— *against* Edward.

'Can we focus on the necessary? Katherine knew this

would come as a…how shall I put it?…a shock. But she was very clear in her request, and felt it was in *both* your interests to see the conditions of her will through to fruition.'

His voice softens and yet strengthens as he speaks, as if he's warming up to the idea as he watches us closely. I don't know what he sees in us to warrant such sudden positivity. Maybe there's more than just water in the crystal glass he's drinking from.

I take a sip from my own glass, wishing it really was something stronger.

'You were friends once,' he adds into the strained silence. 'I think Katherine thought you could readily be so again.'

'And what if we can't?' I say, ignoring the pang his words evoke. 'Stick to the terms, I mean?'

Beside me Edward makes a sound behind his fist—was that a snort? I give him the side-eye, but his gaze is fixed on McAllister.

'Yes. What she said…'

The man clears his throat, studies the papers before him—more to avoid our eyes, I'm sure.

'If one of you leaves before the year is up, the estate goes to the other party.'

'And if we both leave?' Edward presses.

'Well, then it becomes a bit more complicated. Katherine has outlined a careful segregation of the estate, detailing specific areas that are to be donated to local businesses and charities. The—'

'Glenrobin will be *segregated*?' Edward chokes out the last word with the same shock I feel. Was I wrong about Katherine? Had she been mentally unsound? Had I missed it? Paid too little attention?

The guilt rises as Edward continues, 'But that castle, that entire estate, has been in my family for generations.'

'And of course Katherine would like it to remain that way.'

McAllister actually smiles now as he stacks the papers neatly—is the man delirious?

'So, as you can see, it is in your interests to adhere to the terms set out in the will.'

'And what happens after a year?' I ask. 'What then?'

'After you have lived there for one year you can do whatever you wish with your share. Sell it to the other party, donate it, keep it—so long as you both agree.'

'This is ridiculous.'

'That's the first sensible thing that's been said all morning…' Edward mutters, and I flick him a look—*not helping!*—before going back to McAllister and the problem at hand.

'So, just to be clear, Edward's mother inherits a cash sum and the house in London. The rest—the estate, the staff, the heirlooms of Glenrobin—she's bequeathed to us?'

'Along with a sum of money to supplement the income the estate generates to aid with its running costs. The sum should be enough to last for many years to come.'

I nod, numbly. 'A fifty-fifty split between Edward and me?'

'Precisely.'

Edward clears his throat, his eyes pinning the other man down. 'And what if *she* decides to sell it to the highest bidder when the year is over?'

My stomach rolls at the very idea. Rolls even more at his obvious belief that I would do such a thing.

Does he not realise I'm on his side? I *know* I don't deserve this inheritance. I don't even deserve to be sat in the same room as him, hearing Katherine's last wishes. For all my love for her, I wasn't her blood. I wasn't her true family. No matter how much she tried to make me so.

'I asked you a question, Charles.'

But McAllister is watching me. Worrying about me. I can see it in his sympathetic grey eyes. Something else I don't deserve—the man's sympathy.

Unease creeps down my spine…goosebumps break out across my skin.

'Charles!'

The man comes alive, his eyes flicking to Edward, admonishing him. 'In that case you can refuse, as would be your right. Any sale of the assets must be agreed between the two of you.'

Edward nods. 'And the money that comes with the estate? How exactly does that work?'

McAllister stares at Edward long and hard. 'I'm sure you will find a way to make it work, Mr Fitzroy. Katherine asked me to be involved as much or as little as you need. That includes tracking expenditure if it will help you to focus on setting up home amicably. But Katherine did hope that, given time, you would be quite capable of managing it all between yourselves.'

'"Setting up home"?' Edward's upper lip curls, and his voice is devoid of any depth as the phrase revolves around my mind, races through my heart.

I don't have a home. Never have, never will. Glenrobin Castle was the closest I ever got. Eighteen months I stayed. Grew attached. To the grounds, to the people, to Katherine…to Edward.

And then it started to suffocate me. The panic. The *When will it end?*

All good things have an expiry date. I learned that at a very young age. And it's far better for them to end on my terms than to be at someone else's mercy.

But I hadn't been able to let Katherine go.

And she knew it.

Was that what this was? Was she trying to give me roots?

Gifting me a home in death that I couldn't possibly say no to...? It was sick, twisted, manipulative...and it had Katherine's benevolent heart all over it.

'I know this is a lot to take in.' McAllister is filling the strained silence. 'Perhaps if you'd each take the paperwork away, read over it and come back to me with any questions you may have? I will make myself available to you any time you need. Katherine was my dearest friend, my longest client too. This isn't just my job...it's personal.'

Edward gives him a grim smile before turning to look at me, a thousand questions burning behind those rich brown eyes that have haunted my dreams for so long.

I wonder what it would take to have them look at me like they did before. With laughter, with warmth, with—

Leave it alone, Summer! You left for a reason. You ran for a reason. Those reasons haven't gone away.

'Here.' McAllister slides an envelope to each of us. 'She left you each a letter.'

I manage a sad smile, my fingers trembling as I reach for it. The family crest to the bottom right of the ivory embossed paper triggers an ache deep within that I find impossible to ignore. 'Thank you.'

'Is there anything more you'd like to ask?'

I shake my head.

He looks at Edward, whose eyes are trained on the envelope clutched in my hand.

'Mr Fitzroy?'

'No. Nothing that will make sense of this at any rate.'

McAllister gives a grim smile. 'I understand. But rest assured, your grandmother thought long and hard about this. She was never one to make such decisions lightly, as well you know.'

Edward's eyes flash, but his words are measured, 'No. She wasn't.'

'As for your mother—do let me know if I can help relay all this to her. I'm surprised she declined my invitation to be present today.'

'I'm not.'

Edward's tone is clipped as he reaches forward and takes up his letter, tucking it inside his jacket. He's all action now, as though he's made a decision only he is privy to.

'Thank you, Charles, we'll see ourselves out.'

'I'd offer to escort you to the estate…'

McAllister is looking at me, but it's Edward who speaks. 'That won't be necessary.'

Edward's already on his feet and I follow suit, frustrated that he's talking for both of us but too numb to argue. I shove the envelope into my satchel and sling the bag over my chest, hurry to tug my backpack from Edward's reaching grasp.

'I've got it,' I say, throwing it onto my back, my eyes colliding with his in challenge.

He clenches his jaw, gives me a brisk nod and gestures for me to lead the way.

I take my time, refusing to dance to his tune.

It's not like I planned any of this.

It's not like it's my fault.

'Thank you, Charles.' His tone warms with respect for the older man and a modicum of gratitude. 'I'll be in touch.'

McAllister stands, his smile heightened by relief that the meeting is done with, I'm sure. He offers his hand to me and I take it.

'It's good to see you again, Summer.'

'Thank you.'

I shake his hand, return his smile, but inside I'm questioning the 'again'. Have we met before? I guess it stands to reason I might have met him at one of Katherine's many social functions at the estate—many non-social too. But I only had eyes for one man back then.

I suck in a breath as I turn to face that man now. He's still waiting, his brooding presence as heavy as the rainclouds outside. He dominates the room, dominates me, and I stifle a shudder. Why does he have the power to make me feel so small and weak?

Wrong. He makes you feel vulnerable, and that's something else entirely.

I'm known for my strength, my decisiveness, my ability to face a challenge head-on. It's time I started acting like me again. But before I do, I need space without him in it. Space to consider Katherine's wishes and figure out a game plan. A plan that will keep my brain engaged and my heart locked away.

Question is, will he give it to me?

I straighten my spine and stride past him. I can feel his eyes boring through my backpack into me. My skin is alive with his proximity, my heart too… Getting space physically might not be an issue but mentally, emotionally…?

Edward

She's surprisingly quick down the Georgian staircase, the backpack failing to hinder her in the slightest. It would be impressive if not for the fact that I know she's running from me.

Again.

Once outside, she shows no sign of slowing, no awareness of me behind her…

Where's she heading in such a hurry?

Anywhere you're not…

'Leaving without saying goodbye?'

She freezes on the stone steps and her bag lifts with her

shoulders. She blows out a breath before turning to eye me over her shoulder. 'Look, Edward—'

'Don't worry, Summer, you have form for it. I'm hardly going to get offended now.'

She nips her lip, blue eyes flitting between me and the street—her escape.

'But we *do* need to talk.'

'Right now I need space to think.'

I shove my hands into my pockets, try to ignore the pang of her dismissal and the dogged desire to stay in her orbit. *Dammit.* How can twenty years go by and that frustrating need to be near her in spite of everything remain? An intrinsic need that runs so deep it's as much a part of me as the blood pumping through my veins.

'When, then?'

'Soon.'

'How soon?'

'I don't know, Edward!' she blurts, vibrant and alive in her exasperation. 'This whole thing has come as a huge shock and I need to get my head on straight before I can have a sensible conversation with you about it.'

'Very well,' I say. 'Where are you staying?'

'What does that matter?'

'I'll send the car to pick you up when you're ready to talk.'

'That won't be necessary.'

'Tell that to Gran's driver. He'll already be contemplating his future now the estate is under new management.'

She gives a shake of her head, a bitter laugh. 'I hardly think he wants to drive all the way down from the Highlands to ferry me around.'

'It's not about want—it's his job. It's what the estate pays him for.'

She laughs some more and my already frayed nerves snap. 'I'm glad you find this so amusing.'

She huffs at me, raises her brows to the heavy sky above. 'You're a fool if you think my laughter stems from humour, Edward.'

She shakes her head, takes the last step down and turns to look up at me. I steel myself for whatever she has to say. I steel myself against the warmth that pulses through me at having her so close again. Against the age-old anger and hurt that wants to resurrect itself even though its ancient history.

But now I have Gran's betrayal to add to the mix.

'We'll talk at the estate,' I say. It's an order, not a request. 'It's where we'll be living after all.'

My skin crawls as I acknowledge the truth of it. I feel my heart beating harder, faster, daring her to deny me.

'OK.'

I swallow, ignoring the kick to my pulse that her surprising agreement triggers. 'Good.'

'But I'll get to the estate under my own steam. When are you intending to leave?'

I stare off into the distance. The hustle and bustle of Edinburgh is a relief from her and the pressure building inside my head, my chest. Why is it so hard to breathe with her around? To concentrate and think clearly?

Maybe she's right to demand some space—some time apart before we discuss a way forward. A way that gets her out of my life for good with as little of my grandmother's estate as possible…

'Soon.' My resolve builds with my thoughts. 'I have some business to deal with here first.'

'OK…' She's already stepping away. 'I'll message to let you know when I'm ready to talk.'

'Won't you need my number for that?'

She pauses, her cheeks colouring as she inches back to me, her hand rummaging in her pocket. Her eyes don't quite meet mine as she passes me her phone, and for some unknown reason—probably the masochist in me—I let our fingers touch and feel the age-old connection warm me. Tease me.

I'm as attuned to her sharp intake of breath as I am my own, and I see the fire behind her eyes as they lift to mine, dizzying in their intensity. A thousand long-buried wants grapple to the surface and I want to pull her to me. I want to do what I didn't have the nerve to all those years ago…

And then her hand is snatched away and I'm jarred back to reality—it's all in me, not her. I'm the one wanting, feeling more than I should…

I clench my jaw, grip her phone tight, key in my number and dial it so that I have her number too, then thrust it back at her.

'Thank you.' She eyes me warily, wets her lips. 'Goodbye, Edward.'

Goodbye, Edward. The simple phrase launches the past into the present with painful clarity. *Now* I get a goodbye… only twenty years too late.

She starts to walk away and anger rears up…ugly, bitter, cold.

'Summer…?'

She pauses, turning just enough to look at me. 'Yes?'

I breathe in her beauty and feed the pain that is very real and very present. 'You may have found a home in Glenrobin once, and Gran may have gifted it to you again, but I'm not her. And I'll find a way around this if it's the last thing I do.'

Her eyes widen and I turn before she can creep beneath my shield anew. I don't care if I've hurt her—I *don't*…

Although the nails slicing through my palms tell me otherwise.

I walk away before I surrender to the guilt, and raise my shoulders against the knowledge that Gran will be turning in her grave.

I have myself to protect in the land of living, Gran, surely you can see that?

As for Summer… She doesn't get to leave for twenty years—no goodbye, no nothing—and then come back with a claim on the estate. My family's estate. She doesn't.

And it's just the claim on the estate you're worried about…?

It's as though Gran is in my head, goading me into acknowledging the true source of my unease, and I thrust a hand through my hair.

In the distance, my driver steps out of the car, races around to the boot and pulls out an umbrella. Too late. I'm soaked through. And I hadn't even noticed. Not the rain beating down, nor the wetness that's seeped through to my skin.

I wave him away, much preferring the drumming beat of the rain to the panicked staccato of my heart.

CHAPTER THREE

Summer

MY FINGERS HOVER over the keyboard. I've typed and deleted his name several times over, with my tap-tap-tapping getting more and more aggressive if the looks from nearby café-goers are any indication.

Or maybe I'm just more sensitive to their presence because I feel like what I'm doing is wrong.

Nosy. *Gossip Girl*-esque. Wrong.

I'd have done it in the privacy of my hotel room, but it turns out their services don't include free Wi-Fi. So now I'm here, propping up a café bar, with my intent stare on my laptop, my search going nowhere.

I haven't looked him up in a decade. I knew enough from Katherine to understand he was doing well; I didn't need to taunt myself with more. Especially not the gazillion visual hits bound to ensue.

The media appeal of the Fitzroys knows no bounds. Good-looking to a fault, his father's English aristocratic roots and his mother's high society breeding make them regular fodder for the press. Edward is no exception.

But the twenty-two-year-old man I left behind and the man he is now, all suited and booted and so very severe, couldn't appear more different.

And it has nothing to do with age or his impressive frame that suggests he works out—a lot! There's something else. Something dark and dangerous and deeply unsettling.

That'll be his hatred for you.

I throw off the barb. I don't want to believe it. I want to believe it's part and parcel of the man he is now.

He always had an edge, a way of standing out among his peers. Quiet, reserved...his sharp intellect and wit demanding a certain level of respect. But respect and fear aren't one and the same and McAllister had acted like he feared him.

Or was it all about me? His reaction? The lawyer's discomfort? Were they all because of me? Is he all fluffy bunnies and nicey-nice when I'm not around?

No, I don't want to believe it.

But neither do I truly want to believe he's as cold and ruthless as he appeared. Even his accent was clipped, his Scottish lilt indistinct.

And what of the way he touched my hand, held my eye, singed me to my very toes with blatant desire seconds before he delivered his parting remark and cut me to the core.

I shudder and shake it off. I should've known he would be there. I should have prepared myself better, scoured the internet for all the info I could find...

So get it done.

His name glares back at me, the cursor blinking next to it, and I strike 'enter' far harder than necessary. My eyes narrow—part-wince, part-studying—as the results appear.

Billionaire... Billionaire... Billionaire.

The word is on repeat. With every mention of his name it's there, alongside a whole list of accolades, and I'm scrolling and scrolling...

British media magnate…tech and finance entrepreneur…philanthropist…cryptocurrency…social entrepreneur…company founder…net worth…

I swallow… He really is worth billions. *Actual* billions. I shouldn't be surprised…not really…but that kind of wealth…?

Just how ruthless did one have to be to achieve such heights?

How hungry for money?

For me, the stuff's a necessary evil. I live each day to the next, never knowing where my next adventure will take me, let alone the source of my next paycheque. Don't get me wrong. I'm not irresponsible. I always put enough aside to ensure I'm a burden to no one—

A burden?

I choke on a laugh. There's no one I could be a burden *to*. The only person I ever let myself care about is gone… Well, not quite the only one. The other is staring back at me on the screen, his static image enough to make my body warm. Doesn't matter that I know he hates me, wants rid of me…

Not that I can blame him.

I left without a goodbye.

I left, and now he's suffering the injustice of having to share his inheritance with me.

And what if he's married? What if he has an entire family to uproot? Would Katherine really do that to him?

I'm already typing *Edward Fitzroy Wife*.

Enter.

So many pictures, so many articles, all pondering his personal life. Connecting him to society's finest: tech legends, business moguls…women on a par with himself. In looks and brains. Each one so much more than I could ever be.

The past rushes forth, the pain surprisingly acute, and I close my eyes, shut out the memory determined to surface.

You're good enough just the way you are. You have nothing to prove. No one to impress.

I breathe through the tightness, force my fists to relax.

Leave the past in the past and focus on the present, on the situation you're in...

I reach for my mocha, take a sugary soothing sip, and dare to scroll further...

Wait!

The hot liquid catches in my throat and I cough it up, my lips quivering over a hit.

No.

I click the headline, unable to resist:

A Good-Looking Guy, Successful and of a Certain Age, Still a Bachelor... Is our Dashing Fitzroy Gay?

It's an inevitable article, born of an inevitable question, but it tickles me. That's one question I'm sure I know the answer to. We might not have crossed that line, but the look in his eye back then...the look in his eye only yesterday, so strong it rose above the hatred... No, he's not gay.

I only wish I could be as sure about Katherine's intentions. And I know the letter will help explain, but I haven't been able to open it. It's there now, poking out from beneath my laptop, but each time I reach for it my stomach turns over and my fingers refuse to do my bidding. Guilt and grief holding me hostage.

I should have come back sooner. I should have known she was sick. I should have... I should have...

My eyes sting and I grit my teeth, swallow. I'm in a public place, it's no time for tears, but I'm confused...*so* confused.

'What were you thinking, Katherine?' I whisper.

'You mean you don't know?'

I jump as the deep, sexy drawl resonates through my core, my eyes widening as I spin on my stool. 'Edward!'

I can't believe my eyes…but my body does. It's already a hive of activity, my pulse spiking, my mouth drying out.

Does he have to be so goddam sexy all the time? The collar of his herringbone coat is pulled high, his dark wintry look crisp and elegant. His chestnut hair is immaculate, despite the chilling breeze outside, and his eyes, that mouth…

He already looks angry about something. The pink in his cheeks from the biting wind is the only sign of humanity in his face that's set like stone.

'What are you—? Why are you—? How did you know I'd be here?'

And why do I have to sound like a tongue-tied schoolgirl with an impossible infatuation?

Because it's how you feel.

His lips twitch, the sensation inside me deepens—is he laughing at me?

No, I doubt the man ever laughs these days…

'I have my ways.'

'I bet you do.' Every one of them involving the cash he appears to have an endless supply of…it doesn't explain *why* he's here though. 'And you're here because…?'

He says nothing and my brows nudge north. Maybe I'm not the only one struggling with their words. Maybe he's just as disorientated by my presence…

And maybe you're losing it more than you think!

'I'm here to see you.'

'Stating the obvious much?'

Fire flickers behind his eyes and my heart leaps into my throat—*do you want to poke the bear?*

'I mean—'

'I want to apologise,' he says over me.

'You—?' I frown, taken aback…surely I didn't hear him right. 'You what?'

'I want to apologise.'

And now he sounds like a robot…and I'm still not sure I understand. 'You want to *apologise*?'

'I do.'

'You…*do*…?'

My chin tucks in as I look up at him and he makes an exasperated sound that has me wanting to laugh.

'Please don't make this any harder than it needs to be.'

'*Harder?* Begging your pardon, Edward, but did you rush off for a lobotomy last night or something?'

His frown is instantaneous, and the way it makes his lower lip pout…too appealing, too distracting. But an apology…?

I face him full-on, my confidence growing as relief seeps through my limbs. It has to be a good sign, right?

He drags in a breath…pockets his hands. 'It was a shock; *I* was in shock. I had no idea Gran was going to do this.'

'And you think *I* did?'

A V forms between his brows and I have the ridiculous urge to smooth it away, a delicate gesture that is so at odds with his sheer masculinity.

'Well…didn't you?'

'God, no! If I had I would've told her to her face she'd lost the plot.'

A hint of a smile touches his lips and I yearn for a full-blown grin, the slightest of chuckles—anything to suggest the Edward I once knew is still in there somewhere.

'You'd have been given quite the ear-bashing if you'd tried.'

I give a soft huff, feel bittersweet memories choking up

my throat, and I swallow. 'She always was deft at saying just the right thing to get me to fall in line.'

His posture softens along with his eyes as the past shifts between us, wrapping around us, uniting us.

'Well, if you would go around flouting the rules…'

'Says the guy who couldn't flout a single one without breaking out in hives.'

And just like that he tenses, every one of his honed muscles drawing tight.

'I've changed since then.'

It's like he's in my head, but the words are leaving my lips before I can stop them. 'So I can see…'

And the real me—the daring, the confident, usually unperturbed one—comes to life and I let my eyes trail over him, full of provocation. I don't care that I'm eating him with my eyes. I want to devour him. I want him to burn like I do. I want my presence to stir into life that part of him those women on the Internet have enjoyed over the intervening years…

'This apology…' I force my eyes back to his, spy the reciprocal fire I've succeeded in provoking. 'I'm still waiting.'

He scoffs and it doesn't become him… It becomes the old him, though, and I suck my lips in to stop the smile that wants to break free.

'Ever the demanding one, Summer.'

'Well, if you will leave a lady waiting…'

I see the retort burning in his gaze—*I see no lady here*—but he doesn't say it. Twenty years ago he would have come straight out with it. Just for fun. Why not now?

Maybe he's more attuned to what sent me running all those years ago than I give him credit for…or maybe he's just grown up.

In either case, the humour and the passion are no more. I'm chilled to the bone.

'This apology?'

His eyes sharpen and I wonder if he's sensed the shift…

He clears his throat, gives an abrupt nod. 'I *am* sorry, Summer. I've had time to reflect. I've also had time to read the letter Gran left…have you read yours?'

He spies it poking out on the table and I shake my head. 'Not yet.'

I see the question in his eyes—*why not?*

'I—I'll get to it when I'm ready.'

'Right…'

There's a pause, and I know he's pondering my reaction, and all the emotions that feed my hesitancy start to clamber for attention.

'So, you've read the letter and…?' I throw the focus back on him, smother the inner turmoil.

'And I don't agree with what she has done, nor much of what she put in her letter, but this is her last request and I will respect it…to a point.'

'To a point…?' I repeat numbly, wondering how far that point will go. Do I get a tent in the garden? A toilet in the outhouse? Are we really doing this? Living together?

My heart starts to race…

'Yes. And the sooner we can talk it through the better.'

I can't respond. There are no words for this…this craziness.

'So, come with me?'

'Wait. What?' Panic kickstarts my voice. 'Come with you where?'

'To the estate. We can use the travel time to talk.'

'But I… *When?*'

'This afternoon.'

'But…'

Swallow, Summer. Breathe.

It's too soon. I've not had enough time to think. To process.

He dips his head, leans that little bit closer, and his cologne reaches me, floods my senses... Why does he have to smell so good too?

'But what?'

Close your gaping mouth and answer the man.

'But it's a couple of hundred miles away.'

'And? Surely spending the journey with me is not that awful a prospect...'

A shiver runs down my spine as I catch the hint of mockery in his rich, dulcet tones.

'We used to enjoy one another's company once, Summer. I'm sure we can at least be civil for that amount of time.'

The blood seeps from my cheeks and I bluster out a laugh. 'Is that supposed to make the offer more appealing?'

He gives a wry smile.

'No, I don't suppose it does. But I'm sure it benefits the planet in some way, us combining our journey. And I know how much you care for that.'

'Not when there's a train heading that way and...'

Hang on, my voice trails off as my eyes narrow. My eco-warrior efforts came after Glenrobin...after him...

Has he been reading up on *me*? Or is it something Katherine said? What does he know? What has he seen? What's in the public domain? Protest rallies—sure. The odd arrest—maybe.

Oh, God. A certain picture sears my brain and my cheeks are aflame before I can erase it. Please don't let him have seen *that* one...

'Fine,' I rush out. 'When do you—*we*—leave?'

'I'll pick you up at two.'

I wet my lips, my voice failing me again.

'Is that a problem?' he asks.

No. Yes. No. But it's only a few hours away from now…

'Not at all. Two p.m. it is.'

'Great.'

'Great.'

Awkward…

'Is there anything else?' I say, when he still doesn't move.

'No.' He comes alive. 'I'll see you later.'

He turns to leave and then hesitates. My heart leaps. *What now?*

He looks back at me, a curious glint in his eye. 'I'm not, by the way.'

'You're not what?'

His eyes flit to the screen of my laptop and to my horror I'm still on *that* page, with the headline blazing—*Is our Dashing Fitzroy Gay?*

Of all the articles it had to be that one…

Floor, swallow me now!

'I'll take the dashing, though.'

Something glitters behind those chocolate-brown eyes… something that triggers a thousand flutters inside me, each one contending with the mortifying burn.

'Goodbye, Summer.'

And then he's gone, and I want to stick my head and my nether regions in the nearest freezer. Maybe the café will have one out back big enough to take my entire body if I ask nicely enough…

I opt for slamming the laptop closed and pressing my forehead into its solid metal top.

Edward

I pull open the door to the street and can't resist one last look.

She's face-planted on her laptop and laughter bubbles

up inside me, its force as surprising as its presence. I shake my head, step out, grateful for the chill in the morning air.

Nothing about this is funny.

Nothing at all.

She's been back in my life less than twenty-four hours and already turned it on its head. No. Correction. Gran has done that. And as much I loved her, respected her, on this she couldn't have called it more wrong.

Or hurt me any more than she has.

It's not about the money. It's about love and loyalty and my ancestral home. How could she do this? Gift half of it to a woman who's been MIA for twenty years? How could she bring her back into my life and risk exposing me to that kind of pain again?

Betrayed and broken, I have no idea how to fix the way I feel. But I'll stay in control and buy myself the necessary time to eradicate her from my life for good. I have my advisors looking into the terms of the will—if there's a loophole, they will find it.

There's no blood connection and no bond… The woman didn't even make it back for Gran's funeral. What kind of person claims to care and doesn't even turn up to say goodbye?

I clutch the letter in my coat pocket and swallow down the rising sickness, walk away before I storm back inside the café and demand that she tell me.

Now isn't the time or the place. Glenrobin is.

My jaw is throbbing by the time I enter the foyer of my Scottish headquarters, the double-height entrance enhanced by its glass front, white-tiled floor and flashes of chrome. Some might say it's clinical—to me it means business. A space for focus and success. Success I've worked damned hard for, proving that I'm more than just my father's name… My father's title.

And look at Summer now…being gifted a fortune so vast it could feed a small nation and having done nothing to deserve it, too.

Well, over my dead body.

Sorry, Gran.

CHAPTER FOUR

Summer

Dearest Summer,

I know this will come as a shock, but you know me: I never do anything without careful consideration. As the saying goes, there's method in my madness, so please bear with me and the terms of my will. I'm not going to play the emotional blackmail card. I'm only going to ask that you give this old woman the benefit of the doubt and humour me, if you will.

And, yes, I'm smiling as I write that.

Now for the serious bit. And please don't groan—it doesn't become you.

I see the way you spend your life, running from one thing to the next, never settling in one place long enough to put down roots. I worry that if you're not careful life will pass you by, and you will never pause long enough to feel what it is to be content, to be happy, to be loved...

It's my greatest regret that neither you nor Edward ever had a true home. One filled with love and laughter as it should be. Oh, I tried—heaven knows I tried. And I suppose you can say that this is my last hurrah...to try and give you both what you've never had.

Why together?

Because you belong together, and it's high time you realised it.

Call me an old romantic—call me whatever you like—but this is my way of knocking your heads together from above. I should have done it years ago, but I hoped that life would do it for me. Well, life has had its chance and I'm out of mine. So this is it.

Look after yourself, and each other. I believe with all my heart that this is an opportunity for you both to forge a better path to happiness. Please take it.

All my love and hope for the future,

Gran x

I PRESS MY fist to my mouth, fend off the sob that wants to erupt. The sob that's also a laugh, that's also a disbelieving choke.

The carefully crafted words blur with my tears and I lift the sheet away before the first droplet can ruin the ink.

At least I understand her thinking now…

Understand it, yes.

But agree…?

Me and Edward.

It's just not possible.

It wasn't back then. It certainly isn't now.

'I'm sorry, Katherine,' I say into the empty hotel room, wishing I was wrong, wishing she was right, wishing the dream could be real even though I know it's not and can never be.

Because no one has ever loved me enough to want to keep me.

You're wrong. Katherine did.

But then she was one of a kind. And Edward...he's a very, *very* different kind.

The kind that wields the power to break me so completely if I let him.

CHAPTER FIVE

Edward

MY CAR PULLS up outside her hotel bang on time and I'm surprised to find her already waiting on the pavement. Perched on her backpack, one booted foot tapping, her arms wrapping a vibrant yet ridiculously thin kimono around her.

Does the woman not own a coat?

It's not raining today, but the clear sky offers no protection from the chill, and even with the sun's rays lighting her up on the pavement it can't be enough to warm her.

I leap out of the car before my driver can approach her. 'Get in. It's freezing out here.'

She shoots to her feet, her cheeks radiating the same heat as her eyes. I've annoyed her, but I don't care. Where is her common sense?

'Hello to you too.'

I ignore her snippy remark and grab her bag, handing it to my driver as she gives a huff of protest.

'Get in, Summer,' I repeat, holding open her door. 'As much it will save me a headache or two, I really don't want you to catch your death right now.'

She stares at me hard, opens her mouth and closes it again. Whether it's because of the hint that I might actually care about her wellbeing or the cold itself, she finally moves. Shrugging her satchel off her shoulders and slipping inside, she promptly slams the door in my face.

I look over the roof, take a breath and deny the smirk that wants to form. 'Keep it under control.'

I walk around the car and get in the same side I exited.

'Seatbelt,' I say, without looking at her, knowing she won't have fastened it.

I'm saved from a retort by my driver, who catches her eye in the rear-view mirror, and she gives a soft sigh, does as I've asked. More for his benefit than mine, but that's just fine.

As soon as she's secure he pulls away from the kerb and I breathe more easily…until I catch the faint trace of her perfume. Light, sunny…all her.

'Are you always this grumpy, or do you save it just for me?'

Another smile teases at my lips and I beat it back. This isn't amusing. If I could stay grumpy this wouldn't be such torture.

'Behave like an obstinate child and I'll treat you like one.'

'A *child*? What the—?'

She breaks off as the privacy glass glides into position, saving my driver from hearing more than he should.

'How *dare* you?'

Slowly, I turn to face her. Prepare myself for having her so near. The luxurious back seat is far too cosy, and never have I needed us to be at loggerheads more.

'You're stood outside in the freezing cold, paying no heed to the weather—how else should I treat you?'

'"Paying no heed"?' she splutters back at me, laughing, her eyes wide and disbelieving. 'What century did you walk out of?'

'Cut the attitude, Summer.'

'*My* attitude? Have you checked yourself out in the mirror lately?'

Heat collides with heat. Her chest is undulating so rapidly with her breaths that her kimono parts and my eyes unwittingly dip. I fist my hands against the pulse in my groin and she grunts, tugging the fabric back together and throwing herself back in her seat, arms folded, pout to die for.

'For your information,' she blurts to the passing world outside, 'I don't own a coat.'

'You don't…?' I frown. She can't be serious. 'How can you not own a coat?'

She fires a look at me. 'You want to make a big deal out of that?'

'But Summer—no coat? Seriously?'

'I follow the sun, Edward. I don't *need* a coat.'

'Everyone needs a coat.'

'Not when everything you own has to fit on your back, you don't. I carry what I need. Satisfied?'

Her eyes dare me to object, but I'm already pressing the intercom to speak my driver. 'Parker, we're taking a detour. Miss Evans needs to purchase some clothes.'

'Don't be ridiculous, Edward!' She gapes at me. 'We're not going shopping.'

'We are.'

'Don't we have a train to catch?'

'No.'

'Well, if we're driving the whole way it would be nice to get there before sundown, so… What? Why are you looking at me like that?'

'We're not driving.'

'A bus…?'

She gives me a confused frown and now I really am struggling not to laugh. Me on a bus? Is she serious?

'We're taking the helicopter.'

'The *helicopter*?' she chokes out. 'Are you for *real*?'

I say nothing.

'Of course you are.' Now it's her head that's shaking, her lips twisted in disdain. 'I really shouldn't be surprised, should I?'

'I don't know, Summer,' I say evenly. 'The helipad is a recent addition to the estate. It stands to reason you wouldn't know about it.'

I feel her continued censure as she stares out of the window. What exactly is her problem? The fact that I'm highlighting her absenteeism or the fact that my considerable wealth makes such things as a helipad possible?

Would she be so disgruntled if she knew the reason the helipad exists at all?

I have the ridiculous urge to explain, but bite my tongue. I don't care for her opinion. We just need to get through the next few days, weeks, months—a year, even, heaven forbid—without killing each other.

'Where to, sir?' Parker's voice pipes through the car, reminding me he's waiting for a revised destination.

'Harvey Nicks.' It's the most obvious choice—everything under one roof. Quick. Simple. Efficient.

She looks back at me, her blue eyes bright. 'We are *not*.'

I hold her blazing gaze, unperturbed. 'Would you rather House of Fraser, or—?'

'We're not going shopping, Edward!'

'No, we're not. *You* are.'

'I don't have the money to just—'

'Correction. You do have the money—or have you forgotten already?'

'Seriously, Edward, you're—'

'Sir?' Parker prompts as we approach a set of traffic lights.

'Harvey Nicks. And delay our take-off by two hours, please.'

'Two hours! What on earth are we shopping for that will take two hours?'

'As you've just explained, you have a bag full of summer-wear—or am I mistaken?'

'No, b—'

'Then we're going shopping. You can use my card.'

'I don't want to use your blasted card, Edward,' she erupts, her bottom lip jutting out with her displeasure.

It's so perfectly kissable, I can almost taste it.

'No…' Inside, I curse, battling my impossible reaction to her as I go on the attack. 'You'd rather behave like a petulant child—again.'

Her eyes flash. 'Say that again and I'll—I'll—'

I raise my brows at her. 'You'll what?'

She makes a growling sound and slams back into her seat. 'When did you get so *infuriating*?'

'When you left without a goodbye.'

Idiot! Where did that come from?

I race to fill the silence but she's there first, her voice sickeningly soft, 'Edward, I'm sorry for what—'

'Save it, Summer. I'm not interested in looking back. All I care about right now is ensuring you don't die of hypothermia.'

'I don't need you to sort out my wardrobe.'

'Because you've done such a great job of it yourself?'

She re-wraps her kimono around her, case in point. The flimsy thing in no way up to the task of fending off the Scottish weather…even so, I can't deny that I love it. The vibrant colours. The way it sets off her eyes, her wild hair, the sun-kissed glow of her skin…

But then I'd love anything on her—that's the problem.

What the hell is wrong with me?

'I've not had the time to think about something as simple as my wardrobe. My head's been full of all this since I returned.'

I scan her face, see her sincerity for what it is. 'Have you read your letter now?'

'Yes,' she admits quietly. 'I've read the letter.'

'And?'

'And I too disagree with much of it.'

'Common ground at last.'

She gives a huff-cum-sigh.

'In which case, I assume you'll also agree that we need to find a way around the conditions of the will—specifically those relating to where we live for the next year.'

Her eyes probe mine. 'Why?'

'Are you seriously asking me that?'

Her cheeks flush a delectable shade of pink, her lack of make-up offering up no protection from my watchful eye. She used to go in for heavy eyeliner, pale foundation, subtle blusher... Not that she needed it then—or now. Though I'm sure she'd appreciate its concealing benefits if I told her that her skin gives away her every emotion. Anger. Frustration. Sadness... Desire.

'Do you have somewhere else you need to be for the next year, Edward? Or do you simply want to get away from me?'

My laugh is cold and abrupt as I turn to the window. I don't want her to see the bitterness in my face. I don't want her to know how much it stung when she left.

Her shocking departure cut deeper than the emotional neglect I suffered at the hands of my parents and has affected every relationship I've attempted since.

No one gets to see me that weak. Not any more.

'Want to swap letters?' she murmurs into the quiet, and I flinch.

'Hell, no.'

'Spoilsport,' she mutters under her breath.

Silence descends—heavy, strained—and I count the seconds until I can break out of the car, break free of her…

I've never been more relieved to see the front of a department store. The five-storey building a welcome sight of sandstone, granite and gleaming glass. I leap out as soon as the car pulls up and catch the tail-end of Summer's hushed laughter as I go.

I wait for her on the pavement and she strides straight past me, her words trailing on the chilling breeze. 'I never thought I'd see you so eager to shop, Edward.'

I bite my lip. Me neither.

Oh, Gran, if you could see me now you'd be laughing with her…or maybe that was your intention all along.

Summer

I thought nothing could beat the weird adrenaline rush of shopping with Edward.

At first, I was hesitant. 'Uncooperative', to use his word. But I've never been a girly-girl. I've never had the cash to spare or the friends to shop with. Moving from foster home to foster home, school to school, can do that to you.

But under his undivided attention, hearing his honest opinion on what worked and what didn't, what colours, what styles… I was lapping it up by the end.

It sure beat the animosity tainting our every other interaction up until now…even the one when he'd apologised. Sort of.

And with every compliment he paid my body warmed, and my ego with it. Not that he was flirting, or anything close. He said it like a statement of fact. Like it should be obvious to me what shades brought out the blue of my eyes, the honey in my hair…

It didn't mean anything. But it had been so long since anyone had taken charge with my interests at heart. He *cared* that I didn't catch my death and it felt…it felt good. Dangerously good to let someone care for me on some level and take the lead.

But now I'm here, in his helicopter, of all things, with the Scottish landscape drifting by beneath us. A patchwork quilt of greens, browns and hints of purple. Landbound lochs and rolling hills. Seeing it all from the air is incredible—an adrenaline-packed ride, quite literally.

'If I didn't know any better, I'd say you're enjoying this.'

Edward's voice crackles through my headset and I can't help the smile that's busting my cheeks.

'It is stunning!'

'And yet you've stayed away for so long.'

His sudden attack steals my breath and I look back to the window, hide my guilt, my confusion, my pain. How could he begin to understand how I felt? He was born into his world, Katherine's world, and for all his grandmother tried to make me feel at home she couldn't eradicate the doubt. The doubt that Edward's own mother had picked up on and used against me.

'It was better that way.'

I grip my hands together in my lap. *Better for who?* I feel the dig in my ribs—a sharp, acute pain. *Selfish. Selfish. Selfish.* Protecting myself when I should have been…

But I didn't know she was sick! If I had, I would've moved heaven and earth to be here.

'What? Staying away?' he presses, his disbelief audible. 'Even when Gran was diagnosed…?'

I flex my fingers, breathe through the pain. 'No…'

My voice catches as I risk meeting his penetrative gaze. 'Not then.'

'Why, then? Why not come home when you knew she was sick?'

'Because I didn't know.'

I look away in my shame, my guilt, and say it so quietly I'm surprised he hears me over the blades beating loudly above our heads and the static through the headphones.

He leans across the lush cabin—swankier than I ever thought possible in such a confined space—and touches my leg, tries to get my attention.

'What do you mean, you didn't know, Summer?'

'Just what I said…' I swallow the bulging wedge in my throat, blink back the tears. 'She didn't tell me.'

'But all this time you claimed to be in touch. Hell, Charles assured me you'd always been in her life, that her love for you was as strong as it ever had been, that you were close.'

Close? I nip my lip and the tears keep on coming. The retort is on the tip of my tongue. *So close she didn't think to tell me something as important as the fact she was dying.*

But I can't say it. It hurts too much.

'Summer?'

'What, Edward?' I shoot back, my eyes piercing his. I'm angry that he's pressing me on this. Something I haven't been able to come to terms with myself. 'You know what she was like! She didn't want to be seen as weak, as vulnerable, to have people fussing. She wouldn't have wanted me to worry on the other side of the world. She wouldn't have wanted me packing up my life to come back for her. She wouldn't have wanted me…wanted me…'

I fumble for more reasons—reasons that I've told myself a thousand times over. But the only one I truly believe is that she didn't love me enough to think I needed to know…

Or, worse, she thought I didn't love her enough to care.

And if that's the case why the inheritance? Why the letter so heartfelt and full of future promise?

'No, you're right.' He snaps his hand back. The lines bracketing his mouth deepen as he presses his lips together, the rich brown depths of his eyes haunted by his own grief, his own confusion. 'She wouldn't have wanted you to worry or change your life for her.'

I ignore the way his words stick the knife in deeper and ask, 'How long was she sick?'

'I can't believe you didn't know…'

'I didn't, Edward. Please, you *must* believe me on this.' Desperation makes my voice hoarse. 'Do you really think I would have stayed away if I'd known?'

He debates it for longer than I like, his stare intense, and then he blinks and I see the shutters lift, the resignation in his sagging posture.

'She was sick for a while.' He sinks back into his seat, his eyes going to the window, lost in the past. 'Like you say, she didn't want to make a fuss. It was only when she couldn't hide the pain that I forced her to admit something was wrong.'

His voice cracks but he doesn't stop.

'She refused treatment. Said it would only prolong the discomfort, make her feel worse, and she'd prefer to spend her last few months on this earth pretending it wasn't happening…'

He takes a ragged breath and I fight the impulse to reach out for him, to offer comfort that I know he won't welcome.

He turns to look at me. 'You know, I don't think she would have told me either if she could've avoided it.'

He looks so broken, so defeated, and I know what the admission has cost him. Gone is the cold executive. In his place is a glimpse of the man I knew and my heart aches for him.

'She was too independent for her own good,' I say.

'She was too stubborn, you mean.'

'Stubborn, independent—same difference…' I attempt a nonchalant shrug, a sad smile, and I surrender to the need to touch him, to comfort him, to share this moment…especially when I can only guess at how rare it might be. I cover his hand with my own, feel him flinch. But he doesn't break away and I tell him with all the feeling I can muster, 'She loved you, though.'

His eyes reach inside mine, and a thousand shadows chase across his face. 'It appears she loved us both.'

Did she? 'I guess…'

'You guess?'

I look away from his surprise. Of course he won't understand. How can he when I haven't explained myself? I think back to that God-awful phone call a few weeks ago, when Mr McAllister rang me and informed me of her death. Out of the blue. No warning. Nothing.

'I was so *angry*, Edward. Not when I learned of her death—not then. I was shocked, grief-stricken… But when I learned that she'd been sick, that she'd known she was going to—to—' I swallow down the tears. 'That she didn't have much time left. How could she take away my chance to say goodbye? Why didn't she want me to come back? Why didn't she want me here? I would have come—I would have. She should've known that.'

He covers my hand on his. 'Maybe she didn't want your last words to be filled with pain.'

I drag my eyes back to his. 'Like yours were?'

He nods, and in that moment the bond, the connection, is undeniable. The years fall away without the hurt, the distance, and the defensive walls we've erected since.

'How—how was she?'

'Towards the end?'

I nod, and he surprises me with the smallest of smiles. 'Fierce.'

'Fierce?' I mirror his smile and he nods again.

'Like you wouldn't believe. Mind over matter, they say, and she was that through and through, refusing to bend to the illness. But that last fortnight she shrank. She grew tired. She wanted—she wanted it over.'

'And you were with her?'

'As much as possible. It's the reason for the helipad.'

I frown, and he gestures around us. 'I invested in all this when I found out she was sick. I could get to her quicker… more often.'

And I'd been thinking it was just a way of splashing his cash. I feel a stab of guilt and squeeze his fingers. 'I'm so glad she had you.'

Not just your mother, I want to say, but I don't. I can't imagine she will have changed much in all the years I've been away.

'Me too.'

We fall silent, our eyes connected, the mood in the cabin heavy with our grief, our newfound understanding…

There's so much I want to say. So much I want to do. I want to wrap my arms around him, hold him close, absorb his pain like my own.

'Sir?'

I start as the pilot's voice breaks through the headset.

'We're coming in to land.'

Edward looks at me—a look I can't decipher.

'Thank you, Angus.'

He withdraws from my touch.

'You should check out the view. You've never seen Glenrobin from this angle.'

Slowly, I do as he suggests, my head and heart slow to shift focus. I should be grateful for the timely interruption. Should be, but I'm not.

I look at the ground beneath us and press a palm to my chest, comfort my unsteady heart as I take in the sheer beauty below…

'Something else, isn't she?'

I nod as I take in all that has changed and all that remains the same.

The far-reaching loch with its wooden jetty where I first met Edward. The new addition of what looks to be a boat house. The dense woods that punctuate the skyline and run along one edge, up into the mountains, and the rolling fields where the estate's game roam free. And nestled in the heart of its wild surroundings the majestic house itself.

Glenrobin Castle, in all its austere beauty.

'It's even more breathtaking than I remember.'

'And it's half yours now.'

I can hear the continued disbelief in his tone, his discontentment too, and I feel it through and through. *This can't be mine.*

I gaze along the lawn at the vast baronial building with its château-inspired pepper-pot turrets, all granite and slate and irregular in shape. It has a gothic fairy tale vibe, and if I hadn't lived here once upon a time I'd have a hard time believing such mythical beauty exists. Let alone accepting I own any part of it.

I'm mesmerised as the pilot touches down with a gentle bump, the carefully groomed lawn kicking up dirt and grass as it settles into position.

'It hasn't changed a bit,' I whisper to myself as Edward speaks to the pilot, and I'm surprised to hear him respond.

'Not from the outside, but you should see some improvements to the amenities inside, and there are a few holiday rentals dotted about the land now. It needs renovating in parts, but we're getting there.'

If I'm not mistaken, it's the sound of pride in his voice. Is Edward responsible for it all? Has he been helping to take care of Glenrobin for a while now?

Even more reason for him to resent me and my share.

Not for the first time, I wonder at his parents' lack of involvement, their small by comparison inheritance. Now isn't the time to ask him about it, though. I'm exhausted. It's early evening here, but it's the middle of the night in Kuala Lumpur and I'm still on Malaysian time.

How easily sleep will come is another matter. Being back here…with all the memories I've tried hard to forget, all the feelings I've tried to suppress. Last night was impossible enough, but tonight…in a new bed in a new room in a house I know of old…

Where will I sleep? Do I get to choose? Has Edward chosen for me?

'You ready?' Edward looks to me expectantly, his seatbelt already undone as he gestures to the door that has been opened without my noticing.

I release my belt and clamber forward. My legs feel weak. I want to blame the vibrations of the helicopter, but I know it has more to do with him and the castle I'm walking into—the dawning responsibility of it too.

I grip the handrail as I carefully step down to the ground, my eyes fixed on the house and the staff I can see waiting, though I can't make out their faces. Will I know anyone? Will they remember me? Do they know we're now…? What are we, exactly? Their new employers?

Edward's palm presses into my lower back and I inhale sharply, heat rushing to greet his touch.

'Sorry, I didn't mean to startle you!' he shouts over the helicopter blades. 'But unless you want your ears ringing all night we should move!'

'Oh, right…of course!' I scrape my whipped-up hair back from my face but can't find my legs.

'What is it?' He leans into my immobile form.

'Do they—do they know?'

'About us?'

My eyes shoot to his—*us*? Oh, how I once wished that we could have been just that—an us.

'Summer?'

'About the new ownership!' I blurt. 'The conditions—all of it?'

'Yes, they know enough!'

I nod, but still I'm rooted. There are five people standing in the distance, all in the same navy and white uniform, bodies ramrod-straight, hands clasped before them.

'How did they take it?'

'They loved my grandmother and they respect her wishes. That's all you need to know!'

You don't, though, my heart screams as his palm urges me to move.

'Come on! Marie will get tetchy if we're late for dinner!'

'Dinner?' The idea of eating anything feels impossible. But then… 'Hang on, did you say Marie? *Marie* is still here?'

'Yes.'

He smiles now, the closest thing to a genuine smile I've seen him give, and a wave of happiness flows through me. I cling to it, use it to give me the confidence I've been lacking.

'And whatever you do, don't mention retirement to her—

not unless you want something akin to gruel for breakfast each day!'

'Thanks for the warning!' I manage to say, happy to know there will be one friendly face at least.

I only wish it could be his.

CHAPTER SIX

Edward

I INTRODUCE SUMMER to the staff, but my eyes are all for her, watching her every move.

She's nervous. The nip she gives her bottom lip between introductions is so very telling, but then she smiles and I watch it work its magic over everyone. She's wearing one of her new sweaters—a chunky knit in fluorescent pink. It should hurt my eyes. Instead it enhances everything about her…everything that seems designed to entice me.

More layers were meant to be a *good* thing. The less flattering and the thicker the better. But I'm staring at her now and I've never wanted her more. Hot off the back of our emotional exchange, our shared grief and understanding… Is it possible to be starved of someone for so long that their appeal returns so much stronger for the deprivation?

Marie lets out a squeal of delight that jolts right through me, saving me from myself.

'Miss Summer! This is the best news, lass!' She tugs Summer in for a hug. 'The best, I tell ye!'

James, our butler, clears his throat. It's a warning to Marie, but she's been here longer than me and no amount of throat-clearing will rein in.

I tear my gaze away, concentrate on the helicopter being

unloaded, her baggage so light even with the addition of all the purchases I insisted she make.

Is that really all she owns? She's made no arrangements, no requests to have anything else shipped…

'Mr Fitzroy, sir?' Mrs McDougall, James's wife, calls for my attention. She's been the Glenrobin housekeeper for a decade now and still I address her by her title. As does every staff member, including her husband. 'Shall I arrange for tea in the sitting room?'

'Please.' I turn to Summer. 'Shall we?'

I nod for her to go ahead, but she waits for me. I tilt my head, questioning her hesitation, and her smile tightens in return. She doesn't want to walk in first.

And now the staff are staring, their curiosity mounting, so I move before we can look any more out of place.

I guess it hasn't been her home in so long returning to it must be strange. Particularly when it's not just a home now. It's a responsibility, a job, an estate that needs managing twenty-four-seven to keep it ticking over. I wonder if she realises that. It's no free ride caring for such a large estate—a two-hundred-year-old one at that—no matter how temporary I hope to make this entire arrangement.

I cross the entrance hall, my shoes clipping the rich wooden floor, and that's when I realise it's only my footsteps I can hear. I turn to find her in the middle of the room, the double-height space dwarfing her form as she stares up at the crystal chandelier and then all around. At the wood-panelled walls, the hunting regalia, the portraits of ancestors gone by…

I want to read her mind. I want to know exactly what she's thinking. Is her head racing with the same questions…? How is this supposed to work? What was Gran playing at? How do I resist the way my body reacts to her at every turn?

OK, so that latter problem is all me…

The staff disperse behind her and we're alone once more.

'Summer?'

Her eyes fall to mine, wide, unsure.

'The sitting room is this way.'

Like she needs the reminder… She might have been gone twenty years but her memory is intact.

Still, she nods as if she doesn't already know, then takes another look around, her eyes landing on the tapestry of the family crest that hangs above the inglenook fireplace. Its dominant presence leaves guests in no doubt as to who this house belongs to…even if Gran has now stuck a dividing line down its middle.

But to Gran, Summer was family. She became family the second she moved in all those years ago.

'Summer?' I try again, and this time she moves, tucking a loose strand of hair behind her ear and avoiding my eye. 'Are you okay?'

I'm angry at myself for asking. Even more angry that my heart insists on caring.

She gives another nod, but I know she's not. *She* knows she's not. And it should make me happy, but I'm not.

I want to howl with frustration. Instead I clench my jaw shut, don't open it again until we're settled in the sitting room and the tea has been poured. I thank Mrs Mc-Dougall and tamp down the desire to ask for something stronger—neat.

'You're welcome.' She pauses on her way out the door. 'Which rooms would you like your luggage in?'

I glance at Summer and she's nipping at her lip again.

'I'd be happy with my old room…' She directs it at me and I shake my head.

'That's not going to work.'

'Why not?'

'Because those rooms haven't been occupied in years—and besides, you are to all intents and purposes the lady of the house now.' I can't hide the bitter tinge to my words. 'You should have Gran's old room.'

She pales. 'No…' she whispers. 'I couldn't.'

It's like a knife twisting inside my chest, her obvious upset, and I want to take it back. The pain I've inflicted. But what of *my* pain? Why can't I fixate on that and use it to protect myself and keep her at arm's length?

'And may I remind you,' she continues on, her voice stronger now, 'that not two days ago you made it clear I would never be seen as—'

'One of us needs to,' I interject quickly, knowing what she's about to say and not wanting Mrs McDougall to bear witness. 'My mother will have the east wing for her visits—for now. And many of the rooms to the rear, including your old one, are in desperate need of renovation.'

'I think what you class as "desperate need" and what I class as "desperate need" are very different. I'm sure my old room will be plenty good enough, Edward.'

Mrs McDougall's eyes are flitting back and forth between us. Her expression is unreadable but she's certainly taking note. I'm not used to being questioned—especially in front of my staff. Coupled with the way Summer's getting under my skin…and in the very house where we share a past… I need this conversation over. *Now.*

'No.' My tone brooks no argument. 'It won't.'

'Fine.' She folds her arms, stares me down. 'But I'm not taking the master suite.'

Mrs McDougall chokes on what definitely sounds like a laugh.

'Fine,' I bite out. 'I'll take the master suite and you'll take the adjoining room.'

Her mouth quirks just a little, and there's no missing the triumphant spark in her eye.

'I trust that is satisfactory?' My voice is as tight as my hand around the delicate china cup.

'Very.' She graces me with a smile so sickly sweet that I want to recoil…or stride across the room and kiss it from her…bury the chaos of this situation in what I know would be explosive. No matter how unwise.

'There you have it, Mrs McDougall. You can prepare the rooms.'

'Absolutely, sir.'

I sip my tea, force my hand to relax, my body too, and listen for the click of the door closing on her exit.

'It would be better if we saved the arguments for behind closed doors,' I say.

Her frown is instant, the smirk on her lips quicker still. 'Edward! Are you serious?'

'I would prefer it if the staff were not aware of our… issues.'

Now she laughs. '*Issues?* Is that what you're calling it?'

'What would you call it?'

'Well, that just now was us discussing sleeping arrangements. I hardly think it's a criminal offence for Mrs McDougall to know that I don't want to sleep in Katherine's room.'

'And what makes you think that I w—?' I snap my mouth shut on the heartfelt admission. Dammit all. Why can't I keep a handle on it when she's around?

She starts to lift out of her seat, her eyes softening as she reaches for me. 'Edward, I'm sorry, I didn't—'

'Leave it, Summer.'

I'm out of my seat faster than her. I don't want to hear it.

I'm sick of feeling…like this. I need to get out of her orbit. I need air without her sunny scent. I need space without the sight of her chewing on her luscious lip, without the familiar flecks of gold in her expressive blue eyes, without the sympathy…no more sympathy.

'Now that the bedrooms are sorted, I have some calls to make.' I rise with my cup in hand, although I intend to replace it with something stronger as soon as I'm alone. 'Can you find your own way to yours?'

'I'm sure I'll manage.' But she eyes the doorway as if at any moment it might bite her…

'You don't look sure…'

Her eyes flit to me. 'It's just…it's so strange, being back here. I never thought… Well, I didn't think. And especially not now—not without Katherine.'

Her voice cracks, and for the first time since she arrived I see her grief written in her face. It runs so much deeper now that we're here, surrounded by my grandmother's legacy.

'I know. Her presence is as big as the house itself…her absence too.'

She twists her hands in front of her and I can't take the sight of her all vulnerable and alone.

'Right, I'll take you up.' The words are abrupt with my frustration, and I grimace as she flinches. 'Sorry. I'm tired. I didn't get much sleep last night.'

'You and me both.'

Her fingers tremble as she reaches for her cup and I step in, lifting it for her. We're so close now—too close—and I keep my eyes trained on the door as I wait for her.

Just show her to her room.
Get yourself to yours.
Get the space you need.
Simple.
Or it should be…

Summer

From the safety of the bedroom threshold, Edward points out the access to the dressing room, the bathroom and, with a bob of his prominent Adam's apple, the interconnecting door to his bedroom.

And then he's gone, leaving a hint of his cologne in his wake and a whole heap of tension in the air. I'm not blind to the banked desire behind his eyes, the desire he doesn't want to feel…

Well, join the club!

'Is this what you wanted, Katherine?' I whisper into the room. 'Is this meant to be a gift and a punishment in one?'

I think about the letter. Think about the way I'd sometimes catch her watching us when we were younger, a smile about her lips and a sparkle in her eye. I didn't intentionally give away my feelings—my body did it for me… Something Edward's own mother took great delight in highlighting once upon a time.

My cheeks burn as the memory threatens to engulf me and I'm saved by a knock at the door. I turn to it, press my palms to my cheeks and take a breath, smile. 'Come in.'

James opens the door, his arms heavily laden. 'I have your baggage, Miss Summer.'

My smile falters. 'Please, just call me Summer, James. I feel like I should be looking for my mother when you say "Miss".' And if I don't want to think about Edward's mother, I certainly don't want to be thinking about my own. 'If you wouldn't mind, that is?'

He seems to think about it for a second more and then he straightens, gives a nod. 'Very well… Summer. Can I send for Mrs McDougall to help you unpack?'

He eyes my luggage, specifically my backpack, and his brow furrows. He probably thinks a rat will run out of the worn canvas at any moment. Such a contrast to the crisp white department store bags with their fussy black bows and block letters, all carefully filled to the brim thanks to Edward.

'No, it's fine. I'll take care of it.'

'Of course. Can I get you anything else?'

'I'm fine, thank you, James.'

With another swift nod he leaves me, his pace far steadier than Edward's was.

Now it's just me, my cup of tea and a thousand memories all making themselves known.

Oh, Katherine, you really have done a number on us both.

I walk to the bed, sink into its edge, careful not to spill my drink. The bedding alone looks like it's worth more than the entire contents of my backpack. And don't get me started on the rest of the room...

The exquisite furniture that looks ancient yet pristine. The heavy tartan drapes in front of the large bay window that curves with the turret and offers space to sit and survey the land. The pillows sumptuous and inviting. The tapestry rugs adorning the floor and the gilt-framed paintings of landscapes and people gone by on every wall.

It's yours now...

Like hell it is. None of this is mine.

And yet the legal documents and the letter from Katherine say it is. Half of it, at least.

I suck in a breath...let it out slowly. Take another...

It's time to stop questioning it and do as Katherine says—look to the future and *'forge a better path to happiness'.* Whatever that means...

I know one thing for certain: looking back isn't going to help us move forward. We need to lay the past to rest, and that means forcing him to hear the apology he doesn't want to listen to.

Mind made up, I unpack, trying to make the room feel like home. I place the photo Katherine gave me as a leaving gift on the bedside table, where it always lives, and Ted beside it. My little bear is so tatty it's a miracle he still has all his limbs. He's the only thing left from my life before foster care and he's travelled everywhere with me.

'Welcome to your new abode, Ted.' I pat his threadbare head.

I'm not sure why I keep him. I'm not even a hundred percent certain he came from my mother. But I guess he's a reminder of where I came from…and he's a warning, too. Not to get attached. That even those who should love you by blood soon realise you're not worth it.

'Not us, though, hey, Ted? We have each other.'

I tackle the dressing room next…or rather it tackles me. My clothes are dwarfed by the sheer size of it. My trainers, walking boots and sandals tuck into one corner, leaving row upon row of vacant space, the clever lighting accentuating just how bare it still is. And just how ridiculous and out of place I feel using it.

I turn away.

You don't belong here, the empty space whispers at me.

But then Katherine's voice from the past overrides it. *'This is your home for as long as you want it to be, Summer.'*

'Home,' I repeat aloud, testing it for size.

I don't do homes. It's not just people I avoid becoming attached to, but places too. I run before I'm pushed. It's served me well until now…

And I know Katherine insists this isn't emotional blackmail, but I can't help feeling it is—just a little.

'She's a monkey, Ted,' I say, walking back into the bedroom and grabbing up my toiletry bag.

I find the bathroom already stocked as I unpack my own toiletries. I eye the expensive-looking body wash and have the silly urge to sniff it, just to see if it smells of Edward, and snap my hand back to my side—*weirdo!*

It's then I see my reflection in the mirror above the sink and grimace. I look like I've been dragged through a hedge backwards.

Jet-lagged me is bad enough. Jet-lagged me with a disturbed night and a body in turmoil over being back here with Edward is something else. I'm hovering between startled rabbit and Mad Hatter. And don't even get me started on my hair. Do helicopters *do* that?

I check my watch and curse. I have ten minutes to get ready.

I strip swiftly and hit the shower. It's vast, the marble tiles spotless, the jets hot and fierce and everything my aching body needs.

Clean and refreshed, I feel more awake and ready to face the music. To face him.

I choose my clothes carefully. Jeans and a cream fine-knit sweater—one that Edward helped me choose that afternoon.

Edward, Edward, Edward.

I grit my teeth, shake out the taunt. I feel like a teenager mooning over him again.

But I had an excuse back then.

I was young, not quite naive—no child can live through foster care and be that—but foolish enough to believe in real-life fairy tales. He was the first guy to show me the right kind of attention, looking beneath the bad-girl exterior, the cocky arrogance, to the girl beneath. He saw the real me, listened to me, and I let him in…started to care…

* * *

'So, the smoking—it's all part of the image, right?'

We'd taken a run up into the mountains, the second summer he'd come home. He'd been determined to get me fitter and I—well, I never could resist seeing him working up a sweat. We'd collapsed against a sunbaked rock, our eyes on the blue sky, our conversation turning deep.

'What makes you say that?'

'Because you rarely roll up any more.'

I'd shrugged. 'I haven't wanted to.'

He'd pushed himself up on one elbow and looked down at me, his hair flopping forward in its sexy habit, and my entire body had thrummed with the possibility that this might be it. Today he might kiss me and fulfil the dream I'd had since the first day I'd met him.

'I think it's more than that...' The sincerity in his chocolate-brown eyes had set my heart racing, my lips bone-dry.

'Oh, you do, do you...?' Husky. Low. I hadn't even sounded like me.

'I think you know you don't need to be like that around me...you don't need the front.'

'No? And why's that?'

'Because I like the person you are beneath the shield, Summer. And you should like her too.'

My laugh had been awkward, cut short by my heart bursting against my ribs as he'd leaned that little bit closer.

'Just remember that, okay...?'

'Oh, how times change,' I say now, into the bathroom mirror.

Now I know better, and I only wish my body would get the message.

I snatch up my mascara, give my lashes a quick sweep, put some gloss on my lips and the slightest hint of blusher.

If anything, it'll give me some protection when my cheeks flush, as they inevitably will. I towel-dry my hair and run a brush through it. I don't have time for more.

'It's not like he expects to be dining with the country's finest, so get over yourself,' I mutter, heading for the door and wishing I'd purchased slippers on our impromptu shopping spree.

These big houses are cold at floor level, and even the thickest socks I have aren't seeing out the chill. But wearing my walking boots to the dining room is uncouth even by my standards, and my sneakers are as threadbare as Ted.

So, cold tootsies it is.

I reach for the handle as the sound of the door opening next door reaches me. I pause, press my ear against the wood. Sure enough, I can hear Edward approach and I hold my breath—why, I have no idea. He pauses just outside and I lean back, eye the door as if it might suddenly explode. And then…the footsteps continue on.

A smile plays about my lips. Edward Fitzroy, future Lord, billionaire CEO, confident, revered, desired by the female population, is afraid to call on me for dinner.

Afraid?

You're the one hiding behind the door!

I leap forward and pull it open before the inner laughter can take hold and pad out after him, my sock-clad feet silent against the floor. He hasn't heard me and I don't call attention to myself. I'm too content enjoying the sight of his rear. How can a man look just as delicious from behind as he does from the front…?

He's freshly showered too. There's a tantalising scent on the air—citrus, sandalwood, patchouli, perhaps—and it's all him. He's swapped his suit for dark chinos and a navy sweater. His hair, still damp at the edges, catches the golden light of the chandelier as we walk down the stairs, its layered style making my fingers tingle with the desire to reach out and play.

James is waiting outside the dining room as we approach, and he gives us a respectful nod. 'Mr Fitzroy, Mi— Summer.'

I'm about to greet him when Edward spins before me, the move so rapid I almost leap back. 'Summer! I didn't hear you!'

I give a smile that's laced with guilt...a tiny shrug too. 'You seemed to be lost in thought.'

I wasn't devouring your rear with my eyes...honest!

He rakes a hand through his hair and my fingers burn with envy... Until his eyes trail over me, and then my entire body is burning at the obvious appreciation I spy there.

He clears his throat. 'I was...' Then he gestures at my top, his eyes looking but not looking. 'That sweater was a good choice.'

The burn becomes a low-down ache, acute, needy, and my heart is pulsing with a ridiculous amount of joy...all over a sweater.

'I like it...' and there go my cheeks with their blushing '...thank you.'

A heated silence descends, broken eventually by the clearing of James's throat. His trademark move, I'm discovering. 'I'll let Marie know you're ready.'

Edward nods and I step past him, enter the dining room before I can give any more of myself away.

Inside, the drapes are drawn against the dark outdoors and the wall sconces are set to low, setting off the austere beauty of the wood-panelled walls and antique paintings. The fire is roaring in the grate, flames dancing and giving up a heavenly warmth.

The highly polished table that is big enough for twenty has been set for two at the end closest to the fire, and I breathe the smallest sigh of relief. I half expected to walk in and find a place setting at either end of the table, and then I would have had to make a scene as I shifted them closer.

Not that I *wanted* to be closer to Edward, but I didn't fancy shouting my apology across the lit candelabra and huge arrangement of dishes that are sure to arrive courtesy of Marie.

It's intimate, but preferable to the gulf that exists between Edward and I.

The man himself pulls out a chair for me and my stomach comes alive. I feel as if a colony of ants are having a rave in there and I cover it with my palm, lower myself into my seat, while he takes the chair opposite.

I haven't eaten since this morning in the café, before he arrived, but now I can't imagine eating anything until I get my apology out of the way.

I open my mouth and James walks in, followed by Mrs McDougall and Marie, all carrying several dishes.

'Wine?' Edward asks me.

'Please.'

He gives James a nod and the man puts down the food he's carrying and does the honours. I grab my glass the moment it's full and take a satisfying gulp. Both men eye me, passing judgement I'm sure, but I don't care. I need this.

Just as Edward needs my apology…even if he doesn't want to hear it.

CHAPTER SEVEN

Edward

WE'RE LEFT ALONE PROMPTLY. As though the staff sense the mood in the air and want no part of it.

Save for Marie, who has a sparkle in her eye—a sparkle that reminds me too much of Gran. Had the two been in cahoots? Had Marie known about this arrangement even before we did?

I should ask her, although I'm afraid of hearing more than I've bargained for.

'I think Marie has outdone herself for your benefit.' I scan the table—game pie with all the trimmings. 'I hope you have an appetite.'

Better than mine, at any rate, because I can't find any desire for food past my desire for her…no matter what's wise, what's sensible, what's fair.

'I can't remember the last time I ate anything quite so wholesome,' says Summer.

My huff is stilted with tension. 'That's one word for it.'

She closes her eyes, inhales deeply, and I can't tear my gaze from her look of sheer, unadulterated bliss. 'It smells amazing too.'

Her appreciative murmur tugs my gaze lower, to her lips, her angled chin, her throat…

She *looks* amazing…

I clench the fork I've picked up. 'I'm sure it'll taste even better.'

Eat. For God's sake eat and focus on that. Not her.

But swallowing proves trickier than chewing. Especially when she makes no attempt to eat herself.

'Are you not hungry?' I ask.

'I am. I just…'

'You just?'

She wets her lips, nips the bottom one—I wish she'd stop doing that. The hint of vulnerability is killing me, triggering a protective instinct that should be long since dead.

'I know you don't want to hear this, Edward, but I'm going to say it anyway.'

I take up my wine, every nerve-ending on high alert. 'Hear what?'

'I know you want to leave the past in the past, and I get it. But I can't do that until I've told you how sorry I am.'

The food sits like a boulder in my chest, the wine sloshing on top of it, and I can't seem to swallow, or speak, or do anything but stare into the intensity of her blue eyes and acknowledge that she means it.

Though it's too little, too late.

'I'm sorry I left without saying goodbye.'

'I was at university,' I say carefully, stripping the emotion from my voice. 'You could hardly swing by.'

It's what I told myself back then.

But that hadn't meant she couldn't call, write an email, send me one of the many postcards she sent Gran.

'No, but I could have told you I was leaving that weekend you were here for the ball.'

My teeth grind…my knuckles flash white around my glass. 'Are you trying to apologise or rub it in?'

She flinches. 'I am sorry.'

I hear her. I feel her. But the anger I've been suppressing overflows like a shaken champagne bottle with the cork shot off.

'Why be sorry? My parents often came and went without so much as a hello, let alone a goodbye, so why would it matter that you treated me the same?'

She pales in the candlelight, her gasp barely audible. 'I'm not—I didn't...'

'You didn't think it was the same? That I wouldn't be accustomed to it?'

'Edward...'

She wets her lips. Her fingers reach across the table but I ignore them. I also ignore the pained look in her eyes and press on.

'Or maybe it never even occurred to you? I'm not sure which is worse—to know me as well as you did, to know of my estranged relationship with my parents like you did, and then to walk away without it even occurring to you...'

Her eyes are wide, her shock so very evident that I have my answer, and it cripples me inside. 'Just leave it, Summer.'

'But I— God, Edward, I'm so sorry. I'd never... I'm nothing like your parents.'

'I'll be honest: I expected more from you. I was foolish enough to think—'

No, don't go there. It doesn't pay to bring it up now, when Gran's intentions are so bloody obvious she might as well have employed a matchmaking agency to stand over us.

'But you're right. It doesn't pay to dwell on it. The past is the past.'

'You don't understand, Edward. I couldn't say goodbye to you. It's not because I didn't care, or that I didn't want to, I just... I couldn't. I've never been good at goodbyes, and saying goodbye to you back then...'

She stops talking, and for the briefest of seconds I see a glimpse of the girl she was. Confident and carefree on the surface…broken and afraid underneath.

'I just couldn't do it.'

My jaw throbs. I want to ask her why. I want to demand a reason that will justify the pain she inflicted. But I'm not that twenty-two-year-old desperate for answers any more. I'm past all that—*I am*. And raking over it is only going to confuse the here and now.

Make you vulnerable to her again, you mean.

'Apology accepted.'

She stares at me. 'Is it, though? You don't sound like—'

'I'm a man of my word, Summer. If I say it is, then it is.'

She nods, but her doubt is as obvious as her eyes are blue. Hell, maybe I'm not so sure myself.

But I *want* to accept her apology.

I *want* to not care about any of it any more.

Because caring about it is one step away from caring about her all over again. And I won't go there. I won't.

'I hadn't—I never even thought about your parents…' she admits softly. 'How my leaving might have…' She shakes her head. 'I was so focused on how I felt I didn't…'

'I said leave it, Summer.' Her sympathy is crushing me, tearing me apart. 'Now eat—before it goes cold.'

She doesn't move.

'Look, it's done with. You've apologised. Now eat, Summer. Please.'

She gives me a hesitant smile, clearly wanting to believe my words as much as I do myself. 'Yes, boss.'

My heart flips over. She used to call me that back when we were friends. My habit for taking charge colliding with her own and sparking the cheeky little phrase. I ache over the memory, ache over what we've lost…

'For what it's worth, Edward, I am deeply sorry. And believe it or not I am grateful to Katherine. Not for the inheritance,' she's quick to clarify. 'I know I don't deserve that.'

I exhale softly. No, she doesn't. Only…

Summer's worldly goods dance before my eyes. Her life is so very temporary, and the pang in my chest is undeniable. All those years ago she acted like she was happy being a lone wolf, desperate to get out into the big, bad world. But I was convinced otherwise.

And didn't Gran's letter suggest she'd believed the same. That deep down what Summer truly wanted was a home… somewhere to feel safe, secure…loved.

'I'm grateful to her because she brought us back together, Edward, and no matter what happens I'm glad to see you again.'

The pang in my chest deepens exponentially, my defences pitiful in the face of her honesty. Because she means it—I know she does. And I hurry to release the wine glass before the thing shatters in my grasp.

'Don't worry, I'm not expecting you to feel the same way,' she says, racing to fill the silence. 'I just had to tell you before I could even contemplate enjoying this.'

Finally, *finally* she lifts her cutlery, signalling the end of her confession, but I can't move past the chaos she's kicked up inside.

I should say something. Anything. She's apologised, told me she's glad to see me again, but what can I say?

There's no response capable of summing up how I feel.

I'm not even sure how I feel.

I try to follow her lead and eat, but I can't taste anything. I focus on what I do know—Gran's intention to give Summer a home after so many years of traveling.

Not just Summer, my mind intrudes.

Gran saw it in me too. All the travelling, all the work, never putting down roots. But I tested the waters once, knowing in my gut that it wasn't what I wanted, and I had a lucky escape. Now...

What do I want? What does *she* want?

Do our lives really need fixing? Is Gran right on some level?

'Where have you been the last twenty years?' I ask.

She shrugs as she swallows down her food. 'Where *haven't* I been might be the easier question to answer.'

'Always on the move?'

'Always.'

'So, where do you consider home to be? If you had to choose...?'

She cocks her head to one side. 'Home?'

'Before now, obviously...' Because we're home now—*our home*—until my lawyers determine otherwise, and I can't forget that.

'What's that song? "Wherever I Lay my Hat, That's my Home"?'

A smile teases at my lips. 'Good old Marvin Gaye. It was one of Gran's favourites.'

She smiles with me, her eyes misting over and making the blue depths shine ever brighter. 'It was, wasn't it? I guess it kind of stuck with me.'

I imagine her on trek after trek, adventure after adventure, her eyes alive with the wonder of the world, no responsibilities, the world her oyster...it doesn't sound so bad.

'I assume it makes you happy, living that way...?'

Another shrug. 'I don't like to put down roots. I get angsty if I'm one place for too long.'

'Is that what happened all those years ago? You got "angsty"?'

It's out before I can stop it and I curse my wild tongue.

'It—it was more complicated than that.'

Complicated by her past, I know—I get that. But what about now? What of the future and Gran's wishes? How long before she gets 'angsty' and bails anyway?

'I was eighteen,' she says. 'Katherine had done everything she'd promised, taking care of me until I was old enough to take care of myself. It was time for me to go.'

'For the lone wolf to leave and find her place in the world…'

She frowns at me, her eyes lost in the past. 'You used to call me that…'

'I used to call you that when I was calling out the front you put on.'

She swallows, her throat bobbing as her chin tilts up. 'Maybe it wasn't a front.'

'Maybe…'

But it's so soft she knows there's no agreement in it.

'And how's *your* front these days?' she asks.

A wry smile touches my lips. Sparring with her is too much fun. Even if it does take me back twenty years, to this very room, collapsed on the rug before the fire after a day of Christmas-present-collecting for the local children's home.

'I'm not the only one with a front…'

The flickering light from the fire had danced in her eyes as she'd wrapped the throw she'd snaffled from her bedroom around our shoulders.

'You're just as bad.'

'Really? How so?'

'You play the prodigal son for your parents—perfect grades, perfect clothes, perfect friends… You laugh more when you're with me, though.'

She'd been teasing me with the last but she'd been right. I'd spent my entire childhood skirting around my parents, trying to get their attention, being on my best behaviour, coming top of the class, top of the sports field too, bringing home the right friends—the ones with the most influential parents. Anything to get a scrap of attention. To feel an inkling of the love I saw my friends receive in abundance. The kind of love Gran had dished out in spades.

Twenty-two and nothing had changed. I'd still been the dutiful son, working hard, networking...playing the part.

'Ever think you would be happier just being you?' she'd asked.

'I could ask you the same.'

'Maybe we should just run away and be ourselves together.'

I'd laughed, but it had caught in my throat, the very possibility of it. No longer a dream but reality. My parents would lose it entirely, and the idea had only served to make my smile widen.

If only she'd been serious in her offer...

'You need to give up smoking first.'

She'd laughed, but cuddled in closer. 'I haven't smoked a cigarette since the summer.'

'Really? You didn't say.'

'I was saving it for Christmas since it seemed like a big deal to you.'

'You were going to gift me your improved health for Christmas?'

'Pretty corny, eh?' *She'd looked up at me, her head resting on my shoulder as she'd given the smallest of shrugs.* 'But I thought it would make you happy.'

Kiss her. Kiss her now. Tell her how you feel.

And cross a line? Take advantage? She's barely eighteen and more vulnerable than she'll ever admit.

I'd tugged my gaze from her appeal, looked to the fire.

'Yeah, you're right.' I'd forced a laugh as I'd pulled her in close. 'Pretty corny...but it makes me happy all the same.'

I drag my mind back to the present, to her expectant face dancing in the flames. To the lines around her eyes and her mouth that hadn't existed before. They give her a maturity that lacks the vulnerability of old. Is that why I want her more than ever?

'I don't need a front, Summer. I haven't for a long time.'

'Your parents finally take notice of you?'

The wry smile returns. 'I stopped needing them too.'

She searches my gaze. 'Did you decide their love wasn't worth the effort?'

Is she thinking about her own love too? Now that she knows I tarred her with the same brush?

'No love is,' I say simply. 'Save for Gran's and she's now gone.'

She falls silent. One beat. Two. So many questions race behind her eyes and then, 'You never needed a front for Gran...or me.'

My throat threatens to close over. No, what we shared was effortless. But at least my parents stuck around. Their love may be superficial at best, cruel at worst, but *they* didn't disappear into the night, never to return...until now.

And she's only here now because of Gran.

I need to remember that.

I need to cling to it.

'So...' I sip my wine, use it to ease the discomfort in my chest.

'So?'

Her brows nudge skyward, and there's an edginess to her gaze now as she waits for me to finish what I started.

'You must meet a lot of people on your travels.'

'I do.'

'You must make a lot of friends.'

She tilts her head. 'Some, but I prefer to travel alone.'

I nod, ignoring the way her confirmation reassures me. 'Doesn't it get lonely—no permanent base, no travel buddies?'

She laughs now. 'I'm a grown woman, Edward, I don't need travel buddies.'

No, she's never needed anyone, she told you that over and over.

'And besides, I have plenty of social interaction. There are the people I meet on my travels—people interested in the culture, the food, the excitement of a new country...'

'Of course.' Though I don't believe for a second that those people can be considered a healthy substitution for real friends.

'And I have followers too—people who are interested in my journey and vice versa.'

'Followers?'

'Yes, you know...social media?'

She's on the defensive now. I can tell by her rigid posture, and her cheeks blazing as deep as her eyes.

'You know—that internet thing that everyone uses.'

'Not quite everyone.'

'Well, not you, obviously.' There's a hint of disdain in her voice. 'Far be it for you to lower yourself to the standard of the masses.'

'What's that supposed to mean?'

'Nothing.'

'It's not nothing.'

Her chin is back at its defiant angle. 'I made the mistake of forgetting who you are for a second.'

There's something more than challenge in her eyes—

something dangerous and taunting—and it runs deeper than this moment here and now.

'Never mind all this talk of me being lonely—what happened to you?' she fires at me. 'Last I knew you were engaged to be married…quite the match, by all accounts.'

I should have expected it…but it hadn't occurred to me that she would know, let alone raise it now.

'That was a long time ago.' Ten years, to be precise. 'Did Gran tell you?'

'No…' She takes a sip of wine, visibly calming herself. 'I got it from the press.'

'You kept tabs on me?'

The colour reaching up her neck, deepening in her cheeks, is answer enough, and I shouldn't feel the rush of satisfaction, or let the unbidden smile touch my lips.

'What happened?' she presses, avoiding my question.

'My mother happened.'

'She didn't approve?'

'Oh, no—she approved. More than approved. Behind the scenes she was one step ahead of me.'

Her eyes narrow with her confusion. 'What's that supposed to mean?'

'It means Analise was handpicked by my mother. I think she figured that holding the puppet strings over my wife would ultimately keep her hold over me.'

'You're joking!'

She palms her chest as her wine catches in her throat. Far more disturbed than I am. But this is ancient history. I can talk about it without a shred of regret…unlike our situation.

'Seriously, Edward!'

'I am serious.'

She coughs. 'But when did you—*how* did you find out?'

'I came home early from a business trip. I wanted to surprise Analise…' The slightest burn of humiliation reaches my cheeks as I remember *that* particular scene. 'Instead, she surprised me.'

'She did?'

'I found her in bed with our gardener.'

'What?'

'Such a cliché, right?'

'Edward…' She shakes her head, sympathy creeping back into her eyes that I truly don't need. 'I'm so sorry.'

'I'm not. It was a relief to be off the hook—to learn the truth before it was too late.'

'But your mother…what part did she play?'

'Analise came out with all. We had a blazing row. She accused me of being a workaholic, said that she was bored, that she only ever agreed to marry me to keep my mother happy and because my mother had promised she would get her every wish fulfilled. She was moulding her into the perfect daughter-in-law—she was moulding her into herself.'

She gives a dramatic shudder. 'Married to your own mother…heaven forbid.'

A laugh erupts out of me. 'You never were her biggest fan.'

'She was never mine.'

Her voice is stripped of any warmth and there's a glint in her eye that I can't read.

'Don't take it to heart. There aren't many who secure her particular brand of approval.'

'No, I guess not.'

Though it's so quiet I struggle to hear her and I feel like I've lost her somewhere, that her head is in another place, another time. Her eyes… Are those…*tears*?

I lean forward but she looks away, reaches for her glass. She's evading me. Or am I just imagining it?

'Your mother hasn't changed much, then?'

She blinks, her eyes returning to mine tear-free, and it

takes me a second to adjust, another to absorb her question. 'Not really.'

She gives a soft huff around her glass, takes a considered sip. 'And there I was, thinking we're supposed to grow as we get older, learn through our life experiences, become better people… Does she know about the inheritance?'

My jaw pulses as I fend off the memory of that particular phone call and nod.

'How did she take it?'

'About as well as you'd expect.'

'Which is…?'

'She threatened to bring in her lawyers, have it contested.'

'You don't seem worried?'

'I'm not.'

'So, you don't think she will succeed?'

'No. Gran did nothing wrong and followed the law to the letter. Charles made sure of that.'

'Yet, you said—'

'I know what I said, but my lawyers are better than hers.'

Are you serious? I cringe on the inside. *How playground do you want to sound?*

Her blue eyes dance back at me and I know she's thinking the same.

'It's the truth,' I swiftly add, which only makes her eyes dance more. 'Hell will freeze over before my mother gets any more of Gran's wealth—movable or otherwise.'

'"Movable or otherwise"?' She frowns.

'It's a legal definition. Things are classified as movable or immovable. In Scottish law you can't disinherit your own children as far as the movable assets go.'

'So, you're saying Katherine had no choice but to give her something?'

'Exactly.'

'But not Glenrobin…the castle, the land…?'

'If I'm honest, I'm not sure Gran would have left her anything by choice.'

'Really?'

'Really, what?'

'Katherine never wrote her off in life—why do you think she'd do such a thing in death?'

I shrug. 'Gran spent her entire adult life trying to make up for the way things had been when my mother was a child. Perhaps this was a last-ditch attempt at making her see the error of her ways.'

She scoffs, the chip on her shoulder coming to the fore. 'Like she had such a tough time of it.'

'You haven't changed your tune.'

She gives a harsh laugh. 'Edward. Your mother wasn't abandoned or rejected; she was spoilt rotten. Everything she wanted she got. Katherine told me how hard she tried to make up for her lack of a father and getting pregnant so young…how hard she tried to protect her from the disappointment that rained down on them from her high society parents. She forgave her everything.'

'But money and indulgence don't make up for love…'

And isn't that what Gran is trying to tell me in her letter? For all the money I've earned, the success I've achieved in business, none of it has brought contentment, true happiness.

'Katherine *loved* her.'

There's a vehemence to her tone, and I hold her gaze as I tell her the truth Gran once told me. 'She didn't know how to love her—not back when she was a child, during all those influential years that shaped her into who she became. Gran was fifteen when my mother was born. Scared and emotionally cut off from her parents. All she had was their money—and she showered her daughter with it.'

'She showered her with love too. She always cared. Unlike…'

She looks away, her eyes going to the fire as she loses herself in her own thoughts. Her own past. Her own child-hood. A mother who didn't fight to keep her…didn't want her, even.

'She could have done a lot worse than having Katherine for a mother.'

'On that we agree.'

My tone is gruff as I read her every thought and feel her pain like a fresh wound. A wound I want to heal even though it isn't my place—not any more. And she wouldn't want me to either. The only person capable of healing her is herself. That was what she always said and what she still stands by now, I'm sure.

'But who knows? Maybe Gran was right to cut her off now. Maybe it will make her question her life choices and have something of an epiphany.'

Her laugh is hollow. 'Do you truly believe that?'

'I can hope. My relationship with my father has im-proved over the years…maybe there's hope for my mother yet.'

A slow smile builds on her lips, and her eyes start to sparkle. 'Have you become an optimist in your old age?'

'Ha! Less of the old.' But I'm smiling, the sudden light-ness far more preferable to the severity that preceded it. 'And, no, I wouldn't go that far.'

'Happy, then?'

'Hmm?'

'If not an optimist, are you happy, at least?'

I stare back at her for a long moment, surprised by her probing question and the way I feel like she should already know the answer…but then how can she? We don't know each other any more.

'I've achieved what I set out to in business. I dominate the industry. I work for my own satisfaction. I do what I want, when I want. When the only person you can disappoint or be disappointed by is yourself, life becomes much simpler. Don't you think?'

'Simple and straightforward...' she reaffirms for me. 'There's a definite truth to that.'

'And you? Are you happy?'

Her lashes flutter. There's a subtle dance flickering in the depths of her eyes—or is it just the flames of the fire... the candles...?

'I'd like to think so.'

She's not sure, though. There's too much hesitation, too much thought.

'There's been no one else since Analise, then? No one serious?'

I straighten. Maybe I should have expected her to dig deeper into my personal life, to push back, and the answer is simple enough, so why I don't give it to her straight is beyond me.

Liar.

'According to the press, there have been many...'

'But according to you...?'

'No, Summer.' I meet her eye, take up my cutlery and stab at my food.

There's been no one because you broke me. Analise didn't even fracture the surface because there was nothing left to break.

'I had a narrow escape,' I permit myself to admit. 'And I have been grateful for it ever since. My life is my own and I prefer it that way.'

She nods slowly, and I think she's about to leave it alone...but then, when did Summer ever leave me in peace?

'What happened to all your dreams of getting married, Edward? Of having children?'

I'm so relieved that my fork hasn't quite made it to my mouth. 'They were the dreams of an inexperienced foolish youth.'

'But what happens to your gran's legacy if you don't marry and have children?'

'I don't know, Summer. You tell me, since it's a problem we now face together.'

She opens her mouth, closes it again, her frown turning her delectable lips down…lips I really don't want to be focusing on…

But has she not even considered it? The future implications of Gran's wishes and how bound together we are now?

'So it is…' she murmurs.

So it is…

No fight, no clever retort, no denial…

As if you really want one.

CHAPTER EIGHT

Summer

I'M STANDING IN *the corner of the Glenrobin ballroom. Around me there are people. So many people. I didn't want to come but Katherine insisted.*

'You're family. You belong here just as much as the others.'

Only belonging can't be handed over. It's a feeling, and I don't have it.

I see the other foster children, so much younger than me, running around the room, enjoying the Christmas festivities that are in full swing. They're not old enough to know better. They've not lived through the disappointment of many Christmases past.

But it's fine. I'm no fool. And, at eighteen, I've decided this is my last Christmas in someone's care. I'll be going it alone. Independent. An adult at last. No more being tossed about in the system. But before I go...

I drag in a breath and scan the room. Edward is here somewhere...the chaotic beat of my heart tells me so...but where?

I spy his companion first. She's impossible to miss. Glossy blonde hair, pinned up in a style that must have taken hours to perfect, her English rose complexion ut-

terly flawless. Her festive red gown fitting her body like a second skin. She's all elegance and poise, oozing money and glamour and everything I'm not.

And she has Edward enraptured.

I fancy he looks at me like that too, with his eyes alive, a charge in the air, a flurry of excitement within him. Is that how it is for this girl too? Have I tried to see more where there isn't more to see?

'She is a vision, is she not?'

I spin on my heel and come face to face with Edward's mother...or Bitchface as I've nicknamed her. Never has there been a woman so beautiful and so sullen in one. A woman who has everything but it's never enough. And don't get me started on how she treats Katherine—her mother by blood, my temporary mother by paperwork.

I refuse to recoil, though every muscle in my body urges me to do so. My skin is crawling under her insipid smile, her hollow cheeks and ice-blue eyes.

Don't get me wrong. She's beautiful...if cool sophistication and high maintenance are your thing. So very different from her son and the warmth he emanates.

'Who?' I say.

She gives a high-pitched laugh and I can't suppress my wince.

'Why, Charlotte, my dear.' She gestures to where I'd just been staring. 'Edward's new girlfriend.'

I must truly flinch now, because she laughs some more, her bony hand fluttering to her neck.

'Oh, foolish child...you didn't think he'd set his sights on you, did you?'

I frown. She's always been a nasty piece of work, but this...this is something else. I want to run, but I don't. I stand straighter. In her three-inch heels she has me on height, but I tilt my chin. I won't cower.

'*You don't know what you're talking about.*'

'*Don't I? Come, now…*'

She leans into me, almost conspiratorially. Her sickly-sweet perfume swamps me and I want to gag, cover my mouth, but I won't. I won't be seen as weak in front of her.

'*You must think I was born yesterday. I see the way you look at him, with those big blue eyes and that besotted smile. Do you really think you could keep a man like him?*'

'*I don't think—*'

Another cackle of laughter cuts me off and my fingers tighten around the champagne flute Katherine gave me earlier. The glass is still full, and warm now in my hot, sweaty palm. My stomach swoops and my eyes dart about the room.

Is it that obvious? Am I that obvious? Is everyone laughing at me, just as she is?

My cheeks are aflame and I can't quite catch my breath. Does he know? Edward?

'*Oh, my dear, I actually feel sorry for you.*' She shakes her head. '*I blame my mother entirely, of course…putting foolish notions in your head. Still, at least you can see the truth for yourself now, before any real damage is done.*'

The truth. The same truth I've been trying to keep in mind for the past eighteen months. But instead I've let Katherine and Edward get inside my head…and my heart. I was fine before—just fine. I didn't need them. I didn't need this world where I could never belong.

Charlotte is laughing now. Her whole demeanour reminding me of his mother. My stomach rolls, my heart aches, tears prick…

Oh, God, not here…not here.

'*You don't know what you're talking about,*' I repeat, trying to move past her.

But my movements are too quick and my glass collides

with her. Champagne runs down her front and she lets out a yelp.

'You silly girl!'

'I'm sorry... I'm sorry... I'm so sorry.'

And I'm running—running so fast I can't draw breath. I can't feel the ground beneath my feet. I can't see past the tears, the burn...

I squeeze my eyes shut, open them again, and I'm in a cold, narrow corridor. Ted is in my hand and a woman is walking away from me. A woman I love. A woman I have done everything to try and keep.

'Mummy! Mummy!'

She doesn't turn and I clutch Ted tighter.

It's not my mother any more. It's Edward. Edward walking away.

'Edward!' I choke on the pain, the anguish. 'Edward!'

He doesn't react. His pace is slow and steady, unbreaking, but I can't make my feet go after him.

'Edward!'

He disappears. Just like Mum. He doesn't care. He doesn't want me...

'Summer.'

My name is faint, far away.

'Summer.'

I shake my head, feel softness all around me, an inviting warmth...

'Summer, wake up.'

It's a nice voice. Hushed, husky, deep. There's a hand on my shoulder, gently shaking. A familiar, comforting scent in the air. My eyes flutter open and I squint against the subtle light of the room. Where am I? Who...?

Rich brown eyes come into focus—'Edward!'

I scramble back against the headboard, clutch a hand to my pounding chest, my dream and reality colliding in one.

'Sorry, I didn't mean to startle you…'

I glance around the room. The door between our bedrooms is open. I can see his bed in the distance, the quilt thrown off as though he's left it in a hurry.

Did I scream? Did I…?

My eyes return to his, the dregs of my dream still pulsing through my veins… If only it was purely a dream and not a reminder of the past—of that scene in this house, of my mother walking away many years before…

I used to have it often, but it's not hounded me in years, and I know our conversation over dinner and my return to this place—to him—are to blame.

'Sorry,' he says again. He's perched on the edge of my bed, his hand now resting on the quilt between us. 'You sounded distressed.'

'I did?' Oh, God, what did I say? Should I ask him outright? Did I scream his mother's name or, worse, *his*?

He looks so concerned, his brow furrowed, the wrinkles that have formed over the years only adding to his appeal, and those eyes… *God*, those eyes… I could lose myself in them a million times over and still come back for more.

'Let me get you some water…'

He's rising, but I don't want water.

I don't want to trouble him more than I already have.

I also need him out of here. Because this room, the soft light, his concern, *the bed*—it's all too intimate. And I don't trust myself not to act on what's been virtually a life-long dream…a fantasy. One that could so easily become real in the sleepy confines of this room, at this late hour.

'It's okay, Edward,' I say. 'I don't—'

But he's not listening. He's already heading to the bathroom. And that's when I realise he's wearing nothing but underwear. Tight black briefs that cling to his honed behind, accentuate his trim waist and his muscular thighs with their smattering of dark hair…

The sight steals my voice, my breath…he's so *toned*. Like…*everywhere*.

Heat ripples through my body. My nipples are beading beneath my ancient grey tee. *Oh, God.* It's one thing for him to hear me begging for him in my sleep, but to be all pert and alert and blatantly wanton when awake… No, no, no.

I pull the quilt to my chin just as he emerges, a filled glass in one hand, the other raking through his hair. The thick strands are all mussed up and his face is flushed from sleep. The soft light plays over the chiselled angle of his cheekbones, his jaw, the taut muscles of his chest, the dappled hair that darkens as it disappears into his briefs…

Breathe, Summer.

But he's a vision, a sexual fantasy come to life, and I'm… I'm a hot mess!

'Here.' He offers the glass, his eyes probing mine, his mouth twisted into a one-sided smile.

'Thank you,' I manage to rasp out as I take it. 'I'm sorry I woke you.'

'Don't be. I'm just glad you're not being murdered in your sleep.'

I wince up at him. 'Was I that bad?'

'Put it this way: if it had gone on much longer you would have had the entire household rushing to aid you with any weapon they could find.'

'Oh, dear…'

I wet my lips and realise they taste of salt. My cheeks are clammy too. Was I crying? I swipe the back of my hand over my face, sweep away the hair that's stuck there. Definitely crying. Definitely humiliating.

I sip the cool water, hoping it will ease the rising heat inside me. I'd like to say it's all down to embarrassment, but the fever swirling through my middle is all for him. The throbbing ache too.

I press my thighs together, bring my knees to my chest. I don't look at him as I say, 'I'll be okay now…thank you.'

I bring the glass back to my lips, sip it like a good girl, hoping he'll get the message.

'You sure?'

His scent is carried on the air, the warmth of his naked body too, and my eyes are drawn back to him. The crease between his brows deepens as I blink up at him. His eyes are so dark in the low light.

Am I okay? Right now? Hell, no.

I want to jump his bones. Every nerve-ending is urging me to reach up and pull him to me, to feel those lips against my own. They're so perfect, so full, and his stubble looks tantalisingly rough, his hair wild now it lacks the care he puts into it each morning…

'Summer?'

I snap my eyes back to his, plaster on a smile. 'I'm much better than I was, thanks to you.'

He studies me intently for a second longer than is comfortable and I feel my smile slip. What would he say if I asked him to come to bed with me? As two consenting adults, beholden to no one. No divide. No promises. No lies. Just this…

If I was dreaming, I'd do it.

But this is reality, and it's reality I need to get hold of.

He reaches out and my breath stalls in my lungs. His fingers close around my glass as he slips it from my weakened grasp. 'You're trembling.'

'I am…?' I look down at my fingers and sure enough they're unsteady. But it's more to do with the wild energy now pulsing through me in the aftermath of my dream, my wild fantasy too. 'It'll pass.'

He places the glass on the bedside table and the photo catches his eye. He smiles. 'I remember when that was taken.'

I look at the picture, let memories dance to the fore… 'It was a lovely day.'

'You and Gran had taken the kids pumpkin-picking.'

'And you'd refused—said it was for youngsters.'

He shrugs. 'Gran still roped me in, though.'

'Because she played on your macho instincts.'

His laugh is gruff. '"You can't expect us girls to carry all the big ones…"' He mimics his grandmother, his voice as soft as his expression.

'Well, they were rather heavy—especially the one we used for the carriage.'

'Ah, yes—that scene for the Halloween Fairy Tale Ball.'

'It was Katherine's favourite event of the year.'

'That and Christmas.'

We both stare at the picture, remembering the woman with the huge heart and feeling the massive imprint she's left on our own.

'I miss her.'

The quiet confession falls from his lips and I put my own insecurities aside to reach for his hand, squeeze it softly.

'Me too. She was an incredible woman.'

His eyes lift to mine and I can't breathe, seeing the obvious pain there, the pain that's now morphing into something else. Something heated and desperate. I feel the fire unfurl deep within me, my fingers burning around his. I wet my lips, search for something to say—something that isn't *Kiss me*.

This connection is about grief. Nothing else. Nothing more.

'I should go,' he says.

I nod. He *should* go. I can already feel the boundaries

between us blurring. Our lives entwining. It's too easy to forget how different we are. That this is the world in which he belongs. I'll always be on the outskirts looking in, no matter what Katherine wanted otherwise.

He lets go of my hand, starts to walk away.

'Edward?'

He pauses, looks at me over his shoulder.

'I know you don't think I deserve all this—the inheritance, the castle, the estate…'

'That's not—'

I raise my hand, shake my head, cutting off the denial he doesn't need to give.

'I *know* I don't deserve it. But it's an opportunity I don't want to waste. It's an opportunity for me to do so much good—the kind of good Katherine did…'

'What are you saying?'

'I'm saying…' I lift my chin a fraction, uncaring that the quilt has fallen to my waist and that his eyes flit down, resting for a second too long. 'Give me a chance to prove myself to you.'

'You don't need to prove yourself to me.'

'Don't I?'

He hesitates, but I see the answer in his eyes and I can't blame him. With parents like his, his ex-fiancée, people who want him for his wealth and status, not to mention what I did, he's bound to mistrust me.

'Whatever the case, you're a busy man. You have a company that occupies you full-time and I sense you've been running this place for a while too. I don't have the same responsibilities, but I do have the freedom and the desire to carry on Katherine's legacy…help children like I once was.'

He faces me head-on, his brow furrowed once more, and that naked torso is on full display as he folds his arms and his biceps bulge—

Focus, Summer! Eyes up!

'You mean fostering?'

'No… No. I know I'm not in the right place for that—not yet.'

Though never say never…

It's not something I've ever considered—not with how transient my life has been. But aren't things different now…? Might it be an option…one day?

'Then how?' he asks.

One step at a time, I tell myself.

'By giving back to the local community. Volunteering. Carrying on the fundraising events she used to run.'

'Like the Halloween Fairy Tale Ball?'

I smile. 'Yes, like the Halloween Fairy Tale Ball.'

He nods.

'You agree?'

'It's an idea…although it's a lot of work— organising such affairs, I mean.'

'I'm not afraid of hard work, Edward.'

'No, I don't suppose you are.'

He stares at me and I wish I could see inside his head… see whatever thought it is causing his eyes to shine back at me. I like that look. I want more of that look. It makes my heart skip, my body warm.

And, oh, God, there you go again. Boundaries—you need boundaries.

'Goodnight, Summer.'

He starts to move off and I stall him again. 'Edward?'

'Yes?'

Nerves almost get the better of me, but I clench my fists. This is important. I need to draw a line in the sand and make it clear—for my benefit as much as his.

'This house is big enough for the two of us to live our lives, yes?'

'Yes.' It's part-impatience, part-resignation.

'And just because I'm here, you shouldn't feel like you can't…you can't bring people back.'

I see his surprise in the flaring of his eyes and bite my lip.

'You mean *women*?'

My cheeks burn but I hold my ground. 'I mean anyone— but, yes, women too.'

His eyes dance in the lamplight and I suck in my cheeks. He's laughing at me.

'Are you giving me permission to date, Summer?'

'No. I'm saying that just because we're stuck together for a year it doesn't mean…it doesn't mean we need to put our lives on hold.'

'Our *sex* lives?'

I nod, swallow, squeak—oh, God, did he hear that?

'Believe me, Summer…' His eyes darken, and colour slashes his cheeks. 'If I want to bring a woman home, I will.'

Well, you deserved that.

And then he's gone, and my legs twitch with the desire to run after him, jump him, kiss him, until the only woman he could possibly want to bring home is me.

Edward

I close the door between us, deliberately slow. I don't want her to know that every sinew in my body is straining to go to her, to prove that the only woman I want to bring home is already here.

The moment I heard her scream my name, I shot out of bed. Racing to her side with no thought as to how I was dressed…no thought as to how she would be dressed either.

Such a fool.

I drag a hand over my face, lean back against the solid door and suck in a breath that's no longer tainted with her scent. How can twenty years have gone by and she still possess the same smell? It's driving me crazy. As is her voice, her smile, her laugh…

Hearing her distress, seeing her twisted up in the bedsheets, her hair clinging to her damp brow… Nothing could have prevented me from going to her side. But the second she saw me and scurried back I knew I'd made an epic mistake.

The way her eyes burned back at me…the way she caught at her lip, her cheeks still damp and flushed from her nightmare. I wanted to kiss her until she forgot it all. I wanted to kiss her more than I can ever remember wanting to before. The sight of one shoulder exposed, of her nipples, teasing points as they pressed through the thin fabric of her T-shirt…

She was distressed—dazed, even—and I was no better than a horny teenager. Frustrated as hell at myself when I should have been focusing on her wellbeing and her wellbeing alone.

And then she had the audacity to taunt me with the possibility of my bringing another woman home. As if I could even *think* of anyone else with her unique brand of temptation on such flagrant display.

It took every ounce of strength for me to turn and walk away, and she made me do it twice over. Forcing me to turn back each time and drink her in.

The attraction was so fierce off the back of that drive to protect her. Her dream and her distress luring out feelings I've been trying to suppress since the moment she walked into Charles's office.

Did she see how much I wanted her? Did she see it and panic—throw the idea of other lovers out there with the intention of keeping that line drawn? As a reminder that whatever this is between us, it isn't *that*?

I stride to my bed, tug the quilt back on top, but sleep is impossible.

I reach for my phone and unlock the screen. There she is, in all her Instagram glory. She wasn't kidding when she said she had followers…thousands and thousands of them. Her photos garner so many likes and comments and it's easy to see why. She's a vision of happiness—stunning, carefree, living her best life.

Stripped to the barest of layers on a cliff-edge, her arms outstretched to the blue sky and even bluer waters.

Chilling on a beach with a coconut tipped to her mouth, the juice escaping her lips, trailing down her neck, her chest, beneath her loose-fitting vest…

I move on swiftly.

To a rainforest with colours as vibrant as her, wildlife of various shapes and sizes, all coaxing a smile from her and filling her eyes with joy.

Sunset on a veranda, with a string of light bulbs adding a soft glow, a sofa filled with plush cushions and her, with her head in some guy's lap, his eyes on her face as she grins up at him. A boyfriend, perhaps, a passing friend…

My grip tightens around the phone and I scroll past that picture. Back to the wildlife, to her and some cheerful locals in Malaysia, to the canyons and sea adventures.

Back to her and that guy again.

He only appears once. It should be enough to stop the fierce ache in my chest. The desire to have her head in *my* lap like that, looking up at *me* like that. At ease, happy…

I throw the phone back on the bedside table and lie back, stare at the ceiling.

No, she hasn't been lonely. She's happy. Every one of

those photos proves it. Gran didn't know what she was talking about.

And now she's stuck here, in the freezing cold Highlands, with the rain and the responsibility. How long before she needs to be free again? To cut her ties and escape back to that life? The lone wolf ready for her next adventure…

Leaving Glenrobin and I, a distant memory once more… regardless of Gran's last wishes.

Then I think about her lying awake too, on the other side of the door, so close and yet so far away. I think of Ted beside her, just as he was all those years ago. Her one true constant, she'd called him.

I think of the pleading look on her tear-stained face as she asked me to give her a chance, and I think of my diligent team of lawyers, now dissecting Gran's will, and I know what I must do. Even though every instinct screams at me not to be so stupid, so weak…

I fork my hand through my hair with a curse, tell myself it's only three hundred and sixty-three days to go and then…

And then what?

This estate will always bind us on some level.

But being bound by the tangible estate and the intangible chaos inside are very different things, and so long as she keeps the line drawn, I can toe it. I won't take advantage of this situation, just as I refused to back then.

And I certainly won't make the same mistake of thinking that she cares for me as deeply as I once did her.

No. Toe the line, keep things simple…and stay the hell away from her in night clothes.

I turn to switch off my lamp but there's a sound. Movement beyond the door. I stare at it, see the handle start to shift, and my heart launches into my throat.

What is she…?

No, she can't be…

The door opens and I throw my feet to the floor, sit bolt upright…

'Summer?'

CHAPTER NINE

Summer

I'M MUTE. There are no words for the desire racing through my veins. To see him, his body mostly naked, the muscles in his forearms flexing as he grips the edge of his bed and plants his feet firmly on the floor...

My head is empty of any coherent thought save one: *Please don't reject me.*

'Summer?'

He says my name again and I'm so hooked on hearing him say it. His impossibly deep voice, deeper still. His brown eyes, wide and questioning. His body taut with a tension I know I've put there.

I close the distance between us, every breath I take loud in my ears, my heartbeat too.

'You can tell me to leave, Edward, and I will.' I know I need to tell him this before I go any further. Give him an escape if he needs it.

'Leave?'

His frown is delectable, his confusion written in every line of his brow. And, my God, is it sexy. His eyes too. There's a hint of feeling lost, of curiosity, and then he glances lower and the burn is there. The burn that gives me the confidence to close in.

In my gut, I know he's fighting the same battle as me. That his tension is about the fear of what comes next. But if you don't think about the future…if you only think about the here and now and the pleasure it can bring…then fear is a waste of energy.

Energy that can be expended in far more satisfying ways.

I rest a hand on his naked shoulder, catch his sharp intake of breath, the jolt that runs through him. He's all hot, hard heat beneath my tingling palm, and the contact is enough to send tiny sparks of electricity coursing through my veins.

'Do you know what you're doing?'

His eyes lift to mine, his voice so raw it rasps over me as powerful as any caress, though his grip on the bed fails to ease. Still fighting. Still resisting.

I slip myself between his legs, raise my palm to his other shoulder. 'Do *you*?'

His Adam's apple bobs…his jaw pulses.

And then I lower my head to his. Slow enough to let him stop me if he so desires…slow enough to let the anticipation build. There's a flush to his cheeks—a flush I feel right through to my core. I search his gaze, the glow of the bedside lamp lancing his darkened depths with gold.

'Edward,' I whisper, our noses almost touching, 'I've wanted this for so long. And I think you want me too. I don't need endearments. I don't need words or empty promises. All I need is you. Tonight.'

And then I kiss him, and it's like I've never kissed a man before. The lightest sweep of my lips over his and the contact pulses through me in a surge of heat so powerful that my knees weaken and my limbs turn molten. But I don't fall because he's got me, his hands flying to my thighs, tugging me against him, and his tongue is delving inside my mouth, his groan so fierce, filled with passion, with surrender.

There's no restraint. No composure. And I revel in it. In the way his hands rake with desperation over my skin, in his tongue as it twists and tangles with my own…

Our breaths are ragged and in tune…our bodies vibrating with such need it feels impossible to get enough. Enough oxygen. Enough sensation. Enough of one another. And I want his all.

'Summer…'

He growls into my mouth, his fingers rough in my hair as I straddle his hips, ride against the ridge of his desire. He tears his mouth away, his groan verging on pained as his erection reaches for me and he holds me back.

'This is a bad idea.'

'Sometimes bad ideas are the most rewarding kind.' I kiss him again, lower my hand between us to caress him, and his thighs shudder beneath me. 'Don't you agree?'

'Yes!' He curses. *'Yes!'* But he tugs my hand away, his eyes firing up at me. 'I'd like to make it last, though.'

Make it last… If only this kind of pleasure could last for ever…

I block the worrying train of thought and chuckle low in my throat, rake my fingers through his hair, deepen the kiss, think about the now, not what comes next.

His palms come to my aid, slipping beneath my tee. I suck in a breath, arch back as the heat of anticipation floods my breasts. My nipples press against the fabric, hard and desperate…desperate for that first touch. From Edward. My teenage heartthrob. My lifelong dream.

I'm delirious. Intoxicated. My fingers claw into his shoulders as he cups each curve. His touch softens, his caress light and teasing. I bite my lip, look down at him as he rolls each pleading peak with his thumbs. I whimper, writhe, nurse the budding sensation…

'You feel incredible…look incredible…' Awe is in his

voice, in his eyes as they burn into his touch. 'Even better than I imagined.'

Has he imagined it? Somewhere deep my heart considers the possibility, but I don't want my heart involved in this.

This is sex. Easy to pigeonhole. Compartmentalise. No deeper meaning. No heart.

But I'm drowning in his gaze, his fevered touch. Strings are being tugged that I have no control over...

His name is a hoarse cry on my lips as I tear my top from my body and throw it aside, take pleasure from his eyes that burn ever deeper. I feel powerful, empowered... I press him back into the bed and tease my body over him, our underwear the only barrier between us.

'Do you have protection?' I whisper.

He squeezes his eyes shut on a hoarse curse, holds me tight against him.

'You don't?' Disappointment swamps me.

'No, Summer.' His eyes open, pierce mine. 'This wasn't— I never imagined—'

'No, neither of us did.' I nip my lip and say meekly, 'But I'm on the pill.'

His jaw pulses, his grip around my hips too. 'It's not enough.'

My brows draw together. Does he not trust me? Does he think I've been unsafe? Or is he worried about himself?

He moves before I can, sliding my body beneath his as his lips claim mine in a kiss so thorough I wonder if it's goodbye. But then his hands are moving down my front, his mouth too... He's trailing kisses along my jaw, nipping at my earlobe as his fingers trace invisible patterns over my skin, teasing swirls that have me writhing and whimpering.

And then his mouth surrounds one nipple, and I throw my head back with a cry. 'God, yes!'

A quiet voice at the back of my mind, the negative one, wants to ask what he's doing? What does *It's not enough* mean? But I can't form a word past the luscious heat inside me, the heated coil that's being wound tighter and tighter.

His fingers reach the lace of my thong and tease gently, deepening the pressure, circling and circling, until my toes curl into the bed and I can feel the edge so very near.

'Edward, please…please, I need you.'

He slips his hand beneath the fabric. 'I know, baby. I know.'

But his fingers are working their magic, coaxing me higher and higher. *Baby.* He called me baby. He's never… not before… I'm panting as he parts me, his touch gentle, dizzying, hypnotic as he circles directly over me. His thighs trap my own, his fingers slipping inside. His thumb is rolling and rolling… And then his teeth scrape over my nipple and pleasure-pain rips through me.

'Edward!'

'Go with it, baby. Go with it.'

Baby. Baby. The endearment is killing me even as he takes me to the precipice. I claw his shoulders. I toss my head against the pillow, throw it forward to stare down at him. This is real. So *real*.

And I'm gone. My body is pulsing with an orgasm so intense, so mind-blowing, so fierce, that I feel like I've lost something of myself. Lost it and gifted it to him.

I'll never get it back.

And I'm not sure I want to.

Edward

I feel her pleasure like my own. Watching her come apart— so wild, so free, so attuned to me—was breathtaking, and perfect, and more than I ever imagined it could be.

She sags into the bedsheets, her orgasm leaving her limp,

and I climb back up her body, kiss a path all the way to her lips.

Could I ever get enough of this? Of her?

Wild laughter punctuates the silence in my brain.

Hell, no. Now I've tasted her I want more. So much more.

And I know this is bad…so very, very bad. I should have sent her back to her room. But I've never wanted anyone like I want her. It would be like Santa gifting you something you've wanted for an entire lifetime and you saying, *Thanks, but no thanks.*

I'm not that stupid.

And you don't think this is more stupid…?

I drown out the inner scorn with an all-consuming kiss, and she gives a blissful murmur deep within her throat.

'You sound sleepy…' I say.

'Do I?'

It's all husky and filled with post-coital warmth.

I stretch out beside her, her back to my front, and hold her to me, nuzzle the skin beneath her ear. 'Yes.'

She gives a soft little laugh, her arms wrapped over mine. 'I'm still on Malaysian time. I don't think I've slept properly for days.'

'Then sleep.'

'But you… I want to…' She draws the words out, all hushed as she snuggles in closer, and the teasing friction of her bum is enough to make my eyes roll.

'Sleep, Summer.'

It's practically a growl in her ear, and she gives the softest murmur of agreement, sleep claiming her whether she wants it to or not.

And I relax against her, savour the warmth of her body, her scent on the air. She feels so right like this. In my arms. She always did. Even as friends there was an ease with which we'd touch, hug, collapse on a bed together...often laughing. I press a kiss to her hair, breathe her in...

That was before she broke you, though.

I squeeze my eyes shut to the pain. Remind myself that this is temporary. Tell myself it's better to have shared something instead of nothing...but not everything.

Because to make love to her fully and let her walk away, as I know she one day will...

I don't think I could come back from that.

CHAPTER TEN

Summer

I WAKE ALONE in Edward's bed. The door between our rooms is still open but it's eerily quiet, not a hint of movement from the bathroom or the dressing room either.

He's gone.

Part of me is surprised he didn't pick me up and put me back in my own bed while I slept.

Another part is surprised that he left without waking me.

Then I see the time and groan. It's almost eleven! *Eleven!*

I curse and throw off the quilt. The cold air of the room assaults my naked body and I shudder... But then I remember why I'm wearing only panties, and just like that I'm on fire again. Recalling his touch, his fingers, his mouth...

Oh, God.

I press a hand to my lips, which thrum with the memory, my smile irrepressible.

What a night! Perfect right up until the point...

I cringe. He took care of me and I repaid him with *sleep*.

And what now? I have no idea where we stand...

Why didn't he wake me? Does he regret it already? Are we going to have to do the morning-after dance?

I fork my fingers through my riotous hair and grip my scalp with a groan. This wasn't how it was supposed to go.

No? How exactly did you picture it going, then?

I don't know. That's the honest answer. I didn't want to know. I just… I just didn't want to wake up without him.

I try to push the disappointment aside and ignore the unease worming its way through my gut.

Get dressed. Go and find him. Deal with it.

The sight of my T-shirt neatly folded on the dressing table eases my shoulders a fraction. He didn't bolt so fast as to leave my clothing on the floor. Maybe that means something.

I return to my bedroom and get ready in record time, opting for a thick green sweater, jeans and the simplest of make-up. I'm keen to get any awkwardness out of the way and reassure him that nothing has changed. Absolutely nothing at all. Not for me at any rate.

I recall the warmth in his brown eyes when he came to me in the night, the concern, the understanding… We may not have the ease and the trust we once had, but we're in a better place than we were in Mr McAllister's office and that has to mean something.

Unless you've ruined it all by seducing him…

I shoot the thought down as I bolt from my room, racing down the stairs only to find James in the hall, waiting for me. He steps forward as soon as he spies me, his kind smile alleviating the niggle of guilt that I've been caught rising so late.

Not to mention whose bed I rose from.

'Good morning, Summer, I trust you slept well.'

'I did, thank you.' My cheeks burn as I remember the reason for that particular feat and I avoid his eye. 'Have you seen Edward?'

I wince at the pitch to my voice—*way to go in sounding normal.*

'Indeed. Mr Fitzroy breakfasted at seven-thirty and is now in his study working.'

'Seven-thirty?'

Okay, so I probably shouldn't be that surprised, but bearing in mind he was up in the middle of the night seeing to me…

My cheeks flush deeper. Not the best way to phrase it!

'Every weekday,' James says. 'Mr Fitzroy visits the gym at six and expects breakfast to be ready no later than seven-thirty.'

Well, that explains the physique…

'If you'd like to go through to the dining room, I'll send for some food.'

'Oh, no, it's fine, James. I'll sort myself out in the kitchen.'

'But meals are always served in the dining room.'

I almost back down in the face of his frown. I know I'm messing with his routine, but the idea of eating in the dining room is enough to rob me of my appetite. It was okay with Edward's presence filling the vast space so easily the night before, but eating there alone…

'I'd like to catch up with Marie, anyway.'

'I see…'

I smile the brightest of smiles. 'Thank you, though.'

I'm already heading towards the kitchen and I feel his perplexed gaze follow me. Not that I can blame him. I'm hardly what he's used to. From what I understand, Katherine stopped fostering a decade ago, when she felt she could no longer give the children what they needed. It's likely James wasn't here when kids like me walked the halls.

I have to pass Edward's study to get to the kitchen, and even though I know he's working I figure it wouldn't hurt to peep in…test the water, so to speak.

Before I can lose my nerve, I rap gently on the door,

push it open a crack. My eager gaze finds him instantly. He's at his desk, his dark shirt setting off his dark hair and even darker eyes. His phone is to his ear, but his attention in that split-second is all for me. It's as though a trail of gunpowder connects us and the fuse has been lit, with the flame crossing the distance and running right through me.

I breathe through the sensation, smile and wave, mouth *Morning*.

A pulse twitches in his jaw...his lashes flutter. 'Yes, sorry, Juan,' he says into the phone. 'I'm still here.'

And then he dips his head to me, the briefest of nods.

Is that all I'm getting?

His attention shifts to his computer and I have my answer.

I ignore the pang in my chest...the little bubble of panic that threatens.

We're grown adults. We can have sex and be okay. Hell, it wasn't even sex. Just a bit of a fumble. Nothing major.

I'm still telling myself this when I get to the kitchen and the sound of Marie's singing reaches me, coaxing out a smile that quietens the nagging doubt.

'Still singing the same tunes?'

She spins on the spot, palm pressed to her bosom. 'Ah, Miss Summer, you are awake at last!'

Her cheeks round with her smile and I step inside the inviting warmth of the room, breathe in the scent of fresh-baked goodies and am transported back twenty years.

The kitchen hasn't changed at all. The same Belfast sink sits before the window with its view of the garden beyond and a vase of freshly cut flowers on its sill. The same dinner service fills the same antique cabinet along one wall. The same cream range sits beside the fire that always seems to be lit. The same oak table stretches down the middle, the ceiling rack above it laden with pots and pans, herbs and utensils.

'You know, you really can just call me Summer, Marie.'

'Pish-posh. You were Miss Summer back then; you'll be Miss Summer now… That is until you find yourself a good man to take care of you.'

'I don't need a man, Marie. I'm quite capable of taking care of myself.'

'And where's the fun in that?'

There's a twinkle in her eye, and suddenly I feel like all last night's escapades are written in my face for anyone to read.

'I don't know about fun…' I grumble '…it's certainly less trouble.'

'More pish-posh. Now, sit. You need to eat. You're far too skinny!'

'I'm really not.'

But I do exactly as she asks, pulling out a stool at the table and sitting myself down. There's no point insisting I get my own food. Marie wouldn't allow me to do it back then, and she'll be even less inclined to let me do it now.

'Still a coffee fiend?' she asks.

'Still a mother hen?'

She laughs with me as she sets the coffee going. 'It's so good to see you… I can't tell you! Though I have to say your travels kept both Ms Katherine and I very entertained. Your postcards were the highlight of our month, and we always shared a cuppa over your emails.'

I smile. 'I did try and get Katherine to follow my social media accounts, but I think that was a step too far.'

'Ha! Not through a lack of trying, mind you, but those apps are a minefield. Far safer to get your news from the horse's mouth than be exposed to all that.'

I frown and laugh in one. 'Fair enough.'

'Now!' She claps her hands together. 'What can I get you? How about a fresh roll stuffed with bacon and lashings of tomato sauce?'

My mouth salivates at the very idea. 'You remember my favourite.'

'Of course! I'll get it made while you fill me on your latest travels.'

'And you can get me up to speed on this place.'

And keep me distracted from the epic mistake I might have made…

'Deal.'

Edward

I'm working. Concentrating so hard that my head aches and my eyes sting against the glare of my screen. Not that I can tell you what I've been looking at for the past hour… and it's that realisation that has me shoving away from my desk and scowling up at the portrait of Gran above the fire.

It's not Gran I see, though. It's all Summer.

She's been a permanent presence since I left her side, dragging myself away from her curled up in my bedsheets, all blissful and serene and unwittingly calling me back. And then she appeared in my doorway, temptation personified, and I behaved no better than an arse. All because I was angry with myself for letting her in again.

Juan, my closest friend and my Director of Legal Affairs, called me out on my preoccupation, my need for him to repeat himself several times over rousing his curiosity…

Hell, if the man knew the cause was a woman, he'd be sending for the doctor.

I don't get distracted.

I live for my work.

And a challenge like the failing start-up we'd recently acquired and were trying to discuss was my catnip.

Until Summer's return…

I push up out of my seat and stalk to the window. It's frosty outside, a low mist sweeps across the grounds and the far-off loch, coating everything it touches in a veil of glittering white.

Gran loved it like this…all mystical and full of the fairy tale magic she lived for. The kind of magic that saw her doing this…forcing Summer and I back together. Her will, those letters, her last wishes…

You were the one who let her back in, though. You were the one unable to tune out your heart when nothing good can come of it.

I curse, desperate to reinstate the walls around my heart, the armour that has protected me for years.

But what if Gran was right? What if we're meant to be? What if Summer could change? Be happy here?

My head is shaking before I even finish the thought. I wasn't worth sticking around for before—why would now be any different? My only hope is to keep my distance, and I know how laughable that sounds when we live under the same roof.

Aye, good luck with that, I can almost hear Gran say— before a very real commotion from the entrance hall has me heading that way.

I'm already through the door before I question who or what I might find, and whether I really want to face it. But I *am* questioning it seconds later, when I'm rooted to the spot by the sight of a delighted Summer, all laughter and light, as she hunches over Rufus, Gran's four-legged adoptee and the cause of all the noise.

'Rufus! Rufus!'

Danny, our gamekeeper, bursts in, a rifle under one arm, a dog's lead in the other.

'Get back here!'

The young lad skids to a halt as he spies me, his freckled face even redder than usual, his auburn hair wild beneath his flat cap.

'I'm so sorry, Mr Fitzroy, sir. I was just about to get his lead on when he got wind of your guest and that was it—he was off!'

Summer snaps her head around to see me and straightens just as quickly. 'Edward!'

I tug my gaze from her to Danny. 'It's quite all right, Danny.'

'I imagine he's happy to see you too, sir. He couldn't wait to get back in here. I think he's missed the place; my house is all well and good, but this—this is his home.'

'He *lives* here?' Summer asks, and I know what she's thinking.

In the shock of it all, I haven't even considered Rufus and where he might fit in the future of Glenrobin…the future we're now a part of.

I force myself to hold her eye and try to ignore the way my body worships her. 'Summer, meet Rufus. He's—'

The dog gives an excited bark at the sound of his name and scurries towards me. His paws are high on my chest before I know what he's about, his tongue making a determined sweep for my cheek. I press him down, forgetting what I'd been about to say as his ungodly stench reaches me.

'When did he last have a bath, Danny!'

Through his thick eyebrows, Rufus blinks his doleful eyes at me and whines.

'I know… I'm sorry, sir.' Danny removes his cap and scratches the back of his head. 'But he hates water. I'm surprised he hasn't scarpered at the mere mention of the B-word.'

'Oh, but he's gorgeous!' Summer exclaims, her excited voice calling Rufus back and he's skidding up against her, quick as a flash. His shaggy mass of black, grey and white hair all a blur.

'Aren't you, darling?'

Her laugh lights me up from head to toe. Her eyes so bright as she tickles his eager head, not a care in the world for the smell that's radiating off him.

'And doesn't he know it,' mumbles Danny.

'So, if this is Rufus…' she looks up '…who might you be?'

Well done on introducing the human, Edward…

I want to roll my eyes at myself.

Danny clutches his cap to his chest, stands to attention. 'Danny, the Glenrobin gamekeeper, at your service, ma'am.'

She turns the full wattage of her smile on him now, and I feel the most ridiculous surge of jealousy. That he's earned it where as I clearly haven't.

And can you blame her after your cold greeting earlier?

'It's a pleasure to meet you, Danny. I'm Summer.'

She offers her hand and he gives it a hearty shake, his redness reaching new heights.

'And you, Miss Summer.' He gestures to Rufus, who is now nuzzling the inside of Summer's palm. 'He certainly likes you.'

She smiles down at the smelly mass of fur. 'And I like him.'

'He's been mighty moody since Ms Katherine passed away…it's good to see a spring in his step again.'

'So he was Katherine's dog?'

Danny nods. 'She found him on the grounds here when

he was a pup—quite wild by all accounts. We reckon he's a cross between an Irish Wolfhound and a Bearded Collie.'

'He's not a working dog, then?' Her gaze goes to the doorway, where Danny's three black Labrador Retrievers wait patiently for their master, probably despairing of their little runaway friend.

'Och, no. He's all about the fun, this one.'

Fun. Summer's middle name.

'In that case,' she chirrups, 'I think we're going to get along famously.'

'Are you ready to have him back, then, sir?' Danny looks to me.

'Back?' And now I sound like the dim-witted fool I am. 'Of course. Yes.'

'Does this mean he's now *ours*?' she asks me tentatively, and I get it…feel the whole 'ours' thing making me squirm and warm in one.

I scratch the back of my head, the move reminding me of Danny doing exactly the same thing. What is it about Summer that has a man's temperature rising, the collar of his shirt tightening and his hormones regressing to uncontrollable teenage levels again?

'I guess you could say he belongs to the castle,' I correct, as if that somehow sounds better. 'When Gran couldn't take in foster children any more and Rufus appeared—well, you can just imagine her joy.'

Her smile widens, her happiness so pure as her eyes fall to Rufus, who is now leaning into her, his head huge against her waist.

I screw my face up as a cold gust blows through the open door, sweeping his wet dog scent right into my face. 'But a bath first, Danny, and then he can come home.'

Rufus whines, his ears pricking at the dreaded word, and Summer pipes up, 'I'll do it.'

Both Danny and I gape at her.

'He really does hate water, miss,' says Danny.

She gives a shrug. 'It's okay. I've had my fair share of working with tricky animals—and humans—over the years. Does the boot room still have a shower?'

'Yes...' I say, my frown deep. She can't be serious...

'Ms Katherine used to hose him down in there,' Danny says, all helpful. 'His stuff should still be in there—shampoo, towels, brushes... But if you need anything, you just let me know.'

'Great. You can trust me with him, Danny. I promise.'

She's already back to fussing over Rufus, and Danny is grinning like a fool, his eyes as joyful as the dog at her feet as he watches them both.

I clear my throat. 'Danny?'

The man starts, his eyes shooting to me as his body straightens and he seems to give himself a mental slap. 'Yes, sir?'

'Is everything okay with the estate? I wanted to talk to you about the food reserves with the freak weather that's been forecast...'

He nods rapidly, all business now. 'I wanted to talk to you about the same. If it's anything like the snow a couple of years back we'll be needing to supplement it for a good while.'

'I'd say a few months at least, while the ground thaws out. Let's take a walk and discuss it.' *And get out of Summer's distracting orbit.* 'I'll get my coat.'

I'm already heading to the rear of the house when Summer races up behind me, accompanied by the scurry of Rufus's claws on the wooden floor.

'I'll get mine too.'

'You're not needed for this, Summer.'

'But I want to come. If I'm to—if we're to live here—I should get to know the lay of the land.'

I shake my head, give a soft huff.

'What?' she asks.

I say nothing as I shove open the door to the boot room and grab a weatherproof coat from the hook.

'What, Edward? Are you implying that because I'm a woman I can't—?'

'No, Summer!' I spin to face her and she's wide-eyed. Even Rufus has frozen. 'It has nothing to do with you being a woman and everything to do with you. Who you *are*.'

'What—? What are you saying?'

I shake my head, choke on a laugh that feels more like a sob. 'Playing at house. Acting serious, like you're going to stick around this time. When just last night you reiterated how you never stay in one place long enough to settle, to create a home.'

'But… Edward, this is different. I want to do what Katherine requested. I want to play my part and look after this place.'

'How long for, Summer? A month? Two…?'

How could she not see how much this was killing me? Or maybe she could and she simply didn't care?

'You know how long for.'

'Oh, that's right—a year. And then you'll leave and not look back.'

'No. It won't be like that.'

I stare down at her hard, trying desperately to calm my pulse. My anger stems from my panic, not her. This isn't her fault. She doesn't deserve my wrath. Gran has put us in this situation and I only have myself to blame for wanting more…so much more than Summer will ever want to give.

I force my shoulders to ease, my voice to soften. 'Whatever the case, you don't need to be involved in this. I've been running the estate for Gran long enough. I know the staff, the routine, the responsibility.'

She wets her lips. 'But I don't want to be a spare part. I like to keep busy.'

And don't I know it? Always dashing from one thing to the next, one country to the next even, probably fearful that her feet might get stuck.

'You're not a spare part. Like you said last night, you have the time and the freedom to carry on Gran's good work. So do it, Summer. Go and do some good and I'll take care of managing the estate.'

I shove my arms into the jacket, make for the door.

'But Edward, I thought—last night—that we—'

She breaks off, her eyes searching mine, as if I can somehow finish that sentence for her. But my mind is racing, remembering her in my arms, her coming apart around my touch, calling out my name, that earth-shattering connection...

Breathe. Speak.

'Last night— Last night was a mistake. We were both in a weird head-space. Returning here, the inheritance, the memories, your nightmare...all of it.'

'You want to pretend it didn't happen?' she asks quietly. 'That it didn't...didn't mean something?'

'Yes, Summer, that's exactly what I want.'

'But we're okay, right?'

I take a stilted breath. 'We're fine,' I lie. 'Have a good day, Summer.'

I don't wait for her to respond. I up my pace and join Danny on the front porch, throwing my focus into him and off the woman with the haunted blue gaze who had looked close to tears as I left.

Was it cruel, after what we'd shared the night before, to dismiss it so readily to her face?

But what was the alternative? To acknowledge it? To admit that it had meant something? To admit that I want more—so much more?

'Dammit all!'

'Sorry, sir?'

Danny's frowning up at me.

'Nothing. Sorry. Let's go.'

Before I race back inside and beg for forgiveness…and for the future I know we can't have.

Summer

'Don't you worry about him, Rufus.' I tickle his head, though I'm talking more to myself as I watch Edward's swiftly departing form. 'He's only in a grump because he doesn't know how to handle last night. He'll come round.'

I hope.

'And in the meantime, it's bath time, buddy.'

He gives the same whimper and I smile at him, hunch down to his level.

'It'll be fun, I promise.'

'Fun' becomes a very interesting and very wet game of hide-and-seek, with Rufus trying to hide his huge frame and me trying to wash him and not the entire boot room. But we get there eventually, and if I say so myself he smells divine.

'One job down, buddy. Plenty more to go!'

Like carrying on Katherine's legacy…

It would've been good to talk through some ideas with Edward—though I have a feeling he'd caution me to walk before I can run. But I'm excited. I've never had the means to do good on such a level.

I've volunteered in exchange for bed and board in places across the globe—Asia, Africa, Latin America—and I've repaired homes, built classrooms, clinics, taught English, given love and care to kids who need it. But to have money now…enough money to give back on an entirely different scale… The idea fills me with enthusiasm and an impatience to act.

And heaven knows I need the distraction, with Edward's tormented gaze and parting words plaguing me, threatening to replay over and over until I want to run away and not look back. Proving I'm no better than I was all those years ago.

But I *am* better. I *am* stronger. I know my own worth and I'm determined to do right by Katherine if it's the last thing I do.

As for Edward's reaction… I can't blame him for being wary, for keeping me at a distance—not with our history and with the way I live my life now. Doesn't make his dismissal any easier to bear, though…

I head upstairs, with Rufus on my tail, and change out of my wet clothes into something comfy and warm.

Now what?

I look at Rufus at my feet. 'How about a tour?' He gives his approval in the form of a bark. 'Getting my bearings again counts as walking before running, right?'

We set off together, and his company goes some way towards softening Edward's chilling departure. I give silent thanks to Katherine for another unexpected gift, while the real gift, the estate itself, brings back so many memories.

The castle is much the same—aside from the bathrooms, which have been upgraded, the surprising lift that's been added at the heart of the castle, and the cinema room that's like a miniature theatre. But as we approach my old bedroom I can see the degradation, the damp that needs treating, the floors that need stripping, the walls that need re-papering.

I reach my bedroom door, see the heart made from

wicker still hanging there and brush my fingers over it, a bittersweet smile on my lips.

Rufus nudges my hand and I look down at him. 'This was my room, buddy, once upon a time.'

I twist the knob and push the door open. The hinges protest as if they haven't been used in years, and inside the daylight is dimmed by the thin drapes that are drawn across the window. Dust sheets cover the furniture, the bunk beds are stripped, and the walls... The walls are still covered in the same pink and white wallpaper, depicting flamingos and clouds.

For a moment I just stand there, taking it all in. Edward's right   it needs work. The damp is worse here, building around the windows, in the corners, and there's a certain chill in the air... But none of it detracts from the memories. I can still hear the laughter in the walls. Still imagine the kids running around and me trying to mind my own business, my head in a travel book, dreaming of the adventures I would one day experience.

'And I got to go on those adventures,' I say, looking down at Rufus, who cocks his head at me. 'Lucky me, hey?'

But as I stand in the room I once planned my future in I can't shift the feeling that something went wrong. Because the sense of achievement, of fulfilment, never came. All those adventures...all those things on my bucket list...and not once did I feel at peace. Happy. Content.

Katherine's letter haunts me...her warning too...

> *I worry that if you're not careful life will pass you by and you will never pause long enough to feel what it is to be content, to be happy, to be loved...*

But maybe I'm broken. Maybe fulfilment is something that will always feel out of reach for me. Or maybe I just haven't experienced enough yet.

Or maybe Katherine is right. Because you felt pretty content when you were in Edward's arms last night, didn't you?

I gulp the thought down. I won't accept it. I don't need another human being to feel happy and fulfilled. The only person who can give me that is myself.

'Isn't that right, Rufus?'

A bark. Definite agreement.

And getting started on Katherine's legacy is sure to be a step in the right direction.

'Come on, buddy. I have charities to speak to, fundraising events to organise, and I know just where to start...'

I stride back to my new bedroom and take up the photograph of me and Katherine, the two of us surrounded by preparations for the Halloween Fairy Tale Ball.

The thirty-first of October is a month away... It's possible to pull off a ball in that time, surely?

'Anything's possible if you set your mind to it, Summer.'

Katherine's soft voice wraps around me, encourages me.

'What do you reckon, Rufus? I've got this, right?'

His bark is more of a whine-cum-groan, and his eyes peeping through his heavy eyebrows are far too sceptical, reminding me of Edward and his cautionary tone...

'It's an idea. Though it's a lot of work...organising such affairs, I mean.'

And if ever I needed added motivation, that was it, right there.

CHAPTER ELEVEN

Summer

GLENROBIN IS IN CHAOS. Literally.

There are boxes everywhere and James is my eager assistant. If someone had told me two weeks ago that James, the estate's very austere butler, is a secret dance lover with a penchant for fairy tales, I would have rolled over laughing. But it's true.

Today we're taking delivery of the background pieces that will set the scene of the ball, and Rufus is as giddy as we are, thinking it's an assault course for his pleasure alone.

'Right, I think if we get these shifted into the ballroom as soon as—'

'What the blazes?'

Edward tumbles into the hall, his feet caught on one of the many boxes, and both James and I cringe, unable to save him. He rights himself quickly enough, with a bounding Rufus more of a hindrance than a help, but the giant dog is unperturbed by Edward's death stare.

'I'm sorry, sir. I'll have this cleared right away.'

'It's my fault,' I'm quick to say over James. 'I insisted we check the items off on the inventory before moving the boxes.'

The death stare is upon me, and for the briefest second

I see the flare of something in his eyes before the look is replaced with the one I have come to expect these past two weeks. A look that would turn the warmest heart to stone.

'What is all this?'

'It's for the ball,' I say with forced calm. 'You know… the Halloween ball I *told* you I was arranging.'

His eyes return to the boxes, widening with what I'd like to think *isn't* alarm. Has he not listened to me at all?

I've had my suspicions, but seriously…

Never mind being told that James is a dance fiend—if someone had told me it was possible to live with someone and tune them out so completely, I'd have told them they were talking nonsense. But Edward has proved otherwise, and I don't want to acknowledge how much it hurts…or how much the staff have picked up on it too.

I've barely seen him since our night together. When he's at home he's confined to his study, working. On the rare occasions he emerges his phone is in hand, his eyes fixed on it. At breakfast, his tablet is his companion. Lunch he takes in his study. Dinner is the only time he graces me with his presence, and even then his mind is elsewhere and we dine in virtual silence.

Not that I've pined for him. Not in the slightest. Honest.

I've spent my time reacquainting myself with the castle and the grounds, trying hard to feel comfortable…at home. I'm so glad of Rufus, who has become my little shadow—okay, my *big* shadow. And of James and Marie, who've been so warm and welcoming, trying hard to make up for Edward's noticeable aloofness.

And I'm so excited to be putting Katherine's money to good use, and her name too, by holding the Halloween ball in her honour.

I've spoken to the local children's home, social services too. They're as keen as me. Katherine's name gets me prompt access to anyone I need, and it's amazing how time isn't an issue when you offer to pay a premium at the last minute. I have charities, caterers, entertainers, set designers, the all-important attendees with big wallets, and guests—young and old—all lined up.

It's going to be the party of the year and I can't wait!

The only thing that takes the edge off the thrill is Edward. I've been desperate to discuss my ideas, to engage him, get his sign-off on the plans—the lot. He'd know about it all inside out if he chose to listen.

Instead he's snubbed every conversation I've attempted, and there's only so much snubbing one girl can take.

Which is why his blank look now makes my blood boil.

I want to stomp right over to him and dare him to take issue with me. A fight would beat the silence I've been treated to this past fortnight. But there's a small part of me—the part that still feels guilty about leaving all those years ago—that holds me back.

'And when is it?'

I gape at him, fold my arms across my chest, tap my foot. 'It's a *Halloween* ball, Edward, when do you think it is?'

He rakes a hand through his hair, blows out a breath. It's then that I notice the lines around his eyes, the shadows beneath too… Did I do that to him?

'Right…right, of course.'

'Look…' I soften both my posture and my tone '…we'll have it cleared away very soon.'

He doesn't look reassured, and if James wasn't a captive audience I'd press him on what the issue is—the real issue. Because it's not the boxes. And if we don't have it out soon, those shadows under his eyes are only going to get worse—as is the atmosphere within the castle walls.

'Just tell me you have a handle on the budget for this event. It does need to *raise* money, not lose it.'

And just like that I'm livid again. I've been working hard around the clock, and James has too, and he has the nerve to question—

The antique doorbell rings through the hall, silencing my inner rant as all eyes look to the entrance.

'That'll be Juan.'

Edward's already moving off, hopping over the boxes to get to the door, unaware that he's leaving me steaming.

'We'll take coffee in my study, James.'

'Of course, sir. As soon as I've got these—'

'*Now*, James!'

Why, the stubborn, obstinate—

'Of course, sir.'

James hurries to put down the box he's holding and I bite my tongue. I want to tell him to forget Edward's rude request, but I don't want to get him into any more trouble.

'I won't be a moment, Summer.'

I give him an understanding smile and off he hurries. My eyes snap to Edward, who's pulling open the door, oblivious to the escalating heat behind him.

'Juan, it's so good to see you!'

His cheeriness is like lighter fuel to my already burning ire and I screw my face up, silently mimic him. *Juan, it's so good to...*

Oh, crap!

Juan is looking past Edward, straight at me, and judging by the sparkle in his eye he saw every second of my performance.

I smile stiffly, eyes wide.

Edward catches his friend's gaze, and if I'm not mistaken the slightest flush reaches into his cheeks. Is he embarrassed by me?

'Juan, meet Summer. Summer, meet Juan—my good friend and colleague.'

'I know who she is. We've already spoken.'

Juan strides towards me, leaving Edward at the door. Rich brown skin, carefully groomed black hair, eyes as friendly and warm as his smile. He is a sight for sore eyes— particularly as I glimpse Edward behind him, with an expression close to thunder.

'It's a pleasure to meet you in person, Summer.'

'And you.' I smile up at him and he leans in, air-kissing both my cheeks in a waft of very expensive aftershave. 'I think Edward's been hiding you away on purpose.'

He throws a teasing look back at his friend and I giggle like a teenager. The light relief is so much better than the anger. Don't get me wrong, I'm still angry, but I'll deal with Edward later.

'Here, I have something for you…'

I sense Edward's curiosity mounting along with the gathering storm as Juan pulls a slip of card from his inside jacket pocket and passes it to me.

'I know you said we could email our RSVP, but I figured since I was heading this way…'

'RSVP?' Edward comes up behind him, frowning down at the pearlescent rectangle with its silver scrawl and embossed fairy tale scene.

'Thank you,' I say.

'You're very welcome.'

'RSVP?' Edward repeats, stronger this time, his brows raised to us both.

'For the Halloween Ball…' I smile sweetly. 'You know… the thing we were just talking about…'

He makes a sound deep within his throat…

Did he just growl at me? Oh, this gets better and better.

'Aww, don't look so put out…' I touch his chest, well aware I'm poking the bear. 'You're invited, too. You're my Prince Charming.'

Juan chokes on a laugh, and I swear I hear Edward curse under his breath. Serves him right. If he'd paid attention, none of this would be a surprise.

I got a grunt from him when I asked for sign-off on the people I intended to invite, another when I said I was going to ask his personal assistant for help, so as far as I'm concerned at this juncture anything goes.

Though I may have made something of a poor judgement call when it came to using Katherine's old guest list as a starting point. I'm either a sucker for punishment or just a tad too soft. In either case it's done now, and the responses are flooding in.

I haven't received *theirs* yet, but never say never…

Perhaps they'll do me an unconscious favour and not attend.

But if they do the black look on Edward's face now might not be the worst I witness in connection with the ball.

'Well, if the weather keeps up,' Juan is saying, 'you'll certainly have the magic of a winter wonderland to add to your fairy tale theme. I was worried we weren't going to make it.'

I look outdoors, to the blanket of white quickly thickening, and grimace. 'It'll certainly help keep the ice sculptures cold, but if the guests can't get here we won't have a ball at all.'

'Don't you worry yourself with that. Edward will make sure the roads are clear—won't you, Edward?'

He slaps his friend on the back…his friend who looks as if he might want to string someone up right now… And I'm not sure if it's me or Juan, my new and wonderful comrade-in-arms.

'Excellent. So I can leave that job in your capable hands—yes, my Prince?'

I bat my eyelashes at him and suppress a laugh at the

look on his face. Okay, so maybe 'my Prince' was a step too far, but winding him up is so much fun. Payback of a sort.

'I'll take care of it.'

It's a grumble under his breath, and for the added fun of it I leap up at him, kiss his cheek. His warmth teases at my lips, his scent at my nose, and all that strength beneath my palm flexes as I lean into him.

Oh, heaven.

'Thank you.'

His eyes collide with mine, their depths wild and dangerous, and then I'm dropping back and turning away before Juan sees more than he should.

I feel the thrum beneath my skin long after he's gone. And if I had the sense to dwell on it I'd likely be worried. But I don't dwell. I act.

And right now I have boxes to shift and a snow-loving dog to walk.

'Right, Rufus. Boxes and then walk. Deal?'

He gives an animated bark.

'At least you still love me...'

Not the wisest choice of words, Summer...

'It's a figure of speech,' I say into the ether.

Just a figure of speech.

Edward

'You look like you could do with something stronger than coffee.'

I flick Juan a look, wanting to flick him something else, but knowing it's not his fault I'm in this state. I can't sleep. I can't eat. She dominates my every waking and sleeping thought.

I've even found her old postcards to Gran and have been re-reading them all...staying connected to her in a way that feels safe, controlled… And I know how ridiculous that is when she's in the same building as me, but I can't look at her without wanting to do so much more.

He places his cup down and eyes my clenched fist upon the desk. 'Okay, I'm making an executive decision. Coffee isn't going to cut it.'

I force my hand to relax. 'It's only three in the afternoon, Juan.'

'What's the saying? It's party time somewhere… I'll pour, shall I?'

He's already on his feet, striding to the antique Japanese drinks cabinet—Gran's pride and joy.

'I'll say one thing for Katherine: she always had this thing fully stocked. You know, I tried to get my hands on this fifty-year-old malt…' He raises up a bottle '…happy to pay a fair sum for it too, and there was none to be had.'

'She was a woman of many talents.'

'You don't *sound* impressed.'

Impressed? It's Gran's fault I'm in this mess.

'Help yourself to it,' I grind out, pushing up out of my seat and heading to the window.

Summer's laughter reaches me through the glass a second before she appears, a bright splash of colour. Her red coat—another excellent purchase—is flaring out as she spins on the spot, blonde waves escaping her green beanie, an excited Rufus prancing around her, chasing the toy she has in her hand.

She's a vision.

And I should have looked away the moment I heard her.

'I don't mind if I do, so long as you're joining me.'

I drag my eyes from the window to see Juan studying me intently.

'I take it you have your driver here?'

'I do.'

As he says it, the arrival of someone else outside snags my attention. 'So you do...'

Juan's driver approaches Summer, who pauses to offer him a smile, her cheeks all rosy, face aglow. He's young and handsome and his instant attraction towards her is as obvious as Juan's had been.

I force my jaw to relax before I crack a tooth.

She's laughing at something the man has said and I feel an ache deep within my chest, a longing... I want to make her laugh like that again. I want her eyes to sparkle up at me. I want... I want...

The driver is digging in his pocket for something that has Rufus bobbing up and down.

'Does your driver always have dog treats in his pocket?'

Juan chuckles. 'There's a story there.'

'I bet...'

'But I'm more interested in yours right now.'

His tone turns sombre and I refuse to look at him.

'Mine?'

'You haven't been yourself since you came back here.'

I haven't been myself since Summer walked back into my life.

He joins me at the window, a glass in each hand. He passes me one as his eyes drift to the view...to his driver, Rufus, Summer...

'Of course. I understand now.'

'I doubt that.' I sip the warming liquid and wish it would quash the churn beneath my ribs.

'I've never seen you like this. Not over work and certainly not over a woman.'

'I'd love to see how you'd fare being forced into living with one for a year.'

'I told you I would pull the will apart and get you out of it, but you were the one who put a stop to that.'

'Because I can't do it. Gran wanted her to live here—she wanted to give her a home.'

'She wanted you to have a home too.'

I grunt—a really unbecoming habit I seem to have developed.

'You forget I've read the letter—the will too. She was pretty clear about what she wanted and why she chose Summer too…'

'Summer was different. She was special…'

'Special to who? Your grandmother, or…?'

The smallest of smiles touches my lips, and my eyes are lost in the sight of her as I fail to answer him.

'Hey, don't get me wrong—I can totally see the appeal.'

A growl tries to rise up within me. It's a misplaced jealousy that I can't suppress. 'She's off-limits, Juan.'

He lifts his glass to me. 'Amen to that. I wouldn't dare.'

I give a choked laugh, throw back more whisky, nursing the burn. 'You forget I know you and your whole bed 'em and leave 'em reputation.'

'What's the alternative? End up like you?'

'What's that supposed to mean?'

'Like you need to ask… But, for the record, I'm insulted you think I'd go after someone else's woman.'

'She's not my woman.'

'No?' His brows arch, his grin disbelieving. 'You could have fooled me.'

I say nothing, my eyes still trained on the outdoors, my thoughts far too occupied with her.

'So, if she's not your woman, and if she's nothing to you, what's the real problem here? Because it's clearly not the inheritance that you once saw her as undeserving.'

I force my eyes to meet his and his own eyes narrow. He cocks his head to one side. 'You're in love with her, aren't you?'

'She's been back in my life a fortnight.'

'That's not what I asked.'

I stare at him, mute, my chest tight, my heart twisting, my pulse racing. Do I? Is that why this is killing me? Why the pressure of being around her again, knowing she will eventually leave, is dominating my every thought and I have no control over it?

There's no teasing in Juan's face now. His smile is soft, his eyes sickeningly sympathetic.

'I know I'm not the best advocate for love, but my aunt swears she knew within seconds of meeting my uncle that he was the one for her. Love at first sight, she reckons—and, hell, they've been married forty years and counting. They're still like those lovesick teenagers who fled Colombia together. It's stomach-turning…but also kind of sweet.'

I give a gruff laugh. 'If I didn't know any better, I'd say you were a little envious.'

'Because you look so good on it yourself?'

He's got you there.

'Look, Edward, if she's the one…and, let's face it, you've walked the earth and bedded enough women to know the difference by now…do something about it.'

'I can't.'

'"Can't" isn't in your vocabulary. You told me that over a decade ago, when I told you we couldn't save that renewable energy company. But we did it. And achieved a whole lot more with it too.'

'That's business.'

'You say potato…' He shrugs. 'Sounds to me like you're just running scared.'

'And what if I am?' I say, sick of fighting it, denying it.

The look of surprise on his face is a picture. 'You really do have it bad.'

I do.

I swallow. Not that I can say it out loud. Not when I have no idea what to do about it.

'So what's the problem? She doesn't like you? Is that it?'

Like me? Ha! She liked me well enough two weeks ago. Until I shut down and pushed her out.

'She likes me well enough…when I'm not behaving like an arse.'

'So fix the attitude and go after her—what have you got to lose?'

'Her.' That's the simple and painful answer. 'She won't stick around. By her own admission she never stays in one place long enough to form connections, have a relationship…'

'Sounds like someone else I know.'

Another grunt.

'Seriously, look at yourself and your own history—who's to say it won't be different for you both this time?'

I give a huff…but isn't he talking some sense?

'Rather than being an arse, why not try being a man worth sticking around for?'

A flicker of light sparks inside me. Hope. 'Using my own words against me?' I ask.

'Something like that.' He grips my shoulder in encouragement, support. 'You've never been one to shy away from risk in business. So why start now with your personal life?'

CHAPTER TWELVE

Summer

'EDWARD!' MY HEART leaps into my throat as I spy him not two metres away, rooted in the snow as if he's been there a while.

The collar of his coat is drawn high, his hands are deep inside his pockets, and his eyes strike out beneath the rim of a navy beanie. He looks good in a beanie—less executive, more everyday, and my betraying heart gives a little flip as it settles.

How did I miss his approach?

You're rolling around in the snow with a great big Heffalump of a dog and you ask how?

Said Heffalump yaps excitedly as he launches himself at our new arrival. He has none of the wariness I have. But then, Rufus hasn't been shut out like I have.

'Sorry.' Edward reaches down to pat Rufus, but his eyes stay fixed on me. 'I didn't mean to startle you.'

'You didn't. We were just having fun. Has Juan gone?'

Rufus rolls around in front of him, demanding his attention, and Edward rubs his belly, the sight making my skin prickle and my chest bloom with envy.

'Aye.'

I dust snow off my clothing as I step towards him, my

anger from earlier weak in the face of this new Edward. Appeasing Edward.

'I'm sorry about the mess in the hall, I just didn't want anything moved until I'd gone through the list.'

'I know. I get it.'

He looks up at me and those soft brown eyes render me speechless, their sudden warmth so unexpected.

'I'm sorry I was such a grump.'

I fold my arms, purse my lips as I side-eye him. 'Have you had another lobotomy?'

He laughs, and the sound is so deep and unrestrained and everything I've been craving since our meeting with Mr McAllister.

'No.' He smiles at me, hesitant now. 'I don't know… maybe.'

And Edward hesitant is as sexy as Edward stripped to his underwear. What's going on?

'Can I join you for a bit?'

My laugh is soft with disbelief. 'You're asking if you can come and play with us?'

'I guess I am.'

'Are you sure you can afford to spend the time away from your desk? Because this past fortnight you've barely looked up from your work.'

He grimaces. 'I know. I'm sorry about that too.'

'You're very apologetic all of a sudden. What did Juan do to you?'

'Talked some sense into me. Just don't tell him I said that.'

He's teasing, but I'm not laughing any more. I'm confused. And I'm hurt. Having him come out here, expecting me to welcome him back like everything is fine. Swinging from hatred to aloof, from moody to this… I can't protect my heart if he keeps taking me by surprise like this.

'Come on, Rufus. I owe you an actual walk.'

I turn away and Rufus scrambles up, trots to my heel as I head towards the woods. I refuse to be a doormat. There's only so far my guilt and past behaviour will excuse his behaviour now.

'Summer!'

I hear his feet crunch swiftly through the snow, feel his presence at my back, but don't turn. 'What?'

'I really am sorry.'

'I heard you.'

'I shouldn't have snapped at you.'

'No, you shouldn't have.'

'I'm sorry for snapping at James too.'

'Good.' I pause to pick up a stick poking out of the snow and throw it for Rufus, who bounds after it. 'Anything else you care to apologise for while you're at it?'

He blows out a breath and Rufus sprints up to me, drops the stick. But I'm too attuned to Edward behind me, waiting for his answer.

Rufus is jumping up and down, barking with impatience. *This is important, buddy*, I tell him mentally. *It's time for the big bad wolf to play nice.*

'I'm sorry for shutting you out these past two weeks.'

A small smile touches my lips. 'And...?'

I can sense his frown as he racks his brain for more. 'For keeping you out of the estate business and not helping with the preparations for the Halloween ball.'

I take up the stick, give it a good throw. 'I'm glad you finally—'

'And I'm also sorry for this...'

'Huh—?' I start to turn, but too late. He has the collar of my coat in one hand and a ball of snow in the other and...

'Edward!' I gasp as the ice-cold snow breaks through

my clothing, and arch against the icy trickle as it runs down my back. 'Why, you…!'

He jumps back. 'Hey, all's fair in love and war.'

I have no idea if he knows what he's saying, but now isn't the time to think about it—not when there's a fight to be had…a physical one full of play.

I'm already bending forward. 'You're going to regret that.'

'Is that a threat?'

'It's a promise.' He's jogging backwards and I'm balling up snow. 'Have you forgotten how good my aim is?'

He laughs, his eyes so alive, his cheeks so pink. And I'm high on it—high on him.

I take aim and fire, catching his shoulder as he ducks and scoops up his own ball. I turn and run with a squeal, Rufus leaping alongside me. I feel it rather than see it, the dusting to my right as the snowball misses me and disturbs the hedge. Another one comes, quick-fire, and this time Rufus leaps for it, his great big body rolling into me as he catches it. And then we're both tumbling to the ground, the soft snow breaking our fall.

'Summer!'

I can hear Edward's panic, hear his feet pounding through the snow, and I bide my time. Rufus licks my face with a whimper, but I'm concentrating on keeping my eyes closed and my hands full of snow.

Wait. Just wait.

Cold air sweeps over me as he drops to his knees. His breath is hot on my cheek as he leans in, his hands soft on my body.

'Summer! Summer! Are you okay?'

Now!

My eyes snap open, my snow-filled hands come together either side of his face, my grin is triumphant. 'Gotcha!'

'You minx!'

I laugh, wild and free, and he shakes the snow off, showering me with it, his eyes returning to mine, blazing and full of teasing. But then he stills. The world stills. Our breaths come in short, heavy pants. Puffs of steam fill the narrow gap between us. He's so close. Only inches away.

I swallow, unable to fill my lungs, and even Rufus scoots back onto his haunches with an intrigued whine.

'Summer…?'

It's a groan, a growl, a plea, and then his hands are in my hair, displacing my beanie as he kisses me. And, heaven help me, I'm drowning. Drowning in a sea of sensation. So much cold beneath me, so much heat above, and my hands are in his hair, tugging him closer, anchoring my body higher, pressing against him.

I'm scared that he'll suddenly evaporate…stop kissing me…that this isn't real…it's a daydream…a very real-feeling daydream.

And what about when he wakes up and regrets it? Shuts you out again?

I shove against his chest, break the kiss. 'I can't do this. Not again. You shutting me out—it hurts too much.'

'I'm so sorry, Summer. I never wanted to hurt you.' He cups my face, sweeps his gloved thumbs across my cheeks, his eyes mesmerising in their intensity, their sincerity. 'I just didn't know how to behave…how to move forward…'

'Do you ever think you overthink everything?'

He laughs deep in his throat and it resonates through me, warming and thrilling in one.

'Do you ever think you don't think enough?'

'Hey!' I try to shove myself out of his grasp, but he has me held fast. 'You want more snow flying at you? Because I'm ready to go round two.'

'There's only one kind of round two I'm interested in,

and it has nothing to with the bed of snow beneath us and everything to do with the warm variety indoors.'

My breath hitches. 'Are you serious?'

'I've never been more so.'

Panic, excitement, want… It all flutters up, choking at my throat. Can I trust him? I trusted him not to run two weeks ago and look what happened.

'I mean it, Summer. I've been an arse of the highest order. I don't know how long I'll have you back in my life—a week, a month, a year—but I've been so focused on you leaving, on this ending, that I've lost sight of what we can have right now.'

A smile builds with the relief inside me. 'What kind of idiot focuses on the end without enjoying the story first, Edward?'

His eyes glitter…his chuckle deepens. 'What kind, indeed?'

And then he's kissing me, and I'm kissing him, and our bodies are rising up, moving as one.

'Although I think we owe someone a walk,' I murmur against his lips, and Rufus barks his approval.

Edward presses his forehead to mine, slips his hands around mine. 'Okay. Walk and then…?'

'Walk and then…' I give him a flirtatious wink in confirmation and tug him towards the trail. 'I can fill you in on the plans for the ball while we walk, if you're finally ready to listen, that is…?'

He squeezes my fingers. 'I'm all ears.'

'Well, for starters I'll have you know I have the budget in control.'

He grimaces. 'I know. I trust you. I shouldn't have said that.'

'No, you shouldn't have.' And then I let my excitement for the event take over… 'I'm so excited about it, Edward.

I've been using Katherine's old plans as a basis; I want it to pay true homage to her and all that she did. The ice sculptures are an added feature, but the weather is so perfect—and can you imagine the faces of the children as they come up the drive to see horses leaping, princesses dancing, glittering in the moonlight? And the fairy lights I have planned... It's going to be so magical and...'

He's looking at me strangely and my cheeks start to burn. 'What?'

'You know, you're so sexy when you get like this.'

'Like what?'

'Inspired. Passionate.'

I grin. 'I'll remind you of that on the day.'

'What day?'

'The day of the ball...' I wrap my arms around his neck, look up at him, my grin turning impish. 'When you see your costume.'

'My *what*?'

'Did you think Prince Charming was just a name I'd plucked out of thin air?'

'Summer...' He draws out my name, his brows reaching inside his beanie, and I nip my lip again, bite back a giggle.

'It *is* a fairy tale ball, Edward. Costumes are compulsory—especially for you and me as the hosts.'

He frowns. 'Right...silly me.' And then his eyes spark. 'Hang on—if I'm Prince Charming, what does that make you?'

'Cinderella, of course. Quite fitting, don't you think?'

His smile is slow and sultry as he wraps his arms around me, holds me closer. 'Are you saying you're a poor mistreated maiden in need of rescuing?'

'Hardly!' I choke on a laugh. 'I've *never* needed a man to rescue me. However...' I flirt with the hair at the nape of his neck '… I will play the role on the day, if you promise to play yours?'

'Clever, Summer, very clever.'

'Persuasive, I think you mean.'

'Clever, persuasive, cunning…' he drags his mouth over mine '…and very…' he nips my bottom lip with his teeth '…sexy.'

Edward

We race to the bedroom faster than is deemed normal for fully grown adults who should be able to resist long enough to pass the household staff without arousing suspicion, but it's like we're possessed. The frenzied heat coursing through our veins pushing out all sane thought.

Important things are checked off en route, though.

Rufus is walked, fed and watered, left asleep before the fire in my study.

James is instructed to inform Marie that dinner needs to be delayed by an hour. If he thinks the request strange, or our haphazard state of dress, with beanies, scarves and coats askew, he doesn't even cock a brow.

And, unless the house is on fire, no one is to disturb us.

The second I have her across the threshold I kick the door closed and press her up against it. I can't get enough. Of her kisses, her moans, her body—just her, all her. Two weeks of denying myself this has tipped me into insanity, I swear.

'Is it locked?' She hurries out the words against my lips, her fingers tugging at my clothing.

'You think anyone is going to interrupt us after we specifically told them not to?'

She giggles, and the sound is like heaven in my already elated state. 'Good point.'

I thrust my coat to the floor, kick off my boots, all the while walking her backwards to the bed as she does the same. Hats, scarves, tops, trousers, socks, pants, bras— okay, just one bra!—are thrown aside, and then her burning skin is against mine.

'You feel so good…' I groan.

'So do you…' She leaps up, wraps her legs around my waist. 'Please tell me you have condoms now?'

I shake my head, kiss away her disappointed moan as I grip her thighs to me.

'But you said…?'

'I know what I said, but I was a fool. I trust you…if you trust me.'

'Of course.' She holds my face in her hands, stares into my eyes. 'Always.'

It's music to my desperate heart.

I can't believe I've kept my distance for so long. Feared the risk when the payoff is so great, so perfect. It's her, and she's everything. If she'll have me…lay down roots and commit.

Not that I'll say it aloud. Because even through the lustful haze I know she isn't ready to hear it. Not yet.

And so I stay quiet. Tell her with every sweep of my lips, my tongue, my fingers how I feel, what I want and what I dream of for the future.

I know there's a clock ticking away somewhere. Her clock. The time she lives by.

But I'm done with dancing to its tune. I'm done with resisting this.

'Can I ask you something?' she says into the darkness some time later.

We're both spent and stuffed. Dinner in bed was her best

idea yet, and once James got over the blushes it was dished out and cleared away with minimal fuss.

I press a kiss to her hair, pull her in closer as I stare unseeing at the ceiling. 'Anything.'

Because the truth is there's nothing I would keep from her. I'd lay my heart bare right now if I thought it would keep her here rather than make her run.

'Why me, do you think?'

'Besides the fact that you epitomise your name and I could no longer resist your smile?'

'Behave!' She gives me a little shove. 'I mean, why did Katherine choose me to inherit? Of all her foster children over the years, why me?'

'You said you'd read her letter.'

'I did, but…' She gives a tiny shrug. 'It's so much—too much.'

'She did it because she loved you.'

'She loved us all, Edward.'

I take a steady breath, knowing how brutal it will sound, but knowing I must tell her all the same…

'You were different, Summer. You didn't have anyone else.'

She presses away from me, her frown of confusion making my chest ache. 'Neither did the other children.'

I search her gaze. I don't want to hurt her. I don't want to push her away. I'm cherishing the closeness we've found, but it's so precious, so very new.

'Edward…?'

I force myself to put it into words, my arm still around her, holding her close. 'Gran fostered children who were hard to home, Summer. In a lot of cases she took siblings just so they could stay together and wouldn't be separated. But you…you were much older, and you had no siblings, but you were…you were flagged.'

She swallows. 'Flagged as being difficult?'

'Yes.'

'People didn't want me?'

The harsh truth spilling from her lips kills me and my arm pulses around her.

'I wanted you,' I say.

The words are fierce and from the very heart of me, giving me away, but she's too lost in her sadness to see it.

'Katherine did too.'

Her smile is so sad and I return it, my hand soft on her cheek as I sweep a stray tear from her skin.

'She did. She didn't care about all the homes you'd been through. She only cared about giving you this one. She wanted to be the parent who…who…' My voice chokes as her lower lip trembles, her lashes lowering to hide further tears from me.

'She wanted to be the one who saved me?' she whispers.

'Yes.' It's barely audible as I stroke her hair and press a kiss to her head, lift her chin so she will look at me and see the truth in my gaze. 'She chose you because she wanted you to come back home again.'

Her glistening blue eyes hold mine. 'She wanted you to come home too.'

'I know.'

I don't state the obvious. That Gran wanted us to make a home together, to be a real family…

I don't know what Gran's letter to Summer said, but surely she must know her true intentions. That whatever Gran had seen back then, whatever she'd seen in the intervening years, she believed we belonged together.

But this was Summer. Summer who'd never truly felt loved as a child. Her own mother had rejected her, then the system had failed her for a decade, tossing her back and forth foster homes, more and more rejection... Until Gran. Until Glenrobin.

How could I have threatened her with taking it away?

You were sitting on a twenty-year-old hurt. You felt betrayed by your grandmother. You were grieving and confused.

But does that justify how I've treated her?

I don't know.

I know I need to fix things now, though.

'This place will be your home for however long you want it to be, Summer.'

'You can't promise me that.'

'I can.'

She shakes her head, pushes against my hand to hide her eyes from me. To hide herself from me.

'One day you'll want to settle down...make a home with someone,' she says into my chest. 'That someone won't want me around.'

You are that someone.

The words are burning a hole in my heart, desperate on my tongue.

'Never, Summer. That I can promise you.'

A scratching at the door breaks the heavy silence that descends, and she lifts her head. 'It's Rufus.'

She starts to rise and I pull her back gently. 'I'll get him.'

She smiles, but it slays me, her eyes are so haunted by the past.

'You know he sleeps with me every night?' she confesses, and I smile back at her.

Lucky Rufus.

'I've noticed.'

I open the door a crack and he immediately rushes in, making for the bed.

'Can he?' she asks.

I eye the pair of them. 'So long as there's room for me too.'

Now her grin is wide, happiness as golden as her hair all around her as she pats the bed and gives Rufus an excited, 'Come on, buddy!'

Up he jumps, immediately circling to find his spot.

'He has a thing for pinning my feet down. Doesn't matter if I'm lying, sitting or standing…he finds his way to get on top of them.'

I return to the bed, scratch his head with a murmured, 'I like your thinking, Rufus.'

His ears prick, his puppy-dog eyes blink up at me, and Summer, who's puffing up her pillow, pauses. 'What was that?'

'Nothing—nothing at all.' I give him a final pat. 'Night-night, buddy.'

She gives a tired chuckle.

'What's so funny?'

'You.'

I join her under the quilt and she scoots into my side, her naked warmth instantly soothing.

'Why?'

'You've picked up on my nickname for him.'

'I have?'

'Uh-huh. Buddy. Do you think he's gonna get confused?'

Rufus is cocking his head back and forth listening to our little exchange.

'I don't think so. No more than usual at any rate.'

She gives me a playful thrust of her behind. 'Oi! Don't be mean.'

'Mean?' I murmur against her ear, catching her lobe between my teeth and fighting every urge to trail my lips lower. 'Mean would be kicking him out so I can have my wicked way with you again.'

She gives a sleepy laugh that's cut short with a yawn. 'You're insatiable.'

'Are you complaining?'

'Never.'

'What about ten years from now, will you complain then?' I say it in the heat of the moment, the heat of the drowsy connection but as soon as the words leave my lips, I hold my breath, force my body to relax when all it wants to do is tense against her.

'You're so funny, Edward. I prefer you like this, you know. Don't change.'

She thinks I'm joking, only I'm not.

I know that now.

I want her. I love her. And I will do everything in my power to keep her.

Time is all I need to convince her that she wants the same. And, thanks to Gran, I have it in abundance.

CHAPTER THIRTEEN

Summer

'SUMMER!'

Edward's shout jerks me out of my nervous, excited brain fog. The ball is today. *Today!*

I'm just praying nothing goes wrong. But if his voice is any indication, something already has.

I burst from the bedroom just as he arrives and walks me straight back in again, swinging the door closed behind him.

I stare up at his face. He's sporting a deer caught in the headlights look and my hand goes to my neck on impulse. 'What's happened?'

He shakes his head, strides past me to the window, looks out at the driveway, strides back and then returns once more.

'What the hell are my parents doing here?'

Ohhh... I nip my lip, swallow back the nerves.

'James says you invited them?'

He looks at me now, his eyes pinning me with their accusation.

Another swallow. 'I did.'

'Why?'

'Because, like I told you, I used Katherine's plans as a basis.'

'And that included her *guest list*?'

'Katherine would never have excluded your mother from this, and I didn't want to either.'

'But...'

He rakes a hand through his hair just as his mother's voice rings through the entrance hall, demanding attention from the staff. I cringe a little, but I stand by my decision... even if it's now adding to my acute case of nervous belly.

'Why is it such a problem, Edward? There'll be lots of other people here and she's confirmed they're only staying for one night and then leaving again tomorrow. It's just twenty-four hours. And you did say a small part of you hoped that one day things might get better with your mother...isn't the ball as good a place to start as any?'

He's staring at me, his mouth hanging open, his eyes still wide.

'She's your mother, Edward, not an axe murderer.' I give an awkward laugh. 'I'm sure you can get through one evening together. And you can catch up with your father, too. By your own admission things are better between the two of you at least.'

He shakes his head. He looks ill. Beside himself ill. I step closer, surprised at the strength of his reaction.

'I'm sorry.' I reach for his hand. 'I should've told you.'

'Why didn't you?'

'Well, at first, I couldn't get you to listen to anything, and after... I don't know. I guess I didn't want you to talk me out of it.'

He studies me intently and I squeeze his fingers softly.

'It'll be okay.'

'I wish I had your confidence.'

'I'll lend you some of mine,' I tease softly, and it coaxes out the smallest of smiles.

'I'm worried about you.' He swallows. 'I'm worried about how she will take us.'

My lashes flutter over the word 'us'. Are we an 'us' now?

Well, you have been sleeping together for two weeks...

My stomach swoops…my pulse races.

But an 'us'?

What did you expect? It's not like you've been clear about where this is heading or where it isn't. And haven't you been content—deliriously happy, even?

I wet my lips, struggling to find the right words, but then he releases my hand and strides away, leaving a ghostly chill in his place.

'We're hosting this party together. At Glenrobin, Summer.' He forks his fingers through his hair without looking at me. 'Rubbing my mother's face in the inheritance this early on feels like a risky move.'

And just like that the chill and the tension dissipates. He's not talking about our relationship. He's talking about our joint ownership of the estate.

'"Hell hath no fury like a woman scorned,"' he murmurs, and I stride up to him, confident that on this we're OK.

'I can handle your mother, Edward.'

He turns and reaches out to cup my cheek, his eyes tormented as they search mine. 'If she hurts you, Summer… If she says anything, I swear to God…'

My ribs ache, my heart swells. Would he have said something back then if he'd witnessed what she'd done, what she'd said…?

I mimic his touch, palm to cheek. 'And if she hurts you, Edward, or says anything, I swear to God…'

And then I kiss him. I kiss him with my gratitude, kiss

him with my assurance that I can look after myself, kiss him until the world beyond this room no longer exists.

'You know,' he says against my lips, 'a wise person once said to me that the best form of stress relief can be found between the sheets.'

I squeal as he scoops me up and makes for the bed, rousing a sleeping Rufus, who shifts just in time for our arrival. 'And let me guess…that wise person was Juan?'

'How did you know?'

I laugh as he covers me with his body, turn my head from his approaching kiss… 'Isn't it rude to keep our guests waiting?'

'I shall explain we were otherwise engaged…' he teases my earlobe between his teeth '…with last-minute planning and preparations, of course.'

'I'm loving your thinking…' I tug his sweater over his head, my eyes roving hungrily over him.

'And I'm loving yours.'

Edward

I check my watch for the umpteenth time. She's not late. I'm early. Early and eager and…

I adjust my cravat.

'Will you stop that?' Marie bats my hands away. 'Every time you wiggle it, you ruin the symmetry.'

'The *symmetry*?' I raise my brows at her. 'I'm wearing frills and you're worrying about the symmetry?'

'Nonsense!' She pats her curly white wig that is sprinkled with glitter and waves her fairy godmother wand at me. 'You look very prince-like, and that colour becomes you.'

I look down at the navy satin brocade jacket with its gold trim and grimace. Bad enough that the trousers feel more like tights—breeches, I've been assured—but the floral pattern woven through the jacket and waistcoat…not to mention the satin shirt…

'You know, you're so sexy when you get like this.'

'Like what?'

'Inspired. Passionate.'

'I'll remind you of that on the day.'

'What day?'

'The day of the ball…when you see your costume.'

Our conversation in the snow comes back to me, and just like that I'm smiling. Smiling and remembering her teasing and her promise to play the role. My damsel in distress.

As if.

'Oh, my!'

Marie gasps, her hand over her mouth, as she looks past me. And I know what she's seen—or rather who. Her presence thickens the very air that I breathe, my body warms, and slowly I turn, lift my gaze to the top of the grand staircase, and there she is.

Summer.

Her name resonates through me as my vision narrows and she's all I can see. Her golden hair tumbling free about her bare shoulders…a dusting of sparkle all over…her iridescent dress the colour of the mist that enshrouds Glenrobin on the most mystical of days.

Ethereal. Magical. Otherworldly. She could have stepped out of a fairy tale herself.

And isn't that the point?

Tonight she is a true princess and she's mine. All mine.

Marie gives a soft chuckle beside me. 'Best close that mouth of yours before you catch a fly, Master Edward.'

I choke my agreement. Do as she suggests. But there's no moving—my feet are rooted. I'm incapable of anything but watching as Summer lifts the layers of tulle enough to reveal silver stilettos on her feet and starts to descend.

The light of the chandelier plays across her skin, her dress…over the silver-stitched pattern of birds and butterflies in the skirt and the heart-shaped corset that's a work of art. Its fairy tale scene is so detailed that I want to trace it with my fingers, every millimetre of it—and her.

She gives me a coy smile as she reaches the bottom step—a smile that is so unlike her it makes my heart flip and my hand reach out on impulse. 'Prince Charming at your service, Princess.'

I bow my head but keep my eyes fixed on hers, and her smile grows, stealing my breath and my heart with it.

'I think it's Cinders,' she whispers, slipping her hand into mine.

'Not on my watch.'

I'm vaguely aware that Marie has left us. Vaguely aware that there's a reason why I can't pull her to me and kiss her as deeply as I'd like.

I raise her hand to my lips, sweep her knuckles with the briefest kiss. 'You look breathtaking.'

She wets her glossy lips. 'You scrub up pretty well too.'

I smile. The look in her eye is worth every frill and every revealing inch below my waist. 'Are you ready to greet your guests?'

She gives an unsteady laugh. 'I want to be. But of all the things I've done, this has to be the most terrifying.'

'Come now, Princess…' I encourage her down the last step and place her hand on my arm. 'You've travelled the globe, faced challenges I can barely imagine. You've built classrooms and homes with your bare hands. You've taught English to women when their communities would have had them bearing babies instead. You've protested for women's rights and been imprisoned for it. You, my darling, have no need to be afraid.'

She's staring up at me, her eyes reaching wider and wider with every word. 'You really have been reading up on me.'

Reading up on you, devouring your postcards, falling in love with you...yes, that's me.

'When the subject is so fascinating, how could I stop?'

'Edward...' She shakes her head in wonder, her lips pursed, her eyes shining.

'Now, if I'm not mistaken that is the sound of the first guests arriving, and although James is dressed to receive—thank you for also putting him in breeches, by the way, I'm not sure I could have done this alone—I think it's customary for us to be at the door too.'

'Of course. But your parents...will they want to join us?'

I give a short laugh. 'My mother likes to make an entrance. She'll be fashionably late—which gives us plenty of time to enjoy your efforts before she tries to taint them.'

Her eyes tighten, her smile too. 'She might surprise you.'

'She might.'

But she won't.

I tried to speak to my mother earlier, to warn her to be on best behaviour, but she wouldn't even deign to speak to me. Too busy getting ready was the excuse she gave. Avoiding me, more like.

I can only hope that an audience of the rich and powerful, not to mention the great British press, will do what my undelivered threat couldn't.

I can hope, but not even the sight of Summer's unparalleled beauty can ease the prickle of unease at the base of my spine.

I didn't miss the panic flaring in her gaze when I referred to there being an 'us'. I backtracked well enough, using the inheritance as my cover, but she gave herself away so clearly and I'm worried.

This relationship we've built is far too fragile, far too new, and one barbed comment from my mother could see it crumbling to the ground. And I'm not ready for this to be over…nowhere near.

Summer

The evening is everything I dreamed of and more.

The look of wonder in the eyes of the guests as they take it all in—the ice sculptures, the hand-carved pumpkins, the autumnal decorations that lead them to explore each fairy tale scene in its own little nook… The adults are loving it as much as the children, and with all the compliments they shower me with, the gratitude too, I *feel* like a princess.

Me. Summer from the wrong side of the tracks. Holding court with my handsome Prince…

I giggle with the craziness of it.

'What now?' Edward groans as he spins us around the dance floor to an old classic. The soft light of the candelabra and the fairy lights add to the sparkle in his rich brown eyes.

'What do you mean, what now?'

'That laugh… An hour ago it was because my breeches were giving me grief. I can't bear thinking what it might be now…'

'You'll laugh at me.'

'Right now, I feel like you're laughing at *me*—again—so have at it.'

'If you must know I was laughing at the fact I actually feel like a princess.'

His grin lights me up inside. 'Enjoy it. You deserve every royal second.'

'I had a lot of help.'

'This is all you, Summer.' His eyes turn serious, his arm around my waist pulling me closer. 'What you've managed to create, the world you've built…'

He gestures to the room around us. Kids and adults alike are all dancing, talking, laughing, racing between the fairy tale scenes, raiding the dress-up boxes, creating pictures in the photo booths… Everyone is happy.

'You took Gran's vision and made it your own. Just look at the fun around you. As for the donations—I have it on good authority you're going to break Gran's record and then some.'

'I just want to do her proud.'

'You've—'

'It's so juvenile! I don't even know why we agreed to come, do you?'

That voice pierces the music…pierces me and I stumble mid-step. If it wasn't for Edward's grip, I would have face-planted for all the world to see.

Okay, so not everyone is happy.

He sweeps me past the bystanders, but his posture is as rigid as mine. I know he heard her too. I wet my lips, glance up, but he's not looking at me. His eyes are on his mother and projecting fire and ice in one.

'Edward, it's okay.'

'It isn't okay,' he says between his teeth.

'Please, I don't want a scene. Like you say, it's a success—a huge success. The auction went far better than I could ever hope for.'

'The auction *she* didn't even participate in.'

'Did you really expect her to? Besides…she at least made the effort to dress up.'

'Dress up?'

'Yes. Do you think she knew who we were going to be when she chose the evil stepmother get-up?'

He laughs against me, the tension easing from his body. 'You know that's no costume, right?'

I blink up at him in mock innocence. 'Are you serious? But it's all black and angular—and, frankly, quite scary.'

'Ah, don't worry, Princess…' He leans in, whispers beside my ear, and a thrilling shiver runs right through me. 'I'll protect you.'

'Lucky me.' It's as breathless as I feel.

'Lucky you, indeed.'

He twirls us further away, but I can't help bringing the focus back to her. 'Have you spoken to her yet?'

The tension ripples through him again and I bite my lip. Maybe I should leave well alone—but she's still his mother. Still his blood. Though I should know better than most that blood means nothing.

'We exchanged pleasantries…once she deemed herself ready for me. I think I came after Charles but before the caterers.'

He's teasing, and I hate it that he feels he must tease about something so hurtful.

'Actually, poor Charles had something of an ear-bashing about the inheritance, so I was forced to step in.'

'Oh, God, poor man.'

'Don't worry—he can hold his own when it comes to my mother's viperous tongue. I take it she hasn't spoken to you yet?'

I give a choked scoff, try to brush off the sting of it. 'Clearly I'm beneath the caterers.'

'You're the hostess of Glenrobin's event of the year. It has nothing to do with society's hierarchy and everything to do with the fact she can't see past her own bitterness.'

I grimace. 'I really did make things worse, didn't I?'

'You did what you thought was right.'

'But *you* were right. It's too soon. I shouldn't have invited her. I should have given her more time to come to terms with everything.'

'I don't know, Summer… Excluding her would have made her angry, too. You can't win.'

I search his eyes, see the truth of it and feel the sadness it brings. 'Just like Katherine couldn't…'

'Hey, don't let her spoil tonight. This is on her, not you.'

I can't bring myself to agree.

'I mean it, Princess…' He bows his head, brushes the lightest kiss to my ear. 'Forget about her and enjoy your ball, because everyone else who matters is.'

I let my gaze drift over the room, catch sight of Juan at the bar, surrounded by a group of attentive women, and manage a smile. 'Your friend certainly is.'

He follows my line of sight. 'It never takes him long to garner an audience.'

'He does have a certain something about him.'

Edward's eyes come back to me, sharp, probing. 'Don't tell me you go in for that tall, dark and handsome thing?'

'Oh, I don't know…his Spanish can be quite the aphrodisiac.'

He's jealous—it's as obvious as the warmth radiating off his body into mine. And provoking him is sending me a little dizzy.

'As for the tall, dark, and handsome thing…it certainly appeals. But I prefer mine quintessentially British.'

I stroke the base of his neck as I let my meaning hit home and feel rather than hear the soft growl that he gives. 'You'd better believe it, Princess.'

My laugh is breathy. 'You know, I could get used to that.'

'What?'

'You calling me Princess.'

'Stick around long enough and I'll call you it all you like.'

My heart pulses with the vehemence in his tone—but he's teasing, right? So why does it feel like a proposition of sorts? A demand? A desire for this to be something more…?

But how much more?

I press my cheek to his chest, hide my eyes from his and lose myself in the dance, the music, and the steady beat of his heart beneath my ear.

His mother continues to hover on the outskirts, like an annoying gnat that keeps buzzing, close enough to be heard but not close enough to take out. Not that I'd dare.

And she's hurting too…in her own way. She's lost her mother and what would have been her home.

As for me—I'm not that scared teenager trying to find a place in a world that doesn't make sense, running away from her cutting words. I can hold my ground… Although that doesn't mean I belong here, with her son, any more than I did back then.

For now, though, I snuggle in closer, let his warmth ease away the chill. For now, I can hold on to this feeling and get through tonight and tomorrow and the next day…until the day comes when I have to say goodbye.

'Are you ready to give your speech?' he asks.

I press away from his chest. 'Not particularly. Public speaking isn't really my forte.'

'You'll be fine.'

'Are you sure I can't persuade you into giving it?'

'I'm going to present you, but this amazing achievement is all you, and I'm not stealing your glory.'

His encouragement teases out a smile. 'Well, when you put it like that…'

He leads me towards the band, releases me with a gen-

tle squeeze of his fingers. I watch as he negotiates ownership of the microphone and the flutters inside me multiply.

You can do this, I silently tell myself. *Just speak from
the heart—that's all you need to do. Tell them your truth
and be thankful.*

Thankful.

I can do that.

Edward's talking. The music has stopped, the chatter
in the room too. The waiting staff are handing out glasses
of champagne and everyone is listening to Edward's deep,
resonating tone. And then he's looking right at me, his
hand reaching out…

'Ladies and gentlemen, Princesses and Princes, Knights
and—'

'Fairies!' a little girl shouts, and he chuckles.

'And fairies… Please put your hands together for the
woman who made all this possible: Summer Evans.'

I step towards him, accepting a glass of champagne from
a passing waitress on autopilot.

'Do fetch me the sick bucket, Rupert.'

My step falters, my fingers tremble around the glass.

Ignore her…she's just acting out…don't look…

'Hush, darling, people will hear.'

'You think I care?'

I tighten my hold on my drink and drown out Edward's
parents with the look in his eye. The warmth, the admi-
ration…

Camera flashes go off as I take the microphone and I'm
reminded of the press there amongst the masses.

'You've got this,' he whispers in my ear as I take his
place and plaster on the biggest, warmest of smiles.

'Thank you, my Prince.'

I swear I hear his mother scoff, but I can't really—not

from this distance. I take in my audience and focus on the children...focus on the child I once was...

'Thank you all for coming.' I raise my glass in salute. 'When I took on this challenge a month ago, I have to be honest, I wasn't sure I could pull it off. But Katherine's name opened a lot of doors, just as she opened many of our hearts—including mine. I also had her encouraging voice in my ear, telling me I could do anything I set my mind to. There weren't many people willing to take on the challenge I presented as a child, but she did. She welcomed me into her home, gave me a safe space to live, to learn, to love and to grow. She believed her purpose in life was to give to others what they otherwise wouldn't have—to help children become the best possible version of themselves. Without her, I don't know where I'd be now...'

A scuffle to my left draws my attention, but I can't see through the spotlight that's been placed on me. I'm very much centre stage, and Edward's vanished.

I hurry on before my silence draws attention. 'To have this opportunity now, to continue Katherine's good work, in her name, means the absolute world. And I don't say that lightly. Thank you so much for your generosity this evening—your donations have surpassed our highest hopes. To the band, the caterers, the staff...thank you for such an amazing evening. This Princess couldn't be prouder. And to all the guests, kids and adults alike, please continue to enjoy the evening. It is our absolute pleasure to entertain you here at Glenrobin. May we do this all again next year! To the children!'

I raise my glass to the crowd and they do the same to me, their cheers resounding off the walls...

Wow. I breathe it all in and know the moment will stay with me for ever.

I return the microphone to the band leader, and when

I turn back people are rushing forward to talk to me, to thank me, to congratulate me. It's fabulous, wonderful, but where's Edward? I want him by my side. I want him to share in this.

A reporter steps forward. 'Miss Evans? How about a photo of you with some of the children?'

'Yes. Yes. Of course.'

But I'm scanning the crowd, peering through the gaps and over the heads. And then I see him. With his parents. His mother's animated, her face full of colour, her eyes blazing even from across the distance, and Edward…

If looks could kill.

'Just here, Miss Evans.'

'Huh?'

It's the reporter, gesturing to where she has a few of the kids gathered, all with excited grins and a definite sugar-high shining in their faces.

'Of course…sorry.'

I hurry to their side, all smiles and encouragement, but my heart races in a panicked staccato, and my eyes are trying to keep abreast of Edward and his parents while also performing for the children and the camera.

'Now, if you'll all just face me and smile…'

It's then that his mother slaps him. One deft crack across his cheek. And I swear the room freezes, my blood runs cold. Cold, but hot. Hot with rage.

How *dare* she?

She might be hurting, but—

'Miss Evans? Miss Evans…?'

I blink, refocus. The journalist is talking to me, the music is still playing, people are talking. I look back to Edward, but all I see is his exiting form, steering his mother firmly from the room, his father trailing behind.

I look back to where they were standing. No one else

seems to have noticed. In fact, most eyes are trained on me and the children, having our picture taken…

And if you don't start performing soon, they'll know something's amiss.

I force my grin wide. 'Let's try that again, shall we, kids?'

I crouch down to their level and pull them in for a hug. I have a job to do. I'm the Princess and this ball is for them… I can deal with the evil stepmother in due course.

And deal with her, I will.

If Katherine's wake-up call wasn't enough, she's about to get another…with both barrels.

CHAPTER FOURTEEN

Edward

'DO YOU REALLY want to make a scene in front of the press, Mother? Are you out of your mind?'

'Look, son…'

My father tries to come between us but I'm almost past caring. A red haze has descended and I'm ready to throw her out through the door, snow and all.

'I don't think this is going to help.'

'Help?' I don't even look at him. My fury is one hundred percent directed at my mother. 'What kind of person accepts an invitation to a ball that is all about raising money for underprivileged children and behaves like you have? Looking down your nose at everything, constantly bitching, with a complete disregard for the work that has gone into this night…'

'The *work*? The money, you mean. *My* money.'

'It was never your money.' The words vibrate with my anger.

'It should have been. Just as all of this should have been.'

'Come now, darling—'

'Will you shut up, Rupert? He needs to hear this.'

She rounds on me, her fury filling my study.

'You think some silly inheritance means that girl belongs in your world? Seeing you both together, canoodling on the dance floor…it's an embarrassment, Edward, an utter disgrace.'

'You're the disgrace, Mother.'

She moves to strike me again, but this time I'm quicker and I grasp her wrist before she can make contact, throw it down.

'Why don't you try that on someone your own size?'

All heads snap to the doorway as Summer strides through it and I bite back a curse. I'd hoped by extricating my mother from the ballroom I could save Summer from further upset…instead she's walked straight into the firing line.

'I'm not even going to lower myself to speak to *you*,' my mother spits. 'An upstart who can have nothing to say that's worth listening to.'

'Mother, I'm warning you—'

'Edward, it's okay.' Summer presses a hand to my chest, all gentle, but her eyes are on fire. 'I've got this.'

She turns to face my mother and I watch my mother's nostrils flare; Summer's strength and dignity in the face of her wrath only serving to rile her further.

'This "upstart" may not have been born into money, or had the greatest start in life,' she says smoothly, 'but thanks to Katherine I've made something of it and helped people along the way. I'm proud of what I've achieved. Can you honestly say the same?'

'I— You…' my mother splutters, her puffed-out cheeks turning puce.

'You were born into money, Lady Fitzroy, and you married into a title too. What have you done with it?'

My mother's mouth flaps like a fish but nothing comes out.

'Precisely.'

Oh, God, I want to laugh. She has the woman hung, drawn and quartered with barely a word spoken. She has more of Gran in her than my mother can ever hope to.

'Now, you listen here…'

My mother takes a threatening step towards her, and I'm so in awe of Summer that I'm a second too late to step in. But my father is there, his hand on my mother's arm, his eyes flashing in warning.

'That's enough, Carina.'

Summer hasn't even flinched. 'I'm not saying this to be cruel, Lady Fitzroy. I'm saying it because you need a wake-up call.'

'*I* need a wake-up call! A bit rich coming from you, don't you think?'

'Actually, no. I think I'm best placed to tell you so.'

'*You?*' she sneers. 'A girl who's come into an inheritance that she doesn't deserve, acting above her station? I don't think so. This is ludicrous—this whole situation. I don't even know why I'm standing here speaking to you. You take my mother's attention when she's alive, and now you take her home in her death. It's unbelievable.'

'Mother, I've already warned you!'

But Summer's hand is back on my chest, soothing me, reassuring me.

'The truth is, this house would have been yours, Lady Fitzroy, if you'd returned an ounce of the love Katherine tried to give you over the years. All she ever tried to do was make it up to you. For the way her parents ostracised you both. The way she was barely more than a child when she had you, scared and alone. She tried, but all you were interested in was taking. Financially, not emotionally.'

My mother is stunned and still, and Summer has us all captive.

'It won't have been an easy decision for her to make, but

she wanted to provide me with a home. She wanted Edward to have the same. She loved him, and she was proud of him—his achievements, his good heart. The fact he possesses all of those in spite of the way you treat him is some kind of miracle. And she hoped that one day you would see sense and return to Glenrobin as his loving mother and not…' Summer nips her lip, her cheeks flushing just a little '…not as you are now. I didn't invite you to rub your nose in my good fortune, as you see it—'

'Like hell you didn't,' my mother scoffs, but Summer's unperturbed.

'I invited you because this whole night is in memory of your mother and co-hosted by your son. You belong here.' She tilts her chin up. 'But now you've outstayed your welcome. I'd appreciate it if you packed your things and left. I don't want bad press to taint what has been a lovely evening, and I certainly don't want the kids to witness the kind of violence you displayed in the ballroom.'

'Don't you— Why, you—? Rupert! Edward! Are you really going to stand there and let her speak to me like that?'

I have to smother the grin that wants to crack my face in two. I have never seen my mother so unsettled, or Summer so utterly empowered and stunning with it. My chest swells with pride as my heart pounds with my love for her. If I could sweep her up into a kiss and ravish her senseless, I would.

Definitely not what my mother is asking me to do…

There's a rap on the door and James steps in. 'Lord and Lady Fitzroy's car is ready.'

'Thank you, James.' Summer sends him the most dazzling smile and folds her hands in front of her. 'Now, if you please…?'

My mother blows out a flustered breath, looks from me to my father and back again, but neither of us are moving.

She pins Summer with her frosty stare. 'You haven't heard the end of this, you foolish woman.'

And then she's off, storming out of the room.

'At least I've progressed from being the "foolish child" I was, Lady Fitzroy,' Summer calls after her.

I frown over the reference. Foolish child? Summer's tone resonates with meaning. Did my mother once call her that? All those years ago?

'I'm sorry, son,' my father says into the sudden silence. 'She's confused. Things have been a little odd since Katherine fell ill and—'

'It doesn't excuse her behaviour tonight.'

'No…no, of course not. But—please don't write her off for good.'

My nod is very slight, because I can't make that promise. It hinges so much on my mother, and she's too unpredictable. She could have ruined everything tonight. If not for Summer's courage, her strength, her performance just now, I'd be convinced she had.

'Miss Evans…'

My father turns to Summer, his respectful form of address taking her by surprise, judging by the way her brows lift. Hell, it surprises me too.

'If you will permit me to speak openly?'

She nods. 'Of course.'

He smiles his gratitude. 'I will admit I had my doubts when I heard the news regarding your inheritance. And it came as a huge shock to my wife—which I'm sure you can understand. There was no forewarning. And, if I'm honest, Carina hasn't come to terms with Katherine's death. Their relationship was always strained at best, but that's not to say she doesn't feel her loss or mourn what might have been. I know you thought the worst when she refused to return for the reading of the will, Edward. But if you'd seen her lately you'd know how much she's struggling… Anyway, I digress—and I'm making excuses again, I know. But what I wanted to say—'

'Rupert!' my mother hollers from the hall, and I pray that most of the guests are still ensconced in the ballroom and distracted by the music.

My father spares the doorway the briefest of glances before coming back to Summer and taking her hand in both of his. 'You have done Glenrobin and my wife's family so very proud tonight, Miss Evans. Katherine obviously saw in you what some of us missed…to our own detriment, might I add.' He gives me an odd look. 'But I see great things in Glenrobin's future with you and my son at the helm, and I wish you every success with your charity ventures. If there is anything I can do to help, please don't hesitate to call.'

Summer blinks…blinks again. Like me, she can't believe her ears—her eyes, even. My father looks moved to tears. Hell, *I'm* moved to tears.

'Right, I'd best go. I think your mother's going to need some talking down—or a talking-to. Maybe it's high time for the latter.'

I *think* he's teasing, but after tonight's turn of events I can't be sure.

He places his hand on my shoulder. 'Let's get together soon for a drink, son. It's been too long.'

I clear my throat, nod.

'Goodnight to you both.'

And with that he walks away, leaving us staring after him.

Dumbfounded doesn't even come close.

But a flicker of excitement comes alive inside me—a surge of emotion that builds and builds as I recall the whole scene… The way Summer stood up to my mother, the way she defended me, talked about me, the way she acted.

Is she finally ready to accept her place here?

To accept that she belongs?

And not just temporarily…

The future fills with possibility—marriage, children, family…a true home in every sense of the word. Everything Gran wished for.

I can't breathe for the excited rush I feel, and as she turns to me, her blue eyes so bright, her cheeks so flushed…

'Wow!' she breathes, her hands on her hips as she gives a rapid shake of her head. 'Did that just happen?'

'Sure did, Princess.' I reach out and tug her to me. 'You were incredible.'

'Not too much?'

'No, definitely not too much.'

'It's just that when I saw her strike you in the ballroom, I was ready to give her both barrels.'

I wince. 'You saw that?'

She nods, her eyes sad as she strokes her finger over my smarting cheek. 'I pondered dragging her out by her hair and telling the children it was all part of the entertainment, but then I'd have been lowering myself to her level.'

'Now, that would have been a sight to witness—but you're right. What you did was far more powerful.'

'You reckon?'

'There's no doubt in my mind that your words had a greater impact.'

'I hope so, Edward, I truly do.'

'I couldn't stand it any longer—the snide little comments, the digs…'

'I know. She needs to realise she's brought this on herself. I came in here determined to make her see why Katherine did what she did, and how different things could have been—how different things could *still* be—if she saw the error of her ways, but I don't know… Has it gone in? Any of it?'

'You've done all you can. So has Gran, so have I. The rest is up to her.'

'I think a good counsellor wouldn't go amiss.'

'Baby steps, Princess.'

'Maybe your father could take on that battle?'

'Maybe. But tell me something: what did you mean when you told her you'd progressed from being a foolish child?'

She falters before me and I know she wishes I hadn't asked. But I had to. I had to know…

'Did my mother call you that?'

She swallows, hooks her arms around my neck. 'Do we have to talk about her any more? Can't we just—?'

'Summer…tell me.'

Her lashes flutter and I lose her gaze to the past…some memory she's never disclosed…

'Do you remember the last time we saw one another?'

I frown. 'Of course. It was the day of the Christmas party. We'd been helping prepare the presents and you'd left to get ready. But then you never showed up.'

'I showed up.' Her throat bobs. 'I saw you at the party.'

'But—but Gran said you had a headache, that you'd gone to bed.'

She wets her lips. 'Heartache, more like.'

Heartache…

My stomach twists, my frown deepens. 'But I don't—'

'I was there, Edward. I saw you with Charlotte and your mother saw me. She took great delight in pointing out my inadequacies, and the fact that I would never stack up to her…'

'To who? My mother?'

'No. To Charlotte. Though I guess in hindsight she meant both.'

'But there was never anything between Charlotte and me. She was simply the daughter of one of my mother's friends. We never shared anything more than polite pleasantries at social functions.'

'I… I didn't know that. And your mother…well, she noticed the way I was looking at you and saw fit to intervene and put me in my place.'

My heart pulses. 'The way you were looking at me?'

'Apparently my feelings for you were written in my face.'

Oh, God. I can scarcely breathe, let alone speak. 'Your *feelings*?'

She nods.

'What are you saying, Summer?'

'That once upon a time this teen dared to believe in her own fairy tale and fancied herself in love with the Prince.'

I wet my lips. 'You mean me?'

She doesn't confirm or deny, and I feel I've lost her wholly to the past now.

'Your mother took the opportunity to save me the humiliation of a public rejection. She likely thought I'd be grateful.'

'My God, Summer, she had no right! Why didn't you come to me? Why weren't you honest with me?'

'Because I was scared, and I was weak, and your mother had only confirmed everything I believed back then.'

'*She* was the reason you left?' I choke out.

All that pain, all that wasted time—*two decades!*—because my mother couldn't keep her mouth shut.

'And still you're trying to help her?'

'No, Edward. I might have thought she was the reason back then. A month ago, even. But the truth is *I'm* the reason I left. She only brought my departure forward; I would have left eventually. We both know that.'

I stare at her. Unable to believe it…not wanting to believe it. Much preferring to blame my mother for my heartache than the woman I've never stopped loving…

But was she right? Back then, would she have left anyway, to pursue all those adventures, all those charity expeditions? Would she have kept on running for fear of being rejected, like her mother and so many foster parents had rejected her before?

I can't deny it's possible.

But not now.

Things are different.

She's different.

I know that, having witnessed her tonight, this past month…

Surely now she can see how worthy she is and how perfect our life could be if we walk it together…follow the path Gran forged and make it our own.

I know I need to lay my heart bare—that it's the only way to make her see. And then our life together can start in earnest. No more wasting time, no more doubt.

'Perhaps. But what of now, Summer? What of the future?'

Summer

He looks serious. More serious than I've ever seen him. And he wants to talk about the future…

'The future?' I say…wary, unsure.

'Don't you see?' Passion heats his words, and his chocolate eyes are molten. 'If you stay here you can carry all this on. You can keep Glenrobin at the heart of the community. Use the estate, its wealth, its connections, to give back on another scale. There is so much more you could do… so much heart you have to give, Summer. You and Gran came from very different backgrounds, but you have no idea how similar you are. And with your childhood, your insight into what it's like…'

My childhood, my background…

I swallow down the feeling of inferiority, because in Edward's eyes I'm no less for any of it. He's trying to tell me I belong here—and, hell, didn't I feel it? Standing up against his mother. Feeling that sense of belonging deep in my bones.

But for how long? How long before he peels away the layers and realises I'm not worthy of his attentions, his praise, his love…? Because that's what I see in his eyes right now, and I don't want to stick around and see that light go out.

'You could take these charity efforts to the next level, Summer. Go national—international, even.'

I give a heady laugh. 'And there I was thinking you'd caution me into walking before running.'

'Not when you're as capable as you are.'

For a second I lose myself in that look, those words. Feel his warmth, his encouragement, his passion seeping beneath my skin, heating my heart, making me want so much more than I can ever possibly have.

'Now you're just trying to big me up after your mother's attack, but I don't need you to.' I try and dismiss it all. 'I'm fine.'

'I *know* you're fine. That's not what this is about.'

'No?'

He stares at me long and hard, with something desperate in his gaze, and then he parts his lips and I hold my breath.

'I love you, Summer.'

'You…' My voice dies, my gut rolls, my heart— Hell, I don't want to think about my heart.

'Did you hear me, Summer? I love you!'

The air rushes from my lungs, his confession ricocheting through my body—very real, very much heard. I shake my head...shake it again as my arms fall away.

'Don't say that.'

He frowns at me. 'Why, when it's the truth?'

'You can't love me!'

He gives a strained laugh. 'I'm afraid that ship's sailed.'

'No, Edward, you don't understand. No one can love me. There's something wrong with me. Not even my own flesh and blood loved me! Not even people who'd committed their lives to helping people like me could love me! How can you possibly even *begin* to love me?'

'Oh, baby, baby, baby...'

He tries to pull me to him but I back away and he blanches, his eyes pained and so full of sorrow. For me.

'How can you not see how incredible you are?' he asks.

I want to press my hands to my ears, block out his words and the sickness rising inside me.

'You lived through a nightmare childhood and still you smiled, still you cared. You were so full of sunshine and laughter. And, hell, you were a nightmare, too. A hellion with a chip on her shoulder. But you kicked the attitude and kept all the charm. You could have gone down that dark road and kept on walking, but you didn't. How could I not fall in love with you?'

'But you didn't—you never—not back then...not really...'

I wave a shaky hand at him. He can't be saying that he loved me then. Fancied me, sure. Loved me as a friend, absolutely. But more than that?

'You had girls flocking around you...girls who belonged in your world. You had Charlotte, and she was so right for you.'

'So right for my mother, maybe, and what she wanted

for me. But she wasn't you and I wanted *you*. To hell with what my mother told you. I only kept it from you because I was scared of taking advantage. You were young, vulnerable, mixed-up, I didn't want to make things worse for you.'

My whole body trembles. 'This is crazy, ridiculous…'

'No, what's ridiculous is you rejecting my love for you… my dreams for a future with you. The future that Gran so clearly wanted for us.'

'Don't bring Katherine into this.'

'At the risk of sounding like a child…' the hint of a spark reaches his eyes '…she started it and now I intend to finish it. I'm done with being afraid, Summer. I want to make Glenrobin a family home again. For *us*.'

'Please, Edward…please, don't do this. Don't spoil this moment, this night, with heartfelt promises that—that can't stand the test of time.'

'It's a declaration of love, Summer.'

'Love is fickle, Edward.'

His frown deepens. 'But that's where you're wrong. I loved you twenty years ago and you left before I could tell you. I'm not making that same mistake again.'

'Edward, please…you're upset after what happened with your mother…you're shocked at your father's kindness.'

I turn away. I can't bear the pain in his eyes as I reject him. Because the heart *is* weak. It is changeable. It's why I always run before it has a chance to change on me.

My mother taught me that.

Foster homes taught me that.

Run before you're pushed.

Run before you suffer the pain of rejection.

Run because that is in your control.

'I'm all of those things, Summer—upset, shocked…disconcerted, even. But it doesn't change how I feel about you. It doesn't change the fact that I love you and I always will.'

What blood is left in my face drains completely. My heart tries to fight its way to the surface, tries to cherish his words. To hell with the fear, to protecting myself…

I start to pace, desperate to keep moving, desperate to force it all out…the confusion, the shock, the temptation. 'You're upset…you don't know what you're saying…you can't…'

'I'm forty-two, Summer. Credit me with enough maturity to know my own mind and what is in my own heart. So when I say I love you and I want to marry you, I mean it.'

'Let's just pretend this didn't happen,' I ramble on, acting as if I haven't heard him—although I have, every word brands my well-bitten heart. 'We shouldn't have started sleeping in the same bed every night. It was bound to blur things…confuse what this is and what it isn't. Stupid, *stupid* woman.'

I slap my forehead and he moves to stop me. I leap out of his reach.

'What the hell were you thinking? You've ruined everything!' I rub my face. It's damp. And I can't catch my breath through the sobs racking my body.

'Summer, stop and breathe. Just breathe.'

I shake my head, shake it more, my eyes wide as I refuse to look at him—not that I can see through the tears.

'Look at me, Summer. *Look at me.*'

He reaches out, gently clasps my wrists to pull me round to face him, his expression so earnest, his brown eyes ablaze.

'You've done nothing wrong; *we've* done nothing wrong.'

I wet my lips, but I can't put words to my deepest fear. My mother's rejection almost broke me—a wound that Katherine helped to heal. But Edward… Edward's rejection would tear me in two.

And there'd be no fix for that.

'Tell me you don't love me, Summer. Tell me you don't feel the same.'

'I can't do this, Edward,' I sob out. 'I can't.'

He rests his palm against my cheek, his thumb sweeping away the tears that fall.

'Why? Why can't you love me?'

'I just can't.' My body shudders as I force it out.

'The thing is, Summer, you don't get a say in it. Falling in love isn't something you can control. It happens to you, and it changes you. It makes you yearn to be with that person, to live your life with that person, shape your life around them. That's what I want—if you can let yourself want it too.'

I shake my head. Wanting it. Yearning for it. That life… so full, so happy. And so very far to fall…

'I can't…' I whisper, weaker but no less adamant.

'Why? Because I'm not giving up until you explain it to me in terms that I can understand and get on board with.'

I hold his eye and let my confession fall with the tears. 'Because the day you stop loving me will crush me.'

The faintest of smiles touches his lips. 'Oh, baby, who says anything about stopping? I want to love you for the rest of my days—that's what a real marriage is.'

'Want and doing are very different things.'

'They don't have to be.'

'You'll wake up one day and want me gone. Just like my mother. Just like all those foster parents…'

'Not Gran. She loved you from the moment she met you.'

'Because I left. Because I stayed away. Don't you see? If I'd tried to make a home here, eventually she'd have seen the real me. She'd have turned me away just like all the rest.'

He's shaking his head. 'You couldn't be more wrong.'

'Life has proved otherwise.'

'No, Summer. This doesn't have to end—not if we don't want it to.'

'All things end, Edward. It's a universal truth.'

'Yes, but we can choose that ending. And I'd rather go to my grave loving you than live the rest of my life without you.'

My body gravitates towards him, pleading for his warmth, his kiss, anything to fill the emptiness inside me.

'Open your heart to the possibility, Summer.'

'It hurts…'

'Life hurts. There are no certainties. I know that. But I also know that the hardest things in life—the things that hurt the most—do so because they're worth it. *You* are worth it. Don't turn your back on what we have out of fear.'

He lifts his other hand, cups my face in both as he looks into my eyes.

'Let me love you and make a future with you and prove you otherwise.'

And then he kisses me, and the world seems to settle. The ground beneath my feet solidifies, my heart calms… and then I'm transported back, standing in a cold corridor, Ted clutched in my hand, watching the woman I'd tried to be everything for walk away, and I'm shoving at his chest.

'No. No. *No.*' I can't breathe… I can't see. 'I can't do this. I *can't.*'

I race for the door, for the back of the house, away from the guests, the press, and the ball still underway. I break out into the garden and the cold wraps around me, invades me.

But it's not enough.

I don't want to feel any more. I want the heat of his touch off my skin. The heat of his words out of my heart. I need to escape. I need to be free.

I need it to be just me.

Safe. Known. Protected.

CHAPTER FIFTEEN

Edward

'JUST MAKE SURE she gets it, won't you, Marie?'

'Of course, Master Fitzroy. But… Don't you think it would best coming from you? If you could just say good-bye and—'

'I don't think she's ready to be in the same house as me, let alone the same room.'

I eye the empty staircase as if I can somehow see her closed door, and beyond it her. Alone and avoiding me. Torturing me with her silence.

Two days since the ball and not a word. She's taken food to her room, had the entire household worried sick, and me… I can't stand it any more. Being so close to her and never more distant.

'No, it's better this way.'

Rufus whimpers at my feet. I'm not the only one she's shut out in her desire to cut ties, and as my hand falls to his head I feel the ache of it…

'I know. I know. I'll try and bring her back to you, I promise.'

'And what do I tell her if she asks where you are?'

'The truth,' I say to Marie, who's still unconvinced.

'Edinburgh's a big place.'

'And what does that matter? She's hardly going to hunt me down, no matter how much I might wish it.'

She simply stares back at me and I blow out a breath. 'I have a suite at The Balmoral.'

She nods, her eyes shifting to James as he approaches. 'Your car is ready, sir.'

His sombre expression is the same one worn by every staff member. Without Summer's sunny presence everyone is lost. But no one wants her back more than me...

'She'll come round, sir.' Marie's smile is full of encouragement. 'I just know she will.'

'I hope so, Marie,' I say, though I fail to muster a smile in return. 'I really do.'

One last glance up the stairs, hope that she will appear and put everything right giving me pause... But all I see is the ghost of a memory...her standing there two days ago, all ethereal and breathtaking. But that's all it is—a memory.

I blink it away, force one foot in front of the other as I seek to make things right the only way I know how.

Gran wanted Summer to make Glenrobin her home, and I'll do everything I can to make sure that happens...

Even if that means I'm the one who has to go.

Summer

I stare up the stone steps at the brass plaque on the wall bearing Mr McAllister's name and ignore my nagging conscience that's telling me it's the wrong man I've come to see.

Katherine's letter to Edward, handed to me by Marie at his request, is clutched in one hand, my letter from her is in the other, and I'm not even sure why I've bothered bringing them both.

They're identical.

Short, sweet and to the point. She's managed to write a personal message that's so specific and yet it fits us both.

I wonder if she suspected we would share them…that we would see them as a sign that we were meant to be. I can just imagine the sparkle in her eyes, the soft smile on her lips as she penned them to us.

The only change is her salutation. Both are signed off *Gran*. I only truly noticed when I had them side by side. Her way of including me in the fold even at the very end.

A solitary tear trickles down my cheek and I wipe it away.

What am I doing?

The question has been on repeat since I ran away from Edward, almost giving myself hypothermia in the process. If James hadn't found me when he did I dread to think what state I would have been in.

Not that I feel much better now.

The freezing wind whips my hair into my face, and I move before I make the same mistake again.

The warmth of the building envelops me, but the chill inside is impossible to shift. I find McAllister already waiting for me in Reception, and he takes me straight through to his office.

'Coffee, tea…something hot? You look frozen through?'

'I'm fine, Mr McAllister. Thank you.'

Though it's obvious I'm not.

'Call me Charles, please.'

I give a weak smile, a nod. 'Charles.'

He waves away his receptionist and ushers me into a seat. The same seat I occupied on my previous visit…only Edward isn't here now. I look to the empty chair, feel the emptiness inside me swell. I conjure up his face, his eyes, his smile…

'So, what can I do for you, Miss Evans?'

I drag my gaze to his, his friendly face a balm to my tormented soul. 'I need your help.'

His eyes drop to the letters clutched in my lap and I know he recognises them. 'That's what I'm here for.'

'I need you to tell me if there's any way I can sign away my rights to Glenrobin so that Edward can have it all.'

It's not what he's expecting, and his frown says it all.

'As I've already explained…' he interleaves his fingers, rests them upon his desk '… Katherine's wish was that you both live there for one year and then—'

'I know what Katherine wished…' my grip around the letters tightens '…but I can't live there.'

'I see.' He clears his throat, eyes me over his spectacles. 'Though I have to say, you and Mr Fitzroy seemed quite… *happy* with the situation at the ball last weekend. Do you mind me asking what's changed?'

Everything. Nothing.

'We were. Happy, I mean. But that was before…' I shake my head, empty it of Edward's declaration before it breaks me. 'It doesn't matter. I just can't live there any more, Charles, and I want Edward to be able to keep it.'

The silence extends between us and my heart throbs in my chest. What is the man thinking? Why isn't he speaking? Am I going to have to plead with him to help me?

'Katherine was a remarkable woman, Miss Evans. One of the most remarkable women I've ever met. And it seems she was also something of a soothsayer.'

I frown. 'A soothsayer? I don't understand.'

'This should explain it.'

He reaches into a desk drawer and pulls something out. He slides it across to me. It's like *déjà vu*. The same envelope as the two crushed inside my hand.

'Another letter?'

He nods. 'I'll leave you to read it in peace.'

'You don't—'

He's already rising, and as he passes he rests a gentle hand on my shoulder. 'Take as long as you need.'

And then he leaves, and the silence is so very heavy... the new letter heavier still...

Oh, Katherine, what are you doing to me?

I open the envelope, pull it out. My gaze goes to the grey outdoors as I take a deep breath and blow it out slowly.

And then I read, and I keep reading and reading and reading, the same paragraphs on repeat...

Dearest Summer,

I know you are scared. The day I met you, behind that brazen smile and tough attitude, I saw a scared little girl desperate to be loved and terrified of it all the same.

I should have stepped in all those years ago when I saw the magic you and Edward shared. It reminded me so much of what I had with Ben, God rest his soul.

We were together ten years before life cruelly took him away and, yes, it hurt. Ripped me apart. But would I have chosen differently? Would I have chosen not to love him and be loved in return? Never in a million years.

The truth is, going through life alone may well be safe, and it may well stop your heart from breaking, but your heart will never feel full or satisfied.

You will always be seeking the next adventure, Summer, until you realise that Edward is yours.

Open your heart to it. Let him in. And in turn he will give you the greatest adventure of all.

Make Glenrobin a true home again. Fill it with children, with dogs, with whatever your heart de- sires. But above all fill it with love and laughter and

find your true happiness, my daring girl, because
you deserve it all.
Love,
Gran x

I press a hand to my quivering lips but it's no good. I'm shaking from the inside out. Tears are streaming down my face.

This morning there was nothing, no scenario I could think of, that would have changed my mind, but I didn't anticipate this.

I feel like she's in the room with me, her eyes soft and sincere—hard and severe, too.

'Oh, God, Katherine.'

I stare at the paper, the words a blur. I've prided myself on my strength to go through life alone, to run when I need to, to protect myself because no one else will. To go on adventure after adventure, seeking a happiness that's always out of reach.

Not in Edward's arms, though. In Edward's arms I had it all—just as Katherine predicted. Happiness. Contentment. Love.

And I threw it all back at him out of fear when he chose to be so very brave.

'Oh, God, Edward...'

I shoot out of my seat. I need to get to him. I need to get to him now.

Please don't let it be too late.

Please, please, please...

Edward

'Is she in there, Charles?' I stride through his reception area, interrupt the conversation he's having with his secretary. 'Answer me, man.'

'Why, yes…' He straightens away from her desk, eyes wide with surprise. 'How did you…?'

'Glenrobin.'

It's all the explanation he needs. He knows I mean the staff. The staff who care about her, care about us, and know Gran's wishes through and through.

'I'd wait if I were you,' Charles says as my hand closes around the handle to his office door.

But I'm done with waiting.

I've left it a week, hoping, praying that she'll change her mind. That she'll come to me. Well, no more.

'Sorry, Charles, this needs to be—'

The door handle shifts in my grasp. The heavy oak swings open…

'Edward!' She's standing before me, frozen in place, pale, drawn, and never more beautiful to my Summer-starved gaze. The urge to sweep her up in my arms is painfully acute…sharper for the knowledge that I can't.

I kick the door shut behind me. 'We need to talk. I won't let you do this.'

'You're here…?'

'Yes, I'm here.' I pace before her startled form, unable to keep still.

'But why?'

'To do exactly what you're trying to do—gift the other half of Glenrobin and walk away.'

Her eyes flicker with some emotion that I can't identify. 'I *did* come here to do that. I *did* want to move on and leave you the house that I feel belongs to you… I *did.*'

'Did. Did. Did…' The way she keeps stressing it…it's driving me crazy. 'Are you *trying* to hammer the message home, Summer? Isn't it enough that I already know you don't want me? That you don't love me?'

'I never said that.'

'You did. Last week you said all that and more. Then tried to give yourself hypothermia in the process of leaving me. Do you know how hard it was not to come after you myself? To send James in my place?'

'I'm sorry for that, Edward…'

She says it so quietly and it hurts—it *really* hurts.

'Don't say sorry for that. It was my fault, I was the one without any patience, I was the one pushing you before you were ready—'

'Maybe I needed pushing…'

'—I shouldn't have said any of it. I shouldn't have— hang on.' I freeze. 'What did you just say?'

'I said…' She steps closer to me, her eyes wary, the nip of her lip warier still. 'I said maybe I needed pushing because for all I thought I was being brave, I was a coward.'

I frown at her, unable to speak.

'You're the brave one, Edward. Your childhood was no better than mine when it comes to parental love. You craved it and Katherine was the one who had to step in and give it to you. And yet you didn't let that fear of abandonment, of rejection, stop you from loving me. Not then and not now. You confessed your love for me, and out of fear I kept mine from you. I behaved no better than your mother, and for that I am deeply sorry.'

'Summer…?'

I can't catch my breath. I can't believe what I'm hearing…what she's implying. And I don't want—I don't want to feel like I felt a week ago. On a high, so in love, only to have it ripped away with such chilling force.

'Please, don't tease me, or beat around whatever bush this is. Because I don't think my heart can take a repeat of last week.'

'Good, because this isn't a repeat, Edward.'

She closes the remaining distance between us and lifts her hand. In it are letters—three if I'm not mistaken.

'Katherine sent me another letter. It appears she anticipated all of this.'

'Another letter?' I repeat, my voice hoarse, my head and heart struggling to keep up.

She nods. 'Do you want to read it?'

'Do you *want* me to read it?'

She gives me a smile so full of warmth and nods. Her cheeks are bathed in a sheen from the tears she must have shed before I entered.

I take it from her and it trembles in my grasp. 'Though if it caused those tears, I'm not sure…'

'*I* caused these tears, Edward. Our pain is my doing.'

My arms ache with the desire to hug her, to comfort her, to tell her she's wrong. But she's already backing away.

'Just read…and then I hope you will believe me when I say what it is I need to tell you.'

Hesitant, I lower my gaze to the familiar scrawl and read the words, feel the smile and the tears well.

'Dammit, she was shrewd.'

'Shrewd. Loving. All-knowing. She saw what I refused to believe all along.'

'And what's that?'

'That we're perfect for one another.'

I force myself to hold her eye. 'Is that so?'

Her nod is so slight, so hesitant.

I give a shaky laugh. 'You don't seem sure?'

'Because I'm worried it's too late. I'm worried I've hurt you too much…' Her brow puckers, her eyes swim. 'I'm sorry for throwing your love back at you. For not believing in you. And I'm sorry—I'm sorry for not being honest with you and brave enough to tell you that I love you too, Edward. Please forgive me?'

My heart tries to burst through my ribs. 'I'll forgive you on one condition?'

Her frown deepens. 'Which is…?'

'That you tell me again.'

'Which bit?'

I grip her hips, tug her to me with a growl. 'You know which bit.'

She laughs—the sound so joyous and happy.

'I love you, Edward! I love you! I love you!'

And I kiss her. I kiss her so deeply, and so passionately, and I claim what I've been missing all this time.

She breaks away far sooner than I'm ready, dropping back just enough to gaze up into my eyes. And softly now, with all the gravity the moment will allow, she says, 'I love you, Edward.'

'I love you too, Princess.'

Fresh tears well in her eyes. 'I don't think Katherine could have chosen my next adventure any better.'

'Nor mine.'

She tilts her head to the side, flashes a cheeky smile. 'Travel buddies?'

'I prefer the term husband and wife.'

'Deal.'

And she seals her promise, our elation, with a kiss.

Somewhere Gran is smiling down on us, a glass of sherry in her hand, toasting her greatest achievement. And I don't doubt the future she painted—not for one single, solitary second.

EPILOGUE

Three years later

Summer

THE SQUEALS OF excitement from the living room echo through the castle as Edward and I approach, our hands entwined.

'I think they've seen the presents,' I say, and he laughs.

'You reckon?'

Up ahead, Rufus comes tearing out of the room, a golden-haired toddler stumbling on his tail.

'Has he been?' I ask Lucy, whose eyes are like fishbowls, her curls bobbing around her head as she nods, her chubby hand pointing back towards the room.

'Santa!'

Her eight-year-old brother Liam skids up behind her, dragging along his six-year-old sister Lila. 'Summer! Edward! He's been! He's been!'

Lucy gives a piercing squeal and I wince up at Edward. 'Do you think that woke your parents?'

'With my father's snoring and my mother's earplugs, I wouldn't think so. This moment is all ours…until the sun comes up, at least.'

'Lucky us!'

My grin is so wide, my heart so full at the obvious joy in the children and the knowledge that this is to be our first proper Christmas with Edward's parents too.

The last few years have seen many a turnabout, especially where his mother is concerned. Her counselling sessions, and our family therapy sessions too, have helped to bring us closer together.

We're not the perfect family, not by far, but then I'm not sure such a thing exists...

We have our love, and that's what matters.

Especially today of all days.

'Well, we'd best go and take a look.'

Edward's palm is soft on my back as he encourages me forward. His brown eyes glisten in the fairy lights we've strung around the entrance hall, in amongst the holly and the ivy that I crafted with Carina, Marie, and our eldest foster child Lara.

'But where's—?'

And then I see her—Lara. She's hovering in the corner of the living room, her arms folded, her eyes wary as she takes in the tree with its array of presents beneath. She's the big sister, twelve going on twenty, and my heart aches for her.

Her smile is small when she sees us enter, her gaze on her siblings as they race for the tree, their excited chatter filling the air. It's our first Christmas as foster parents. Our first opportunity to give them the kind of Christmas I never thought possible when I was their age.

Edward squeezes my hand, and I give him a little smile before stepping away from him to go to her. We've come a long way since they joined us at Easter, and we've spent the build-up to Christmas feasting on all the traditions possible. Crafting, baking, carol singing, ice skating, a trip to see Santa… We didn't want to overwhelm them, but neither did we want Christmas to pass them by.

'Merry Christmas, Lara.'

I give her a tentative smile, pause a step away, and she lifts her gaze to mine. It's the tears I spy that steal my breath, and then her arms are wrapped around my waist, her head is on my chest.

'Merry Christmas, Summer.'

I hug her to me, kiss her hair, and try not to choke on the overwhelming rush of emotion inside.

I blink back the tears and spy Edward looking on, his smile full of love and happiness. He has Lucy in his arms, an excited Liam at his feet, and Lila is laughing as she rolls about with a barking Rufus on the floor.

It's noisy, it's perfect, and it's ours.

Thanks to Katherine.

Glenrobin—our family home.

* * * * *

FALLING FOR HIS STAND-IN FIANCÉE

NINA MILNE

MILLS & BOON

To my family with love xx

CHAPTER ONE

THE HONOURABLE ADRIANA MORRISON looked up as she heard the sound of her name being called. Damn! She'd been sure that she'd be alone for the next few hours. Swiftly she covered the easel and moved it out of sight into a small alcove, pulled the curtain across. Glanced down at herself—thankfully she'd only just got started, so there was no paint on her as yet.

She glanced round the room for any tell-tale signs of her artistic endeavours and, once satisfied there weren't, she walked to the door and pulled it open, smiled at her elder sister with the familiar mix of love tinged with the tiniest hint of envy that, try as she might, Adriana couldn't shift. However much she loved Stella.

And she did try, understood that it wasn't Stella's fault that she was beautiful, smart, vivacious and all-round perfect. Nor was it her sister's fault that she was the loved one, the child who could do no wrong, the daughter her father adored, in so much as Lord Salvington was capable of adoring anyone.

Whereas their father literally couldn't bear the sight of Adriana, the daughter who should have been the son he longed for. The son he had been promised—the gender scan had been sure she would be a boy. Sometimes Adriana tried to picture the moment Lord Salvington had been told he had a second daughter, the bitter disappointment, the anger and rage etched on those sneering features. Compounded by the fact her mother had suffered such complications during the birth that she would never fall pregnant again.

The all too familiar stab of guilt pinched at her and she shook her head to dislodge the thoughts. Her brain knew it was not her fault she was a girl, that she deserved her father's love regardless of her sex, that she hadn't intended to put a stop to future pregnancies. But years of witnessing her father's disappointment, years of watching her parents' marriage disintegrate, years of her father's constant putdowns and her mother's sadness told her that it *was* her fault. Because, unwittingly or not, she was the cause, the catalyst that had led her family down a path strewn with misery and bitterness.

And, unwittingly or not, she was the reason that Salvington could pass to some distant cousin who knew how many times removed. A man called Bobby Galloway, an American who had no interest at all in being 'lumbered' with the responsibilities of an estate and had been clear he would sell Salvington to the highest bidder.

Adriana understood her father's deep sadness, frustration and anger that this should happen, all due to an archaic, outdated system that insisted on male primogeniture, decreed that the estate and title pass down the male line. To give him his due he had fought tirelessly to try to change that system, so that Stella could somehow inherit. That had been Strategy A. His Strategy B had been a disaster, a cold-hearted affair, a 'try before you buy' attempt to get another woman pregnant that culminated in a scandal that rocked their house. Because when a scan revealed the sex to be a girl, Lord Salvington had rejected the woman, who went public with the story. Adriana could still feel the sear of sorrow and shame and misery. Made worse when the woman had lost the baby. After that for some reason her father's dislike of his second daughter had intensified. As if the failure of Strategy B was her fault.

Thank goodness for her mother and her sister, who both loved her and did their best to protect her. Though Stella was always careful not to show love or kindness to her sister in front of their father. The sisters had learnt early on that that was the way to infuriate Lord Salvington and trigger the caustic edge of his tongue against both Adriana and their mother. That the best course of action was for Adriana to be as invisible as possible.

But that didn't stop them from forging a real bond, and now worry touched Adriana as she took in the pallor of her sister's face, the panic that clouded the beautiful blue eyes. 'What's wrong?' She glanced at her watch. 'And what are you doing here?' Stella was supposed to be on her way for her first date with Rob Wilmington, Viscount Rochester, heir to the Earldom of Darrow.

A different type of envy, a different type of guilt threatened to surface and Adriana pushed it down. The fact that she had once harboured some sort of foolish crush on the man destined to marry her sister was a secret she planned to take to the grave. Even more so as the whole thing had been toe-curlingly stupid, the only saving grace being she was sure Rob had never suspected. In truth it was extremely unlikely that Rob even remembered her.

'I can't go through with it.' Stella's voice was low, the words so utterly unexpected that Adriana was sure she must have misheard.

'Sorry?'

'You heard me.' Stella came in, started to pace in front of the battered mahogany desk.

'What do you mean? It's all arranged; you're the one who planned the whole thing.'

'I know,' Stella wailed. 'And I meant to do it, Ria, I really did. I *wanted* to do it.'

Adriana tried to think; she truly had not seen this coming. The proposed marriage had been welcomed by Stella as the 'grand alliance' she'd always been destined for. Always wanted. A duty she welcomed. For this was Strategy C. Although the Salvington estate and title could not pass directly to a daughter, due to a legal quirk set back in the history of time, it could pass on to the male offspring of a daughter, provided that offspring was born 'in wedlock' and was born whilst the existing Lord was alive. So it had always been essential, if Strategies A and B failed, that Stella would marry and have a son and heir. In addition their father expected a 'good' marriage, wanted his heir to be worthy, with the correct blood running through his veins.

Stella had been happy to go along with that, bound by a duty to her ancestral home. In the past weeks she'd surrounded herself with bridal magazines and pictured her life as the future Countess of Darrow. Her only stipulation that, although the marriage was to be one of convenience, it would appear to be a love match. She and Rob would be the fairy-tale aristocratic couple, present the celebrity magazines with interviews and photographs, attend balls and dinners. Stella had surely been looking forward to bridal glory and today should have been the first sweeping step towards that. A romantic lunch in one of Oxford's most expensive restaurants. Champagne and a discreetly alerted journalist in attendance.

'I don't understand. What's happened? What's changed?'

Stella twisted her hands together. 'I'm pregnant.'

'What?' Shock conflated with confusion. 'But if you and Rob are…'

'It's not Rob's. He and I haven't even kissed.' Stella gave a strangled laugh. 'I had that planned for date number three in full view of the press. We were going to hold hands at date two. A peck on the cheek was scheduled for today—date one.'

'But…' Adriana's brain desperately tried to compute the information. 'Then who *is* the father?'

'It doesn't matter.'

'Yes, it does. It matters a lot, given our situation. Are you going to marry him?' That way, at least, if the baby was a boy there would be an heir.

Stella's strides increased. 'No. That is not an option. But neither is marrying Rob. I can't pretend the baby is his.'

Adriana studied her sister. 'But you thought about it?' she asked, keeping all judgement from her voice. 'Is that why you've left it this late to pull out of this date?'

'I only did the test today. I know that was stupid, but I thought… I *hoped* I would be wrong. I even thought if I were to be pregnant it wouldn't matter. I'd have an abortion. But now…' She rested her hand on her tummy. 'Now… now I know it's a disaster but I want to keep the baby.' She stopped. 'Please don't give me a hard time. I know I've messed up, messed up our whole plan, but I'll make it right somehow in the future…'

'Whoa. Slow down. I'm not going to give you a hard time—I would never do that. You're my sister and you've always been the best sister I could wish for.' The plan had been concocted when they were young, when they'd vowed to save their ancestral home somehow and to share it.

It was decided that one day Stella would be Lady of the Manor, carry out all the high-society duties, be the public face of Salvington, whilst Adriana would do what she loved most: look after the land and manage the estate.

'As for the plan, you don't need to worry about that right now. Because we have far bigger worries. If you don't go through with marrying Rob, Father is going to go ballistic.'

Her own fear was reflected on Stella's face, a fear that she had lived with all her life, an underlay of darkness that clouded the brightest day. Fear of her father's anger.

Though once, apparently, her father had been a different man. Kind and loving; their parents' marriage had been a love match and often Lady Salvington would look back, tell Adriana of their happiness, their courtship, had described a man Adriana could not imagine as her father.

Because disappointment over the lack of an heir had curdled love with bitterness; and slowly, slowly, as the barren years had passed love had morphed into dislike and a need to belittle; vitriolic words that put his wife and daughter 'in their place'. Stella and Adriana had often begged their mother to leave but she had refused, too scared that she would lose custody. Known too how much both sisters loved their ancestral home—felt too that it would be wrong to take them from it even if she did.

So, life continued and Adriana kept herself as invisible as possible. Spent hours away from the family, roaming the estate or shut away painting. Painting landscapes of Salvington, trying to capture the beauty and reality of a place she loved, a place she felt she had in some way let down. Her art, the silver lining to her cloud, a means of expressing her feelings, a hobby she loved and told no one about. Refused to expose something precious to her to the sneers and derision of her father.

But now there would be worse than derision—and when Lord Salvington discovered his favourite child had failed him, that Plan C was down the pan, there was no strategy that would stem the tide of his anger.

'What are we going to do?'

'I'll have to tell Father,' Stella said. 'And there's another problem,' Stella said. 'Rob will be in the restaurant by now.'

'You need to tell him. We can't leave him stranded.'

'I know.' Stella frowned, resumed pacing. 'The problem is, I've got press all lined up to catch us. I've dropped all the right hints and I'm pretty sure there will be at least one celebrity journalist in that restaurant to scoop us. So they will see him take my call, or get my text.' Her stride increased. 'I can't think straight. But if the press get even a glimmer of suspicion about my condition, then…'

'We are up the creek without a paddle or a stick.'

'More than you know. I can't risk the paternity of this baby coming out. I can't.' Stella's voice broke. 'But there is one thing we could do…'

Rob Wilmington, Viscount Rochester, heir to the Earldom of Darrow, glanced surreptitiously at his watch. Where was Stella? He could only assume she was planning a grand entrance. Not for the first time he questioned the idea of a public 'romance'.

He understood that a positive, happy spin would hopefully undo the horrible negativity of scandal for both families. Even now, two years later, he could taste the bitter tang of his own humiliation. Recalled seeing Emily, his fiancée, the woman he'd loved, splashed across the tabloids locked in a passionate embrace with her ex-boyfriend.

So he'd agreed to Stella's suggestion, understood, too, her point when she'd said, *'I have no wish for true romance but I would like to enjoy the trappings of it.'* So she'd planned a campaign, laid a trail so that their first date would garner some publicity, had the whole next few weeks mapped out.

As for Rob, he had no interest in romance whatsoever. Would never be fool enough to make the mistake of believing in love again.

He'd risked everything for Emily; at one point his parents had even threatened to disinherit him, they had been so dismayed by his declaration of love for a girl so far 'below them'. But Rob truly hadn't cared, hadn't thought her background mattered a jot. So what if she came from a rough council estate, so what if her father and brother had done time in prison, so what if her past boyfriends left a lot to be desired?

And he still didn't believe any of that mattered. What had mattered was the fact that, whilst he loved Emily, that love hadn't been reciprocated; Emily had been taking him for a ride, had joined the train because she expected glamour and riches, had been dazzled by his title and position. Shades of his parents in a way. They loved him because he was an heir, and would ensure the Darrow line remained unbroken for at least another generation. Before his birth they had all but given up hope of having an heir, after years of miscarriages and failed treatments, and then he'd come along, late in their lives, a 'miracle baby'. They had never seen him as an individual in his own right, he was a treasured commodity to be moulded to continue in the traditions of all the Earls of Darrow. As a result, in the name of love and duty they had tried to control his life. Decided it was too risky for him to ride a bike, had sent him to boarding school, but with the diktat that he wasn't allowed to play rugby, go swimming, do anything in case he got injured.

But at least they loved him in their own way. Emily hadn't. When his back was turned, she'd hooked up with her ex, fresh out of prison and more than happy to make a quick legitimate buck from the press. Once it was out in the open and Rob had wised up, the ex convinced Emily to jump on his bandwagon and they milked the scandal for all it was worth.

When he recalled some of the 'truth' Emily had revealed, the intimate details, hot anger still welled up, not only with her but also with himself for falling for her act.

The pretence of passion, the fakery of love. When in fact, as she had so cheerfully admitted to all and sundry, she'd been 'lying back and thinking of her ex', although she'd felt so bad. 'I tried, I really did,' she explained, 'because Rob is a decent man, a man who was trying so hard.' Pause and a small, cheeky smile. 'I didn't mean it like that.'

Enough. Not now. It was over. He'd been a fool once... he wouldn't be again. After Emily he had decided to take control of his life, wouldn't let anyone call the shots any more. He would do his duty because it was the right thing to do but on his own terms. First he'd brokered a deal with his parents. That he would go away for two years, but then he would come back, settle down, create an heir, take over the running of the estate, so his parents could semi-retire, spend more time in their villa in Portugal, stand down after a lifetime of dedication to Darrow.

But he knew he wanted more than to continue in their footsteps, knew he wanted to forge his own path. The knowledge was reinforced in his two years away. Because he had revelled in the freedom of being plain Rob Wilmington. He'd enrolled on a business course, a creative design course, a web design course and somewhere along the way an idea had germinated for a business. An idea he'd run with, with the help of a fellow student, Fleur Hardcastle, and for which he'd got funding, and he knew Easel Enterprises would be a winner—he knew it in his gut.

And he took pride from the fact it had been set up by plain Rob Wilmington, only Fleur had known that he was an English aristocrat. And soon the company would launch properly, taken forward by Fleur. He'd decided to remain in the background, as a consultant for now. Because it was time to keep his promise to his parents, time to take on the mantle of duty. Because he understood his parents' need for continuity. They were in their early seventies, they wanted to see a next heir, to know the Earldom would continue.

But once he'd got married, once he'd got the hang of the estate, Rob intended to also have a life of his own. Intended to take Easel Enterprises to great things.

But that was in the future; first the marriage. A marriage of convenience, as he would never give any woman power over him again, the power to inflict hurt or humiliation. This would be a partnership, a mutually beneficial arrangement, part of his aristocratic life.

So here he was. The question was, where was Stella? Unease touched him as he resisted the urge to pull out his phone and check for messages. Where was she? Here he was, ready to play Romeo—all he needed was the other half of the duo.

He looked up as the glass revolving door of the on-trend Oxford restaurant swung open, allowing in a blast of air and the noise of the shoppers that thronged outside. His gaze landed on the woman who came in. Not Stella—the hair not blonde, the clothes not right.

Instead this woman had shoulder-length light-brown hair, with an overlong fringe, her shoulders were ever so slightly hunched and she looked more than a little apprehensive. Realising that his gaze had lingered on her way too long, he looked away and then back again as a definite sense of familiarity struck him. He knew who she was—of course he did.

And it wasn't only him who had worked out her identity; he sensed the interest of a couple sitting at an adjoining table, wondered if they were from a paper.

Before he could work out what to do, she brushed her fringe from her eyes, straightened up and hurried towards the table.

'Rob.'

On automatic, he rose to his feet, the welcoming smile stuck in place. What the hell was going on? Just as she stumbled. Instinctively he moved to catch her, and as his arms went round her waist he felt a sudden unmistakeable jolt of awareness, so unexpected he froze. Recovered himself, gently steadied her and stepped back, saw heat tinge her skin, and as his gaze met hers he saw an answering response before she looked down.

'Adriana? Is Ste—?'

Before he could finish the sentence she rushed into speech. 'Hello, Rob, I am so sorry I am late—and on our first date as well. But I am so glad to be here now.'

Rob blinked. Right. The options were that he was going nuts and had mixed up the sisters. This seemed unlikely. But there had to be some reason for Adriana to be here. Another brush of her fringe showed large grey eyes that now surveyed him with a hint of apprehension and an unmistakeable plea. All too aware of the glances from the neighbouring table, he decided he'd play along. Though an underlay of anger rippled inside him; he didn't like being manipulated and this stank to high heaven of exactly that. Even worse, it was in full view of the press.

'Don't worry at all—I'm glad you made it.' He kept his voice smooth, saw her small exhalation of relief.

As she sat down he took the opportunity to study her properly; he hadn't seen her recently—for one reason or another she hadn't attended the family dinner that had been part of the pre-romance campaign. But he did remember their encounter from a few years back. It had been a party at Salvington Manor, perhaps a birthday party for Stella. He'd spotted her then, intrigued by how different the sisters were. Unlike Stella, Adriana shunned the limelight, seemed to flit about in the shadows, tidying up, almost as though she wished to render herself invisible.

He'd found her in the kitchen. 'I'm sorry, Stella isn't in here,' she'd said.

'Don't be sorry,' he'd said. 'I'm more than happy to find you.'

That had elicited a smile, one that spoke of disbelief but also appreciation. 'That's kind of you,' she said.

'I didn't say it to be kind. Why don't I help you with this?'

And for the next fifteen minutes he had done exactly that, chatted as he helped tidy away glasses, loaded the dishwasher, watched as she restocked the fridge, put snacks and canapes on trays.

'So how come you are doing all this?' he asked. There were hired caterers and he was sure there would be additional staff available.

She shrugged. 'I'm not really a party person. I prefer to have something to do and then it's not so obvious I'm not socialising. And anyway…'

She broke off as her sister entered the kitchen, a wide smile on her face, blonde hair rippling past her shoulders. 'There you are, Rob. We've been looking for you. We're about to start a game of Jenga.' Stella turned to her sister. 'Rob is apparently king of the wooden blocks. Come on, Ria—join us.'

'Thank you but I'm actually a bit tired, and you know how bad I am—I don't want to ruin it for everyone.' Rob frowned, watched as Adriana seemed to almost step back into the shadows. Her voice perfectly friendly but it held no hint of regret, her smile for her sister both sweet and absolute.

He hesitated, about to ask again if she was sure, but before he could she'd turned and headed for the door. 'Thanks for the help, Rob. Enjoy the game. I hope you win.'

But he hadn't. Had in fact spent the next hour vaguely

unsettled, distracted by those large eyes, the sudden sweet smile, the wariness and reserve in her expression.

But that was then and this was now. Odd, though, how clear that memory was. As he studied her he realised in some ways little had changed. There was still the overlong fringe that drew attention away from her face, yet now he could see how striking her features were, wondered why she wore her hair in a way that obscured them. Her grey eyes were large and the colour of a stormy sea. It was a face that would age well, keep its classic cast. Her nose aquiline straight, her lips generous and…as his gaze lingered on them he suddenly became aware of what he was doing. Enough. Why on earth was he checking her out? Noticing her mouth, the gloss of her hair? When she was the wrong sister? Realised too that he'd never checked Stella out at all.

'So…' she said. 'I hope this restaurant is OK for you. It's one of Stella's favourites.' Adriana looked directly at him, picked up the menu. 'She said to say goodbye as well. She is off to Spain for an extended holiday.'

What? He bit the word back as the ripple of anger returned, threatened to tsunami, and then he saw exactly how tightly Adriana gripped the thick, scripted card. However justified his ire, he would never be guilty of shooting the messenger. So he schooled his features into one of polite interest. 'I wasn't aware that she was planning a holiday.' He put the slightest emphasis on the last word; after all, he'd thought she was planning a wedding.

'It was a last-minute decision. I left her packing up a storm as she's not sure how long she'll be away for. A couple of months at least.'

'I see,' Rob said in a voice that he hoped indicated quite clearly that he didn't.

'Is Spain somewhere you would like to go?' The words

stumbled out and he sensed her rising anxiety. 'I mean, not now obviously,' she added.

'Obviously,' he said, realised he'd infused the word with sarcasm, saw the tiniest of flinches from Adriana and the quick glance she shot round the room.

Come on, Rob. Pull it together.

There was press nearby and the last thing he wanted to see splashed the next day was *Viscount in Awkward First Date Since Heartbreak and Scandal!* or *Heir to Earldom Reduces Honourable Adriana Morrison to Tears!* He and Stella had been in agreement that their first date had to generate positive spin, be the first step towards good publicity for them both. 'Because right now I'm here with you and there's nowhere I'd rather be.'

Adriana looked as though she wanted to flinch again in defence against the sheer cheesiness he'd uttered. 'How sweet,' she said softly, and this time it was her voice that held a hint of sarcasm, though her smile didn't waver. 'Anyway, Stella sends her best and I'm under strict instructions to tell her how it all goes, seeing as *she* set us up!' So that was the story and he had to admire the way she had manoeuvred the conversation.

Before he could respond the maître d' approached. 'The champagne, as ordered.'

Rob glanced at Adriana, saw her ever so slight nod of the head, knew it meant that Stella had primed her for this bit of the date. 'How lovely,' she said as the cork was expertly popped and the amber liquid poured into the delicate crystal flutes.

He lifted his glass. 'What shall we drink to?'

'New beginnings,' she said, exactly as scripted by Stella, but then added in an undertone, 'Wherever they take us.'

As they clinked Rob was aware of the woman at the next table taking a photograph, ostensibly of her table, but he

had little doubt that the real target was them. Stella's journalist, no doubt. In the aftermath Adriana leant forward.
'Sorry,' she whispered as she rose from the table. 'I need
to pop to the loo.'

Rob watched as she walked away, one hundred per cent
sure that the apology had not been because she needed
a bathroom break, but for this whole situation. So in the
space of ten minutes Adriana had managed to apologise,
let him know that Stella was absconding to Spain and that
the new story for this date was that it was a set-up. Later
he'd demand an explanation but for now he had no wish
to generate negative publicity, so he'd go along with it—if
the Honourable Adriana wanted a first date, damn it, he'd
give her one.

CHAPTER TWO

ADRIANA RESISTED THE urge to rest her forehead against the cool of the mirror, all too aware that right now there was every chance she was being watched. She knew exactly what lengths the press would go to for a picture, so she knew better than to let her guard drop even in the supposed privacy of the restaurant bathroom. But she did need a few moments to pull herself together, even if it was just to get her hormones under control. Because, mortifying though it was, the second she had seen Viscount Rochester her hormones had stood to attention. Not helped by her stupid stumble into his arms; Adriana glanced down at her unaccustomedly high heels with loathing.

The only saving grace was that if he had clocked her awareness of him she could put it down to her acting skills. Because they needed to make this date believable—she could only hope she'd got that message across.

The last thing any of them needed was some enterprising journalist putting two and two together, wondering why Stella had pulled out at the last minute and figuring out the truth. So somehow she had to make this look good. The question was, how? She had no idea how to flirt or hold witty conversations or play to the press. That was Stella's domain—by now she would have dazzled Rob, captivated him, had him halfway on the road to falling in love with her. Even though that wasn't part of the plan, Stella had always been very clear that she had no interest in love, yet such was her charm that men fell for her like proverbial ninepins, dazzled, lured, captivated.

Adriana glanced at her reflection and sighed. Stella had certain assets that she quite simply lacked. Glossy corn-blonde hair that never ever frizzed, sparkling blue eyes framed by impossibly long lashes, delicate features, and a figure that wouldn't look out of place on the catwalk.

Adriana, on the other hand—genetics had graced her with light-brown hair that had got more than a fair share of frizz factor. Her grey eyes were her best feature but her eyelashes were too light, her nose too 'aristocratic', in other words too large, and her mouth a tad too generous. Average height, average figure…average—that was what she was. No one would ever give her a second glance when Stella was in the room.

Enough. Stella wasn't in the room and Adriana would not let her sister down, would not be the one responsible for unleashing another scandal on the family. All she had to do was make one date look *believable*; it didn't have to look successful.

Picking up her bag, she returned to the restaurant, paused for an instant as her gaze lingered on Rob. And there it was, the thing that was making this 'date' even worse. The stupid little lurch in her tummy, the hardly acknowledged tiny wish that this was a real date.

Then again, it wasn't surprising—by anyone's standards he was gorgeous. Thick blonde hair, dark blue eyes, and the craggy good looks that could easily grace the silver screen. Tall, broad-shouldered, lithely muscled and…so far out of Adriana's league she may as well live on a different planet.

Yet for the next hour or so she had to make this look real. A quick glance at the table next to them showed her

that the woman who had been taking photos was still there
and unless Adriana was imagining it she had inched her
chair round the table so she was closer to Rob. No doubt her
plan was to have a go at either recording their conversation
or indulging in some good old-fashioned eavesdropping.

So as she sat down she smiled, picked up the champagne and sipped it, resisted the temptation to gulp the
bubbles down. Tried not to focus on the shape of his forearm as he reached for his own glass, tried not to focus too
much on the deep blue of his eyes, or the slight unruliness
of his hair or…

Aaargh!

She stared down at the menu. 'Have you decided what
to have?'

'I thought I'd have the lamb. What about you?'

She studied the menu. 'Hmm. Stella always says…' She
broke off. What was wrong with her? Why on earth would
she bring up Stella? Probably because she had no doubt at
all that Rob was thinking about Stella. Just like Steve…
her one serious boyfriend, the one man she'd believed preferred her to her sister, had turned out to be a crackpot,
a secret stalker who had fabricated a whole relationship
with Adriana to be nearer to Stella. You couldn't write the
script. But unfortunately it hadn't been fiction and her skin
still crawled when she remembered Steve. Recalled finding his cache of press clipping about Stella, the pictures
on the wall, his secret shrine to her sister and worst of all
his diary—that described his feelings for Stella. He hadn't
even denied it when she'd confronted him, had expected
her to understand and accept how he felt, to feel grateful
for his attention.

*'I know I am not worthy of her, but at least through you
I feel closer to her.'*

She'd felt such a fool, felt as though no shower, no body

scrub would wash away the mortification—because for a few stupid months she'd allowed herself to believe that someone loved her for her. Preferred her to Stella. She should have learnt from her father that she wasn't worthy of love, could never be equal to, let alone better than Stella. It was a lesson she wouldn't forget again.

'What does Stella always say?'

Sensing that this wasn't the first time he'd asked, she pulled herself together. 'Not to have salad on a first date in case you get spinach stuck in your teeth. And to avoid linguini or spaghetti or you'll spend more time on working out how to eat it properly than you will listening to your date.'

'Are there any other rules I should know? I am guessing soup is out—in case you slurp it by mistake.' She glanced up at him, saw that he had relaxed, could see amusement in his eyes, and as for his smile...she was pretty sure her toes were curling in her despised high heels. Some tension drained away; it looked as though Rob was going to play along.

'That's true.' She considered for a moment. 'And I suppose garlic is only OK if you both eat it.' Adriana broke off as heat touched her cheeks. 'I mean...in case you end up driving home together.' Fabulous. She'd made it worse. Defiantly she stuck her chin out. In for a penny, in for a pound. 'But FYI one of my rules is no kissing on a first date. So you can order extra garlic if you want.'

Now his gaze lingered on her lips and she'd swear they tingled. '*I* always think rules are made to be broken,' he said softly.

She stared at him, her senses suddenly awhirl even as she reminded herself this was all a show for the cameras. 'In that case I'd better order linguine with a side of salad.' She smiled. 'But I'll avoid garlic. Just in case.'

His smile morphed into a grin. 'Or how about this? Let's

both order exactly what we want. But we'll make a deal. I'll tell you if you have spinach in your teeth and vice versa. Deal?' He held out his hand.

'Deal,' she said, told herself it was a simple handshake as she placed her hand in his.

But there was nothing simple about the feel of his skin against hers; logic told her electric shocks were the stuff of myths but no way was the tingle that ran up her arm a figment of her imagination. Her startled glance met his and she was almost sure his reaction matched hers.

Almost.

'Right. In all seriousness, I'll have the lamb as well. There's nothing worse than staring at someone else's plate wishing you could have their food.'

'Is that another first-date etiquette thing?'

'Nope. That's just me.' And she knew why. When she was a child, if they went out for dinner as a family and she couldn't be left behind her father made a point of allowing Stella to order whatever she liked and getting Adriana the cheapest thing on the menu. The same principle had run through the whole of her upbringing—only the best for Stella, only the worst for Adriana. In the end Adriana had accepted it as her lot.

Rob looked as though he was waiting for an explanation and it was a relief when the waiter arrived to take the order.

'I'll have the leg of lamb with salsa verde, please.'

'Same for me. Thank you.'

'Of course,' the waiter said. 'And perhaps you would like the chef's special recommendation with that? Wild garlic fondant potatoes?'

Adriana glanced at Rob and saw a glimmer of amusement light his eyes, and she couldn't help it. 'That sounds divine,' she said. 'Yes, please.'

'Then the same for me as well,' he said.

Once the waiter had gone he leant back and picked up his champagne. 'To garlic,' he said. 'And breaking the rules.'

As she met his gaze she could feel desire melt over her skin at the huskiness of his voice. The clink of the glasses somehow momentous as though the echo reverberated.

'I… That reminds me of a joke,' she said hurriedly. 'What does garlic do when it's hot?'

He considered, then, 'I give up. What does it do?'

Too late she remembered the punchline, wished her brain hadn't scrambled. 'Takes its cloves off.'

There was a silence and he chuckled. 'I like it,' he said.

And then she was laughing too at the sheer inanity of it.

'Though I do wonder what brought that particular joke to mind.' His words were deep and flirtatious and teasing and they caused a breathless gasp to fall from her lips.

'It's the only joke I know about garlic,' she said with as much dignity as she could muster, and he chuckled again.

'Touché. Though I could come up with a few about taking one's clothes off.' With that he wiggled his eyebrows and she full-on laughed.

'I'll pass, thank you.'

'Probably wise. But on a serious note, tell me how you've been. Do you still not like parties?'

'Oh.' Surprise and a funny sense of warmth touched her. 'You remember. And no, I still don't, but now I can choose not to go. Though if I do I still end up tidying up. What about you? Are you still the King of the Wooden Blocks?'

'I haven't tried my hand at that for a while.' He sipped his drink. 'I also remember that you said you were hoping to start work on your father's estate. Did you do that?'

She paused as the waiter arrived with the food, smiled her thanks and sampled a first mouthful before replying.

'Yes, I did.' She'd always known that Salvington was destined for Stella, that that was Plan A and Plan C. It had never even occurred to her father to have a Plan D that involved Adriana, even though Salvington could be safe-guarded if Adriana had a son. In truth she believed her father would prefer for Salvington to go to a distant relative, rather than risk a son of Adriana's becoming heir.

But it didn't stop her from loving Salvington with a deep, instinctive love, her connection to her home an invisible thread that linked her to the woodland, the farmland, the earth, the sheer majestic beauty of the place, steeped in history.

Perhaps that link had been forged in childhood, when, in her quest to be invisible, she'd spent hours and hours wandering and exploring the acres of fields and country, the woods and stables. Knew every inch, every nook and cranny, had spent hours looking at wildlife, inspecting the soil, climbing the trees. When she was older she'd taken a sketchbook with her, capturing different bits of the estate on paper, with pencils and charcoal. Sketches she'd later try and paint in the privacy of a seldom-used room she'd turned into her 'study'. It had been a form of escape, even if in some ways it had compounded her guilt, that all this may be lost because of her.

She could only hope that the law would be changed or that Plan C would work and Stella would provide an heir. If that happened then one day Adriana could become estate manager, if not whilst her father was alive then at some point in the future.

But Adriana knew that plans changed, that this may be her only chance to work on the land she loved. So she'd summoned up the courage to suggest to her father that she could help, and he'd agreed, though his consent couldn't be classed as gracious.

'I suppose the least you can do is try to earn your board and food.'

'Do you enjoy it?' Rob asked.

'Yes, I do. I really do. Though sometimes it's a bit frustrating.' She broke off, suddenly aware how easy their conversation had become—he'd had the ability to make a shy twenty-year-old hold a conversation and clearly he still did.

'Why is that? I'd really like to know. Seeing as I am about to take over running the Darrow estate from my father.'

Envy touched her as she tried to imagine what that must feel like, to be able to say those words. 'These aren't the type of frustrations you'll have. You'll have free rein.'

'So you have ideas you'd like to implement but you aren't allowed to?' His tone was puzzled. 'If they are good ideas surely your father would be happy to consider them.'

It was hard to keep the snort from escaping. For a start her father belittled every idea she had on principle. But to be fair there were other considerations as well. 'Not really,' she explained. 'He feels there is no point in making innovations if the estate ends up in the hands of the current heir, who is more than likely to sell it and doesn't care if it turned into a golf course or an industrial park. So he thinks any innovations should be up to Stella once she is married and has a son.' She broke off. Why, oh, why was she so gauche? Everything had been going so well but those words had plummeted lead-balloon-like into the atmosphere.

He picked up his glass, a frown furrowing his forehead. 'So in some ways Stella getting married would be…problematic for you. It would be hard for you to see Stella step in, take over, be allowed to implement innovations.' His blue eyes had narrowed slightly and Adriana could almost see the cogs whir in his brain as though he suspected she'd somehow sabotaged his plans with Stella.

'Absolutely not.' And in any case she knew one day Stella would listen to her ideas, would implement them.

But that was the sisters' secret. 'I want what is right for Salvington and that is for Stella to get married and have a son.' She kept her voice low and a smile on her face, aware of the nearby journalists. 'My love for Salvington means I will happily step aside knowing it will stay in the family. So when Stella marries my plan is to go forth and have a life of adventure—I'll go travelling, maybe help run a cattle ranch in Australia or work on a vineyard in the South of France. The world will be my oyster.' In truth these plans were less than completely formulated, but they held good. As a stop gap. 'I want Stella to get married sooner rather than later. Because once she has a son Salvington is completely safe.'

Really, Adriana? Worse and worse—this was not the way she wanted the conversation to go at all. A hint of anger showed in the twist of his lips and she couldn't blame him. After all, he'd believed he was going to marry Stella within weeks.

His expression still hard, he nodded. 'Understood.' She finished her last mouthful, saw that he'd also finished eating, had pushed his plate away. Knew that the mention of Stella had reminded them both of why they were here. 'I've got an idea. How about we go somewhere else for dessert? Somewhere more private,' he added. The smile was back in place, the charm-filled tone of his voice sounding like a man on a first date suggesting a dalliance. But this time his smile didn't reach his eyes and Adriana felt a little lurch of trepidation. It was time to face the music, explain the reason for Stella's no-show in more detail. A conversation she was not going to enjoy. This may not be her fault, but life had taught her that facts were irrelevant. Rob had the right to be upset but she couldn't help wishing she wasn't the one in the line of fire. But as his date she was presumably supposed to look pleased at the suggestion.

'Oh…um…yes. That sounds…lovely,' she managed.

'How about we go for a walk in the park? We could get hot chocolate and cake.' It probably wasn't what he had in mind but at least she was pretty sure he wouldn't lose his temper in a public place. So they would have a civilised conversation and then go their separate ways. It would be fine. Though as she glanced at the clench of his determined jaw, trepidation touched her anew.

CHAPTER THREE

ROB STRODE TOWARDS the open spaces of the park. At least he would now get some straight answers. The past hour had been confusing to say the least. He still had no idea why Stella was absconding to Spain and even less idea why that had necessitated Adriana taking her place. Could Adriana have sabotaged the wedding plan in order to keep her job? That seemed far-fetched. Or was it? He glanced down at his companion; her hands shoved in her jacket pocket, she looked distinctly nervous.

Because she was about to be found out? Or perhaps because he was marching along like a man about to go into battle. Forcing himself to slow down, he said, 'I'm pretty sure no one has followed us but let's grab some hot chocolate, double-check we're unaccompanied and then we can talk.'

Adriana nodded. 'Sure.'

Five minutes later, cups in hand, they strolled down a wide, tree-lined pathway. 'OK. So now we can talk. Or rather you can,' he said. 'What is going on? Where is Stella?'

'She really is going to Spain.' Adriana's voice was quiet. 'I'm sorry, Rob, and so is Stella. Truly. But she has changed her mind. She can't…doesn't want to go through with it.'

The words seemed to ricochet through the air, carried

back memories of another woman. Of Emily, who had never said those words to his face, but her actions behind his back had screamed the truth loud and clear.

'Can I ask why she has changed her mind?'

'She has feelings for someone else and she doesn't think it's fair to you to go ahead.'

Brilliant. History truly on repeat. Feelings for someone else. Exactly like Emily, only in Emily's case she'd acted on those feelings and had been caught on camera.

Perhaps he should be grateful Stella hadn't done that, but…

'Why didn't she tell me herself? Cancel the date? What was the *point* of that whole charade?' Adriana flinched, looked away, and he thought she wouldn't answer. Then she turned, her face slightly pale.

'She was planning on going through with it until the very last minute. By the time she changed her mind you would most likely have been in the restaurant—she didn't want you to be captured on camera being stood up. So we thought if I came along the press would hopefully think it was always meant to be me. Unlikely but just about possible.'

Curiosity surfaced through the sensation of ire and disbelief. Why was it unlikely?

'So now all we have to do is fade away—say the date didn't work.'

Only oddly enough it had; a memory of that frisson when they'd touched hands, of the ease of conversation once they'd overcome the initial awkwardness, hit him. The sound of her laughter. All fake, he reminded himself, all done for the sake of the press.

'But please believe that Stella entered your agreement in good faith, she's just been…blindsided.'

He shook his head. 'Blindsided by love. I hope it works out for her.'

'You don't sound like you think it will.'

'I'm not a great believer in love. That's why I'm on the market for an arranged marriage. I thought Stella agreed with me. That love, lust…those are transient feelings. I was offering her certainty, a future that could be relied on.' He could hear the bitterness in his voice.

'You had feelings for her?'

The words made him pause. 'I liked her but I suppose that's the beauty of an arranged marriage—it is a business arrangement first and foremost. So I am upset in the same way I would be if a deal fell through. It's an…'

'Inconvenience?' she offered. 'And you'll be looking for a new partner forthwith?'

'Yes.' Aware that she was looking at him oddly, he said, 'Look, I realise that sounds…'

'Insulting?' Now there was a definite spark to her grey eyes, her lips pressed together in obvious annoyance, and his gaze snagged on her mouth. 'I understand this wasn't a love match but… Stella is a person, not a convenience.'

'I understand that. But we planned a marriage of convenience. So her pulling out is by definition inconvenient.'

'In the same way as a supplier letting you down when you need the parts to manufacture an order?' she asked. 'In which case I'm sure you won't have any problem finding a host of replacements for Stella—a veritable conveyor belt, in fact. You're rich, young, good-looking and you're heir to an earldom. I'd imagine you have women falling all over you.'

There it was again—a flash of how it had felt earlier when she'd literally stumbled into his arms.

He blinked, focused on what she'd said, stung by the slightly derisory tone to her voice. 'It's not that easy. Because if you are going to carry this analogy on, Stella was a rare part, hard to find.' How many women could he trust not to be taking him for a ride, taken in by the glamour and wealth as Emily had been? How many women would genuinely be happy without love? Understand the duty that lay behind being the Countess of Darrow, the commitment to the land, the commitment to staying married, because the alternative was unacceptable, a divorce with the heir not brought up on the estate?

'Of course she was,' Adriana said quietly, and now her voice had lost its tartness, held an understanding. 'And yes, it *will* be hard to replace her—I wish you luck in your search. I will leave you to concoct something for the press if they show any interest in why we aren't taking things further.' She gave a half-laugh. 'You could say I don't fit your business model. Or blame the garlic.'

'Or...' They could go on a second date. The idea came from nowhere. Ridiculous—Adriana was not on the market for a marriage of convenience, whereas he and Stella had been and that made another date redundant, however attractive the idea of putting the garlic theory to the test was. Even more ridiculous. 'I'll come up with something. In the meantime, thank you for saving me the embarrassment of being stood up.'

'No problem.' She hesitated and took a step closer, stood on tiptoe and brushed her lips against his cheek, evoked a scent of jasmine and chocolate and warmth and, oh, how he wanted to prolong the contact. 'Goodbye, Rob.'

'Goodbye.' As she walked away he raised a hand to his cheek, dropped it and turned to walk away.

Adriana climbed out of the taxi and thanked the driver, looked up at the sprawling yet elegant proportions of Salvington Manor. The stone-façade house exuded splendour and history and as always Adriana felt that sense of con-

nection to the edifice that had housed her family for so
many generations.

She took a deep breath as she approached the curving
arch of the front door—she had heard nothing from Stella
and hadn't dared contact her in case she was talking with
their father. A call or message from Adriana would do nothing but exacerbate his anger.

She pushed her key into the door and entered as softly
as possible. Wanted at all costs to avoid her father. Took
her shoes off and held them in one hand and walked quietly
along the parquet floor of the hallway, paused suddenly, her
senses alert, though she wasn't sure why. Could she hear
her mother crying? A distinct possibility if her father had
delivered one of his shattering tirades to his wife.

Not for the first time she wondered how it had come to
this, recalled her parents' wedding photos, the love shining in their eyes. Followed by a stream of happy photos,
the honeymoon, her mother's first pregnancy, Stella's birth,
pictures that showed love and laughter and happiness.

Then the stream had dried up with Adriana's arrival. She
had been the cause, the catalyst, the turning point that had
turned her father into a bitter, vitriolic man, her mother a
mass of nerves and misery, Stella still loved but bearing a
burden of duty too heavy to carry.

It was then that she saw the figure crumpled at the bottom of the stairs.

Saw that it was the prone figure of her father.

She ran forward, knelt by his side and, fingers fumbling
in her haste, she managed to pull her phone out to dial the
emergency services.

The next day Stella twisted her hands together as she paced
the plush carpet of the lounge of Salvington Manor. 'Oh,
God, this is all my fault.'

Adriana shook her head. 'No, Stella, it isn't.'

'It is. When I told him I was pregnant he completely lost it, Ria. He smashed my phone, he shouted, screamed such awful things and told me to get out.'

'Then he yelled at Mum, then he shut himself away with a bottle and then he must have realised something was wrong and got to the stairs. None of that is your fault. The doctor says he believes he has probably had a minor heart attack in the past as well.' Adriana took a deep breath. 'Now they will put in a stent and hopefully he will recover.'

'What if he doesn't?' Stella asked. 'Then Salvington will be lost and it *will* all be my fault.'

'No. It isn't anyone's fault. Unless you want to blame the stupid laws that mean a daughter cannot inherit.' They could not let an archaic, outmoded, outdated system take their land. 'Stella, the father of your baby—is there any way you can marry him, make the baby legitimate? Even if you divorce again once the baby is born?'

Her sister shook her head, eyes wide in her pale face. 'I'm sorry, Ria, but it's not possible. I can't explain but it's not possible. He's…'

'Married already?'

'No. He's engaged to someone else and he's…very high profile. It was a mistake. I just never thought it was possible for me to feel like that, that attracted to any man.'

'Not even Rob?' The words were out before she could call them back. 'Sorry, Stell. That is none of my business.'

'No, not even Rob. I mean, I can see that he is a good-looking man, but I didn't feel it, I just didn't think it mattered. But with…the baby's father it was all-consuming. The slightest touch and there really was some sort of reaction, a spark, an ignition…anyway…none of *that* matters now.' Another twist of her hands.

'No, it doesn't,' Adriana agreed. 'The bottom line is we

need a legitimate baby boy and the sooner the better. The doctors have said with care there is no reason for Father not to recover well, but obviously they can't guarantee that and equally obviously he may not take care. So I need to do something.'

'Such as?'

'I've got an idea. I'm not sure if it will work but I have to give it a try. I'm going out. Call me if there is any news from the hospital.'

'But…'

'I promise I'll explain when I get back.'

As she climbed into the family estate car Adriana wondered if she'd completely lost the plot. Perhaps, but all that burned in her was a determination to save Salvington; in her mind images streamed of bulldozers razing the manor to the ground, diggers pulling up the soil with no care for the generations past who had cultivated and loved it. The loss for the local wildlife. She shuddered.

The thoughts churned through her mind as the car covered the miles to the Darrow estate. She wouldn't, couldn't let that happen.

She drove up the wide gravelled driveway without pause; she wouldn't stop now, wouldn't let any doubt cloud her actions, prevent her from this path. Carefully she parked next to the row of cars and went up to the front door, knocked on the ornate knocker shaped like a lion. Her mind took in the detail of the mane, the fierce expression that almost looked as if it was warning her off.

The door was pulled open and she blinked as she took in the majestic form of a butler—she hadn't realised that Rob's family still maintained a high level of staff.

'Hello. I'd like to see Rob…um… Viscount Rochester. It's urgent. I am Adriana Morrison.' She glanced down at herself and then rummaged in her bag. 'I've probably got my driving licence somewhere or...'

'That won't be necessary. I recognise you. Please come this way. Viscount Rochester is in his study. If you will wait in the drawing room I will get him.'

Left in the massive environs of the drawing room, Adriana glanced round, tried to focus on the interior to keep the growing doubts at bay, but the dark red velvet curtains, the heavy antique furniture with brocaded seat covers, the imposing sideboard all intimidated her, and she was convinced the portraits on the panelled oak walls were looking at her in disapproval. Realised it wasn't only Rob's ancestors who disapproved—so too would her father. She knew that her father would hate the idea of her being Salvington's saviour, but circumstances meant he no longer had the luxury of that opinion.

Then the door swung open and Rob entered. As she took in the broadness of his chest, the width of his shoulders, the craggy features Adriana gulped, the enormity of what she was about to do hitting her. If only he didn't have such an impact on her, an impact almost made worse by Stella's description of her mystery man. Because right now she could not afford to be distracted by attraction. This was a business proposal—that was what he wanted—a manufactured marriage constructed on the blocks of convenience. That was what she was here to offer.

Hands outstretched, he approached her and she stepped backwards, knew she couldn't risk touching him, however much she wanted to.

'Adriana, I am so sorry to hear about your father. I was going to call but I didn't want to intrude. I was also worried that it was the situation with Stella that may have triggered his attack and I wasn't sure if my call would be welcome. How is he?'

'He is stable. They are going to put a stent in and they think with proper care he should recover and hopefully not have another attack. As for what caused it, there is no point in speculation. Anyway, that's not why I'm here.'

'Of course not.' He studied her face. 'So why are you here? If I can help in any way of course I will.' He hesitated. 'But I won't marry Stella. If that's what you are here to suggest. Whilst I am sorry for what has happened, that wouldn't be right.'

'I know. That's not why I am here either. I…' All her carefully rehearsed speeches vanished clear out of her head. 'I want you to marry me instead. I'm proposing a merger.'

CHAPTER FOUR

ADRIANA'S WORDS TOOK a while to register in his brain. 'Marry *you* instead,' he echoed, just to be absolutely clear he'd got it right.

'Yes. I know I am not what you wanted. I know I am not Stella. I get she was a rare find and I won't tick as many boxes. But I still think I can fit your business model.' Her voice held an edge of desperation under the calm tone of her voice and he could see the tension in the set of her shoulder, the clench of her delicate jaw.

'Whoa.' Rob raised his hand. 'This is a highly emotional time for you; it is not the right time to make a decision of that magnitude.'

She inhaled deeply, made a visible effort to pull herself together as she nodded acknowledgement. 'I understand that and in different circumstances I would agree with you. But time is of the essence. So would you at least discuss the possibility?'

This would be the moment to shut this conversation down; but...somehow the idea had started to circulate in his brain, to put out a few tendrils of curiosity. And...he couldn't simply send her away—she looked exhausted, her skin pale, her brown hair tangled, and as she pushed her fringe back he could see the strain in her grey eyes. He was tempted to move over and hug her, reminded himself they were barely acquainted, had clocked too her reluctance to take his outstretched hands. But there was something he could do.

'Of course we can talk,' he said. 'But first you need to sit down and I will get us something to eat. Wait here.'

'No…really…'

'I insist. And you may as well eat whilst we talk.'

'Then thank you.'

Ten minutes later he handed her the tray and watched as she selected a sandwich and bit into it.

'Thank you. I hadn't even realised I was hungry—I haven't eaten anything since our lunch yesterday.' Two sandwiches and a mini Scotch egg later she put her plate down and said, 'So… I realise my idea is a bit out of the blue.'

'It is,' he agreed. 'Yesterday you thought the whole idea of replacing Stella quickly was incongruous. You mentioned conveyor belts.'

'I did. And I realise it's a bit rich me climbing aboard the conveyer belt I was so derisive about. But circumstances have changed. Of course I hope and pray that my father makes a full recovery and lives for many more years, but there is no guarantee of that. Yesterday it was important there be a male heir, now it is imperative.'

'Perhaps Stella will marry the new love in her life.'

There was a heartbeat of a hesitation and then, 'It's not that easy—she has feelings for someone. There's a long way to go from that to marrying someone and having a baby. It takes time. And even if that did happen instantly the baby may be a girl. It makes sense to double our chances. For me to get married too.'

'Just like that?' he asked. 'You're willing to change your whole life on a—?'

'Whim?' Her grey eyes sparked with ire. 'Do you of all

people believe this to be a whim? Don't you understand what it would mean to lose Salvington? To watch my home torn down, our land desecrated?' There was no denying the depth of her emotions. 'Wouldn't you do anything to save Darrow from that fate?'

Of course he would—duty was the bedrock of his existence, imbued in him since he'd taken his very first breath… hell, before that in all likelihood. Darrow was bred in his blood and bones. And he would do anything to save it.

But it was different for Adriana. 'Yes, I would. But our marriage wouldn't necessarily save Salvington. We may have a girl, or not have a child in time. Plus, if Stella does marry and have a boy in time you would have sacrificed yourself for nothing.'

'I understand that, but I cannot sit back and *do* nothing.' The set of her lips, the twist of her hands spoke of her sincerity. 'There is a chance that Stella won't do that, there is a chance I will have a boy, and once I have a boy Salvington is safe.'

Rob continued to look troubled, though he said nothing more.

Adriana leant forward, her fists clenched. 'I love Salvington and the risk is worth it to me. I want my children to have the chance to explore the land and places that I roamed as a child. I want to keep Salvington in the Morrison family, to see it prosper and grow. I want to be part of that. I will do anything I can do to make that happen.'

'Including having a loveless marriage of convenience?'

She waved her hand in dismissal. 'Love is overrated.'

Whilst he agreed whole-heartedly, he reminded her that, 'Those are words. Similar to those that Stella said, and she changed her mind.'

'That wouldn't happen with me.'

'You can't know that.' After all, he'd taken Stella's words

at their face value, blithely accepted that she held the same beliefs about marriage as he did, sure that what he had to offer was acceptable. With hindsight he could see now how foolish that was, that he should have probed and questioned. 'Most people want to fall in love, to love and be loved, to have the happy-ever-after.'

'I don't.'

'Why not?'

'I don't see why my reasons matter. They are personal.'

'Marriage is personal.'

That drew a reluctant smile from her, and as his gaze snagged on the upturn of her lips he felt it again, that insidious dart of desire. 'Fair enough. I get you need an explanation. I am sure you know from the press how tumultuous my parents' marriage has been—yet once they loved each other. I've witnessed that roller coaster and I'd rather avoid it. Love doesn't last.'

'Your parents are one example of love gone wrong. I am sure you could cite plenty of examples of happier marriages where love did last.'

'Of course, and I don't believe all relationships based on love are doomed. But I do know that for me personally it isn't worth the risk.'

'Just because of your parents?'

'No. That is a big factor but there is more than that. I did take the risk once and it didn't work out. I loved him, I thought he loved me, turned out he didn't. I will not put myself through that again. Love made me blind and stupid. Left me hurt and exhausted. I would rather live in calm and peace, be my own person.'

He blinked—he couldn't have put it better himself. 'I get that. I am sure you know of my previous ill-fated matrimonial venture.' You'd have had to live on Mars to miss the publicity.

'I know you had a very public break-up, but I didn't read the detail. I avoid stories like that wherever I can.'

'It wasn't pretty and I have no wish to repeat it. So I am not offering or expecting love.' He hesitated. 'But I do want a life-long commitment. Our child would be heir to the Darrow estate; would need to live here, be brought up here.' That was an absolute, though a part of him apologised in advance to this potential child, whose fate was already being written before he or she had even been conceived.

'I understand that.'

The words were quick, too quick, and he shook his head. 'I'm not sure you do, or rather I am not sure you really do. You are thinking about the here and now, your present need.' His eyes narrowed. 'I am not just a temporary convenience, this is a marriage of convenience, and that means thinking about the future, the rest of your life. You cannot give birth to a son, then discover that our marriage has become "inconvenient" and take him off to Salvington. Neither can you give birth to a girl and decide to take her away from her birthright.' Darrow was one of the few peerages in England that allowed descent through the female line, so his first child regardless of sex would inherit.

'I wouldn't do that.' She hesitated. 'Though if our son does end up inheriting Salvington then we would have to work something out. I would want him to grow up knowing Salvington too, so we would maybe have to live some of the time at Salvington. But of course I wouldn't take him away from Darrow.'

'No, you wouldn't,' he agreed. 'I would ask you to do as Stella agreed. Sign a prenup that states if you instigate a divorce I get custody.'

'And Stella agreed to that?' He could hear incredulity

in her voice and then she rolled her eyes with a muttered, 'Of course she did.'

'Yes, she did. She was sure there would be no question of divorce. So it made sense. Just as we both agreed to have a full health check before the wedding.' Another thing that made sense.

'Well, I am not Stella. I wouldn't sign something that gives you carte blanche to behave however badly you want, all the while knowing I couldn't leave you without losing my child.'

He raised his eyebrows as annoyance rasped. 'That's rather an insulting assumption. That I would *wish* to behave like that.'

'It's an equally insulting assumption to think I would take our baby and run,' she snapped.

They glared at each other and it occurred to Rob that when he and Stella had come to their agreement there had been no sparring, no arguments; instead there had been quiet, calm negotiation. He inhaled deeply. 'OK. Let's take a step back. I wasn't trying to insult you—I was trying to point out that you haven't thought this through. I have.'

'On the contrary, I'm thinking very clearly about an element of your plan that could prove hugely detrimental to me and our children.'

Rob frowned, trying to damp down the anger she provoked in him. Realised that part of that anger was because Adriana was in fact correct, and yet a sense of outrage remained that she would even consider that he would behave in an abusive way. Do anything detrimental to his children. Yet logically she did have a valid point, and using logic was paramount here.

'OK. Point accepted.' He did his best to keep the tightness from his voice. 'We could word the prenup in a way that protects us both. So in the case of my being abusive, or whatever you are envisaging in this carte blanche be-haviour, then I wouldn't get sole custody.'

'That would work for me.'

Whoa. How had the conversation moved so fast? And why had he let emotion in? Emotion clouded logic, got in the way of a properly negotiated, mutually beneficial agree-ment that would lead to a calm, well-oiled marriage that would leave him free to do his duty by the estate *and* take on a proper role in Easel. So the sooner he got the mar-riage box ticked the better, but only to the right woman. One who fulfilled all the necessary criteria. And he wasn't at all sure Adriana did that.

'Hold on. That was a strictly hypothetical scenario. I have a whole heap of concerns about this idea. I won't take advantage of your situation. You are grieving and scared and worried—you can't commit the rest of your life on the off chance it may save Salvington.' Plus, Adriana had spo-ken of travel, of adventure. He wouldn't marry someone who would regret it, wouldn't let her give up her dreams.

'Yes, I can. That is my decision, my choice to make. You are willing to marry for duty's sake. You were willing to marry Stella when she was marrying for duty's sake. So what is the problem?'

He opened his mouth to explain, but before he could speak her expression changed. She shook her head and rose to her feet. 'It's OK. You don't have to answer that. I'm sorry. You're right. This is a stupid idea. I apologise for disturbing you. Thank you for the sandwiches.'

Huh? Confusion froze him to his chair as he tried to figure out what had caused the volte face. Swore he saw hurt flash across her grey eyes, saw the lips he'd tried so hard not to dwell on tremble before setting in a line. What was going on here? And did it matter? It made sense to let her go—after all, it was a daft idea. Yet…he didn't want to, not like this. Not if she was upset, when she was already worried about her father and the future. 'Adriana. Wait.'

Adriana didn't want to wait—could still feel mortification roil inside her. She was an idiot. Rob had been planning on marrying Stella. That was hardly much of a sacrifice. So, yes, he wanted a marriage of convenience, but there was a big difference between a convenient marriage with Stella and a convenient marriage with Adriana.

Rob was not in her league and she had been a fool to come here. He'd even told her Stella had been a rare find and yet she'd waltzed in here, offering herself as a substitute. What had she been thinking?

Clearly she hadn't or perhaps, most mortifying of all, she had been acting on the vestiges of her own stupid crush on him, on the pull of attraction that she couldn't shift. Even now. As she reluctantly turned to face him, still she noticed his looks, his stance, the strength of him. But she wouldn't show it, somehow she had to retreat with dignity. Forcing a small smile to her lips, she said lightly, 'Really. There is no need for further discussion. I'd be grateful if you forgot this whole conversation.'

'I don't think that's possible.' He studied her expression and she forced herself to meet the dark blue gaze. 'And I want to answer your question. Tell you why, if I was going to marry Stella, I have a problem with your proposal.'

She didn't need an answer, certainly didn't need to listen to a litany of her sister's many virtues. Better if she got in first. 'You don't have to explain. I get it. Stella is beautiful, witty, and she is perfect countess material. I know that—and I know I'm not.'

'What?' Rob looked genuinely confused. 'That's not what I was going to say at all. I mean, yes, Stella is all those things, but that's not the problem. I was going to marry Stella because I believed she wanted a convenient marriage. That she has been brought up to marry for duty, to provide an heir. You weren't and this isn't what you want. Yesterday you told me you want to travel, to run a cattle ranch in Australia, to have an adventure. That is your dream. I can't allow you to give that up for a convenient marriage that may not even achieve its goal.'

She studied his expression, could see nothing but sincerity there, and a small tendril of surprise touched her. 'I understand your reservations. But the ranch, the travel, they weren't my dream. They were a *plan*, something I thought I may enjoy for a while. But they weren't inspired by a yearning or a compulsion.' Not like her art—that was a passion, a necessity, something she loved though would never dare to dream about. 'Travel was more of an idea.' A stopgap. 'Not travelling is not a sacrifice for me, it won't cause me sadness. Standing by and doing nothing to save Salvington—that would devastate me. I know it may be lost anyway but I have to know I tried everything to save it.'

There was a long silence and then he shrugged. 'In that case, here's what I'll offer. Stay for dinner. Let's talk about this more, see if it really is a possibility.'

Relief rocked through her. 'I'd like that.'

'Then come with me. I have a separate annexe that I use when I stay here. I'll get dinner on and we can start talking.' A sudden rush of adrenalin jolted through her, heightened by the enormity of it all, and further still as he rose to his feet and she caught her breath. Was she really about to discuss the idea of marrying this man? Blond hair a touch unruly, his dark eyes held a hint of a smile. 'Call it a preliminary discussion.'

One that she had to focus on, rather than the fluttery feeling in her tummy. A feeling she was going to put down to nerves—would not let it be attraction. Attraction had no place at the table. Look where attraction had got Stella.

She returned his smile with one of her own. 'Bring it on.'

CHAPTER FIVE

ADRIANA FOLLOWED HIM through the grandeur of the hallway and up a massive curving staircase, along a narrow corridor into the annexe.

She liked the area at once; it had a comfortable feel to it. The lounge had a large, over-stuffed sofa and two mismatched armchairs. A computer was set up in one corner and there was a flat-screen TV on one wall. The other walls were dotted with pictures and she walked over to look at them.

'I like these,' she said, as she studied the line drawings, deceptively simple yet emotive. Clean and beautiful and expressive.

'So do I. My parents don't think they are grand enough—they prefer the family portraits and landscapes and oils. I found these in the attic—I have no idea who the artist is, they aren't signed, but I like them.'

'Perhaps one of your ancestors drew them,' she said, liking that idea. Sometimes she wondered if one day one of her own descendants would find her drawings hidden away in an attic and hopefully find something to like in them. 'Anyway, can I help with dinner?'

'As it happens I made a venison stew last time I was here and froze some portions—so it shouldn't take long to rustle that up. We can have bread and I can make a salad to go with it.'

'I'm impressed,' she said. 'You made the casserole.'

'With these very hands.'

She couldn't help herself: she looked down, studied his hands, and for an absurd moment desire melted through her. The shape of his wrist, the length of his fingers all evoked a yearning to feel those hands on her skin, evoked too an urge to draw them, to try and capture their sheer masculine beauty.

'Adriana? You OK?'

'Of course—absolutely.' She could hardly say that she was distracted by his hands, or ask permission to draw them. He'd think she'd lost the plot. Anyway, she didn't tell anyone about her drawings.

She watched as he made a salad, tried not to fixate on the deftness of his movements, the tang of vinegar in the air, the sound of the knife thudding on the chopping board. Every detail seemed seared on her mind, made conversation almost impossible. The sheer intimacy of it all threatened to overwhelm.

Get it together. This was nothing to do with cosy intimacy—this was a working dinner that by necessity needed to be a private one. This was about a need for her to somehow convince Rob that she could be a good choice of bride. Not up to Stella's standard maybe but still a viable choice. Second best, but in truth she had lived with that all her life. The realisation was enough to snap her out of her hormone-induced trance.

'I could set the table if you tell me where everything is.'

Ten minutes later they were sitting at the square wooden table in front of a bay window that overlooked the expanse of a kitchen garden. Adriana gazed out in the gloom of the dusk, tried to gather her thoughts together. 'Maybe you should tell me what your expectations of a marriage are. What you're looking for from a wife.' As she said the words she glanced at him, the way the lighting glinted on his blond hair, the strength of his features, watched the strong column of his throat as he sipped his wine. And all of a sudden her question seemed to take on another meaning, a double entendre she hadn't intended.

His blue eyes studied her and she wondered if he could read her thoughts, wondered whether his own thoughts had taken the same errant turn. But she couldn't wrench her gaze away, couldn't stop looking at him. Her mouth dried and her brain seemed to fuzz as her gaze lingered on his forearms, sleeves rolled up as he ladled a portion of stew onto her plate. The rich aroma almost dizzied her as she took the plate from him. Next her eyes zoned in on the shadow of stubble on his jaw, saw a small scar on the side of his chin, and her fingers tingled with a desire to touch the determined square…

Enough.

Clearing her throat, she somehow forced her vocal cords into compliance. 'Sorry. I got distracted by this delicious meal. Where were we?'

'Our expectations from a marriage,' he drawled, and as his voice melted over her skin she was sure, almost sure, that his eyes had darkened, that he felt the same way she did.

'Why don't you go first?' she said. 'I assume you want someone who will be a good countess.' Her emphasis on the last word would hopefully move this conversation to the proper footing.

He nodded. 'Yes. My mother is on various charitable committees, she also organises the annual fairs on our land and helps with the village fair as well. Then there are various dinners and events.'

All things Stella would have revelled in. And things she would have to learn about. 'My mother will be happy to talk you through what she does. But my wife will have to hit the ground running to a degree as my parents are planning on spending a few months every year in the family villa in Portugal.'

Adriana nodded. 'I understand. Any other expectations?

'No scandal.' He met her gaze fair and square, but now she could see the grim set of his lips, hear the harsh rasp to his voice. 'Both our families have suffered because of the press—I do not want that to happen again. So my wife must behave in such a way that there is not so much as a hint of scandal.'

'I assume that this rule goes for you as well.'

'Of course.'

'But just to be clear, by that do you mean don't get found out or don't engage in any scandalous behaviour?' Heat touched her cheeks. 'I understand that fidelity is a big thing to ask for, but it's important to me…' She'd seen her mother's grief and humiliation first-hand when her father embarked on his affair. As for Adriana herself, the idea that every time Steve touched her he'd been thinking of her sister was an act of unfaithfulness that still made her skin crawl.

'It isn't a big ask.' The words were sharp and she remembered that, whilst she didn't know the details, she did know his fiancée had been unfaithful to him. 'I am asking for fidelity and I intend to return the favour.'

Relief trickled through her, but alongside that was scepticism. It was easy to promise loyalty, and if he'd been marrying Stella she doubted that he would have any issues. But with her…it seemed too much to expect.

'But our marriage will be one of convenience—over the years there will be the temptation to stray.'

'Will there? Are you trying to tell me something? That I won't be enough for you, or that you find me completely unattractive?' There was a glint in his eye, one she couldn't interpret, and his tone was edged. How had she got herself into this conversation and what could she do now? No way would she, could she admit she thought he was drop-dead gorgeous, so she settled for her wooden expression, the one she deployed when she hoped her father would abandon whatever conversation was working him up. The one where she did her best to project invisibility.

He looked at her and exhaled a long sigh, ran a hand through his hair. 'I'm sorry. I don't mean to make you uncomfortable, but Stella and I didn't discuss attraction or fidelity—and it seems clear that we should have. Compatibility is all very well at dinner but it's important in the bedroom as well.'

To her intense annoyance she could feel a blush touch her cheeks. Of course he and Stella hadn't discussed it. Why would they? Stella was infinitely desirable and attractive—so every man in the world would assume compatibility. Anger laced her voice. 'Well, I'm not really sure how we can test that out.'

Now he smiled and it was a smile that made her dizzy with awareness. 'I can think of a few ways.'

Confusion whirled in her head—was he flirting with her? Surely not—he was the one who wanted a business partnership. Yet…as she looked at him all she wanted to do was lean over, grab him by his collar and kiss him. But she couldn't—damn it, she didn't have the confidence, was too scared that he'd reject her, and so she'd do what she always did. Play it safe. 'Perhaps we should just wait and see how we feel—I mean, attraction doesn't necessarily spring up straight away.'

His withdrawal was instant as his face assumed polite

neutrality. 'Of course. You're right. This can wait for another time.' Yet she'd swear that for an instant rue and regret tinged the blue of his eyes as they lingered just a fraction of a second too long on her lips. Had he been thinking about kissing her? Surely not—just her fevered imagination having a wishful think. He rose to his feet.

'I'll get dessert,' he said.

As he stood in the small kitchen, Rob was aware of a disproportionate sense of disappointment—was he really so rusty that he couldn't read the signals? He'd thought there was a spark, been sure of it. Now he wondered if it was wishful thinking. Again. He'd believed Emily had been attracted to him and it had turned out she'd been pretending, acting, faking. So clearly, reading signals was not his forte.

'Rob?'

He turned and saw Adriana standing in the doorway, two plates in hand. 'I thought I could help?'

'Thank you.' But now they were standing there he felt rooted to the spot, mesmerised by how elusive a grey her eyes were, a beautiful, expressive grey, fringed by long lashes, that contrasted with the light-brown of her hair. Hair that held a glossy sheen that begged his fingers to smooth it over. Now that he studied her face he could see the character in the planes and angles, the high bridge of her nose, the shape of her mouth.

'I'll take them.' Aware that his voice sounded rough, he cleared his throat and stepped forward, saw the spark in her eyes, the slight darkening of her pupils, and again he was sure that he was right, that she too felt the pull.

'Sure.' She handed over the plates, and his hand inadvertently brushed against hers. With an audible gasp she stepped backwards and one of the plates crashed to the floor. 'Oh, God. I am so, so sorry. That was so clumsy of me. I'll clear it up and replace it obviously. Is it part of a set? I hope it's not an heirloom or a—'

'Whoa. It's OK. They aren't heirlooms and it was my fault as much as yours. Really, leave it for now. It doesn't matter.'

'It does to me. I hate being clumsy. I'll clear it up. Where is your dustpan and brush?'

'You weren't clumsy.' Though perhaps that was a more palatable explanation than the truth—that the sheer jolt of attraction had caused them both to recoil in shock. Moving away, he opened a cupboard and took out a dustpan and brush, squatted down to brush the pieces up.

'I'll do it.' She dropped down and he forced himself to continue sweeping, not to tense up at her nearness.

'It's fine.' The words were jerky. 'Really. And again I apologise for bringing up the whole attraction factor. It seems to have…derailed negotiations a bit.'

'And I don't want it to do that. That's what I wanted to say really. I completely understand that it will take you a while to adjust to the idea of me rather than Stella. Please don't think I expect you to feel a spark instantly or any time soon.'

Huh? The penny dropped with a clang and he quickly placed the dustpan and brush down, rose, held out a hand and helped her to her feet. 'Adriana, I am an insensitive idiot. But… Stella and I…we never so much as held hands. And it seems clear now why—there was no spark.' And he'd been so busy outlining all the advantages of a convenient marriage he hadn't even thought about it. If anything he'd been pleased, because after Emily the last thing he wanted were the emotions that attraction could bring.

Her eyes held disbelief. 'I find that difficult to believe. Stella is hardly an antidote.'

'No. Stella is a beautiful woman—I get that, I see that

she is attractive, and maybe that's why I didn't really question that side of things. I just assumed…'

'That it would all be all right on the night?' she asked, and he saw the glimmer of a smile.

'Yes. After Emily I was so focused on a marriage of convenience, one without emotional roller coasters, that I didn't see instant attraction as a necessity. I wanted to make decisions based on logic and the long-term, not attraction.'

'And now?' she asked, and her voice was almost a whisper.

'Now…' He looked at her and his breath caught in his throat as desire jolted through him. Warning bells started to clang at the back of his mind. He would not let his decisions be governed by desire, by the magnetic pull of attraction. But, 'Now I can see that perhaps I was wrong not to consider attraction—if Stella and I had discussed it, perhaps we would never have agreed to marry at all. Because attraction is important.'

'But not the be-all and end-all.'

'Agreed. Attraction is a factor but not the most important one.'

Adriana nodded, her gaze not wavering from his. 'And how do we assess the attraction factor?' Her voice was slightly breathless and he wondered what was going through her mind. He could see a pulse beat in her throat and his finger tingled with a need to test her heart rate, check it against his own.

He knew he should back off, but he didn't care, knew that it would be impossible not to kiss her. 'Like this,' he said, and he stepped forward as Adriana did the same.

Then he was kissing her and nothing else mattered except the glorious feel of her lips against his, the scent of her, the taste of her. As he tangled his fingers in the glossy silk of her hair, as he deepened the kiss and heard her small gasp of pleasure, the world spun and he lost himself entirely in the kiss.

Until the ping of the oven recalled them both to the here and now and they both stepped back, stared at each other in mutual shock. 'I…um…' Adriana visibly pulled herself together. 'I guess that means dessert is ready.'

Rob nodded, even as he urged his vocal cords into action. 'Yes. I'll dish it up. It's just a shop-bought chocolate pudding. I hope that's OK.'

'Absolutely. That sounds perfect.'

The words were forced, meaningless amid the after-effects of desire.

On automatic pilot he found plates and cutlery, noted she made no move to help him. Keeping their distance seemed like the best plan for now, whilst he tried to work out what the hell had happened there. He'd expected a kiss, not a Kiss with a capital K that rated somewhere off the Richter scale.

As they sat down again he cleared his throat. 'I suggest we…'

'Put the kiss firmly behind us. Tick the attraction-factor box and don't let attraction affect our decisions.' The words were said in a rush.

'Exactly.' Though he couldn't help wondering how easy it would be to close Pandora's box. Not when his whole body still strummed and hummed with desire.

'So what now?' she asked.

'You asked me what I expect from a marriage; now I need to know what is important to you.'

The question caught her attention and he could almost see her push away the aftershock of the kiss. She paused to marshal her thoughts, pushed her fringe away from her face in an impatient gesture.

'I need to know you will be a good father. That we will be good parents. Part of the reason we would be entering this agreement is because we both want an heir, but our child needs to be more than that to us. I don't want love for myself. But I would expect our children to have your love.'

'They will.' He kept his voice gentle, not wanting to insult her but knowing this was important. 'Regardless of their sex. But I know that's easy for me to say. We do both want an heir but the heir to Darrow can be a girl or a boy. You need a son to save Salvington. So I am sorry to ask this, but how will you feel if our first child is a girl?'

'I will love my child regardless of its sex, and that is a promise. I will never let my daughter be anything other than loved and cherished. Never feel disappointed in her. I swear it.' Her hands clenched into fists. 'I'm not capable of that.'

He could hear the emotion in her voice, sincerity and pain as well.

'I hate the system. I hate that Salvington can only be saved by a son, I loathe the laws that say that, and I intend to keep fighting against them as my father has done ever since I was born.' Rob nodded—it was no secret that Lord Salvington was extremely vocal on the need for the laws to change. 'I wish, so wish that I was planning a family just because I want one, that there wasn't this need, that it wouldn't make any difference if the baby is a girl or boy.'

'I know,' he said softly.

She shook her head and he could see a tear glistening on the ends of her eyelashes. 'You don't. You can't.'

Only a little bit he did and somehow it seemed important to tell her that. 'I can in a different way. I don't like the idea of bringing a child into the world with their destiny preordained—that they will have to do their duty, have to be an earl or a countess simply by dint of their existence. Like you I wish I could have a family without any expectations or rules involved.' Since he'd drawn his first breath he'd been brought up to understand the importance of being heir, had duty drummed into him. He wouldn't bring up his child the way he had been brought up, but he couldn't change some facts.

'But if we do it right our child won't see it as a duty they don't want, they will see it as a duty they embrace. I hope they will love their land and their home.'

'So do I, but I wish they could just love it rather than be responsible for it.'

'I understand, but... I don't know about you, but I'd like a large family.' Her tone dreamy. 'A whole brood of kids, and I think that will make a difference. It will take the pressure off the heir and they can share the responsibilities of the estate. If the eldest doesn't want the title, maybe it can be abdicated to the next in line? Maybe it won't be straightforward, but the important thing will be that we are there for them. To talk and listen and help.'

'And love them for them, whether they are a boy or a girl, the eldest or the youngest.'

Her grey eyes were wide and dreamy and an image filled his mind: himself and Adriana sitting in front of a roaring log fire with a mass of kids around them. Two boys, two girls—why not?

She blinked, took a deep breath, pushed her fringe away from her eyes. 'So will you do it? Will you marry me?'

CHAPTER SIX

MARRY. MARRY. MARRY. The word seemed to dance in front of her eyes, hop and twirl elusively out of her reach as she waited for his answer. Would he marry her?

'Are you sure this is what you really want?' he asked.

'Yes.' She wanted to save her land, her home, the home of her ancestors. She wanted her children to play in the woodlands, roam the fields. She wanted to be part of Salvington's future. She had no problem with the lack of love—she was used to that. If she could live with someone who offered her respect and liking it would be a massive improvement on her current status. So it was a no-brainer really.

The only shade of doubt was about whether it was fair to marry him. Could she be the countess he wanted? Step into his mother's no doubt fashionable shoes? Stella could have. Could she? She'd have to.

'Yes,' she repeated. 'It is. It is what I really want.'

'Then this is what I propose.' He leant back in his chair, sipped his wine. 'I am still worried you are rushing into this. So let's give ourselves a few weeks. Time for us to get to know each other better. Make *sure* this is what we both want.'

Relief flooded her and she knew her smile bordered on goofy. 'Fair enough. So what shall we do to get to know each other better? Maybe something we can do just you and me?'

A heartbeat of a pause and the words seemed to hover in the air, swirl and twirl and glitter with an innuendo she hadn't meant at all. Worse, her hand went up to her mouth, brushed her lips, which tingled in memory of the kiss. His lips quirked upwards in amusement and she tried to think of something to say, anything at all. 'You choose.'

He raised his eyebrows. 'You sure?' He stroked his chin. 'Hmm. Something for just you and me. Let me think...an activity of some sort, just you and me...something fun...'

His eyes met hers, then dropped to her lips and she shivered, would have sworn she could feel the heat of his gaze caress her skin.

Then he grinned at her. 'How about ice skating?' The suggestion was so unexpected she blinked. 'Unless you have something else in mind?'

Her eyes narrowed but she couldn't help grinning back; it felt strange to be teased like this. But it was a short-lived smile once she actually considered his suggestion properly. 'Ice skating sounds fine.' Though actually it didn't—she hadn't been skating since she was a child, when her father's glowering presence had caused her to stumble and fall whilst Stella had glided and twirled. It hardly seemed a milieu where she was going to exhibit the grace and poise a wannabe countess should possess.

But, given she was proposing to marry the man, she could hardly refuse to go ice skating. *Marry. Marry. Marry.* Once again the word swirled in her mind and Adriana wondered if she had lost the plot completely.

'Have you completely lost the plot?' Stella's voice was agitated as she paced the floor of Adriana's bedroom.

'No,' Adriana said quietly. 'I want to do this. If I have a baby boy it makes us safe. Makes Salvington safe.'

'And what if I then have a legitimate son in the future?'

'Then I am good with that. Your son will be heir.'

'But the sacrifice will be yours. This is my fault.'

'No, it isn't. You couldn't have married Rob and pretended the baby was his. And you couldn't have married Rob if you have feelings for someone else.'

Stella shrugged. 'Yes, I could have. My feelings for this man are irrelevant, pointless, and most of all they are foolish.'

Adriana studied her sister's face. 'If you could turn the clock back, would you change things? Do you wish you'd never met him?'

'Of course I do.' Stella twisted her hands together and gave a half-laugh. 'No, dammit. I wouldn't change a thing. How can I wish this baby away? I can't. As for the father... I don't know, Ria. I never thought I could feel like this. Feel so much.'

'Then...surely you need to tell him about the baby.'

'I'm not going to do anything yet. But this is not about me. You can't marry Rob.'

'You were going to.'

Stella hesitated. 'That's different. I was brought up knowing I would need to marry and have an heir. I chose a marriage of convenience, I wanted to be a countess and it felt fair that I should do it. After everything, after the way Father treats you, you don't deserve to be the sacrifice.'

'It's not about sacrifice. Salvington is ours, our family home, and it is wrong we should lose it. Plain wrong.'

'OK. But why Rob? Isn't there someone else? Someone you like, someone who makes you feel something? A spark?'

Adriana focused on the wave and swirl of her printed

duvet, traced the outline of the flowers with her eyes. Imagined painting the actual flower. Hoped her sister couldn't see her face, the tinge of heat as she suddenly recalled the kiss. The way it had sent her body and brain into a whirl and swirl of feeling, desire, need.

'I do like Rob. I think we can make it work. But it's not a done deal. We're going to see how it plays out over the next few weeks.'

Her sister sighed. 'Keep me posted.'

'I will. And what about you?''

'Mum says Father still doesn't want to see me and it's better he is kept as calm as possible, so I am going to go away for a while.'

Adriana couldn't help but wonder if she was going to find her mystery man. 'Good luck. And you keep me posted too.'

Rob knocked on the front door of Salvington Manor, stepped back as the imposing door swung open to show Adriana. There it was again, a tightening of his chest, an urge to step forward and drop a kiss on her lips. She was dressed simply in dark blue jeans and a chunky-knit jumper that reached mid-thigh, her hair pulled back into a ponytail.

'Morning,' he said.

'Good morning.' She pushed her fringe away and looked up at him briefly. 'I'm ready to go.' She smiled. 'I think, anyway. Though I have the feeling I may be about to make a complete fool of myself.'

'You'll be fine,' he said easily, though he caught a note of what sounded like genuine anxiety in her voice.

'That's easy for you to say. I'm assuming you know how to ice skate,' she said as they walked towards his car.

'Yes, I do, and I'm sure you'll pick it up easily.'

'Hopefully. But last time I tried I spent most of the time flat on my face. I think it's because I was born clumsy.'

'No one is born clumsy and you don't seem clumsy to me.'

She raised her eyebrows. 'I tripped into your arms in the restaurant and yesterday I broke a plate in your kitchen. I rest my case.'

'I think nerves played a part in both those mishaps—you don't need to be nervous now.'

'Hard ice, skates and me; the combination isn't promising.'

'I think it's very promising, and anyway, you're forgetting the magic ingredient.'

'What's that?'

He grinned at her. 'Me.'

Satisfaction touched him as she returned the smile. 'You're magic, are you?'

'Yup. With me you have nothing to fear.'

'I think you're overestimating your talent.'

'And I think you're underestimating yours.' On impulse he took her hands in his, felt her body freeze for an instant, knew the contact had jolted her as much as him. Sensed too that she did always underestimate herself, he just didn't know why. 'This is going to be OK. You can do this—I know you can. We'll take it slow. OK?' He squeezed her hand gently.

'OK.' Her smile was slightly tremulous. 'Sorry. I'm being a complete baby about this.'

'No need to apologise.' That was something he sensed she did far too much of. He squeezed her hand again. 'Let's go.'

He watched as she pressed her lips together as they approached the ice. 'It's fine to hold on to the side for a bit.'

'Why don't I watch you for a turn? Maybe I can learn by osmosis.'

'Nice try. I'll get you started first. So hang on to the edge and find your balance, get comfortable on the ice. Walk round taking small steps.'

'That's it?'

'To start with, yes. If that's OK.'

'That's perfect.' She smiled at him, as if in relief, and he watched her small frown as she focused on finding her feet, her concentration absolute as they circled the rink. 'Right. I think I've got it. What now?'

'Move away from the side a little, bend your knees a bit and relax…again, just feel comfortable. I'll be right here.'

Belatedly it occurred to him that perhaps this was foolish, because the proximity was doing funny things to his head. Her light floral scent cast some sort of spell on him and close up he could see the gloss of her hair, see the slanted angle of her cheekbone, the curve of her lips and…

'Oh, I forgot. I thought this may help on the ice. Hold still.'

He dipped his hand into his pocket and pulled out the small bag, opened it up and showed her what he'd bought. Suddenly wondered if she'd be insulted. 'I thought, just for skating, it may be easier…' He held out the hair clips, dark red barrettes. 'But…'

'That's really thoughtful.' Her smile was wide and genuine as she reached out to take them and stumbled. Swiftly he reached out and caught her, steadied her before she could fall.

'I'll do it,' he said. Oh, so carefully, he unclipped one of the barrettes, desperately aware of her nearness, the feel of her hand on his arm. As he gently brushed her fringe back, the silken glossiness captivated his fingers. He slid the barrette in and now he could see her eyes close up, large, and

clear, the grey pulling him in, eyes that could glimmer silver, or cloud to stormy grey, sparkle or cast allure. Any
which way they were beautiful, fringed with long brown
lashes, and the words fell from his lips without thought.
'Why do you hide such beautiful eyes?'

'I…don't hide them.' Yet she looked away as though she
missed the safety of her fringe.

'You are hiding them now,' he countered, and, gently
putting a finger under her chin, he tipped her face up. 'You
shouldn't.'

'I prefer it,' she said lightly. 'I've always thought people
will know what I'm thinking if they see my eyes.'

'And is that a bad thing?'

'It depends what I'm thinking,' she said softly.

And now their gazes meshed together. 'I bet I know what
you are thinking now.'

How he wanted to kiss her, and he knew he would have
if life hadn't intruded in the form of a teenager who shot
past, stumbled and nearly crashed straight into them. Rob
moved instinctively to protect Adriana and get them both
out of the way and she gave a small, rueful smile.

'Saved,' she said.

'For now,' he answered. 'But we're here to teach you to
skate. So let's try to start a glide.' He moved to face her.
'I'll skate backwards, and I'll keep one hand under yours
for you to grab if you need to.'

She took a deep breath and nodded, and pushed herself
off the side.

'That's it! You're doing brilliantly. See if you can glide
for a bit, try and coast. Fabulous.' After a moment he took
both her hands in his and skated backwards, drawing her
along, saw her lips turn up into a wide smile. The next
half-hour flew past and by the end of it he was genuinely

impressed. 'See. You're a natural. That's what you were born—a natural skater.'

'You're forgetting the magic ingredient. You. You're a natural born teacher.'

'Then prove it. Have a go on your own.'

At first he thought she'd refuse, and then she nodded. 'OK, but if I fall over…'

'If you fall over that's OK,' he said softly. 'Everyone falls over sometimes. It doesn't mean you're clumsy, or a bad skater. It means you're learning. If you fall over, you get up and off you go. But if you do fall over, fall safely. And I'll be here to help you up. Deal?'

'Deal.' But she didn't fall over. He watched as she pushed away from the side, glided forward, ponytail bobbing up and down as she negotiated around another skater, and a sudden pride slid through him. Because he sensed that this had been harder for Adriana than she was letting on. Seconds later she crashed into the wall next to him. 'Next time perhaps you'd better teach me how to stop. But now the least I can do is buy you a hot chocolate. To say thank you.'

As they walked back to the car, takeaway hot chocolates in their hands, she said, 'Really, thank you. Once you made me see falling over was OK, it made all the difference. It took the fear away, and you were so patient—you didn't expect me to instantly get it and you didn't get angry when I did something wrong.'

The words caused him to wonder who had taught her in the past, but before he could work out how to ask that she continued.

'But you were pretty impressive—did you learn as a child?'

'No.' His parents would never have let him do anything so 'dangerous' as a child, nothing that could possibly hurt him. And no amount of persuasion could make them see that the chances of his dying on an ice rink…a rugby pitch…climbing a tree…riding a horse…were minuscule. 'I learnt in the States.' Fleur and her boyfriend, Jonathan, had been shocked that he'd never been, had taken him along and he'd loved it, the freedom of gliding across the ice, in control of his movements, able to weave in and out, go backwards…it was something he loved doing. Found too that on the ice ideas seemed to come to him, and he and Fleur had spent hours brainstorming ideas for Easel.

'Tell me about your time there,' she said now and for a moment he wanted to. Wanted to tell her about Easel Enterprises, his pride and joy. But he couldn't. Needed to keep his involvement in Easel Enterprises completely under wraps—it was important to him that this company launched and succeeded as the brainchild of Fleur Hardcastle with an honorary mention to a plain Rob Wilmington, but not a whisper of Viscount Rochester.

For now. Once the company was up and running, once he'd sorted out Darrow, then it would be different, but for now he didn't want the press or his parents or anyone to know, and that meant telling no one.

There was no reason not to trust Adriana but equally no way would he risk trusting her either. After all, he'd trusted Emily with a blind trust that had been repaid with betrayal.

'I enjoyed myself,' he said instead. 'I enjoyed being plain Rob Wilmington, I enrolled on various courses, I travelled, I did normal jobs. I worked in a bar, I worked as a waiter, I went to watch American football.'

'Are you happy to be back?' she asked, and the question took him by surprise.

'Yes.' Realising how terse the answer was, he tried to clarify. Because he had no regrets about coming back. 'I do miss the freedom of my life there, but I do know it was time to come back. My parents are getting older, they want to step back, and I am keen to start work here.'

Her large grey eyes studied him and she nodded. 'I know how hard your parents have worked for Darrow and I think there is a huge potential to build on everything they've done.'

Rob nodded, knew he should feel way more enthusiasm than he in fact did, but it was hard, hard because all his life Darrow had felt like a weight rather than a joy.

'Speaking of your parents, have you told them about me?'

'Yes. I told them that Stella pulled out and that you and I are considering marriage.' He kept his voice neutral but clearly not neutral enough.

'I'm sorry. I'm sure they were disappointed.'

'They…' He hesitated as he recalled the conversation with his parents.

Did you even try to change her mind?' his father had asked.

'No. What would have been the point? I could hardly marry a woman who loves someone else.'

His mother had sighed…a small, elegant exhalation of air.

'Darling, I am sure you could have persuaded Stella that what you have to offer far outweighs love. I have no doubt she will soon regret this decision—I do think your father is right. You must at least try.'

'I'm afraid I disagree. I will have no part in forcing a woman to marry me when she doesn't want to. Nor do I wish for a reluctant bride. So I will not be speaking with Stella. However, Adriana and I are considering an alliance. But it is early days.'

'I remember Adriana. She isn't a patch on her sister. Too shy, too gauche.'

Rob had gritted his teeth. *'Well, thank you for your opinion, Mother, but with all due respect it's not up to you who I marry.'*

Her next sigh had been on an industrial scale.

'Given how right we were about Emily, I do think you could listen to us, Rob.'

'You were not right about Emily—you disliked her because of her birth and her status.'

'Very well.' His father's voice had been sharp. *'The important thing is that a marriage may come from this and Adriana's birth is good. Why don't we meet her? Come, Cecilia, from what I remember Adriana is perfectly presentable. We should give her a chance.'*

His mother had nodded.

'Fine. If she wants to speak to me, I'm happy to tell her more about being a countess and what it entails. Why not bring her to dinner on Friday?'

'They would like to meet you,' he offered now, 'but I said it was probably a bit early in the proceedings.' Especially as he suspected his mother's idea may well be to scare Adriana off.

She laid a hand on his arm. 'It's OK, Rob. I'd rather you were honest. I understand why they wanted Stella as a daughter-in-law. I do. She would have found it easy to step into your mother's shoes. In some ways they are very similar—they always know the right clothes to wear, the right things to say. They are at ease in society. Stella was born to be a countess.'

Her voice held no bitterness, was simply factual, but it made him frown.

'Anyone can be a countess,' he stated firmly.

'That is technically correct, but I am pretty sure your parents disagree. But that's OK—it sounds like they are at least willing to give me a chance.' She hesitated. 'And maybe I should meet them sooner rather than later? I mean, who better to tell me about being the Countess of Darrow than your mother? And if they want to meet me and I refuse, that will be bad for any future relationship I might have with them, won't it?'

Her words made sense but a qualm still struck him. One he pushed away—what could go wrong at a simple family dinner? Especially as he would be right there. 'If you're sure,' he said.

She nodded. 'I'm sure.'

CHAPTER SEVEN

ADRIANA LOOKED AT her reflection and wondered what had
possessed her to agree to a family dinner with Rob's parents. Part of it had been the sheer adrenalin that had coursed
through her after their ice-skating session. But some of it
had logic—she had no doubt they would prefer Stella as a
daughter-in-law and she completely understood that. But
they couldn't have Stella so it was her job now to get them
on side with her. Get them to accept that she would at least
be a viable substitute. And she knew the Earl and Countess—had met them at various events over the years—and
she knew Stella had got on with them fine.

Another look at her reflection—perhaps she should have
bought a new dress, but she'd decided it was better to stick
to what she knew and was comfortable in. A simple grey
dress, bought to allow her to blend into the background, but
she was pretty sure it classed as 'smart casual'.

Now for her hair. She'd keep it loose... Her fingers hov-
ered over the barrettes and her skin tingled as she recalled
Rob clipping her hair back, how near they had been to another kiss. Determinedly she clipped her fringe back; a
light layer of make-up and she was good to go.

The knock on the door heralded Rob and she ran lightly
down the stairs, pulled the door open and gulped. Wondered if he would ever stop having this impact on her. If

they did get married would her knees still wobble when they were both old and grey? The thought was enough to stop her in her tracks.

'Hey,' he said softly, and in the dusk she could see that he was smiling down at her, and her heart did a somersault.

'Hey.' With an effort she summoned up some conversation. 'How was your day?'

'Good.' They headed for his car. 'I've been up in London all day. How about you? How was your day?'

'Good too. I spent most of the day in the woodlands overseeing some tree felling. I just hope I don't have woodchips in my hair.'

He glanced across at her quickly before returning his attention to the road. 'So you really are hands-on.'

'Of course. I mean, I do get involved in the books and records side as well.' Thankfully the estate manager employed by her father had a much higher regard for her abilities than her father did. 'Martin, the estate manager, is happy to teach me. Probably because I used to follow him around a lot when I was a child.'

'So he approves of your ideas?'

'Yes. But he does also appreciate my father's position as well.'

'And what about Stella? Is she interested in the land in the same way?'

'No. That's my side of it. I'm focusing on the woodlands right now. Whilst some felling is necessary we need to make sure we are replanting as well. I want Salvington to be environmentally positive and there are so many ways of doing that. I'd like to introduce eco farming and a wildlife area and...' She broke off as she realised they were nearly at Darrow. 'Sorry, I'm rabbiting on. Maybe I am a little nervous about this.'

'No need. I'll be right by your side to make sure my

parents are on their best behaviour. And you aren't rabbiting. I'm interested.'

He pulled into the gated sweep of the driveway, but as he drove over the gravel he slowed down. 'What the hell?' His lips set in a grim line. 'Adriana, I'm sorry. We've been ambushed—it looks like my mother has invited more guests than just you tonight. I didn't know.'

Adriana surveyed the row of cars that lined the parking area. 'More guests? But why would she do that?' Stupid question. It was a test—to see if Adriana could cope, to see how she performed in society. 'Don't answer.'

'I won't. But I won't subject you to this either. We're going.'

Adriana thought, and then said, 'No. I will not run away.'

'But you hate parties,' he pointed out. 'And this is outrageous behaviour.'

'Yes, it is. But if we leave, how does that look? To all the guests she has invited—guests who, if we do get married, I will need to socialise with, need to mix with? That's what you want, isn't it? A countess who can step into your mother's shoes? Then I need to start now, because believe me, if I turn tail and run now they will all remember it.'

'So we're going in.'

'We're going in.' Adriana closed her eyes. She could do this; she'd been to parties before, she'd blend in, be as invisible as possible. Get through it, because if she wanted to marry Rob, save Salvington, then she had to.

Before she could change her mind she climbed out of the car and headed for the front door.

'Hey. Hold up. We're going in together, remember?' She halted and he came to her side, took her hand in his, and she took comfort from his proximity, managed a smile for the stately figure of the butler.

'Good evening,' he intoned. 'Come this way.'

They followed him into the drawing room and Adriana quickly scanned the room, her heart sinking as she assimilated the guest list. Members of prominent society families, the older generation here were mostly friends of her parents, people who she'd known since childhood. That wasn't a massive problem, though she suspected those with daughters would prefer Rob to choose his bride elsewhere.

More of an issue was the fact that said daughters were also present, along with others of her contemporaries, young men and women who had always despised her, sensed her vulnerabilities and insecurities in her childhood, and when Stella wasn't around they had delighted in tormenting her.

And in that moment all those childhood feelings resurfaced, but she forced a smile to her face as the Countess approached them, flanked by Lady Eleanor Maxwell, a dazzling redhead who had been one of Adriana's prime tormentors. Both women, the older and the younger, looked immaculate. More than that, they looked svelte, elegant and poised, casting her grey dress into the category of dowdy, boring and plain.

'Hello, Rob, darling. And this must be Adriana. I haven't seen you since you were a gawky teenager. It is marvellous to see you again.'

'You too.' The words sounded stiff and she felt Rob's hand squeeze round her in reassurance.

'You didn't tell me there'd be company,' Rob said.

'Oh, I'm sure I did. But if I didn't I'm sure Adriana doesn't mind. Do you?'

'Of course not.'

'Well, I do,' Rob said. 'So I'm afraid we won't be able to stay long.'

'But it's a three-course dinner, darling. You don't want Adriana to miss out on Marco's cooking, surely.'

Rob's eyes narrowed, and now it was Adriana who

squeezed his hand, trying to convey that she really didn't want a scene, especially under Eleanor's amused gaze anyway.

As they followed the Countess further into the room, she could feel herself flinch, wanted to tug the clips out of her fringe and hide as everyone turned to look at her. She heard a repressed snicker from the younger people and knew as she looked at them how wrongly dressed she was.

'Come on, Adriana, say hello to everyone,' Lady Eleanor purred.

'And Rob, your father wants a quick word before dinner,' the Countess interpolated.

As she followed Eleanor towards the small group of younger people Adriana could only hope these people had grown kinder since their childhood days. Wished cravenly that she had Stella to protect her as her sister always had. But now she was on her own, and even as she stepped forward she failed to see a rug, tripped and stumbled.

'Oh, Adriana. Still as clumsy as ever,' drawled Eleanor. 'Now tell us what's going on, darling. We simply don't believe you are dating Rob…'

'In fact, we've all got a bet on how long it will take for Eleanor to cut you out,' said her brother, a dark-haired man who she had always loathed.

It was all so beautifully done—they would claim it was banter, but it didn't feel like it. Stella would know how to handle it, but she didn't. So she tried to smile, and when she had the chance she slipped away to hide in the bathroom. Pulled the clips out of her hair—foolish perhaps but it helped her feel hidden.

The dinner bell rang and she exited the bathroom and followed the other guests towards the dining hall. The massive mahogany dining table was set with the gleam of family silver, place mats adorned with the family crest, an array of cutlery you needed a manual to navigate and designer crystal glasses.

Marvellous. A quick look at the place cards showed that she'd been put next to the Countess and one of her father's oldest friends, Sir Roger Montacue. Whilst Rob was at the other end of the table next to Eleanor.

'How's your poor father?'

'He is stable, thank you.' Adriana smiled politely as a bowl of soup was set down in front of her.

'Glad to hear it.' With that Sir Roger turned away to engage in a heated conversation about hunting and recent proposed changes to the law.

Then smoothly from her left, 'I thought it would be nice if we had a chat,' the Countess stated. 'I want you to know how dear Rob is to us and to the estate.'

'I am sure he is,' Adriana said quietly as she followed the Countess's gaze to Rob and Eleanor, saw the red-haired woman lean in towards Rob. Distracted, she lifted a spoonful of soup to her mouth, and to her horror a few drips escaped, staining the front of her dress. And of course it was tomato soup. Or roasted tomato and basil bisque, as it was called on the ornately scrolled menu cards.

The Countess continued, her melodious voice light and low, though her eyes were fixed pointedly on the stain, 'We want only what is best for him. Sometimes Rob gets quixotic ideas in his head, favours doing the "right" or "PC" thing without considering the long-term.' She sipped her wine. 'And don't all children always like to do what their parents don't want them to do? But hopefully Rob has learnt his lesson from the past. Now we are so glad to see him back here, where he belongs. And how is your lovely sister? Such a shame she couldn't be here today.'

Well, that told her, and all Adriana could think to say was, 'Yes. It is a shame.'

Because as she looked round the table she could see exactly what the Countess was trying to show her, the reason for this whole dinner, a stunt, a set-up to show Adriana the stark reality, the truth: Rob belonged here. Adriana didn't. Stella did. *Lady* Eleanor did. She saw the red-headed woman's hand touch Rob's arm, heard her soft laughter, wondered if her touch affected Rob, realised it didn't matter. Lady Eleanor was countess material, Adriana wasn't. They'd agreed that attraction was important but not the be-all and end-all.

At that moment she saw him frown, say something to Eleanor that wiped the smile off her face and made her remove her hand from his arm, a faint flush on her cheek. He looked across the table and met her gaze, and as a footman removed his plate Rob whispered something in his ear.

The man nodded, put the plate back down and came round the table to Adriana. 'The Viscount has asked me to let you know that unfortunately he has just got a message that necessitates your departure.'

Before Adriana could respond she saw Rob rise from his place, and now he came to join them. 'Deepest apologies, Mother, I'm afraid I will have to drag Adriana away from this wonderful dinner. A friend of mine called and he needs my help. It's a bit of a crisis so we'll have to run.'

Adriana saw the Countess's lips compress for a fraction of a second and then she rose to her feet and the occasion.

'Oh, darling, I am so sorry. And I hope the crisis is averted; if anyone can help I know you can.' She clapped her hands together and the conversation around the table stopped. 'Unfortunately Rob and Adriana have been called away.'

'Apologies, but we have no choice. Please, all of you continue with dinner and enjoy Marco's wonderful food. And *we'll* no doubt see you at the next event.'

Adriana managed, 'It was lovely to meet you all. And thank you, Cecilia, so much for inviting me.' She gave a small wave and followed Rob out of the room.

As soon as they reached the sanctuary of the car he turned to her. 'I can only apologise. I have no idea what that dreadful gathering was about or what my mother was thinking.' Anger roiled inside him at his mother's temerity in not only not warning them dinner had meant a formal gathering but also separating Adriana from him and making a blatant attempt to throw Eleanor at him. 'But believe me, I will be having words with her.'

'There's no need,' she said. Her voice was oddly colourless.

'There is every need.'

'Do you really have a friend in crisis?' she asked.

'Nope. I wanted to get us out of there pronto.'

'You mean you wanted to rescue me.'

'Rescue *us*,' he corrected as he started the car. 'Now I intend to drive us somewhere nearer to you to have dinner.'

'Actually, I'm not hungry.'

A quick glance at her showed that her hands were twisted together and her face looked pinched with worry, though her fringe once again obscured her eyes.

'What's wrong?'

'You shouldn't have had to rescue me,' she burst out. 'I should have been able to hold my own in there. And I do understand why your mother did it.'

He didn't reply for a while, waited until he saw a small woodland car park, a local place where people parked to walk their dogs. It was empty now and he pulled in, switched the engine off and turned to face Adriana.

'Then perhaps you could explain it to me.'

Her face was illuminated by moonlight as she nodded.

'Your mother was trying to show me that I don't belong, that I can't step into her shoes. Whereas Lady Eleanor could. I am not countess material. Stella would have waltzed in there and charmed everyone. Eleanor commanded the room. I lack the poise needed, the dress sense, the ability to know what to say. I hid in the bathroom, for Pete's sake.'

Rob shook his head. 'We were ambushed.'

'Yes, we were, but I know I should have coped better and I didn't. I am not sure I can be the countess you want... not sure I can keep my part of the bargain. I want to give you, give both of us the chance to think about that. So if you could drive me home now that would be great. Maybe talk in a couple of days.'

'I...' He could see the misery on her face, knew too that she had loathed the entire time at that dinner. And who could blame her? Every instinct told him to pull her into his arms, kiss away the sadness in her eyes, tell her it would all be all right. But that wouldn't be honourable. If she married him Adriana would be a countess. Dinners like tonight's would abound in her future. That was the way it was. It was imperative that she go into this with her eyes wide open. 'Fine. We'll regroup in a couple of days.'

Adriana opened her eyes to the insistent ring of the phone. Squinted at the window, where dawn was only just emerging. Great. She'd only managed to fall asleep an hour ago, unable to get her dilemma from her mind. Was it fair to marry Rob to get what she wanted when she wasn't sure she could provide him with what he wanted? She didn't know the answer, only knew that the thought of not seeing Rob again felt... wrong.

Irrational hope flared that maybe the caller was him, but of course it wasn't. It was the manager of the riding school they leased the stables to.

She listened and then swung her legs out of bed. 'It's not a problem. I'll be down in fifteen minutes. It's fine.'

And actually it was. In some ways this was exactly what she needed—two stable hands had called in sick and they needed some help. Well, good. The company of horses was exactly what she needed today—better than bloody human beings. An hour later she was immersed in her tasks, wiped a mud-encrusted hand across her face.

'Good morning.'

Adriana whirled round and gave a small gasp, blinked and stared at Rob. 'What are you doing here?'

'I came to talk to you.'

She narrowed her eyes. 'I thought we agreed to wait a couple of days.'

'I thought it was more of a guideline. You said we should go away and think—well, I have, and here I am, ready to share my thoughts.'

'I'm working.'

'I'll help.'

'I don't think it's your sort of thing.'

He raised his eyebrows. 'Based on?'

'Intuition. I mean, have you ever mucked out a stable?'

'As it happens, no. So are you saying I don't belong here?'

Now she narrowed her eyes further. 'Why do I feel I just walked into a trap? Anyway, that's not what I am saying. I am saying you don't know how to muck out a stable.'

'Because I've never done it before. It doesn't mean I can't learn. If I want to. And I do. So tell me what to do. And I'll help.' He shrugged off his jacket and she couldn't help it; her eyes drank in the fluid movement, the powerful breadth of him.

'You'll get your clothes dirty.' The inanity of the warning struck her.

'I get I'm not dressed right but that's because I wasn't prepared, didn't know I'd be mucking out a stable. Remind you of anything?'

She sighed. 'You cannot compare you being in a stable yard to me being at that dinner yesterday.'

'I think I can. Anyway, I don't mind a little dirt.' He squatted down and scooped up a handful of mud and smeared it on his shirt. 'There, see?'

The laugh was startled out of her. 'Do you even like horses?'

'Time to find out. But if I don't I'll still give it a try. And I'm pretty sure they can't be worse than some of yesterday's guests.'

She watched as he approached the horse she was standing with, saw that his stride was easy, showed no sign of anxiety.

'This is Rusty,' she said. 'He's one of the children's favourites. All these horses are part of a riding school we let the stables to.'

'So what's the best way to approach him?' he asked.

'Are you nervous?'

'A little. He is larger and more powerful than me and I respect that. So I know to be careful but I'm not scared. But I don't want to spook him either.'

'You can stroke his nose. He likes that, don't you, Rusty?' The horse nudged her gently and she smiled at him affectionately, watched as Rob reached out to do the same. 'You can give him a treat. I don't do treats often, because it's not good for them to expect a treat, but I think Rusty is due one. Here.'

She reached into her jacket pocket and pulled out a finger of carrot, which she handed over.

'So what's the best way of doing it? I can see how big his teeth are.'

'Hold the carrot in the palm of your hand and curl your fingers slightly.' She placed her own hand under his, felt an extra frisson to add to the hormonal tumult of his proximity. 'You need to guide your hand upward and don't flinch from the teeth. That's when a horse may start to lunge for the treat.' She knew Rusty wouldn't, he was a prime favourite with the kids and an expert at taking treats from small hands let alone an adult's. She couldn't help studying the shape of Rob's hand anew, marvelled that a hand could evoke such a tug of desire in her. Perhaps it was the sheer capability of it that gave it such beauty. Whatever it was, the contact played havoc with her senses even as she focused on his reaction to Rusty as the horse gently nuzzled from his hand and he smiled.

'You're a good boy, Rusty.' He turned to her. 'Now put me to work,' he said.

'OK. We need to muck out another stall. Basically, use a pitchfork to get together all the manure and soiled straw and then we heap it into the wheelbarrow. But don't pile it up too high. Then we repeat till we've got rid of it all.'

'So is this part of your regular duties?' he asked as he worked.

'No.' She realised that she had stopped work, seemingly entranced by watching the flow of his muscles, the lithe strength of his back, the powerful movement of his shoulders. 'A couple of stable hands called in sick, so I said I'd help out. It's on more of an ad hoc basis. But I do enjoy it. Sometimes I think I prefer the company of horses to people.'

'And if the company behaves like last night's did, who can blame you?' He paused, leant the pitchfork against a wall and turned to her. 'You cannot judge your ability to be Countess of Darrow based on last night.'

She shook her head. 'It's more than that and you know

it. Last night showed me how…ill-equipped I am for the position.'

'Rubbish.'

'Excuse me?'

'I said rubbish.'

CHAPTER EIGHT

ROB WATCHED THE play of emotions dance across Adriana's features, could see confusion, a hint of ire and a touch of frustration. And the temptation to pull her into his arms, smooth the crease from her forehead, and kiss her nigh on overwhelmed him. She looked ridiculously endearing, with her hair in a messy ponytail, a smear of mud across her nose. Dressed in a wax jacket, leggings and boots, she also looked part of her surroundings, as though she belonged. Which brought him to what he wanted to say.

Now she folded her arms. 'Perhaps you could clarify exactly what you mean by "rubbish"?' She mocked quote marks in the air with vehemence.

'I'm happy to explain. I disagree with your assessment. The bit where you said you couldn't be a countess, couldn't step into my mother's shoes.'

'You saw me yesterday. I let myself be laughed at and bullied, I hid in the bathroom and I even managed to drop soup on myself.'

'That's not what I saw. I saw that you were tricked into a social occasion orchestrated to make you uncomfortable. You didn't turn tail and run, you went in, and in the face of rudeness and provocation you were polite. So what if you spilt some soup? Other people would have poured their soup on my mother's head. Or Eleanor's.'

Now surprise widened her eyes as she studied his expression. 'Thank you. I truly appreciate what you are saying, but part of being a countess is social poise, knowing how to dress, how to talk the talk, host events.'

'Yes, but only part of it. Because I've been thinking and I've realised that when we first discussed our marriage, my expectations, I was wrong. I should never have said you needed to step into anyone's shoes. You can be Countess of Darrow however you want to be. In your own shoes. Or Wellington boots come to that. I wondered if you wanted to be involved with the estate management.'

Now her jaw dropped and he could see a glimmer of a smile in her eyes along with more than a glimpse of disbelief.

'But I thought that was what you wanted to do.'

'It never occurred to me that it is something you would want to do. And that's my bad.' It was. As he'd driven home the night before, as he'd tossed and turned through a sleepless night, he'd realised how hidebound and pig-headed he'd been and cursed himself for a fool. He'd been so busy ticking boxes, getting the Darrow side of things sorted out so he could get back to also focusing on Easel Enterprises, that he'd done the very thing his parents did to him. He'd not seen Adriana as an individual. 'You can be a countess however you want to be,' he repeated. 'It doesn't have to be done the way my mother did it, or the way Stella or Eleanor would do it. You can do it your way.'

'But… I would love to be involved in the estate but all the other things your mother does are important too.'

'I get that, but I believe you can learn how to do that. Like I am learning how to muck out a stable. I think the only reason *you* think you can't is because you don't believe in yourself.' He just wished he understood why. 'You do have poise. I can see it in the way you move, the way you are here, the way you ice skated. You are more than capable of holding your own—you and I have never had a problem with conversation.'

'That's because you don't scare me. And neither do the horses.'

'Then what does scare you?' he asked softly.

Her eyes held shadows now, that swirled in the grey depths. 'Being judged and found wanting, making a fool of myself, not being good enough.' She blinked as though surprised at the directness of her response.

Again he wondered what made her feel like that, sensed she'd said as much as she wanted to say, or perhaps more as she turned away, headed towards Rusty and stroked the horse's nose.

'Perhaps you judge yourself too harshly,' he said softly. 'And worry too much about what other people think.'

'It's hard not to, though, isn't it?' she asked. 'I do care about being liked. Don't you?'

'To a point,' he said. 'I care about being respected by other people, providing they are people I respect myself. And liked as well, I suppose, and it's important to me to be liked for myself, not for my title.'

She sighed. 'You're the sort of person people do respect,' she said on a sigh. 'I'm not.'

'If you are talking about people like Eleanor and that crowd, I wouldn't give them a second thought. Why would you want them to like you?'

'Because it would have made my life a whole lot easier as a child, and last night for that matter. But you're right. I don't want them to like me, I want them to respect me.' She turned away from the horse. 'I'm guessing you've never had a lack-of-respect issue.'

Part of him wanted to let that assumption lie, didn't want to remember times past, but he wanted to help in some way, wanted to show Adriana that she should believe in herself, that she deserved respect from everyone.

'Actually my childhood held its share of bullies. My parents were so relieved, so happy to have a son. They tried for years and years, went through countless IVF attempts and who knows what else? My mother went to every type of doctor of every type of medicine and eventually when they had given up all hope I came along. A miracle baby. An heir. And they were terrified they'd lose me—that an illness or an accident would carry me off.'

'That's understandable,' she said.

'I know, but they took it to extremes. They wouldn't let me ride a bike, climb a tree, have a scooter. They vetted anyone who went anywhere near me. But my father insisted on sending me to boarding school.' Like all the Earls who had gone before him. 'But under strict instructions not to let me do anything dangerous including sport or pretty much anything extracurricular that held even the possibility of me stubbing a toe. As you can imagine, that put a bit of a downer on my school life. I was teased and bullied.' Mercilessly. He could still recall the taunts, the tricks, the names. The time they'd held him still and poured buckets of water over him, or held him down in a freezing shower to 'teach him to swim'. The pink ribbons they'd put in his hair because he was 'girlie'.

'But didn't you talk to your parents? Explain?'

'I tried, but their take on it was that I needed to "man up" because everything they were doing was for the estate, to ensure the future of the line. To make sure I grew up "to be an earl that history and future generations would be proud of".' He could hear bitterness in his voice and hastened to add, 'But the reason I'm telling you is I do know what it feels like to be bullied and have no respect whatsoever.'

'What did you do?'

'I worked out. I saved my money and I sent off for weights and training stuff. I found a shed on the edge of the school grounds and I set up a makeshift gym. In the holidays I managed to persuade one of the staff to cover for me whilst I went running and I followed a regime. And it worked. My parents were suspicious but so pleased I was apparently bulking up naturally they didn't investigate too hard. When I was ready it was a simple exercise—I challenged the head bully to a one-on-one fight.'

'But surely he saw that you were a real threat.'

'I don't think he did. To him I was still a weakling.' A snivelling cry baby, because once, just once, a single tear had escaped him.

'What happened?'

'I won.' He could still hear the satisfaction in his voice. 'It wasn't the most scientific fight in the world, but the end result was a win for me.'

'And after that?'

'He stopped picking on me or anyone else. And after that I got people's respect.' Especially as in the inevitable aftermath he hadn't 'snitched', though he'd made it clear he would if the bully or any of his mates laid a finger on anyone again.

'I'm glad. Not glad about what happened to you because it makes me angry, but glad that good won out in the end. You saved yourself and others.' Now she grinned at him. 'So what would you suggest? That I challenge Eleanor to a brawl, or perhaps your mother?'

He grinned back. 'I was thinking more subtle than that. Prove them wrong. Show them your way is the right way. Outdress them, outsmart them, make them sit up and take notice. Or show them you don't give a damn. But whatever you do, don't roll over and give up. If you don't want to be Countess of Darrow that's fine, but if you do then do it your way. Don't give up on this, on us, because of those people. Or because you don't believe in yourself.' He stopped. 'So what do you think?'

'I think… Thank you. For believing I can do this. And I'd like to give it a try.'

As she stepped towards him, looked up at him, the air seemed to shimmer, charged by a sense of momentousness. And it seemed inevitable that as she took another step forward he too moved and then the gap was closed and then he was kissing her and she was kissing him. Mutual desire, mutual relief, the same need for each other, and it felt *right* as she melted into his embrace. His whole body hummed with desire for her, for Adriana, as her lips parted under his and he revelled in her taste, her touch, the brand of her hands through the cotton of his shirt. The smell of the stable yard, the rawness of their desire, the vanilla scent and gloss of her hair heightening his every sense.

The sound of someone clearing their throat broke into the moment, slowly penetrated the fog of desire, the bubble of need where only he and Adriana existed, and they moved apart and he saw the interested face of a young woman.

'Clara,' Adriana said in a credible attempt at assurance. 'This is the manager,' she said to Rob by way of explanation.

'Nice to meet you,' he said.

'The stalls are mucked out, and the saddles are pretty much cleaned,' Adriana continued brightly.

'Thank you, Adriana. I really appreciate you coming down to give us a hand.'

Clara was clearly speaking on automatic; her attention was solely on Rob, her eyes slightly narrowed as if she was trying to work it out.

'Right. I need to get back to the house,' Adriana said

briskly. 'Let me know if you need me tomorrow or this evening.'

'Of course. Thanks again.'

Clara turned and left with one more backwards glance, and Adriana shook her head. 'That was a bit embarrassing.' Yet she didn't look embarrassed, her cheeks still flushed and a smile still tipping her lips. 'So what now?'

And just like that Rob knew exactly what they should do next—as each moment went on he became more and more sure that he and Adriana could make a go of a marriage. A wife who actually loved the estate would be a massive bonus—would allow him more leeway to balance Darrow with Easel quicker. 'I have an idea. We've got to know each other better now so let's take it to the next stage. See how we survive spending proper time together.'

'Define proper time,' she said, a hint of wariness in her eyes.

'A week? Spent together away from here, away from our normal lives, away from family, where we can see what it would be like to actually live in the same place. Obviously the beauty of a marriage of convenience is that we can shape it however we like, spend as much or as little time with each other as we want. But we will still be living together and that means spending some time together. We'll get back from work and then what will we do every night?' He paused and gave a sudden smile. 'Don't answer that.'

Heat touched her cheeks. 'I wasn't intending to.' She grinned. 'But if I had been I would have suggested play Monopoly, of course.'

Now he chuckled. 'Of course. But in all seriousness this will give us a chance to see if we are comfortable together, can spend time together without getting on each other's nerves.'

'You mean you want to see if I have any annoying habits?'

'Absolutely. And of course make sure you can put up with mine.'

'So where would we go?'

'How about Portugal? For a week. My parents have a villa there.'

A heartbeat of hesitation and then she nodded. 'Let's do it.'

Adriana looked at her mother. 'So Father still doesn't want to see Stella. Or me.'

Her mother shook her head. 'I'm sorry, Ria. He says he can't. I think…' She hesitated. 'The attack has changed him; I don't know if it will last or not, but he is gentler, kinder, more like the man I used to know. But he's also emotional and depressed—he says he needs to get his head together before he sees anyone. Needs to be more himself—the doctors say it's normal to have a lot of emotional change after an attack. But it's important for him to be positive and rest and look after himself.'

Adriana looked at her mother. 'Will you tell him what I've done, what I'm doing?'

'Yes, I will. When the time is right, but Ria…'

'Yes.'

'Are you sure you want to do this?'

'Of course I am, Mother. I want to make Salvington safe; you know how important that is. It is our home, our place, it belongs to *us*.'

'I know, Ria, and I know how much you love it.'

'So do you, don't you?'

There was a silence. 'I understand how you feel about it, but… Salvington is a place—you are a human being with one life. If, God forbid, your father had died Salvington would have gone to Bobby Galloway, and you would have had to get on with your lives. Salvington is just bricks and stone and mortar and land. It's not more important than your happiness.'

There had been a hint of bitterness in her voice and Adriana got it. 'Oh, Mum. I'm sorry. Salvington has always been put above your happiness.'

'You're right. Everything in my life has revolved around Salvington since I married your father. I don't want it to ruin your life. If you go ahead with this you give up the chance of love, of a fairy-tale ending.'

Adriana went to her mother and hugged her. 'I don't believe in fairy tales and this won't ruin my life. Truly it won't. I love Salvington. To me it is more than bricks and mortar and soil, it feels like part of me, I feel connected to it and I want it to be part of my life, my children's lives. I *have* to do this.'

'Well, you've always known your own mind, sweetheart. All I can do is wish you luck.'

'Thank you.' Another hug and though her mother smiled Adriana could see the sadness in the smile and the tiniest flicker of doubt pervaded her mind. A flicker she quenched instantly. This was the right thing to do. She knew it. She and Rob had a plan.

CHAPTER NINE

ROB GLANCED SIDEWAYS at Adriana, silhouetted against the plane window, a background of blue sky and cloud. She had a book in her hand and was absorbed in it, and as he studied her he realised how much he liked what he saw. There was something tranquil about her, her fringe was clipped back with the barrettes he'd given her, and she seemed more at ease. All positives that augured well for their plan—a sense of the surreal ran through him—he was possibly— no, probably—looking at the woman he would marry, have children with, a family.

Someone who shared his own values and beliefs, who didn't want love and was happy to broker a partnership. And then there was the spark between them; the kisses they'd shared imprinted on his mind and body.

Whoa. Careful here, Rob. Attraction was what had triggered the whole disastrous relationship with Emily. She'd reeled him in like an expert, teasing, tempting and sweetening it all with a shyness and a pretence that she was falling in love. But attraction had blinded him to the falsity of her words, her actions, her gestures. He'd been played, sure, but he'd let it happen because he'd desired her, because he'd let himself fall in love with her, or with who she pretended to be.

With Adriana there was no risk of love, he'd made that

clear from the outset, but he didn't want his judgement clouded by desire. They needed to decide whether they could make a life together, raise a family and live in mutual respect and liking. That was where his focus needed to be.

His email pinged and he looked down to see an update from Fleur: plans for a company launch, how she and Jonathan wished he could be there, how excited they were and ending with a request to call him.

Quickly he typed a reply, promising to call when he could the next day, and for a moment he wished this flight was going to the States, that he was taking Adriana to a dazzling launch, could introduce her to Fleur and Jonathan, tell her about the company, show her the designs, the concept...

'You OK?'

Instinctively he lowered the laptop screen and turned to look at Adriana, who narrowed her eyes. 'I'm not trying to read your emails,' she said, and ice encased her voice. 'You just seem a bit transfixed, and the pilot has announced we're arriving soon and to put our seat belts back on.'

'Oh.' He clicked his seat belt in and his laptop shut, told himself he couldn't tell her about Easel. It was strictly need-to-know and Adriana didn't need to know. Not yet. Because he could not be one hundred per cent sure he could trust her. He didn't think she'd go public, but how could he be certain? He would never have believed Emily could betray him so thoroughly. In fairness his assessment of Adriana was way more balanced, but even so...if it would benefit Salvington in some way maybe she could be persuaded to break his confidence. An unlikely scenario, but why take the risk?

But he had been rude. 'I apologise,' he said.

She shook her head. 'Sorry you closed the laptop or

sorry you weren't more subtle?' she asked, and he couldn't help but smile.

'Touché.' He paused. 'The latter, but I am sorry.'

'Then apology accepted. I understand.'

But he could hear the hurt in her voice as well, a hurt he understood, but could do nothing about. So it was a relief when the plane began its descent and she turned to look out of the window.

Once they'd got their luggage, they picked up the car he'd hired and soon they were headed towards the villa. 'This is utterly beautiful,' she stated. 'What an incredible place to come to for family holidays.'

'It is beautiful,' he agreed. 'We could drive via the road tunnels, which are an incredible constructive feat in themselves. I believe there are over one hundred tunnels and goodness knows how many bridges. But today I thought we could go the scenic route if you don't mind, although it will take a little longer.'

'I'd like that. Thank you.'

Minutes later she gasped. 'The road is so steep it feels impossible that the car can move forward. But the views are utterly breathtaking.'

'I thought we could stop at the top. It's called Cabo Girão and it's the second highest sea cliff in the world. I believe it's about five hundred and eighty metres above sea level.'

She fell silent after that, clearly allowing him to focus on driving until he pulled into the massive car park at the summit.

He turned to face her. 'About ten years ago they built a glass walkway at the lookout point, a suspended platform of transparent glass. Apparently it is utterly incredible, though it can be a little bit scary. I should have checked if you suffer from vertigo.'

'Nope, not a bit. Let's go!'

As they approached the walkway they fell silent. It was late in the day so the tourists were sparse, and Adriana stepped forward and stopped.

'Whoa.'

'You OK?'

'I'm a tiny bit dizzy, but it's one hundred per cent worth it.'

Instinctively he placed an arm round her shoulder to steady her, and perhaps to steady himself as well. The platform jutted out over the sheer drop that plunged down to the swirl of the ocean below.

'It's like walking on air,' she breathed and now she wrapped her arm round his waist as well, the sensation giving him a funny sense of warmth as they stepped forward together. They stood at the railing and stared out over the panoramic vista, the jut and angle of the landscape, the cliff fronts and sweep of mountains, the stretch of rooftops and then down at the churning surf.

'Look. You can see the fields down there,' he pointed out. 'It's odd to see them so near the sea, but they are dried-up lava streams which makes the soil extra-fertile.'

'They are called *fajas*, aren't they?' She smiled up at him. 'I looked up interesting facts about Madeira. But nothing prepared me for this. It is truly spectacular.'

He nodded, knew that the experience was made better in some way by sharing it with Adriana, seeing the genuine appreciation and awe on her face, the feel of her arm round his waist.

'Thank you for bringing me,' she said. 'It must have been amazing coming here as a child and getting to see all these wonderful things.'

'We didn't really do much sightseeing when we were here,' he said. 'And if we had my parents wouldn't have let me anywhere near a cliff edge. I mean, this wasn't built but they didn't even like driving on any road other than the motorways. They thought it was too dangerous. Some of the roads are pretty narrow and near the edge of very vertiginous cliffs.'

She looked thoughtful. 'Do you think you'll feel like that with your children?'

'No. Or at least if I do I won't act on it. It didn't help me being wrapped in cotton wool. I understand why they did it but at the time I hated it.'

'Of course you did,' she said softly. 'I imagine you must have wanted to take all sorts of risks, and after what happened to you at school it must have been even worse that holidays felt restricted too.'

'Yes. It was hard.' And it had been lonely as well: his parents had wanted him to get to know the 'right sort of people' but it had made making friends with any people impossible because of the swathe of restrictions on his activities.

'Speaking of your parents, your mother called me yesterday. To apologise. Was that your idea?'

Surprise touched him. 'Actually, no, it wasn't. I mean, I did make it clear that I thought her behaviour was abominable and we would not be returning to visit them any time soon, but I didn't ask her to contact you. She did that off her own bat. Was it a real apology?'

Adriana grinned. 'Well, to begin with she said she was sorry for "springing" extra guests on me yesterday—that she should have realised it might be a "bit much".'

He sighed. 'So more of a non-apology.'

'Maybe. So I said she didn't need to apologise, that I was *flattered* that she wanted me to meet old family friends.'

Rob emitted a crack of laughter. 'Good for you. What did she say to that?'

'Actually, she laughed too and said, and I quote, "Admirably said, my dear. I deserved that." Then she apologised again and said she hoped we have a good time in Portugal. So I am going to take that as an olive branch.'

'You should. And see?'

'See what?'

'You handled my mother brilliantly. That was the exact right thing to say to her. Which shows you *do* know the right thing to say.'

Her arrested expression made him laugh and he squeezed her a little closer to him.

'What about your parents?' he asked. 'Have you told them?'

He felt her tense slightly and then she spoke, the words careful. 'I told my mother, but she is going to wait to tell my father. When we have made a final decision.' Before he could respond she stepped away from him and turned. 'I guess we'd better get going. Before it gets dark.'

'Sure. Let's go.'

Adriana was aware of Rob's sideways scrutiny as they walked back to the car and she kept up a bright flow of conversation, having no wish to discuss her conversation with her mother, because she still hadn't really had a chance to process it. Perhaps because she didn't want to.

And once they were in the car she fell to silence so he could focus on driving and she could focus on the scenery, the dusk lit by streetlights that illuminated a village full of thatched cottages, flashes of green fields and everywhere the steep cliffs and curves and bends. Until he said, 'Nearly there,' as they wound their way up another vertiginous mountain road.

And then there it was, a glorious villa that looked as though it was nestled into the cliff itself. Dazzling white walls, blue shutters and a terracotta roof all seemed to gleam in the last few shards of sunlight. 'It's beautiful,' she said.

He parked outside and they climbed out of the car, and she inhaled the smell of the sea, the tang of salt mixed with the scent of hazy sunshine and hibiscus that bloomed in the dusk.

'Come and see inside,' he said, and she followed him in. The villa was open-plan, the large kitchen area well-equipped, the dark marble countertops polished, and leading to a living space complete with wicker armchairs and sofas and luscious green potted plants.

But what caught her attention most was the view, the jut and crag of the mountains, the undulating dark blue of the waves topped with gleams of silver that stretched to meet the horizon, the terracotta roofs of the village houses. As she looked her fingers itched to draw, to try and capture the colours and vibrancy.

'This is amazing—no wonder your parents want to retire here.'

'If you like we could have an evening stroll through the village, find somewhere to eat.'

'That sounds like a plan.'

Ten minutes later they were walking through the picturesque village, and it seemed the most natural thing in the world when he took her hand in his. The village was tiny, only a few hundred metres from end to end, filled with cobbled streets and narrow alleys lined with pretty stone houses and gardens that scented the air with bougainvillea. The whole was interspersed with allotments that boasted grapevines and vegetables galore, and in the middle was a village square with shops and restaurants and a small, white-walled church.

'It's like stepping into a fairy tale,' she said and then

almost wished she hadn't. Because the words were a reminder that this wasn't a fairy tale that ended in love and romance and a happy-ever-after.

As if he guessed her thoughts he looked down at her. 'Well, I am very happy to see that this fairy-tale setting has an actual restaurant, so we don't have to rely on finding a gingerbread house.' He gestured towards a small, busy eatery. 'Does this look OK?'

The restaurant overlooked the sea, its glass-fronted exterior showing a scattering of square tables and booths mostly full with customers, families that crossed several generations, young couples and a few people on their own. The door opened and a tantalising aroma of garlic, seafood and spices wafted out. 'Definitely.'

Once inside they both studied the menu.

'What are you going to have?' he asked.

'I'm not sure. What have you chosen?'

'Trying to avoid food envy again?' he asked, and she shrugged, knew it was foolish. 'I've got an idea. Choose whatever you like and I'll do the same and then we'll go halves.'

The sheer thoughtfulness warmed her and she smiled as the waiter approached. 'Thank you. In that case I'll be adventurous and try the *filete de espada com banana frita e maracujá*. The description written in both Portuguese and English sounded amazing. The swordfish fillet would be soaked in a mixture of flour, egg and parsley and slowly fried, then lemon would be added, and it was accompanied by fried banana and passion fruit.

'And I'll have the *arroz de polvo*.' Adriana quickly scanned his choice before handing the menu back and nodded approval. Octopus, rice and a rich base of tomatoes, onions and the chef's very own spice mix.

'Excelente,' the waiter said.

Once the waiter had gone Adriana glanced round the restaurant, this time paying more attention to the people. Smiled as a woman she assumed to be a grandmother reached out and tickled a toddler safely ensconced in a high chair; the whole family laughed as the child giggled with glee and his parents linked hands behind the chair. Next to that table sat a young man and woman, and as she looked the man reached out for the woman's hand and they exchanged a smile so full of love that Adriana felt a sudden unexpected tear prickle her eyelashes.

'Adriana? You OK?' Rob asked.

'Of course. Just people-gazing. I wonder what we look like to them. A couple? Two friends? Work colleagues?'

'I'm not sure.' He frowned. 'Is something wrong?' He turned slightly, studied the tables she'd been looking at. 'If you're having any doubts, tell me.'

'I'm not.' And she wasn't. She knew it didn't matter, knew that once her parents had been like that young couple and after Stella's birth had even been like the other one. It hadn't lasted and yet for a minute she'd wanted to experience what it felt like to be looked at like that.

'Are you sure? You mentioned fairy tales earlier. Are you sure that isn't what you want?'

She smiled sadly at his perceptiveness. 'I am sure.' She waited as their food arrived, thanked the waiter and then looked down at her plate, carefully halved her portion as he did the same. Looked up and met his gaze, saw the slight crease in his brow and knew he didn't fully believe her. 'It just reminded me of something my mother said— that Salvington was only bricks and mortar and wasn't worth giving up the fairy tale for. I guess her saying that surprised me.' She tasted the food and gave a small appreciative nod at the tang of salt and lemon, that complemented the sweetness of the banana and the sour hint of the passionfruit.'

'Because her fairy tale crumbled around her?'

'Exactly. I also hadn't realised that she feels differently about Salvington from the way Stella and I do. I suppose it's natural.' In truth she felt stupid that it hadn't occurred to her before. 'My father's concerns about Salvington destroyed her marriage.'

'It won't be like that for us,' he said. 'I believe there are different types of happy endings. I want us to be happy but our happy-ever-after won't be based on love with its roller coaster of emotions. It may not be a fairy-tale happy ending but I think it has a chance of being a real one. After all, do you really believe Prince Charming and Cinderella had a great marriage based on one party?'

Adriana grinned suddenly. 'That she went to in a pumpkin.'

'And Sleeping Beauty didn't even get the party.'

'Just one kiss.'

The kisses they had shared shimmered across her mind and she knew the same thought crossed his mind as his gaze snagged on her lips.

'I think we're doing this the right way,' he said softly. 'And it's OK for us to get to our happy ending our way. I think our foundations will be stronger than Cinderella's.'

She nodded. 'You're right.' Of course he was and it was time to put her doubts behind her. Her mother couldn't be right—why would Adriana want a happy-ever-after that was based on something as transitory as love? Answer was, she didn't. So, 'Now hand over your plate,' she said as she picked up her own, ready to swap. 'The swordfish was incredible and now I'd like to try the octopus.'

In fact the whole sharing was symbolic of their partnership, a mutual negotiation and agreement that benefited them both. Their relationship wouldn't be based on deceit and illusion like her relationship with Steve had been. Nor on love like her parents' had been. Nor on the vagaries of an attraction that might not last. This was the right way forward.

CHAPTER TEN

ADRIANA OPENED HER eyes, looked up at the bright white of
the ceiling, turned her head to see the closed slatted blinds
that had plunged the room into darkness and realised she
had no idea of the time. Glanced at the luminous dial of
her watch and swung her legs out of bed. Eight-thirty, definitely time to get up, follow the tantalising smell of coffee and freshly baked rolls. She showered and pulled on
a long grey sundress, pulled her hair back into a ponytail
and ventured into the cool, spacious kitchen.

'Good morning. I went down to the bakery and got
breakfast,' Rob said.

'That looks divine.' Mind you, she thought, so did he.
Hair shower-damp, jeans and a T-shirt that showed the
sculpt and breadth of his shoulders, the muscular strength
of his legs. Enough. Focus on the food, on buttering bread,
dolloping on jam.

'So what would you like to do today?' he asked.

'Honestly? I'd like to have a lazy morning on the beach,
take my book, soak up the sun, then go and do something
more energetic in the afternoon.'

'Sounds good to me.' He rose from the table, refilled
the cafetiere, his back slightly turned. 'I do have to make
a few calls first, some unexpected business—if that's OK.
I'll only be an hour or so, if you want to go without me.'

'That's fine.' Though she had the impression he was over-casual, hiding something, wanting to be rid of her, but dismissed the idea as sheer paranoia. Realised too that this would give her an opportunity to spend an hour alone, a chance to get some sketching done on the beach. She'd brought simple pencils and a sketchbook on the off-chance.

He nodded. 'I'll give you a call before I head down.'

'Sounds good.'

An hour and a half later Adriana was set up on the beach, felt the familiar sense of absorption take over, her whole being focused on trying to get her concept of the landscape onto the paper in front of her. To somehow convey the sense of nature's majesty, the unique beauty of the colours and hues and how they made her feel.

So absorbed in fact that she completely lost track of time until she heard Rob's voice.

'Here you are.'

Panic touched her and without even thinking she rose and spun round, every instinct telling her to hide her work.

'Sorry I was so long.' He looked slightly puzzled. 'So what have you been doing?'

'Nothing.' Spinning back round, she picked up her folder, moved to stuff the sketches into it.

'Adriana? What's wrong?' He stepped backwards. 'If you don't want me to see, that's fine. I'll move away. Sort it out slowly.'

She didn't need telling twice. Quickly she put the pencils back, carefully put the sketches back into the folder, cleared the easel away and turned back round. 'You said you'd call,' she said, aware of how petulant she sounded.

'I thought you might be absorbed in your book or napping. I didn't realise you needed to be warned.' He sounded puzzled rather than angry. 'I am guessing you were sketching.'

'It's a hobby. Something I do for myself, so I don't really talk about it.'

'So not something you feel comfortable sharing.'

'Exactly. As I said, I don't want to talk about it.' Forget petulant—now she was being downright rude. 'I'm sorry,' she said.

'Sorry you were rude or sorry you didn't hear me in time?' he asked.

'Touché,' she responded, echoing their conversation on the plane. Only with the roles reversed. In this case she was the one hiding something. 'And the latter. No one knows about it, that's all. Now you do. So…it would be great if you don't mention it. In the unlikely event it ever came up. With my family. With anyone.'

'Fine.' To her surprise he didn't sound at all judgemental. 'If this is something you want kept private, then of course I will make sure it is.' Calmly he placed the rucksack he was carrying on the sand, opened it and took out a blanket. Shook it out and sat down. 'I hope one day when you're ready you'll feel comfortable showing me your work, but I won't pressure you. We're here to get to know each other better but not to intrude on each other's privacy.'

The words should have been reassuring and yet they made her wonder what he was keeping private from her. What hadn't he wanted her to see on his laptop? She could hardly ask, not when she was unwilling to share her own secret, not when she would have hidden her art from him if she could. And what if his secret was a dark one? After all, she'd trusted Steve, believed in him, and his secret had broken her heart and taken her to the depths of humiliation. She shook the fear off. It had been different with Steve—he'd used her, lied to her, conned her. Rob wasn't doing that— they were negotiating a partnership and within that they were agreeing that each of them had the right to privacy.

She'd just have to trust his secret was as innocent as her own.

'Agreed,' she said and lowered herself onto the blanket, hugged her knees and looked out at the azure blue of the waves.

'Any other hobbies you want to tell me about?' he asked, and now there was a smile in his voice and she told herself to relax.

'Not really. You know I like horses, and I enjoy reading, but most of my spare time I paint.' She pressed her lips together.

'If I promise not to ask to see your work, would you mind telling me a little bit about it? Like when you started?'

She supposed there was no harm in that. 'I started when I was about twelve—Stella thought she'd like to take up art but then she lost interest. I came across all the stuff one day and thought I'd have a go and I was hooked.' It had provided a safe haven, a way of escaping, of losing herself in another world.

'Were you tempted to take it further, study art at college?'

'No.' The idea of showing her work made her feel too vulnerable, the idea of losing something that gave her so much joy too scary. 'I draw and paint for myself.'

'And that's enough?' He lay back on the blanket, looking up at the sky, and she sensed it was so that she wouldn't feel pressured to reply, and that knowledge did seem to make it easier to speak.

'I love the challenge of getting how I feel onto paper. Capturing a moment and what that is all about. I mean, this landscape here—I don't think it's ever really the same from day to day, maybe superficially it is, maybe one summer's day is very like another, but it isn't really. And not just because the cloud formation is different or the sun slightly less bright. It's also about how a person is seeing the world. If I'm happy, a stormy landscape may look different than it does if I'm sad. I find it interesting how much feelings filter through into our pictures. But it's more than that. It's trying to convey beauty without it being wooden. I mean, it's frustrating sometimes because I don't always know how to achieve a perspective I want, but mostly I love it.' She broke off. So much for not talking, once she'd started it seemed she couldn't stop. 'Sorry. I spouted on for ever.'

'No need to apologise. There is nothing wrong with feeling passionate about something. But…are you sure you don't want to do something with all that passion? Exhibitions and—?'

'No.' The idea was terrifying in the extreme. 'It's something I do for myself. The way other people might go running or cook a lovely meal or go to the gym.'

He frowned. 'I have to admit I am now very curious to see what you were sketching.'

For a second she considered the idea. After all, it wasn't as though he would be rude or put her work down the way her father would. At least he'd be polite. But wouldn't that be just as bad? At the moment she could look at her work and it was hers. She could tell herself that it wasn't too shabby, that it didn't matter if it was. But subjecting it to anyone else's gaze was too risky…think how embarrassed Rob would be if he had to try and find something nice to say whilst inwardly laughing. Or worse still, pitying her delusions.

'Sorry,' she said firmly, shaking her head. 'I…can't.' And she needed to close this conversation down, should never have opened up as much as she had. 'How about we build a sandcastle?' she suggested.

He sat up and turned to look at her, a slightly odd look on his face. 'A sandcastle?'

'Yup. I think it would be fun. I haven't built a sandcastle for years. If you need a better reason, it'll test our ability to work together as a team.'

'I don't need an excuse,' he said. 'I was just remembering the last time I built a sandcastle here. I'd made friends with a local boy. He was called Juan, and he spoke Portuguese and I spoke English, but we managed to communicate well enough to start building a castle. But we only got halfway through before we were stopped.'

'Why?'

'My parents didn't approve of me mingling with the locals. Ridiculous, I know, but they marched me off and that was that. When was the last time you built a sandcastle?'

'Funnily enough, mine never got completed either. My mother took Stella and me on a holiday.' One of her mother's few acts of rebellion. Her father had been in the midst of his affair and her mother had said, 'Right. We're going on holiday.'

It had been wonderful. Relaxed and full of laughter, and the three of them had been engrossed in building a sandcastle when her father had arrived. 'He took over, decided it would be better to turn the whole thing into a contest. Him and Stella versus my mother and me. He and Stella raced ahead and finished and I never got to finish mine.' Hadn't wanted to, all the fun sucked away. 'I've always regretted that lost castle.'

'And I've always regretted mine. So I suggest you and I build the best castle ever. Better than anyone's. Deal?'

'Deal. The key, *I* think, is to have wet sand.'

He nodded. 'Agreed. So I suggest we dig a well so we don't have to keep going and getting water from the sea.'

'Sounds good. But we need spades.'

'I'm pretty sure there were some back at the villa. Probably the same ones I used all those years ago.'

A quick trip back and he returned, holding out two spades. 'Red or blue?'

'I'll take blue,' she said, and looked down at the choice for an inordinately long time, suddenly way too aware of him, the sculpt of shoulder muscle, the lithe shape of his forearms and those hands that she still craved to feel on her. As she looked up their gazes met and the flash of desire in his blue eyes sent a shiver through her entire body, wobbled her legs and clenched her tummy with an answering tug of need.

Focus.

'Right. Let's start digging.' Her voice was a husk of its usual self as she forced herself to turn away and set to work.

He nodded and squatted down beside her and she gulped at his sheer proximity, focused on the movement of the spade, the trickle of sand, the quest to dig deep enough for water. But somehow the actions, the rhythm, the scent of the sea, the beating of the sun on the back of her neck all combined to heighten her senses, her awareness of him.

He paused to reach for a water bottle, took off the lid and handed it to her, and now she felt the heat of his gaze as she tipped her head back to drink.

To her fevered imagination it seemed that as they built up the layers of the castle, the tension built up alongside it, her awareness of Rob growing alongside the upward spiral of the smooth sand walls, the turrets shaped so carefully— how could his hands be so deft and sure, pay such attention to detail? As she watched the movement of his fingers, the dextrous flick of his wrist, her mouth dried.

And it wasn't only her—she knew it, even if she didn't quite believe it. She caught the lingering of his gaze on her, could feel the tension in his body as they worked together, and most of all she could see it in his eyes, the dark pupils sending goosepimples over her, and when their hands accidentally touched she thought she might actually combust.

Instead she placed the final seashell in place and jumped to her feet. 'Ta-da!'

'Ta-da, indeed.'

'It's…'

'A work of art,' he said, his deep voice full of meaning as he looked not at the castle but at Adriana, and each word shivered over her skin.

'It is,' she agreed. 'I'll…take a picture.' Send it to her mother and Stella. To give herself something to do so she didn't simply throw herself at him. 'It is a masterpiece and it feels very satisfying to have completed it.' She was babbling now.

'Hmm…' he said. 'I'm not sure satisfied is the exact word to describe how I'm feeling.' Her startled gaze went to his and to her annoyance she could feel a blush rising on her cheeks. 'When I said let's go away together I hadn't factored in how…awkward it might be, fighting the attraction factor.' He paused. 'Assuming I'm not the only one feeling it.'

She shook her head. 'Nope. You are definitely not alone.' She gulped.

'Remind me why we're fighting it?'

'Because we both agreed that the attraction box is ticked and to explore it further is unnecessary and may cloud our judgement when it comes to assessing whether or not this marriage is truly a good idea and whether we are compatible in other ways. More important ways.' The words came out in a rush and felt completely meaningless, syllables that were whirled away by the sea breeze. Because right now nothing felt more important than the simmer of desire. She looked at him across the tartan blanket, against the backdrop of sun, sea and sand, and suddenly judgement seemed irrelevant. She tried to think. 'Or…'

'Yes?' He spoke like a parched man who had seen the glimmer of an oasis.

'Or maybe we're looking at it the wrong way. Right now attraction is still clouding our judgement because all I can think about is the attraction. So maybe acting on the attraction will help. And if it doesn't, well, it doesn't matter.'

'Damned if we do and damned if we don't?' he asked.

'That's about it.'

'In which case…' And then, before he could say any more, she moved across the rug; he exhaled a small sigh of relief and then he'd pulled her down next to him and he was kissing her. Kissing her as though their lives depended on it and in truth that was how it felt as need escalated through her, her hands slipped under his T-shirt and she gasped at the wonder of finally touching him.

'We need to get back to the villa,' he said raggedly. 'Before we get plastered across social media. And I don't think it's the castle they'll be interested in.'

She gave a half-hiccup of laughter and dazedly got to her feet. They quickly grabbed all their stuff, her easel, her sketchbook and the spades, before dusting the sand from themselves briskly and hurrying off.

The walk back seemed interminable, her whole body yearning, desperate, her calves aching as she tried to move faster up the dusty terracotta track.

Then they were inside the villa, dropped everything any which way, and headed to the bedroom.

'Thank God,' he said as they entered, and he was kissing her again, and now his hands were tugging at the sundress, and then her phone buzzed.

'Ignore it.'

She tugged it out of her pocket, about to switch it off, when an image of Stella filled the screen. Both their gazes fell to it and Adriana couldn't help it—the image of her sister's face triggered an instant reaction and she froze.

Unwanted memories streamed through her mind—of Steve, of the last time a man had kissed her, wanted her, made love to her. That was a man who had been fantasising about Stella, thinking of Stella.

No, no, no! Rob wasn't Steve.

No, but he was man who had wanted to marry her sister, spend his life with her, sleep with her, have children with her.

But he never even went on a date with her.

But…it no longer mattered, panic swathed her, an insidious fear that she was being made a fool of yet again.

'Adriana?'

'I'm sorry… I…'

'It's OK. We don't have to do anything you don't want to do.' He moved away, his voice abrupt. 'Just give me a minute though.'

'I am so sorry, Rob.'

'It's OK. I would never want you to do anything you didn't want to. Or pretend…'

'No.' The word fell from her lips with vehemence. Because she could see more than confusion in his blue yes. She saw hurt and something she couldn't quite comprehend. 'I wasn't pretending.' How could he think that, why would he think that?

'You changed your mind.' He lifted a hand as if to take hers and then dropped it. 'That is OK.'

'No, it isn't. I mean, it is, but it's not that. I mean…' Oh, God, why couldn't she think straight? Probably because her body was on edge, roiling with frustration and hurting from the poisonous slew of memories. 'I did but I wasn't faking.' She took a deep breath. 'I'd like to explain.' Well, she wouldn't like to, but she knew if she didn't this would become something that could cause an ongoing problem. Because he didn't believe her even if she didn't understand why. And she wanted to soothe the hurt she could see shadow his blue eyes. 'But not here.'

He nodded. 'Come on. I know where we can go.'

CHAPTER ELEVEN

As THEY WALKED to the car Rob breathed in the flower-scented air and wondered if he even wanted to hear Adriana's explanation. Yet it was always better to know and face the truth. Even if it meant being hurt. Because better to know now if the attraction factor was fake on Adriana's side.

Yet could she have faked the kiss, the passion, the need? Stupid question—of course she could. Emily had, after all, taken him in completely.

Why shouldn't this be a rerun? Adriana wanted to marry him for the sake of Salvington—she had said herself she would do anything for Salvington. So why wouldn't she do what Emily had done? Lie back and think of…in Adriana's case, the splendour and beauty of her ancestral home?

As the thoughts streamed and whirled in his mind, he forced them into abeyance and focused on the drive, followed the sat nav to his chosen destination—a glorious botanical garden, a place where he sensed it would be easier for them to speak, a setting where if it became too much, the beauty of the place, the warmth, the colours would help. Give them breathing space.

Once they'd parked they walked to the entrance, purchased tickets and entered.

'Is it all right if we walk for a bit?' she asked. 'Then talk? It'll give me a chance to gather my thoughts.'

He nodded and for a while they did exactly that, wandered the beautifully structured paths, took in the array of exotic plants, Azaleas and orchids from the Himalayas, Scottish heather, and a collection the placards informed them were cycads. They surveyed the thick trunks and the sprouting crown of large, stiff, dark green leaves.

Then onwards until they came to a massive lake. 'Shall we sit?' he asked, and she nodded.

'Yes. Thank you for bringing me here. I feel a bit more together. And I want to tell you, explain what happened back there.'

He tensed, tried to relax his shoulders, studied her face as she pushed her fringe away in the familiar impatient gesture.

'Go ahead,' he said. 'I'm listening.'

'I wasn't faking. I was worried *you* were.' Her voice was small now, small and sad and vulnerable.

Her words made his head swim. 'Me?' He could only hope utter incredulity could be housed in such a short syllable.

'I saw Stella's image on the screen and...'

Rob took a deep breath. 'I'm sorry. I don't understand.'

She looked toward the lake where Koi carp floated and occasionally gave a lazy jump. 'Stella is... Well, Stella is Stella—she is beautiful, smart, funny, and she does have that wow factor. If you put me and Stella next to each other any man would choose Stella, given the choice. When we saw her I panicked.'

'But why? I told you already I'm not remotely attracted to Stella.'

'But you were going to marry her. She was your first choice.'

He sensed he was on complicated terrain. 'Yes. But it wasn't a choice between her and you. Your offer wasn't on the table when Stella and I made our plans. What happened between us was between us. You and me.'

'I want to believe that.'

'Then why don't you?' He was trying to get it, he really was, but it didn't make sense to him. And he couldn't help but wonder if she was trying to spare his feelings in some way, find an excuse.

She twisted her hands together, looked around as if to take strength from their surroundings, the verdant greens and the bloom and the splash of the waterfall as it flowed smoothly into the blue waters of the lake. 'I told you that I had a serious boyfriend who I loved but he didn't love me. There was a bit more to it than that. I met Steve at a party, one that Stella dragged me to. It was a charity shindig and she was really insistent, so I went. Steve was there. He started talking to me and it was…nice. Extra-nice because it was unusual as he didn't seem to be interested in Stella. And at the end of the evening he asked me on a date.'

She said it as though she couldn't understand why and he wanted to say, But of course he would, why wouldn't he?

'And after that…he swept me off my feet. I mean, with hindsight I should have seen the cracks, but I didn't. He was very interested in meeting the family and sometimes we'd double-date with Stella. But he seemed to adore *me*. So I fell and I fell hard. Then one day I found a key at the back of one of his drawers—I was looking for a stamp or something. I wouldn't have given it a thought except there were some photos with the key. I wasn't snooping to start with, but I saw the top of a photo and I recognised Stella. Turned out all the photos were of her. I can still remember the coldness in the pit of my stomach as I tried to tell myself it was OK.'

He recognised that feeling all too well and he reached out to take her hand in his.

'Rightly or wrongly, then I did snoop. I found a locked shed at the bottom of the garden. It was…like a shrine to Stella.'

Jeez. He could only try to imagine how that must have felt, to walk in and see that.

'Massive photos of her everywhere, press cuttings, printed-out internet stories, glossy magazines. And a diary. Saying how he felt about her, talking about me, how every time he touched me he thought of Stella, fantasised about my sister. How he adored me as a sort of conduit, the closest he could ever come to her.'

Anger filled him, a desire to go and find Steve and make him see the error of his ways. 'What a creep…what a low-level, slimy waste of space. I wish… I wish I could have spared you that, I am so very sorry that he put you through that.'

'I haven't dated anyone since and today when I saw Stella's picture on the phone I…it all came back to me and I froze, all I could remember were those awful memories, the humiliation of it all and how I couldn't go through that again.'

'I get it.' Of course he did. He moved forward, squatted down in front of her, still holding her hand. 'I swear to you that the only person in my mind, the only person I was thinking of was you. That is the truth. I wish I could make you believe me. Because I know how horrible it is to go through what you did.' He hesitated but knew that he wanted to tell Adriana if sharing his own hurt would help her with hers, make her know that he understood her pain. 'Shall we walk whilst we talk?' he asked.

She nodded and he rose, pulling her gently up with him,

kept her hand in his as they started to walk the cobbled paths lined with Portuguese tiles from centuries gone past.

'Emily was like Steve in a lot of ways,' he began. 'Her interest wasn't in me…it was in my wealth and position. With hindsight that should have been obvious, *I* should have seen the cracks. But I didn't. I believed her, believed she loved me for me, believed she was attracted to me. But she didn't and she wasn't. The whole thing was fake. She was still in love with her ex, who was in prison. But she wanted the glory of being a countess, and when I proposed she accepted. Then her ex came out of prison and she started seeing him. Faking it with me whilst seeing him. Eventually she got caught on camera and the proverbial hit the fan.' Her hand tightened around his and she moved closer to him, their steps completely in sync. 'She thought she could sweet talk me back, thought I'd forgive her, but I didn't. Suddenly I could see how fake it all was.' It had been a true eye opener and the worst of it was how sure she'd been that she could bring him round, lure him back in, so sure of her absolute power over him. A power he would never give a woman again. 'I told her it was over and she was furious.'

Adriana nodded. 'As though it were your fault.'

'Exactly.'

'Steve was like that. He couldn't see that he was at fault. It was as though he expected me to understand how he felt about Stella and actually be grateful that I was "the moon to her sun". He seemed surprised when I told him it was over.'

'That's how Emily was.' Her beautiful face had contorted with confusion and then when she realised her hold on him was truly broken she'd lost her temper. 'She said she'd make me pay and she did. She took her story to the press and she milked it for all it was worth. Tore me to shreds in the most humiliating way possible.' His skin still crawled at the memory. 'Emily discussed my prowess in the bedroom, or lack of.' In ways he wished he could eradicate. 'In one of her interviews she told the interviewer she'd lain back and thought of her ex. She also made it plain what a credulous fool I'd been, but somehow she did it in a way that made me look like an upper-class twit and she was wholesome and naïve and taken in. That somehow I'd tricked her, dazzled her with money but in the end true love had won through.'

'Even as she was pocketing the hefty fees from the press.'

'Yup. Got it in one.'

He kept his tone mocking, light and full of self-deprecation, braced himself for the pity that he would see in her grey eyes. But there was no pity, there was compassion and there was empathy—of course there was, because she understood implicitly what he had gone through just as he understood her pain.

But there was anger in her eyes too. 'I am so sorry, Rob. Sounds to me like she and Steve would have been a perfect match. Thank you for telling me and I understand now why you thought maybe I was faking. I wasn't.'

The last two words were simple and impossible to disbelieve.

'I believe you.'

'Good.' Now her face lit up in a smile so delightful that it almost hurt him to look at it, his chest squeezing with a warmth he didn't understand. She gazed into his eyes and he could see a tentative trust dawn. Then she leant over and brushed her lips against his, the sweetness, the hesitation, the sheer momentousness of the gesture blasting him with a wave of warmth and desire. She pulled away. 'Good,' she said again. 'Because I believe you too.'

'Good.' Now he pulled her back into his arms, oblivious of other tourists strolling past them. And he kissed her. Properly kissed her, savoured the taste of her, the scent of the flowers mingled with her vanilla shampoo creating a sensory miasma that dizzied him as she wrapped her arms around his neck, pressed her body against his in the language of yearning and need.

Until finally, as a reminder of where they were, a pointed cough broke the spell. They broke apart and she gave a gasp of laughter. 'I... What now?' she asked.

'Now? I think we need to go, get back to the villa. As fast as we can.'

'Let's go.'

They walked hand in hand, and as they walked the beauty of their surroundings made only the most distant impression on him, a sense of contrasting colours, the red of tiles on pagodas against the dark green fronds and bursts of colour from exotic flowers. A glimpse of two marble dogs that he vaguely recalled were mythical animals from the Orient, usually found guarding the entrance to temples.

They gathered pace, barely paused even when they spotted a flock of swans, pristine white, floating lazily on the lake, a stray peacock seen from the corner of his eye. All of this served as a mere backdrop to Adriana, a scene that preceded the sight of their destination. Finally they exited the gardens, made their way down the steep decline to the car park and he noticed almost mechanically that his fingers were shaking as he fumbled with the keys.

Once in the car he focused, resisted the urge to put his foot on the accelerator and speed all the way back. Deep breath and a quick smile at Adriana, who smiled back at him, a smile full of promise.

Then, with a muttered curse at every red light, a sense of disbelief as they got stuck behind the slowest lorry in the whole world, finally they were back at the villa.

They scrambled out of the car and raced inside straight to her bedroom, and instinct took over as he gathered her into his arms, revelled in the glorious rightness of the sensations, the taste, the smell, the feel of her against him. And this time, as he tumbled her back onto the bed, he knew there was nothing on this earth that would or could stop them.

CHAPTER TWELVE

ADRIANA OPENED HER eyes, aware of a hazy sense of wellbeing, of glorious, exhausted satiation. She kept her breathing steady, not wanting to disturb Rob, revelled in his arm flung over her chest, his breath warming her bare shoulder.

The previous hours had been magical in their beauty, the joy, the laughter, the intensity and the aftermath, and the idea that they could share this for ever seemed impossible to contemplate. Adriana didn't understand it, hadn't known it could be like this, knew now what Stella had meant, knew too that, like it or not, it would be hard not to let the wonder of this connection affect how she felt about wanting to marry him. Who wouldn't want this for the rest of her life?

Warning bells began to peal. Slow down. Perhaps her parents had started out with this level of attraction—it hadn't led to happiness. Rob had been honest about his attraction to Emily—but attraction could be faked, could change, die, wither, and so she must not let it taint any decision they came to.

But getting to know Rob better here in Portugal had shown her other good things. He'd been understanding of her need for privacy with her art and he'd been more than understanding about Steve. She felt a strange sense of warmth and lightness at having actually spoken about Steve, told the horrible truth to someone.

She'd told nobody, not a soul, unable to share the depths of her humiliation, endure the scourge of pity her tale of woe would evoke. But she hadn't seen pity in Rob's blue eyes, she'd seen empathy. And she understood why. When she thought of Emily her hands clenched into fists—at least her own humiliation had been private, not splashed across the papers.

She glanced sideways at Rob, momentarily distracted by the length of his dark eyelashes, which contrasted with the blondness of his hair. Hair spiked by sleep, his features more relaxed now but still craggy and well-defined. And a sense of optimism warmed her.

They had both endured pain and hurt because of love—maybe now they could forge a calm, contented union. Calm? Contented? Her hormones jeered—there had been nothing calm about last night. But that was attraction—that was separate from the day-to-day life and arrangements of a convenient relationship.

She shifted slightly and smiled a sleepy, happy smile just as he opened his eyes.

'Morning,' he said. 'That's a big smile.'

'I was thinking if we did get married how much fun it would be having you on tap, so to speak.'

He blinked sleep away. 'Feel free to turn me on any time you like.'

She gave a gurgle of laughter even as desire shivered through her, and then in one deft movement he swung her up so she straddled him and smiled the wickedest smile she'd ever seen. 'No time like the present,' he said.

An hour later they were entwined together in a tangle of sheets and, dropping a kiss on her shoulder, he sat up. 'You stay here and I will go and sort out breakfast, and then I think we should spend the day exploring. There's a town near by that I'd like to show you.'

'Sounds good.' Right now she suspected anything would sound good.

'Give me half an hour.'

It was more like an hour before the tantalising waft of coffee and croissants drifted into the bedroom, and as Adriana entered the kitchen it was to see the patio table set with a delicious array of food.

'I am ravenous,' she declared as she heaped her plate, then said. 'So where are we going?'

'It's a historic town, with a magnificent cathedral, beautiful churches, cobbled streets and lots of restaurants. And…something else I think you'll like.'

'Tell me.'

He shook his head. 'Nope. It's a surprise.'

Warmth touched her—no one had ever surprised her before. But Rob was surprising in more ways than one and her earlier optimism burgeoned inside her. They could make this work—they were building a base for a future together. Why would they need love when they had this? They liked each other, were forging a friendship, and on top of that they had attraction. Rob truly found her attractive. He was kind and civil and polite. They both needed to marry someone quickly, they both wanted a child, neither of them wanted love. This could work.

She took one last gulp of coffee. 'Then what are we waiting for? Let's go.'

Half an hour later they reached the bustling historic town, parked the car and started to wander through the winding streets that dipped up and down. Paused to browse the market stalls where fruit and flowers burst with colour and her fingers tingled to paint the scene. Poles were hung with bright bunches of dried chillies, wicker baskets of wares. Green guavas, a sample cut open to display the succulent pink inside, purple passionfruit with vivid yellow-orange flesh speckled with seeds sat alongside the more familiar bananas and grapes.

'I'm not even sure I know what some of those fruits are. Look at those—they look a bit like oddly shaped tomatoes.' She pointed at the small, round, ridged fruit that were varying shades of orange and red.

The stall owner overheard her question. 'They are called *pitanga*. They come here from Brazil. Try one. The more orange the fruit the more bittersweet…the darker it is the sweeter.'

As they walked on the scent of fruit mixed with the fresh bloom of flowers, the stalls all bustling, the sound of the vendors' chatter and cries floated on the balm of the breeze as they left the market behind. Walked along mosaic-tiled pathways towards an older part of town.

'We're nearly there,' he said. Now curiosity did start to unfurl inside her, his smile looking so full of excitement, anticipation even, and she came to a halt.

'Where?' she asked.

'You'll have to wait and see.'

'OK.'

They walked a little further and then slowed down as they approached a long, winding cobbled street, ablaze with colour and artwork.

She paused, trying to assimilate it all. Realised that every door on the street hosted a different picture, a rectangle of individual artwork, the variety so immense it blew her mind.

'This is… I don't have words.'

'It's pretty awesome,' he said. 'I've never seen it—it wasn't here when I was a child but my parents mentioned it a few years back. This area was very run down, and the local government decided to try and change that. So local artists were all given the chance to paint the doors and now people come here specially to see this street, which has made it busy and so local businesses are thriving—cafes, shops and a couple of art galleries.'

As he spoke they walked down the street and she studied the different styles and techniques on display. 'That is so clever—I wish I could do it...the trompe l'oeil style. I'd love to do a massive canvas and manage to make it look three-dimensional. Manage to actually deceive the eye like this does. I mean, it feels as if I could walk straight into the garden. Oh, and this—this is brilliant, I love it.'

'Thank you.'

She whirled round to see a dark-haired woman smile at her. 'I am Isabella Rocha, the artist,' the woman explained.

'Oh, wow. That's amazing.' Adriana smiled at the woman. 'I love it, the colour, the lines, how alive it is. And how you've captured the detail.'

'Thank you. I think you must be Adriana.' Isabella Rocha turned to Rob. 'And you must be Rob.'

Adriana blinked as Rob said, 'Surprise. I did some research, saw that Ms Rocha was exhibiting here at a new gallery and I had the feeling you'd like her work. I thought you may want to meet her.'

'Call me Isabella, please. I also said I would give you a sneak preview of the exhibition,' she explained.

'That is really kind.'

'Well, yes, but I also persuaded Rob here to help a little with a charitable foundation I am part of, one that helps impoverished artists.'

Rob nodded acknowledgement and then smiled at Adriana. 'I'll meet you back here in an hour or so. I thought you may like to spend some time with Isabella on your own.' Warmth touched her because she knew why he was going; because she'd said her art was private to her and by going it would allow her to ask Isabella questions she may not feel comfortable doing with him there.

Adriana followed Isabella into the art gallery where she studied the paintings, listened to Isabella talk about her inspiration, where she had trained, how she worked. The whole experience was wonderful, and she couldn't believe an hour had gone past when the door opened and Rob came in.

'Thank you so much for showing me round. I feel truly privileged.'

'I enjoyed myself,' Isabella said. 'I was wondering… there's an opening party tonight. Would you like to attend? I am quite nervous. The owner is a celebrity, a famous actor. It would be nice to have a genuine fan of my work there. And a couple of friendly faces.'

Adriana's mind raced. A celebrity party? Nightmare scenario, surely. And yet…maybe it wasn't. For a start it would be the height of rudeness to decline, but more than that, this was a chance to see if she could put her money where her mouth was. See if she could fulfil Rob's faith in her. He'd said she could be a countess if she wanted to. Could hold her own in social situations—maybe this was the place to start.

'We'd love to,' she heard her voice say, and saw the look of surprise on Rob's face.

'Yes. Thank you,' he added. 'We would.'

'Marvellous.' Isabella took out a card and scribbled on the back of it. 'Here are the details. I look forward to seeing you both tonight.'

Once they had left, Adriana turned to Rob.

'She is amazing. Thank you so much for arranging that.'

'I'm glad you liked her. And I'm sorry about the party. I didn't know about that.'

She shook her head. 'Don't be sorry. I want to do this—

maybe parties can be fun.' If you had the right person by
your side, if you felt liked and desired. It occurred to her
that this must be how Stella felt all the time and it was a
way she had never felt before. 'But I need to go shopping.'
She glanced at her watch. 'How about I meet you back here
in, say, two hours? Is that OK?'

'That is fine. Unless you want some help.'

'Nope. I'm good.' Because now *she* wanted to surprise *him*.

Rob knotted his tie and gave his reflection a cursory glance.
Everything in place, shirt properly buttoned, cuff links in,
dinner jacket not a bad fit for a hired suit. He felt a sense
of anticipation as he exited the bedroom and stood in the
lounge area of the villa. Adriana had seemed pleased with
her purchases and, whilst he had sensed that she was nervous about the upcoming party, he also believed her when
she said she wanted to go.

'Here I am.'

He turned at the sound of her voice and his breath
hitched in his throat. She looked absolutely stunning, and
all he could do was stare at her. The dress was grey, her
favoured colour, but it was a silvery grey and the material
shimmered over her body. The spaghetti straps, the V-neck,
the artfully placed necklace, the subtle slit down the side
all combined to render him speechless, inspired a burning
desire to tug her into the bedroom and remove the dress
inch by tantalising inch.

'You like it?'

'I definitely, one hundred per cent like it. You look incredible.' And it wasn't just the dress. Her hair shone and
was pulled back in an elegant yet simple arrangement, so
for once her face was in full view, no fringe in sight. Her
grey eyes sparkled and she'd applied a light layer of make-

up that emphasised the beauty of her lips and the classic slant of her cheekbones.

'You don't look so bad yourself,' she said, walking over to him, and again his lungs threatened to give up the ghost as she reached him and her sheer proximity dizzied him, the vanilla scent, the sheer kissability of her lips.

She smiled up at him, clearly read the desire in his eyes, and her own eyes darkened and she caught her lip in her teeth.

'Later,' she said on a whisper.

'Is that a promise?'

She smiled at him again, a smile that lit up her whole face as she grabbed his tie and pulled him towards her. 'It's a cast-iron guarantee.'

'I'll hold you to it.' He took her hand in his. 'And you're OK?'

'Yes. I'm nervous, but I'm OK. I've worked out that if I want to give this proposed marriage of ours a chance then I need to be able to do this, and today… I think I at least look the part.'

'You've nailed it. So let's go and wow the room.'

And Adriana did exactly that. From the moment they entered the room, a large, clean space with white walls on one side and cork walls on the other, ambiently lit with strategically placed lights that highlighted the different exhibitions, she didn't put an elegantly high-heeled foot wrong. And as he watched her chat about art, discuss local politics, and circulate whilst expertly managing to sample the canapes and hold a glass of champagne he wondered why on earth she had ever felt she couldn't do this. He was aware too that with each passing hour it became more likely that they would be able to conclude a successful negotiation, that this was most likely the woman he would spend the rest of his life with, would be the mother of his children.

A life where he managed the family estate and ran Easel, where she fulfilled all the roles and duties that befell a countess, and helped on the estate as well, a job he hoped she'd enjoy. A niggle of doubt touched him—would she enjoy that, working for Darrow where she didn't have the love of the place, the love that came of family pride and ancestry? But of course there would be their children, children he knew she would love and cherish. But children she was having now out of duty and, whilst he knew that wouldn't compromise her love for them, he was sure that if you took Salvington out of the equation Adriana may not choose to have a family right now. Wouldn't choose to have a family with him. Was this arrangement truly what she wanted, underneath it all?

He looked at her, so vital, so enthusiastic about Isabella Rocha's paintings. She was studying a picture now alongside the artist and another painter, asking questions, so focused, so alive.

And he saw she was in her element, her milieu, and he could no longer believe that art was simply a hobby for her; the equivalent of a morning run.

This was something truly important to her and a qualm struck him. He'd made a decision to keep his role in Easel alive, to do what he wanted to do alongside his duty. Why wasn't Adriana doing the same, and could he really believe she wouldn't come to regret prioritising Salvington over everything else?

'You OK?' Now she was by his side, looking up at him with a hint of concern.

'I'm fine. I've been enjoying watching you.' He smiled at her. 'I take it you're enjoying yourself.'

'Yes, I am. Isabella is incredible. And she's so kind as well—she doesn't mind me asking questions. She's inspirational.'

'Did you tell her you draw and paint yourself?'

'Of course not.' She looked aghast.

'Why not? Why don't you show her your work? See what she thinks.'

'No. There is no way I would impose on her good nature like that. Really there is no point.'

He frowned and she looked up at him and he could see panic in her grey eyes, cursed himself for being a fool. Talk about raining on her parade. 'That's fine,' he said lightly. 'It was just an idea.'

'Well, I've got a few ideas too for later,' she said. 'I think it's probably time to head back now, don't you?'

CHAPTER THIRTEEN

ADRIANA GLANCED ACROSS at Rob as they drove back to the villa, the darkness outside dotted with the occasional car light, the air thick with the sweet scent of hibiscus. His expression still held the same seriousness it had at the party and for a minute a sense of foreboding touched her.

'Is everything OK?' she asked, wondering suddenly if she'd done something wrong.

'Everything is fine.' The warmth of his voice reassured her. 'I've just been doing some thinking.'

'Sounds ominous,' she said, trying to keep her voice light.

'Nope. There's something I want to talk to you about. That's all.'

Talk was the last thing she'd been planning on doing. 'Can't it wait till morning?' she said softly. 'I thought we had other plans.'

This drew a smile. 'I hadn't forgotten, but I still want to talk first.'

The rest of the journey was completed in silence and once back at the villa she watched as he clicked the kettle on, made tea, which they carried to the kitchen table, sat down.

He'd shrugged off his jacket and now he unknotted his

tie, and despite everything she felt the now all too familiar tug of desire in the pit of her tummy.

'So what do you want to talk about?' she said.

'You,' he said. 'Or more specifically your art.'

Adriana frowned. Whatever she'd expected, it hadn't been this. 'I told you. It's a hobby. I also told you I didn't like talking about it.'

'I know and I'm sorry, but we need to talk about it. Because I watched you tonight and earlier with Isabella. You were in your element and it sounded to me as though you really know what you are talking about, that this is a passion with you, something really important. So I don't understand why you don't want to talk about it. Why you haven't pursued it.'

'Because I don't want to,' she said, her voice flat.

'Because of Salvington?' he asked, gently. 'Because you feel you should work on the estate? At the expense of your art?'

'No! I told you, art is a hobby.' She was beginning to feel like a parrot.

'But are you sure you don't want it to be more than that?'

'Yes! I'm sure. Really.' She frowned. 'Why is it bothering you?'

'Because I don't want you to give up on something important to you because of Salvington. It doesn't have to be a choice. I want you to know that you can be a countess and an artist if that's what you want. I don't want your love of Salvington, or a sense of duty, to prevent you from pursuing this.' Warmth touched her at the fact that he cared, truly cared.

'This really matters to you.'

'Yes, it does.' He couldn't marry her if he knew she would regret it, knew he had to make her see the lesson he'd learnt himself. Even if that meant trusting her. Could he trust her? He could—he knew now that he could. Knew too that he wasn't getting through to her, could see it in the set of her chin, the fold of her arms. 'And it should matter to you as well. You only have one life, and you mustn't be bound by duty alone. I know how that feels.'

'I don't understand.'

'I told you how for my parents I was a miracle baby, and as such they were over-protective. But they weren't over-protective for *me*—it was the heir to Darrow who had to be kept safe at all costs.' Rob continued, 'I do understand their pride in our lineage—I do. And I do love Darrow. But…' He looked across at her and she could see the shadows in his eyes. 'But I don't feel it the way my parents do, or the way you do.'

'That's hardly surprising. I know your parents meant well but that isn't the way to engender love—you must have resented something that held you back from doing what you wanted to do.' How could a boy forced to do his duty, burdened and weighed down, not allowed to do anything he wanted in the name of that duty, made to fear he wasn't good enough, actually embrace it wholeheartedly? 'I love Salvington because I was allowed to forge my own connection with it, and maybe in times to come you will do that with Darrow.' And she vowed there and then to help him do just that.

'Perhaps. At the very least, I believe that it will be possible to do my duty to Darrow and have more than that. Find a balance. And I have found a way to do that.' He hesitated. 'I am telling you this in absolute confidence.'

'I understand.' She reached out and covered his hand with hers. 'I give you my word I won't break that confidence.'

'After Emily, when it had all gone so spectacularly wrong, I brokered a deal with my parents. They are get-

ting old now and they want me to take over, which is fair
enough. I asked for two years, two years in which I could
go and do whatever I wanted. I thought it would give me
a chance to get over Emily, so I promised after that time
I would come back, settle down, take over the estate and
marry suitably. They agreed.'

'So you went to the States and you discovered a different life.'

'Yes. As I've said, I was plain Rob Wilmington there.
And I loved it.' Of course he had, after a life bound by
duty, weighed down by his identity. 'The opportunity to
discover what my life might have been like if I wasn't who
I truly am was exhilarating. That's where I met Fleur and
Jonathan, a couple in the house I was renting a room in.
We became friends. One night we ended up talking and I
got an idea. For a business. An idea for a website that offers people the chance to make their own websites—I know
there are a few of those around but we came up with a way
to make it super-easy and almost free. We had some added
angles, ways of using social media, video clips, and a way
to not only use stock clips and artwork but also make your
own and market it. Anyway, the next day I thought, why
not actually go for it?' He gave a half-laugh. 'I persuaded
Fleur it could be a success and she agreed to it and Jonathan agreed to front it.'

'Because you wanted to keep out of it?'

'Yes. I didn't want anyone to work out who I really
was—I wanted to be sure I'd achieved this as plain Rob
Wilmington. And I did.' The simple words held a simple
pride. 'Our partnership worked and we went for it and…
it was amazing. In those two years we've got to the point
where we are ready to launch Easel.' It was a good name,
she thought. Combining the ease of use with the artistic
side of it. 'For now I am going to keep out of the limelight,

take a more background consultancy role. I don't want anyone to know of my involvement yet.' That was why he'd told no one, she realised—realised too what a leap of faith it was for him to trust her with this. 'Because I will keep my promise to my parents, I will learn the ropes on Darrow, I will be a good earl when my time comes and I will do my duty by my land, ready to pass on to the next generation.' She could hear pride in his voice, understood that he did love his land, but not exclusively. 'But then I will get a good estate manager and I will do both. I will be part of taking Easel global, to growing my company alongside working for Darrow.'

'That sounds…like a fantastic plan. I am truly happy for you.'

'Thank you, and if you wanted to play an active part in helping run Darrow of course you can. But my point is, you don't have to. If you want to pursue your art I would support you in any way I can. I understand how much you love Salvington but that love doesn't have to be exclusive—you can follow a different dream too.'

'I… I don't know if I can,' she said. Wasn't even sure if she wanted to.

'Why not?' he asked. 'I know it's a scary idea, doing something different, but I also know the joy it can bring. Building up Easel, there were times when we thought it would fail, times when I wondered if I could do it, if anyone would pay attention to my ideas without the glitter and shine my title and position gives them. But… I believed in my idea, and that belief got me through the doubts.'

'Maybe that's it, then. I don't believe.'

He frowned. 'Truly? You don't believe your work is good?' He looked at her as if she were a puzzle he was trying to unlock. And whilst the thought unnerved her, the idea that he was interested, that he cared, still warmed her.

Adriana sighed, cradled her mug in her hands and gave the question some thought. 'I… I don't know. Sometimes I think it is awful, rank amateur stuff that a child of five could do better, and other times, occasionally, I think it's OK. But mostly I try not to analyse it because I don't want to put myself off doing it.'

'But why not show someone? Your family? Why keep it a secret?'

'Because I can't bear for something precious to me to be destroyed,' she said softly. Knew Rob deserved a real explanation, deserved the truth after what he'd shared with her and because he did truly care, believed it was important.

'Tell me,' he said softly.

'When I first started drawing it really was a hobby, but I soon realised how much I loved it and that's when I knew I needed to keep it to myself. You see, my father…' She paused, twisted her hands together, and then in a deft movement reached up and let her hair out of its bun, ran her hands through it and for the first time in days allowed her fringe to hide her eyes. 'My father…he blamed me for all the problems with Salvington. My parents were told I was a boy at the gender scan—they weren't as sophisticated in those days, I suppose, and there is always some margin for error. Anyway, they believed I was the son and heir. I wasn't. Even worse than that, my mother developed endometritis after me and, rightly or wrongly, my father blamed me for that as well. Well, blamed me and my mother, really. The bottom line is he has always loathed the sight of me.'

'I had no idea—that is appalling.'

She shrugged. 'I sort of get it. I mean, I know it is completely wrong but his love for Salvington isn't rational, any more than perhaps your parents' is for Darrow. But your parents got what they wanted—an heir. My father didn't. He has never blamed Stella—he adores her. No matter what she did. It's not her fault and I know she has tried to show him that she isn't perfect but to him she can do no wrong. But me—he takes any opportunity to show his dislike. So as a child I learnt the best thing to do was for me to keep out of sight. That protected our mother. I mean, he never hurt us physically but…'

'Words can be weapons too,' he said. 'So you didn't tell him about your art because you knew he'd tear it to pieces, tell you you had no talent. I'm guessing too that if he has spent your whole life putting you down it's hard for you to believe in yourself. Even more so when it is something so important to you.' He leaned forward now, took her hands in his, and his clasp made her feel safe. 'You said you "sort of" get it. Well, I don't, and I don't think you should either. The way your father has treated you…it's wrong, Adriana. Truly wrong—it makes my blood boil with anger. It is unfair, unwarranted, unjustified and you did not deserve it. Now you've told me this it makes me admire you even more, for who you are despite what you've been through. And it makes me even more convinced that you should take your art further. Though I truly understand why you haven't.'

'Thank you. I feel…lighter. Maybe I can pluck up the courage to think about doing something more with my art.'

'Would you show me?' he asked and then immediately shook his head. 'Sorry. Forget that. I have no right to ask that.'

'Yes, you do. But it feels unfair to show you—if it is totally pants I don't want you to have to tell me.'

He shook his head. 'I think lots of famous artists' work is pants,' he said. 'That's the beauty of art—it is an opinion. I wanted to see it because it's important to you, not to judge it.'

Adriana took a deep breath, knew that Rob had entrusted her with his secret, knew she could trust him not to hurt her feelings, knew too that if her work was rank and amateur he would be the best person to break it to her.

'I don't have much with me, only the sketch I did on the beach and a few bits that were in my portfolio.' She got to her feet. 'I'll go and get them.'

A few minutes later she entered the room, her heart pounding in her ribcage. This was the first time she'd ever shown anyone anything she had created and her nerves fluttered and twisted as she handed the sketchbook over.

He took it, gave her a reassuring smile, and she forced herself to keep her gaze on him, wanted to see his reaction, wanted the unvarnished truth.

His face remained smooth as he studied the sketches. The unfinished one of the beach and some others, a drawing of woodland, a field of flowers... 'I used the sketches as a basis for some paintings.' She scrolled down her phone and found the woodland painting. He took the phone, studied the painting and then looked up at her.

'I think they're amazing,' he said. 'There's something about them, a way you have of capturing a mood, or a moment in time. I think for authors it's called having a "unique voice", and you have something. I know I've only seen a sample of your sketches, but when we get back I'd love to see more and I'd love to see the paintings. And I think you should do something with this, Adriana. I do.'

A surge of happiness washed over her, because she knew he wouldn't say that, wouldn't let her risk making a fool of herself by showing Isabella or anyone else if they were rubbish.

'Thank you.' She didn't know what else to say—instead she moved over and leant down to kiss his cheek. 'Really.'

In an instant he'd tugged her down onto his lap.

'Thank you for showing me. For trusting me with something so precious to you.'

They sat in a comfortable, warm silence for a while, and then she rose and smiled down at him. 'I think I have a promise to keep and right now I could use some help taking this dress off.'

'Then I'm your man,' he said.

The words seemed to resonate round her head. Her man. The idea was heady enough to make her dizzy.

CHAPTER FOURTEEN

ROB PUT THE kettle on, whistled as he scooped coffee into the cafetiere and cracked some eggs into a bowl. Today he was opting for a breakfast of omelettes served with fresh bread. He chopped the green peppers he'd bought at the market early that morning and smiled as he recalled the rest of his purchases and arrangements.

He watched the onions sizzle in the pan and switched off the potatoes he'd brought to a boil. As he did so his mind revolved around his plans and his smile widened as he turned to see Adriana enter. In one hand was a towel she used to dry the glossy brown hair.

'Good morning.'

She glanced at her watch. 'It's barely still morning,' she said. 'Why didn't you wake me up?'

'You looked too beautiful lying there asleep.' And he'd had things to do. 'So I went to the market, picked up some provisions and, *voilá*.'

'It smells amazing.' She poured water into the cafetiere. 'What shall we do today?'

'I have a plan. I think we should go in the cable car up the mountain and then we can toboggan back down again.'

'Sounds like fun.'

'I also thought if you want to take a sketchbook you can

sit and draw the cathedral and I can catch up with some paperwork for Easel.'

'Better and better.' She grinned at him. 'Life is easier without secrets.'

A leisurely hour later and they were in the surprisingly short queue for the cable cars, but instead of keeping his eye on the blue cars as they made their jaunty way up and down the mountain he found himself watching Adriana. The way her eyes scanned her surroundings, the interest that lit the grey depths, and he realised how much he'd learnt about her, knew she was thinking now about how she would draw or paint the scene, how she would capture the glint of blue, the wisp of white cloud in the sky.

So much made sense—her dislike of social situations, her fear she wasn't good enough, her assumption that her sister was better than she was. All down to her father. He suppressed the quick surge of anger, told himself there was no place for it now. Lord Salvington was an ill man and whilst that didn't excuse his behaviour it certainly pre-cluded Rob giving him a piece of his mind.

A cable car came to a stop and a few minutes later they were aboard, lucky enough to have the car to themselves. They sat opposite each other, hands clasped, as the car glided upwards.

'Look at that,' she said as she gazed out, and his gaze followed hers. Took in the stretch of red rooftops, a vivid contrast to the whitewashed walls of the houses, glimpsed the vibrant colours of people's gardens and the steep down-ward sweep of ravine gorges. 'The people look so tiny, it's almost like looking at a play world.'

At the end of the twenty-minute ride they reached the summit. 'I thought we could stroll along to the church first.' It was a place he thought she would like but he also needed to kill time, couldn't take her back to the villa until dusk.

'Sure.'

They walked along the cobbled paths, past the start point of the toboggan ride, down some stairs and then up another path that meandered between green hedges. Until they reached the church and she came to a halt.

'Oh. That's not how I imagined it would be.' He knew what she meant. The church was a symmetrical structure with white walls outlined in black, with large windows embedded in the walls.

'I read that the façade has a "baroque pediment",' he said, and she gave him a quick glance.

'Anything else you can tell me?'

'Yup. Originally there was a chapel built here in 1470 by someone called Adam, and Adam and his twin sister, Eva, were apparently the first children born on Madeira. This church, though, was built in the 1740s, then an earthquake damaged it, and then it was rebuilt and consecrated in 1818.'

'Anything else?'

He pointed to the stairs that led to the church. 'There are seventy-four of them.'

'Have you made that up?'

'Nope.' He grinned at her. 'Bet I'm right and if I am I get to claim a kiss whenever I want.'

'Seems like a win-win deal to me. Let's go.'

'Seventy-two…seventy-three…seventy-four!' he said in a tone of exaggerated triumph and she gave a small chuckle. They stood and looked at the imposing outside of the building for a moment. 'Shall we go in?'

'Definitely.' She gave him a sideways glance. 'I have the feeling there's lots to see inside and that you know all about it.'

'Correct. If we go inside we can see the tomb of Karl the First. He was the last Emperor of Austria, and when he was forced to cede his position he was exiled here, where he died. He was only thirty-four.'

'That's sad,' she said softly. 'He had to leave the place he loved, his home and give up something integral to his identity, to his being. Maybe it's no wonder he died young.'

'I read that his heart is in Switzerland but the rest of his body is in here.'

They entered the church and looked around the ornate interior, stood in front of a statue of the Virgin in a silver tabernacle.

'Legend says a shepherdess was given the statue centuries ago and lots of miracles occurred because of it. Also the main festival of the church, the Assunção de Maria, is held on August the 15th annually. It's a place of pilgrimage and those coming here often climb those seventy-four steps outside on their knees.'

She glanced at him and now there was definite speculation in her eyes. 'All of this is genuinely interesting, but I can't help feeling you had some ulterior motive in finding all this out. In fact, why do I have the feeling you know something I don't know?'

'I have no idea,' he said blandly, even as he glanced at his watch, checked the time, mentally went through the preparations for later on.

'Hmm. I do realise that that isn't really an answer.'

'How about we go and check out the toboggans?' he suggested. As they left the church and headed back along the path he realised how comfortable she was to be with—the silences were easy not awkward, both of them content to walk hand in hand and soak in the sun and scenery until they arrived.

As they waited in the queue she glanced up at him. 'So are you also a font of all knowledge on the toboggans?' she asked.

'Absolutely. I wanted today to be…special so I did all the research.'

Standing on tiptoe she brushed her lips against his cheek. 'Thank you. So tell me what you found out.'

'The toboggans are made of wicker and wood, eucalyptus wood to be precise. They run on greased slats, the grease used is tallow and there are ropes to help the drivers steer the toboggans. The drivers drive in pairs and they all wear white trousers, white shirts and straw hats with a black ribbon. Oh, and specially soled boots as well.'

'How fast do they go?'

'Anywhere up to thirty miles per hour. So it should be exhilarating.'

'Oh, we're about to find out.'

They climbed into the basket car and a few minutes later they were off, the two drivers expertly steering the toboggan. It was definitely exhilarating as they swooped and swerved downward, the scenery whizzing past as they both braced themselves.

'They are going to need to stop at the junction! How…?'

'I think that's where the boots come in—they help them brake,' he said as the car came to a surprisingly smooth stop, before restarting the journey.

'I love this,' she said and when he saw her smile, saw the graceful lift of her hand to hold her hair off her face, he felt a sudden thrill of anticipation for the evening ahead. But first they disembarked from the toboggan and elected to walk down to the city, holding hands as they navigated the steeply inclined back. Once there they wandered the cobbled paths, found a small restaurant where they ate spaghetti cooked in a Chouriço sauce before moving on to a café near the cathedral where Adriana sketched the simple façade of the building with its Gothic archways, and Rob focused on the Easel launch.

Then a quick glance at his watch, a hurried message to check everything was in place and then he said, 'Are you ready to head back now?'

'Sure.' She smiled at him. 'I've had a lovely day.'

'So have I.' As he looked at her, a small warning bell pealed at the back of his mind. One that he pushed away. There was no *need* for alarm. This was all going according to plan. He and Adriana had come here to Madeira to make sure they got on, make sure they liked each other enough to commit to a marriage.

So enjoying time together was a good thing. The attraction was a good thing. All ticks on a criteria list for a marriage of convenience. And he reassured himself he didn't feel the same way about Adriana as he had about Emily. There was no sense of agony, no fear of loss, no pangs of jealousy or hour upon hour spent trying to decide the best way to entertain her, or please her.

'Then let's go,' he said, a small smile on his lips as he anticipated her reaction once they got back.

Adriana glanced across at Rob, wondered what was going through his head, knew he wouldn't tell her but knew too it was nothing to worry about. They'd shared their secrets now, confided in each other, and that felt good. So she leant her head back and watched the scenery go by, felt the warm evening breeze ruffle her hair, braced herself against the now familiar dips and inclines of the roads.

Then they were back and as she climbed out of the car she sensed that something was different. Following him into the house, she glanced round, couldn't see anything amiss, and then she followed him across the lounge as he pulled open the sliding doors and she gave a small gasp.

The patio had been transformed. Fairy lights twinkled in a cascade of illumination that cast light and shadows over the mosaic tiles, lit up the potted plants and the fronded trees and cast enough light to show the dark blue of the waves that lapped and frothed down below.

The circular table had a white damask cloth over it with a centrepiece of blooming flowers that filled the air with a floral scent that she knew would be embedded in her memory for ever along with the vibrancy of colour and light. A silver wine cooler held champagne and silver platters with covered dishes were artfully scattered.

'It's beautiful,' she breathed as he walked forward and pulled out a chair for her to sit on.

It was then that she saw there was a package next to her plate, a long rectangular shape encased in thick gold paper and tied up with a pretty bow.

'It's for you,' he said.

'For me?' Carefully Adriana opened the beautifully wrapped parcel. 'Thank you.' Inside the wrapping there was a box of artist's pencils, ones she recognised as being top-notch, not just because of their price tag but also because of their name.

He smiled. 'I cheated a little. I asked Isabella for a recommendation. Have a look inside.'

She lifted the lid and then froze. Nestled amongst the pencils was a jewellery box. With trembling fingers she opened it, stared down at the ring inside, a ring that her artist's mind could see was a burst of colour that matched the flowers in the centrepiece, a detail that for some reason made her blink back a tear.

'Adriana, will you marry me?'

She nodded and he reached over, took the ring and carefully slid it onto the ring finger of her left hand. 'I promise to always try to make sure our marriage is a happy one.'

The words were full of seriousness and yet somewhere deep down Adriana felt a pang of sadness, one she quelled instantly. There was no reason for sadness—this was what she wanted. She had known from the start their marriage was a deal, one that would be protected by a prenup agreement. But that didn't mean they couldn't broker a happy marriage. A marriage that could save Salvington *and* provide them with a union that would be a happy one. With a man she liked, a man she respected and a man she desired. That was enough—of course it was.

'And so do I,' she said, and if her smile held a hint of sadness she could only hope he didn't see it.

'And here we have a selection of tapas,' he said. 'I ordered them in, and there are even numbers of them so we can share them equally, so you definitely don't miss out on anything.'

Now her smile was genuine and as he lifted the plates and showed her the delicious dishes, he told her exactly what each one was, the *polvo à galega*, octopus and potatoes cooked with garlic and paprika, oysters served with lemon juice, *peixinhos da horta*—green beans fried in a tempura batter—and *gambas na frigideira*—prawns fried in a special sauce of whisky, port wine with garlic and sweet peppers. Then he opened the champagne and as they ate and drank, dusk turned to night and she looked down at her engagement ring as it glittered in the moonlight.

And seemed to send her a message: this is enough. Be content.

CHAPTER FIFTEEN

A week later

ROB LOOKED AROUND his annexe at Darrow, noted the evidence of Adriana everywhere, small, subtle reminders that he was engaged, that she was definitely now a part of his life on the estate. A stray barrette, an upturned book, a piece of paper, entitled *Things You Need to Do*—things she wanted him to do before their engagement announcement and party. They'd decided to hold a small party at Darrow itself, not too large, as the wedding itself would be a massive affair, so the engagement party would be low-key, just family and close friends. Plus Adriana was keen to announce the engagement and then get married as soon as possible. Whilst her father was stable, he still wasn't recovering as quickly as the doctors had hoped, still seemed lethargic and fragile. Though news of the engagement had definitely sparked a positive reaction and he knew Adriana hoped that the official announcement would bolster that.

His gaze went back to the to-do list; it reminded him of things on his own list. He needed to sort out the prenup agreement, but he was unsure why he kept putting it off. It was important to ensure that Adriana couldn't get sole custody of his heir, as long as the prenup protected her as well—they'd agreed that at the outset. Difficult to believe how short a time ago that was. Yet reluctance still touched him, one he must overcome. But in the meantime there was something he could do—he could sort out a health check for himself. The other thing they'd discussed.

He'd just dropped his phone back in his pocket when there was a knock at the door and he looked up to see Adriana, rose to his feet, knew the smile on his face was ridiculously wide, considering he'd seen her only the previous day.

'Was I expecting you?' he asked.

'No, and I haven't come here to check on the to-do list either,' she said with a grin, no doubt clocking his guilty glance towards it. 'I've come to take you on a picnic. I'd like you to show me round Darrow, seeing as I'm going to help you run it.'

'OK. But would you like to meet the estate manager or…?'

'Nope, I want you to show me.'

He looked at her, wondered why he had the feeling there was some ulterior motive to the request.

'Take me to your favourite place on Darrow. And we can eat there. And then I'd like to maybe see the Woodlands. It's a lovely day after all.'

It truly was. The sun shone and the smell of freshly mown grass pervaded the air as they walked alongside freshly ploughed fields until they reached a woodland glade. And somehow walking with Adriana, answering her questions about the farming done on the land, discussing eco methods, he felt a sudden muted pride in his land.

'I think there are so many things you could do here. There are places that you could preserve for wildlife, there are grants you can get to help with that. And I know you have the capacity to grow market produce; you could start a farmers' market. One day perhaps it would even be worth having an area set aside for the public, you could have a play area and a small farm for children to visit, with pony rides and…' She broke off. 'But right now I know what I'd like to do.'

'What?'

She narrowed her eyes as she looked towards the glade. 'Climb that tree over there. And you could climb the one next to it. What do you think?'

'You want to climb trees?'

'Yes,' she said. 'I told you that when I was a child I spent hours exploring Salvington, roaming the land, climbing trees, building shelters and all the stuff we've just been talking about that is really important, but so is forming a connection with the estate, and I thought today…maybe we could start doing that. Together. Because I'd like to love Darrow as well. And I'd like our children to feel a connection to their land, but I'd like us to teach them that in a way that you weren't taught. That way they won't feel like you did, won't feel burdened or weighed down with responsibility. But to teach a connection you have to have a connection. Does that make sense or do you think I've run mad?'

'No. That makes sense.' But he could still see worry on her face and reached out to smooth the crease from her forehead. 'What's wrong?'

'I don't want you to think that I was trivialising all the things we were talking about, about farming methods and crops and eco management. They are so important, the nuts and bolts of running an estate. And your father was right to teach you that. I also know how much I have to learn about those nuts and bolts.'

'I don't think you are trivialising anything. You're saying that having a connection to your land makes you want to learn how to look after it to the best of your ability. In the same way I have a connection to Easel because I created it,

spent blood, sweat and tears getting the funding, getting it
right, and now I will always do all I can to take it forward.'

'Yes, and I believe you can feel like that about Darrow
as well.'

'I'd like to try,' he said. And he would; as he looked at
her now, seeing the serious look on her face lighten as her
lips turned up in a smile, his chest seemed to squeeze tight.
'So let's start. I'll race you to the top.'

And as he climbed, figured out which branch could take
his weight, trusted his instincts to help him alight the sturdy
breadth and height of the tree he felt a sudden sense of exhilaration, akin to how he felt when ice skating, and when
he'd reached as high as was safe to go and looked down he
had a boyish urge to proclaim himself King of the Castle.
He saw Adriana in the next tree seated on a sturdy branch,
one hand resting on the trunk, her legs swinging.

'This is amazing,' he said.

'I know. I used to spend hours in my favourite tree with
a book and some snacks. Maybe when we have kids we
can build them a tree house—that was always one of my
dreams. My father would never have helped me do it but
I'd love us to help our children.'

He could hear the wistfulness in her voice. 'Deal,' he
said. He could picture it now, Adriana and himself helping an exuberant little boy and a determined little girl lay
some planks. 'I promise that I will be a better father than
either of ours.' He shook his head. 'Though that's not setting the bar that high, I know. So how about I will be the
very best father I know how to be?'

'I know you will and I truly believe you will be a great
father.'

He glanced across at her. 'How is your father?'

'Stable but still frail.' She sighed. 'I think he is glad
about our marriage, but I know he wishes it were Stella.

He is still refusing to see her. So she won't come to the engagement party.' Another sigh and then a small shake of her head, as though to dislodge thoughts of her family. 'So where shall we have our picnic?'

'There's a river near here. Let's eat next to it and then paddle.'

'Sounds perfect.'

And it did; for a moment foreboding touched him. Though he wasn't sure why. After all, he had it all, didn't he? He'd found the perfect wife for a convenient marriage. 'Oh and whilst I remember we need to sort out some of the legal side of things before the engagement announcement.' He forced himself to continue. 'Like the prenup,'

The words acted like a cloud that obscured the sun, though he knew that was only in his imagination, knew if he hadn't said it now he would never have said it. Would have let the dream of the perfect family take over from the reality. And so what if they signed a prenup? It wouldn't stop them from building a tree house for their children, or being a happy family.

Yet as he descended the tree he knew some of the exhilaration of the day had seeped away.

A few days later and Rob stared across the desk at the man who had just delivered such devastating news, in such a clinical fashion. 'I see,' he said.

'I'm sorry, Mr Wilmington. But it isn't all bad news—as I said…'

Rob nodded. 'I fully understand the situation. I have a low sperm count. Conceiving a baby may take a lot of time. There are also possible treatments but no guarantees.' A completely uncharacteristic sense of anger threatened, urged him to tip the fancy desk over, lean across and shake the consultant till his teeth rattled.

But of course he didn't—it wasn't this man's fault.

'Thank you. I'll be in touch.'

It took all his iron will to allow him to rise from his seat unhurriedly to leave the room at his usual pace, though once out on the street he started to walk faster, his brain churning, analysing, trying to find a way out, a solution.

Tried to fight off the bleak knowledge that there wasn't one. That there was no way he could now marry Adriana. The knowledge was like a punch to the solar plexus and the pain spread through his body, through his heart, his very soul.

Enough.

This reaction was extreme and yet he felt clammy, ill... sick. Perhaps it was a reaction to the diagnosis—that would make more sense. After all, getting an heir would now be more complicated than he'd foreseen, and his situation could be a rerun of his own parents' quest. And if he failed so did the line of Darrow. Yet those facts didn't seem to be having an impact; all he could think of was the immediate consequence: he could not marry Adriana.

He tried to focus on the positives—at least he had found out now, before the marriage, before the preparations were truly underway. But that lining was so thin it may as well be a near-invisible glimmer of silver.

He could not marry Adriana.

And that thought was clouding everything, casting a shadow, causing a deep, raw pain that he couldn't seem to wrestle under control.

He forced himself to stop, saw that he was outside a café, forced himself to go and order a coffee, hoped the scorching hot caffeine would somehow allow him to think beyond the pounding echo of *You cannot marry Adriana.*

Because he had to think, to see if there was a solution, a way.

Cradling the coffee cup, he resumed walking, oblivious of the London crowds that thronged the pavements. He had to get a grip—why was he feeling like this? Yes, it was unfortunate, but it wasn't the end of the world. When Stella had pulled out of their agreement it hadn't mattered apart from a sense of aggrieved inconvenience.

His conversation with Adriana echoed in his head.

'You had feelings for her?'

The words had made him pause.

'I liked her, but I suppose that's the beauty of an arranged marriage—it is a business arrangement first and foremost. So I am upset in the same way I would be if a deal fell through. It's an...'

'Inconvenience?' she'd offered. *'And you'll be looking for a new partner forthwith?'*

'Yes.'

The words mocked him now, because this wasn't an inconvenience, this was...devastating, the knowledge he no longer had a future with Adriana, and now images streamed through his mind. Her laugh, her smile, waking up with her wrapped in his arms, her hair tickling his chest, his cheek, her arm flung over him. Listening to her, her listening to him, the way she pushed her fringe off her face, the small frown, the infectious laugh, her scent, her taste...the life they'd planned together.

A life with a brood of children.

All over.

A burn of pain scalded his hand and he realised he'd inadvertently crushed the coffee cup and allowed the liquid to spill over him.

Enough. He had to get himself under control and he had to admit to himself that somehow the unthinkable had happened. He loved Adriana.

And there was nothing he could do about it. Because he also remembered her other words,

'I love Salvington, and the risk is worth it to me. I want my children to have the chance to explore the land and places that I roamed as a child. I want to keep Salvington in the Morrison family, to see it prosper and grow. I want to be part of that. I will do anything I can do to make that happen.'

That was what mattered to her. She'd spoken of her connection to her land, and he knew the most important thing in the world to her was to try and save it. That meant the best thing he could do for the woman he loved was to pull out of this agreement and never let her know of his love.

Because he knew that would tear her in two, that she would already feel compassion for him because of the fertility issues he faced, and if she knew how he felt about her that would only deepen the compassion and cause her conflict. What if she loved him too? The question whispered at the back of his mind.

Then, even then, their marriage couldn't work. He wouldn't let her choose the transience of love over what mattered most to her. Wouldn't let their marriage become an echo of her own parents'.

He clenched his hands into fists. The bleakness intensified as he realised exactly what this meant. That he'd never kiss her again, never wake up next to her, never watch her push her fringe off her forehead, never…

Never happening. Adriana wanted to marry him for a child, an heir, a chance to save Salvington. That had been the cornerstone of negotiation, the only reason she'd approached him, the only reason she'd contemplated marrying him. With or without love, without that stone the whole edifice collapsed in a cloud of debris and dust. That was the stark truth and he knew exactly what he had to do and he'd do it. Man up and do his duty, do the right thing. For her.

He glanced at his watch—he was due to meet her in his London flat in half an hour. Ironically enough to discuss the prenup. No need for that now.

Adriana let herself into Rob's London flat. She hadn't been here before but he'd said she should have a key. In case she was doing 'wedding things' in London and needed a place to have a cup of tea.

She pushed the door of the lounge open and entered, saw that he was sitting at his desk.

'Rob?'

He turned and she halted at his expression. He looked... hard, his expression withdrawn, the set of his lips grim. As though he'd steeled himself to an unpleasant task. She knew the prenup was a sensitive subject but surely it didn't warrant this.

'What's wrong?' She headed forward, hands outstretched as he rose to his feet, kept his own hands by his sides, the distance on his face, in his body language, the tension in his legs and shoulders and jaw absolute. He gestured to a chair, the movement awkward as though he was directing his arm with an effort.

She sat, perched on the edge of the chair, hands clasped on her knees as she waited.

'There is no easy way to say this. The deal is off the table. I can't marry you.'

Shock froze her. 'Why not?'

'I went for a full health check. Like I said we should both do before the wedding. I figured I'd go first.'

Panic escalated as nightmare scenarios crossed her mind.

'It turns out I have a very low sperm count.'

Her first reaction was sheer relief, that he wasn't dying, wasn't stricken with a life-threatening disease. But then came understanding as she put the statements together. *Low sperm count.* Adriana stared at him as the fact lodged in her brain, nudged the first domino and sent the whole lot tumbling down, crushing hopes and dreams, obliterating engagement-party plans and wedding-venue arrangements. *Can't marry you.*

Desperately she tried to stem the crash, reverse the domino effect. 'But that doesn't mean it's impossible for you to have a child. For us to have a child.'

'No. But it's very unlikely to happen quickly. Timing is everything for you.' She stared at him, hands twisting in her lap, nails in her palms as she forced her mind to think. 'You told me that your father's recovery is slower than you'd like. So logically there is no choice but to call the marriage off. Dissolve the partnership.'

'Without discussion?'

'There isn't anything to discuss.'

'There must be something to discuss. How can you sit there like that? And talk about logic? Don't you care?' He flinched at that and she rose, moved towards him. 'This is me. This is us. We had a future planned. You must feel something, that this is more than just an inconvenience. Please, Rob. I am not your parents. You don't have to man up and only think about the earldom.'

Finally his body sagged a little, the awful tension lessened its taut hold, and now he too rose, moved towards her. 'I do care, Adriana. And I'm not thinking about the earldom. I am thinking about you, about us, about our agreement.' He took her hands in his and she knew with awful finality that it was the last time he'd do so. The last time she'd feel his touch. 'We did have a plan. And that plan centred around having a family. The whole reason you wanted this marriage was to give yourself a chance to have a son, to save Salvington.'

Oh, God. He was right.

His voice was gentle now. 'Your home, your place, your land. You told me you would do anything to save it, asked me to imagine a scenario where your father dies and you know you did not do everything you could to save Salvington, how you would feel to see the diggers wrench up the earth and soil of a place you love. Desecrate it. So I have imagined that. Imagined us married, trying for a baby and trying for a baby whilst your father's health hangs in the balance. It's not your father I am thinking about—it's you. What that would do to you. To us. I couldn't bear to watch your unhappiness and know that I am the cause. Don't want our marriage to go the way of your parents'. Or mine.'

She bit her lip. What to do about her father, about the situation with Salvington? And more importantly, what about Rob? What must this news have done to him?

'What about you? I won't desert you because you…'

'Can no longer provide you with what you need?' he said. 'Yes, you can. You are not deserting me. That was always the point of our marriage—it was a partnership based on a provision of mutual benefits. I can't give you what you need.'

'But…' She took a deep breath. Now it was sinking in and she could only imagine how he must feel, given that his whole life he had known it was his duty to carry on the line of Darrow, to have an heir. Now that was no longer straightforward and the weight of responsibility must be heavier than before. The anxiety of failure. 'Forget about us for a moment. This is a massive shock. You must be reeling from it.'

'Things happen. There is a chance I will have a child, but possibly not a large family unless there is a treatment.'

Now she heard the slight crack in his voice. Knew how much that would hurt. There was a chance he would end up having an only child, just as he had been, a child who would bear the whole burden of familial expectations. He stepped back now and she could see his withdrawal. 'But all this is for me to manage.'

For him to manage. With another woman. The idea took her breath away, as a deep, visceral pain twisted inside her. Enough. There should be no pain, no hurt. That was supposedly the beauty of their arrangement. No reason to feel pain.

This was an agreement, a deal, exactly what they'd discussed just weeks before. But that had been then, before they had got to know each other, before she'd learnt so much about him, the way he smiled, that strong sense of duty, countered by a sense of humour and an ability to make her laugh, before she'd discovered he cared about her, before she'd confided in him about Steve, about painting, about the way her father had treated her all her life. Before he'd confided in her, before they'd climbed trees together, goddamn it, before they'd gone tobogganing. Before they'd made love, before she'd got used to waking up next to him... Her brain caught up with the slipstream of thoughts, focused on the word, the taboo. Love. They had made love because she loved him. Had fallen for him, heart, body and soul. She loved him.

The realisation froze her, caused her skin to come out in a cold, clammy sheen of panic. How had this happened, how had she let him find a way under her skin, into her heart? She'd been so sure love would not come into play, sure she was immune from even the slightest possibility. Because she'd only ever approached him for Salvington's sake.

Or maybe that wasn't true, maybe that stupid crush from years ago had never abated, maybe that was all this still was, some sort of foolish infatuation.

But right now she couldn't think straight, knew she had to keep this from him at all costs. With her heart aching, she reached up and slipped the barrettes from her hair, those barrettes he'd given her and she'd worn like a talisman since. But now she didn't want him to read her eyes, couldn't bear to see the pity in his if he guessed, and there would be pity because he would know exactly how she felt. He'd loved Emily and Emily hadn't loved him back. But in his case he'd been duped. Rob had never lied to her, never led her on, had been more than clear love was never on the table, never a possibility.

But then, she'd been so sure of that herself; for a mad moment she wondered if there was any way that his take on it all had changed, that he had fallen in love with her. And an impulse nearly overcame her—to tell him the truth, that she loved him. But she couldn't—the words wouldn't come. The risk of humiliation was too great, because if he loved her, why wouldn't he tell her? There was nothing in his stance, in his expression, in his words to indicate anything other than a man calling off a business deal.

But she needed to at least try to give him a chance, a hint to tell her if he had any feelings for her at all. 'For you to manage with another woman?' she asked. 'Is it that easy for you?'

She'd swear he winced, rocked backwards on the balls of his feet, but then he steadied himself, shook his head. 'No. It's not easy. I swear it. But one day, yes, I will need to marry someone.' The words were delivered in an even pitch, and all of a sudden she recalled their conversation from weeks ago.

'I am upset in the same way I would be if a deal fell through. It's an...'

'Inconvenience? And you'll be looking for a new partner forthwith?'

'No! Not forthwith,' he answered her now. 'Of course I won't.'

'But in the fullness of time. A month? Three months?' Hearing the bitterness in her voice, she knew she had to pull back; she would never let him know how she felt, she had too much pride to open herself up to mortification again— so better to keep this pain to herself and treat her wounds in private. Her pain was not his fault, she knew that, and right now he was going through enough.

And so she pulled herself together. 'Rob, I am sorry. I don't know what else to say.' Except that she loved him. 'But I am sure, I really am, that you will find a solution, that treatment will be successful, or maybe you will be plain lucky. With whoever you marry.'

Those words cost her more than she could say and she saw something fleeting across his blue eyes, a shadow of what was surely sorrow and pain.

'I didn't want it to work out this way. I am so sorry that I can't come through for you, that I can't fulfil my part of the bargain. More sorry than I can convey to you.'

She looked at him, saw and heard the sincerity in the catch in his voice, and she knew that any minute now she would either break down in tears or throw herself at his chest. Instead she stepped forward. 'Goodbye, Rob. Thank you for the past few weeks…thank you for…everything.' She slipped her engagement ring off her finger and handed it to him. 'And I hope it all works out for you.'

A gulp and she turned and walked away.

Three days later

Adriana clicked the link to join the video meeting and seconds later saw the familiar face of her sister. Stella looked tired, but even in her tiredness her beauty shone through.

Her smile was tentative, her eyes worried as she surveyed Adriana.

'Ria, what happened?'

'Rob and I called it off.'

'Why? Because you couldn't go through with a marriage of convenience? That's OK.'

'It doesn't matter why. I really don't want to talk about it.' The last thing she wanted to do was discuss her own sorry state. She had done her best the last few days to throw herself into work on the estate by day, and by night she painted, sketched, but to her own horror all she could picture as she drew was Rob, had found herself trying to draw his forearm in charcoal, to capture the expression on his face...until she'd given up. 'I'd rather talk about you. Are you OK? Have you decided what to do?'

'No.' Stella gave a small laugh. 'I don't want to talk about me. All I still know is that I want this baby and as each day goes by I love her or him more.' She stopped. 'Oh, Ria, what did I say? I'm sorry.'

'It's fine.' Only it wasn't. She was happy for Stella— she really was. But suddenly she thought of how Rob must have felt when the specialist told him he may not be able to have children and her heart twisted.

'No, clearly it isn't fine. Are you worried you can't have a baby? Is that why you split up with Rob?'

'No!' But her sister's suggestion set off a train of thoughts in her head. If she had found out she had fertility issues, what would she have done? She would have called off the marriage exactly as Rob had. Would have assumed, no, would have known that it made the marriage a non-starter.

'Then what happened? Please talk to me. Because I feel all this is my fault. You don't need to feel bad that you called it off. You shouldn't have to go through a marriage of convenience, just to have a baby. You do not have to sacrifice yourself for Salvington. I told you that.'

The words pinged a lightbulb in her brain. 'I know, Stella. And I know you only want what's best for me. I am truly happy for you and I think you are going to be a wonderful mother, whether you do this on your own or somehow with the baby's father being involved. But listen, I've just realised something important. There's no time to explain right now but there is something I have to go and do.'

Rob eyed his parents in disbelief. 'You want me to do what?'

His father returned his glare with a basilisk one of his own. 'You heard us. Your mother has arranged a date for you with Lady Eleanor.'

'Let me ask another question. Why?'

His mother had the grace to at least look a little uncomfortable. 'I realise it seems a little soon, but your fertility issues mean we have to get a move on. It took your father and me so long and it was so hard and stressful I just want you to get started as soon as possible.'

'And Eleanor is happy to go along with this.'

'Well, obviously you would have to discuss it with her.' The Countess shrugged. 'Darling, you are the one who stood here a month ago and told us you wanted to get married as soon as possible to someone suitable, that you planned to "broker a deal" that would lead to a convenient marriage. That you would provide Darrow with an heir and you would take over the estate. When Stella dropped out you moved on to Adriana and...'

Rob closed his eyes. What an arrogant, misguided, pompous idiot he'd been. But that had been before Adriana, before she'd shown him so much. 'That was different. I didn't really know Stella. I got to know Adriana and I can't and won't just move on from her.'

There was a pause and his parents exchanged glances.

'That's what I came here to tell you. That I'm shelving marriage plans. I will still take over the estate—but I will also be pursuing something else. When I was away for those two years I set up a company—it's called Easel Enterprises and I am truly proud of what I achieved.' He hesitated and then ploughed forward. 'I hope if you are willing to listen to more about it that you will be proud as well.'

He waited, watched them both.

Adriana met her mother's gaze. 'Are you sure it's OK for me to see him?' she asked.

Her mother nodded. 'I think it's best. He knows everything and he said he wants to see you.'

'OK.' Trepidation touched her but she leaned over to give her mother a kiss. 'I wanted to say thank you as well, Mum.'

'Why?'

'For everything you've always done for me. You've always loved me and I'm sorry Salvington has made your life difficult, and also thank you for everything you said about my marriage to Rob. I didn't understand at the time but I do now.'

Her mother returned her hug with fervour and then Adriana left her, walked up the stairs to her father's room, pushed open the door and entered.

'Father. How are you feeling?'

'Not so bad. Your mother is looking after me. Better than I deserve.' Her father surveyed her, an expression she couldn't read on her face. 'I wanted to talk to you. It was good of you to try to go through with the marriage to Rob. I wish it had worked.'

'So do I.' She waited for his expected outbreak of wrath, of jibes of anger at her failure, but none came.

Instead he sighed. 'It's OK. I'm too tired to be angry and I know I've no right to be anyway. The heart attack—it's changed me.'

'It's good you're not angry but I still think you should fight. Fight the law like you always have, use your influence. And...' She hesitated. 'I've got something for you.' Nerves clenched her tummy, even as she told herself what she knew to be true. That his opinion didn't matter. Just as Rob had told her. She handed over a framed painting, one of her favourites that she'd painted, a woodland picture of part of the Salvington estate.

Her father took it and looked down at it. 'This is very good. Who is the artist—' He broke off as he saw her name in the corner. 'Thank you,' was all he said, and she nodded.

'I'll be back soon,' she said and turned for the door.

Rob felt his phone vibrate in his pocket, nearly ignored the sensation. Realised he couldn't. It could be Fleur, finalising arrangements for the launch. A muted sense of excitement touched him, but somehow everything seemed muted without Adriana. He'd spent days walking around Darrow, taking solace from his land in a way he would never have believed possible. He'd thrown himself into the launch plans as well.

But always at the back of his mind was Adriana, her look of hurt when he'd spoken of marrying someone else. But what else could he have done? And what could he do now? Except miss her, and he did. He missed her with a constant ache, one he had no idea how to assuage.

He pulled his phone out of his pocket and looked down at it, and his heart gave a sudden lurch. It was from Adriana. He scanned the message.

Hi Rob. It's urgent. Please could you come to Salvington at your earliest convenience? Adriana

Pausing only to reply, On my way, he dropped his phone back into his pocket, turned and headed at speed for the house. Once there he climbed straight into his car and headed for Salvington, pulling onto the sweep of driveway as soon as was humanly possible.

Braked as he saw Adriana standing a little distance from the house. Tried to calm the pounding of his heart, tried to hide the wave of bittersweet joy at seeing her as he drank in every detail of her—jeans, a white T-shirt, hair clipped back with the red barrettes he'd given her, a tentative smile on her face as he opened the car door and climbed out.

'Is everything OK?'

'Yes, it is. I think. I hope. Thank you for coming. I'm sorry to have summoned you like this. But I didn't really know what else to do. Anyway, is it OK if we walk whilst I try and explain?'

'Of course.' He couldn't help the smile that tipped his lips for a fleeting moment—it was so lovely to hear her voice.

'I wanted to show you some of Salvington,' she said as they began to walk, leaving the house behind them.

Was she perhaps showing him that she knew he'd been right to call off the marriage, show him what he had saved, thank him in some way? He didn't know and in truth right now he didn't care, was happy to be with her for one last time, happy that she was OK. Though of course there was a tiny bit of him that felt affronted that, whilst he had spent the past days hurting, she seemed to have recovered completely.

But then again, he loved her—she didn't love him.

As they walked she pointed out various spots to him,

places she'd roamed as a child, places she'd sketched, places she'd seen different birds or wildlife. The places where she'd picked wild mushrooms and berries, the time she'd tried to fish for trout using a stick, a piece of string and a worm.

Until they came to a leafy glade.

'This was your favourite tree?' He hazarded a guess.

'Yup. And look.'

She led him further forward and he saw that under the wide stretch of branches she'd set a sylvan scene. The green leaves were dappled by the sunshine that made it through the canopy, but she'd also strung lights at differing heights to overhang a wooden picnic bench. The table had an array of covered dishes on it and in the centre was a wine cooler. The whole area was sprinkled with rose petals.

He halted, knew confusion was written on his features.

'Sit,' she said. 'Please.'

Once he was seated she sat too, opposite him so they could see each other clearly.

'I told you it was urgent,' she said. 'And it is. I just don't know where to start but I'll try.' She took a deep breath and then, 'I wanted to tell you this here, at Salvington. I wanted to show you the place I love. Because I do love Salvington and when I came to see you after Father's heart attack I did mean everything I said, about wanting to save it, about it being the most important thing to me.'

'I get that,' he said. 'I really do.'

'But now things have changed.'

He frowned, saw her hand instinctively go up to her barrettes as if to free her fringe, and then she didn't. Placed her hand on the table instead and kept her beautiful grey eyes on him, meeting his gaze full on.

'Because somewhere in the last few weeks I fell in love with you. And that changes everything.'

He could only stare at her as his brain tried to fathom

the words, as happiness, joy started to seep through him, even as he tried to stem the tide. Adriana loved him. He needed to speak, to say something, but before he could she raised a hand.

'I need to finish, to say what I need to say. You see, when you told me what the specialist said I didn't even give Salvington a thought. I only cared about you and I cared about us. I wanted to be with you, I wanted to be by your side. I didn't want to lose you. And that was more important to me than Salvington and it still is. And I thought… I want you to know that.'

He knew he had to say something. 'Adriana, I love you.' Perhaps he should have dressed it up more, perhaps he shouldn't have blurted it out, but he couldn't bear for her not to know for even a second longer than necessary. 'I love you,' he repeated. 'I love you.'

He could see the joy dawn in her eyes, see a hint of disbelief, and he reached out, said the words again. 'I love you. With all my heart. I've loved you since… I don't know when. But when the specialist told me the news about my fertility all I could think of was what it meant for us. That it meant I couldn't marry you, and then I knew that I loved you.'

'Why didn't you tell me?'

'Because I didn't want my love to be a burden to you. I didn't want your pity, or for you to feel you owed me anything, and I knew that for you Salvington would have to come first.' He hesitated. 'And how can you be so sure that isn't true? Your love, our love means too much to me to watch it go sour, to see your unhappiness…'

She shook her head. 'It won't. I can see things more clearly now. I was speaking to Stella and she thought I'd pulled out of our marriage because I didn't want a marriage of convenience. But this isn't a marriage of convenience to me—not any more.'

'Adriana, I…'

'My mother told me not to give up on the fairy tale for Salvington and she was right. To her, Salvington is bricks and mortar and soil. To me it will always be more than that. And that's why I know this sounds mad but I know that Salvington itself doesn't want my misery to go on in its name. We need to still fight—and I will…fight to have the laws changed. Because that is the right way forward to try and save it. And if we happen to have a son in time, or Stella happens to find a suitable husband and they have a son, then great! But if we are lucky enough to have a child or children then I will consider myself blessed whenever they are born. And if we have no children, or a daughter, or four daughters, that's good with me.' Her face was serious now. 'But for me the most important thing is to be with you.'

His eyes searched hers. 'You're sure? Because I'm optimistic that there is a good chance with time I can have a child, but there is no guarantee.'

'I know that.' Her expression was solemn. 'And I know that must be hard for you to come to terms with.'

'It is, but not for Darrow's sake. I already know that there is more to life than Darrow, more to it even than Easel. You made me imagine the joys of building tree houses, spending time with my children, letting them climb trees. They can enjoy the land, but then they can go and do whatever they want. And if I can't have children naturally then we could adopt. I know adopted children can't inherit titles, but hell, maybe we can lobby to change that law too. And if we can't our children would still be happy.'

'I completely agree. And I think adoption is an amazing idea. But the most important thing is that we are together and we can make all those decisions together. If you'll have me.'

He wondered if it were possible for his heart to burst with joy, because he heard nothing but truth in her words, knew there had been nothing but truth in his.

Moving round the table, he got down on one knee and pulled her engagement ring out of his pocket, where he'd kept it for the past few days.

'Will you marry me and make me the happiest man in the world?'

'I will.' Her answer was clear, uttered without even a hint of doubt.

'And I promise to love and cherish you for the rest of my life.' He slipped the ring on her finger and then sat down beside her, one arm wrapped around her. 'You've changed me, Adriana. Shown me how to trust, shown me how to find a connection with Darrow, shown me what having a family truly means. You've brought joy to my life.'

'And you've shown me that it is possible to embrace a life outside of Salvington, to have belief in myself. To believe in my art. If I want to go to college, if I want to study, I can. You've shown me that I am a worthy person in my own right, that I am my sister's equal, that I can be a countess.'

'You will be the most loved Countess in the land,' he said, and as he kissed her, and then as they ate and drank and discussed their future, planned a fairy-tale happy-ever-after full of love, he knew that he was the luckiest man alive.

* * * * *

COMING SOON!

We really hope you enjoyed reading this book.
If you're looking for more romance, be sure to
head to the shops when new books are
available on

Thursday 13th October

To see which titles are coming soon, please visit
millsandboon.co.uk/nextmonth

MILLS & BOON®

Coming next month

WEARING HIS RING TILL CHRISTMAS
Nina Singh

An older couple walking past smiled at them, then paused directly in front of their bench. Evan's response was a respectful nod with a slight bow. Chiara had no idea what to do so she followed his lead and mimicked the action.

But they didn't move on.

The woman pointed to the top of the pole behind the bench and said something Chiara didn't understand. Then she nodded enthusiastically. Chiara shrugged her shoulders and gave the woman a smile in return. Why hadn't she thought to learn a few words of greeting in Mandarin before coming to Singapore? Most of Singapore spoke English but it couldn't have hurt to learn a bit of the second most popular language here. Things had just moved so quickly after she'd yes to Evan's offer. In fact, time seemed to be speeding by since the day she'd met him. She leaned sideways in Evan's direction. "What's she saying?"

He turned to her. Their faces were inches apart. "She's pointing out that we happen to be sitting under some mistletoe."

Oh dear. The couple was still staring at them expectedly. Chiara froze in her spot, at a complete loss as to what to do.

But then, Evan lifted her chin with one finger. Suddenly, despite the chaotic fun and boisterous noise surrounding them, Chiara's entire focus narrowed to just the two of them. She gripped the cone in her hand so tight, it was a wonder it didn't break in her hand.

And she almost dropped it when she felt Evan's lips on hers. Soft yet firm, gentle yet somehow demanding in equal measure. She had no idea if he'd meant to deliver a small peck on the lips in response to a stranger's prompting, but this kiss was quickly turning into so much more than that. Heat and desire curled through her stomach as his mouth remained on hers. Every cell of her being vibrated with desire.

When she finally made herself pull away, she had to take a deep breath to try and regain some of her senses. The older couple wasn't even there any longer.

At some point, their fake kiss had become all too real. For her anyway. Maybe even for Evan…

Continue reading
WEARING HIS RING TILL CHRISTMAS
Nina Singh

Available next month
www.millsandboon.co.uk